A Fistful of Salt
- A Tale of Two Townies -

KEVIN KEELY

Visit the Website
https://kevinkeely.wordpress.com/

ISBN-13: 978-1512188653

©Kevin Keely, August2015

The right of Kevin Keely to be identified as Author of this work has been asserted in accordance with the Copyright, Designs and Patents Act.

All rights reserved. No part of this novel may be reproduced or transmitted in any form or by any means, electronic or mechanical, including photocopying, recording, or any information storage and retrieval system without prior written permission of the Author and without similar condition including this condition being imposed on any subsequent purchaser. Your support for the Author's rights is an imperative that you acknowledge in the reading of this statement.

This is a work of fiction.
All characters and events in this book are fictitious.

Published by Kevin W. Keely, IRELAND

©First Print Edition Dec 2015

Limited Edition 2020..

Copyright 2020.

A Fistful of Salt

Author's Note.

This book is a work of fiction. No person described in this book exists in reality. None of the characterisations herein are based on real people or are in anyway intended to reflect on any part of the human family. There are wonderful people in all walks of life including the excellent individuals, and communities, who identify as gypsies, travelers, taxi-men and sometimes even gingers. So please, just enjoy the story for what it is.

Acknowledgements

The Beta-readers who helped to make this book something that I am proud of.

My Mum, without whom, nothing is possible.

All Art Work by
Dan at Vanguard Designs Ltd., Dublin, Ireland.

For Suzanne

The King did send one thousand knights
And at the walls spent them deep
To keep a promise made in his youth
He spirited her away
Awakening in a snow kept forest
Each day to a perfect crystal silence
Frozen in eternity with a Rose
So his heart would stay
Exactly as she found it.

Chapters

TWO TAXIS	1
THREE WOMEN	6
A DIFFERENT SUNDAY	13
EMERGENCY SURGERY	26
THE GREY MAN	36
THE POSSE	55
MEETING THE STROKERS	63
CONFESSIONAL	73
THE NEW MAN	88
THE KILLER ORPHANS	97
TWENTY PILES OF SHITE	114
SWITZERLAND	134
RED MIST	149
GUCCI TO THE RESCUE	160
CAESAR PERPIGNAN	168
THROUGH THE LOOKING GLASS	181
CARPETS AND CURTAINS	193
PEEPING TOM	200
BEST LAID PLANS	210
OF MICE AND MEN	223

SUKIE'S REVENGE	237
BRODY'S DESCENT	257
KELLY FALLS	261
SNOW WHITE GETS GRUMPY	265
THE LONG ARM	270
END OF THE ROAD	273
POSSESSED	278
POINT BREAK	282
RENDEZVOUS	288
MAGICAL BLUE	291
THE HONEYMOON	296
THE DIVORCE	305
AU BAR L'IRLANDAISE	311
EPILOGUE	315

TWO TAXIS

Melanie Johnson squeezed through the parting doors of the late train and hit the platform running. Sandals clattering on the marble tiles, she slapped her ticket down in front of the inspector who was just arriving at the gate.

'Thanks!' she called over her shoulder.

'Student card,' he shouted after her. But she was in a race against time.

Down the long flight of concrete stairs with her shoulder bag clutched to her side and her light skirt held close to her thighs, she dodged the traffic on the busy street below to burst in the door of Raftery's Pub to wild cheers from the girls sitting around the high table next to the bar. She took a bow. Thirty seconds later and she'd have had to pay for the round of shots sitting on the table. She drained her glass as the clock struck eleven.

In the early hours of the morning, swimming in fragrance and alcohol fumes, the gang tussled in a lively embrace on the footpath outside. Someone hailed a cab and before Melanie knew it, a door was opened and she was pushed inside. Her friends insisted that she should take the first taxi, as she was the only one who had to travel out of town. With a wave and a cheer the car pulled away and headed for the lake road.

'Hiyahh, Mister Taxi-man.'

She was already texting the girls she'd just said goodbye to, then stealing glances at the town as she messaged her father, letting him know she was on the way. The cab looped the one-way system then hit the hill and climbed the last few orange-lit streets before the edge of town. As always, Melanie spun around to catch the view out the rear window, a three-tone painting of a thousand orange rooftops speckled with red taillights, all jumbled around the oily black expanse of the bay. It was no thing of beauty, but it was home. She turned back in time to notice something in the driver's hand as it slid from the dashboard.

The car passed the last street light and was consumed by the night.

Briars struck the windows as they sped downwards and the shimmering lake came into view through the trees. Again she said hello to the dark figure in front of her and this time listened for an answer over the low growl of the engine. She didn't hear anything. Shifting sideways, against the tug of the belt, she scanned the front for his license, then raised her eyes to the mirror and found him staring back—two pinholes in the dark. She turned her face to the window and the hairs on her body went stiff.

'Where's your license, Taxi-man?' Her voice didn't sound as strong as she'd intended and she suddenly had to contend with an urge to pee.

The car swayed as they passed the stretch of road that touched the lakeshore, then they hit the incline that wound back into the trees at Slishwood Forest. She leaned across for another glance, but the dash was still bare and she couldn't make herself look in the mirror again.

'Are you deaf?'

No response—but she was only a mile from home now.

The car slowed to a near halt, making a tight left onto the gravel track that led up to the forest car park.

'What's going on?' Her words were drowned out by the rattling planks on the old bridge.

Sweeping in a wide arc they came to a noisy stop on the stones. The engine died and the driver was out, closing the door behind him. He walked into the blackness under the canopy of low pine branches, just a stone's throw away.

The faint illumination of a phone went to the side of his head and a cigarette flared. She couldn't make out if his lips were moving. Releasing her belt buckle she pulled her phone out of her pocket to check it but everyone knew that on this side of the hill there was no signal for another quarter-mile.

The steady pulse of the meter seared the darkness red while she pressed the roof light in vain a few times, then hammered it once with her clenched fist. Stretching over the seat she fumbled across the dashboard for the radio mic then snatched it up and keyed the button several times to bursts of static.

'Hello?'—more static, then silence.

Through the trees, the headlights of a car swept past on the lake road and her fingers found the door handle. She thought about the flimsy straps on her sandals and cursed them through gritted teeth. She had run in these forests often enough to know that it wasn't an option in the dark. It was sixty yards by the track back to the road, but even if she made it, there mightn't be another car along for half an hour. Another set of headlights came into view then sped past, plunging the road back into darkness.

'Please.' The word lodged in her throat and a tear welled in her eye.

The driver's cigarette flared then arced out from the shadows to hit the front of the car in a shower of sparks. Then he stepped forward and stood with his arms by his sides, no longer pretending to be on a phone call, just staring in the front window. It was impossible to know if he could see into the car or not. Only his outline—blacker than the shadows around him, he just stood and waited.

'Waited?'

'Yeah—waited.'

'Waited for what?'

Melanie was sitting forward on the back seat, recounting her story to her taxi driver on the way back to the train station three days after the events in the forest.

'My guess?' She took a deep breath and let it out. 'He was trying to figure out could he get away with whatever he was thinking.'

She hadn't taken any chances this time, phoning her favorite driver on his own private number. He worked for a company in the town and had driven her and her friends around since they were kids.

Thomas Brody was his name and he didn't look like much but she trusted him. Toady, as he was known by most, offered no excuses for the behaviour of the driver in her story. Compared to most taxi men he never spoke much but was good at listening.

'So what happened next?' he asked her. He pulled his car over at the bottom of the concrete steps that led back up to the train station and put his elbow up on the back of the seat. He looked her straight in the eyes and it was obvious to see that in the cold light of day she was struggling with her conviction.

'Nothing.' She was almost apologetic as she took her hand from her pocket to hold up a steel nail file. 'I was going to stab him.'

He regarded her slender fingers wrapped tight around the weapon. He had known her for so long and had clear memories of his back seat filled by Melanie and her friends, just picked up from the afternoon show at the Gaiety Cinema, all pigtails and squeals.

'Did you get a look at this fella?'

Melanie had her head down. 'Not really. When he got back in I looked away, I was scared—drunk. He said something about a dog, seemed to think it was funny.' She looked out the window and shook her head. 'Then off we went, back down to the road. He took me home. Christ— I'm overreacting, amn't I?'

'No,' Toady said. He pulled her shoulder bag from the back seat and walked her to the bottom of the steps. "He was up to no good."

His vote of confidence bolstered her to say her last word on the matter as she took the bag from him. 'That's not all.'

Her tone drew a worried look from under his brow. But Toady spent a lot of time looking worried. His thoughts constantly etched in the furrows on his high forehead making him appear older than he was. His cheap clothes and lank hairstyle combined with his pained facial expression to imply that he was closer to fifty than thirty.

She gestured towards his cab. 'Those cars are new, aren't they?'

He shrugged. 'If you call eight months new?'

'I haven't been around, so they're new to me.' She pointed at his door. 'That owl's face on the side—he had the same thing on his car.'

THREE WOMEN

The next day Toady sat in his car in the early afternoon sun. All night he'd sifted through the details of Melanie's story. Outside the row of three-storey buildings on Quay Street he was making his conclusions. The old houses on the corner where he had grown up were all converted to apartments now, chewed up and spat out in the boom. His car window was down, his elbow resting outwards. He stared at the sunshine glistening on the river. The two-way radio crackled from the dash, but it was a slow afternoon and there were enough drivers to handle the runs. He keyed his handset.

'Need to get out of the car, I'm gonna take fifteen.'

'Yeh,' came the boss's reply.

He sat on the concrete bollard where they used to tie off the little fishing boats when he was a kid. In the water below, the ribs of an old dinghy protruded from the mud. Seagulls sat on the rocks, waiting for tiny crabs to show themselves on the turn of the tide.

There were over twenty drivers with the company but when he whittled it down, taking out the women and the older guys, he had little doubt who the culprit was. Dominic Kidd, or Nicky, as he liked to be called, was the boss's cousin and he fit the description better than any. Young, male, smoker, not fat and not short.

He'd been with them for less than a year and he'd also been working that night. He hadn't been with them long enough to know that Melanie was a regular. Nicky hadn't done anything illegal, per se, but a wicked notion had slowly crept into Toady's thoughts and would not go away.

A couple of months after Nicky had started with the company, a detective had been down on the rank going car to car with a photo of a missing homeless girl, Flora Mc Carthy. She came and went from the shelter, so the cop wasn't getting too excited about it. But he'd had a tip off from a friend of hers that she'd been talking about a Taximan that took her up to a car park in a forest a couple of weeks beforehand. It wasn't the first time she'd gone with men for money, her friend had admitted, but afterward she'd seemed different, frightened on the streets at night, and that just wasn't like her.

All the drivers knew Flora to see, but they shook their heads as the cop passed by their cars with the photo extended. He came to Toady and shoved it in his window like he'd been waiting to do that from the start of the line.

'She was seen in your car, Brody. Maybe you know what could have frightened her.'

'She's a kid, I'm sure lots of things could frighten her. I bought her a cup of tea, she was freezing.' Toady stared out the windscreen. 'That was months ago. Is that a crime?'

The cop left, but a week later the girl was found in a rancid ditch beside the tidal plains with enough vodka and tranquilisers in her to drop a horse, don't mind a skinny sixteen-year-old. She'd been dead forty-eight hours when they found her but the autopsy showed that she'd spent her last days eating dog food and being sodomised. The detective was back on the rank with the same picture and stuck it in the window again. This time Toady said nothing, he just stared at the pretty face with the vacant smile in the photo and remembered the last words he had said to her.

On a bland Tuesday he had taken his lunch break to coincide with her funeral mass. He sat at the back of an empty church and listened to some woman's lonely sobbing coming out of the shadows near the altar while the priest droned on about God's endless love. When he came out, the same cop was sitting in his car on the opposite side of the road. Toady stared back at him and remembered again what he'd said to Flora.

'A pretty girl should have a boyfriend—and a home.'

'So you wanna take me home and be my boyfriend?' She always spoke more like a woman than a child. He watched her suspicious glances soften a little before she went to get out. He offered her twenty quid and she took it without looking at him. He knew what she was thinking. 'If you're ever hungry just ask,' he had called out to her as the door shut.

But she never asked him for anything. Once, when she was walking by the rank, she raised her eyes from the footpath as she passed his car and a pathetic smile flitted on her pale features and Toady thought his heart would break.

He didn't have time to go to the graveyard to watch them put her in the hole but he went up after a couple of months to put flowers on the grave and it was already lost under a foot of weeds. Nobody was pushing the cops for answers and they knew Flora kept bad company, so when nothing substantive emerged, the investigation petered out—probable death by misadventure.

Gazing at the river drift by, he couldn't stop thinking about something Nicky had come out with the week she went missing.

'Gotta go feed the dog.'

It had sounded so absurd coming over the radio that dead afternoon, especially from the new guy. Drivers were paid for a ten-hour shift and the boss didn't ever tolerate men leaving early for any reason. In the eternal silence of a slow afternoon on the rank the words had hung in the air long after he'd watched Nicky's car taking off. A couple of days later they had found Flora's body. Those words were there again now, etched in the space in front of him, as clear as Flora's face.

'Gotta go feed the dog.'

Toady glanced back across the road, to the line of old cut-stone buildings he used to call home, each one with a new weather-glazed balcony. All the same and not a single sign of life throughout any of them. He could hear the past echoes of screaming kids drifting out to the slow river. His mother was leaning out the kitchen window on the second floor with a cigarette in her hand.

'What d'ye think, Mammy?' he whispered.

'I think it's none of your business, Thomas.'

'But it stinks.'

'So do lots of things. Are you planning on playing the hero now?'

'I'm just going to nudge the tree, see what falls out.'

'I suppose you can expect rotten apples so. Stay out of it, Thomas, you're no detective.'

'Trust me, Mammy, I have a plan.'

'You also have a vile temper, son. Just don't do anything stupid.'

Unfortunately, having a plan and doing something stupid aren't mutually exclusive, regardless of what your dead mother says. He parked his car at the back of the rank and walked over the brow of the hill past the groups of drivers standing, chatting and smoking.

'Toad, Tom, Toady.' The men nodded as he passed.

He got to Nicky's car with butterflies in his gut.

'Ay, Brody.' Nicky's nasal drawl was grating to the ears. 'Wassup, boy?'

He was a townie, from his beanie hat under his hoody, to his heavy black boots. His head bobbed when he walked, usually with a fag hanging from his mouth. When he put the word "boy" at the end of a sentence it was on the soft puckered lips of a Judas kiss.

'Boy,' Toady grunted—and lost his temper. He grabbed him by the jacket collar and tried to drag him out the open window. Nicky let out a squeal as he squirmed to get free. Toady cocked his elbow but before he could get a punch in the other drivers were on him.

'Jesus, Lad—what are ye at?' They dragged him to the railings where Fat Dave pinned him to the steel and latched on either side with an iron grip.

Toady could hardly breathe for the weight of Dave's jiggling torso, then Nicky's beanie hat came into view over Dave's arm.

'What the fuck are you on, ya rehab?' Nicky shouted as he danced around the path. 'Let em go boys, I have it sorted.'

Then the boss arrived into the middle of it. Jackie Ryan, shirtsleeves rolled up to the elbows, his jaw trembling with rage and his bottom lip pushed out to the tip of his nose. He grabbed Nicky by the collar and pulled him backwards, sending him stumbling onto the bonnet of his car, then slapped Fat Dave on the shoulder and Dave eased off. He reached in and grabbed a fistful of Toady's jumper and wrenched him out into the street. Jackie not only had the strength of a gorilla but his meaty, silver head gave him the appearance of one too. Toady stepped backwards and held up a hand, warning him to keep his distance.

'What the fuck, Brody—ye wanna get sacked?' Jackie barked.

'Payback,' Toady declared. 'His dog bit me.'

'What dog?' cried Nicky. 'I have no fuckin dog, ya daft cunt.'

'No shit!' spat Toady. 'What were you doing up in Slishwood with Melanie Johnson the other night?'

Jackie's eyes narrowed to slits. 'Have you lost your fuckin mind?'

'You tell me, Jackie.' Toady pointed at Nicky. 'He's your cousin. Ask him why a taxi driver pulls into a forest at two in the morning. Ask him does he know anything about Flora Mc Carthy while you're at it.'

Jackie shoved him square in the chest and sent him scuttling backwards on the cobbles. 'Alright Sonny, you're not gonna pull this shit on me in front of Town Hall. Get your car back to the depot. I want you off the streets.'

'Woof woof,' heckled Nicky. 'Get yourself some clothes and a haircut while you're at it, ye retard. Ye don't wanna look like that at your funeral.'

Toady paced from side to side, then turned on his heels for the back of the rank.

'You're a dead man, Brody,' taunted Nicky. 'Careful who ye pick up from now on, cos ye never know, boy.'

'Shut your hole,' growled Jackie from the corner of his mouth.

Toady considered taking the day off while he circled the town, but before his anger had abated the radio came to life and the dispatcher's voice interrupted.

'Michelle Kelly—St. Brigid's Close—coming into town.'

Before Jackie had the chance to delegate it, Toady was on his radio. 'Got it!'

Within three seconds his phone rang and Jackie was seething. 'You're a bollox, I told ye to go home.'

'I said I got it.'

'I'm sending Nicky over, now get that car off the road before I fuckin shoot ya.'

'Only send him over if ye don't want him back.'

'This is the sound of your job goin down the shitter. You know me, boy, I don't mess around.' Jackie was livid, but the phone was already dead.

Toady drove to the pick up and he knew that Jackie wasn't stupid enough to send Nicky into a cul-de-sac after him. This was a small town and the shit didn't have to fly very far to hit way too many doors.

As was the case more often than not, a full-blown argument could be heard going on inside Michelle Kelly's house. Doors were slamming, pushing lace curtains against the windowpanes. He surveyed the close while he waited. A terrace of quiet graves, flaking paint and pebbledash, bleached pale by another insipid Sunday afternoon. The sound of shattering glass came shrill from within over the dull thud of a man's voice.

She burst out the door, red hair blazing like wildfire escaping from hell. Storming down the path to the car, she kicked the decrepit wooden gate open and lunged into the backseat, slamming the door. He breathed deep the wondrous cloud of perfume, heavy with the scent of flowers and washed hair. In the mirror her face was calm, her cool green eyes regarded him without a trace of emotion. Two small scratch marks on her cheek.

'Hi, Shelley.'

'What are you lookin at—Freak?'

'Nothing.'

'Go!' She pointed sideways out the window at the shadow of a bull barreling out from the dark hallway. Toady floored it and the wheels spun smoke down the middle of the street to the main road. The short run into town went without a word and he dropped her in the centre.

'I'll pay ye later, when I'm goin home.'

'Sure thing, Shelley, when's that gonna be?'

'When I'm full.' She slammed the door as he cancelled the meter. Every fare she didn't pay came out of his pocket but there was a level of intimacy in that worth more to him than the money. She rapped on the window and he buzzed it down.

She waited, then bending just enough to look him in the eye she said, 'Thanks.'

'Sure thing, Shell.'

He watched her walk away as the lingering fragrance evaporated like a daydream. He'd have given everything he was worth to be holding her hand and walking into a different Sunday, somewhere, anywhere, far away from this unfolding nightmare.

A DIFFERENT SUNDAY

He became aware of the blackness first, both inside and out. He thought to lift his hands, maybe check his eyes in order to know if they were open or closed, but mustering the will to execute that simple action was impossible. Had he been blinded?

He wondered if he was dead but the searing pain in his skull said otherwise. Then, much worse, it occurred to him that he had been buried alive. The air was still, he strained his ears listening for the faint thuds of dirt being shoveled overhead. He wrestled with his eyelids. In the silence he wondered was he even awake, had he ever been awake—had he ever been alive? Pain enveloped his head in a red-hot blanket and his thoughts dissolved.

In his dreams he was on a boat, on a wide grey sea, being driven through the darkness, shunting from side to side with the cold, empty belly of the ocean rumbling beneath. Then he was running away from a pack of dogs. Men hunted him, long blades drawn. Terror was ripping at his heels when he ran headlong into a wall and his head exploded in light. When he went down, the hounds tore at his neck and the blades flashed silver and red. Then that sweet fragrance and a soft voice, begging him not to die. 'We made it to Switzerland,' she said—then silence.

The next time he cracked his sticky eyelids there was light, but the effort of trying to open them brought nausea and agony to every raw nerve. He grunted then let out a low groan and now, at least he knew he was alive. He heard noise and felt movement. Something brushed past his face and the smell of flowers was all around him again.

'Open your mouth, Thomas,' came her voice. 'Open up for painkillers.'

Tablets were dropped into his dry mouth, then water was poured in that overflowed down his cheeks onto his neck.

A face loomed in, speckled with gold dust and surrounded by a fiery halo. Piercing green eyes came into focus for a moment.

'Where am I?'

'Safe.'

He tried to focus on the room behind her, but it was a hopeless blur. He wanted to rise, but her hand was on him.

'No!' she said. 'You can't. They took your legs.'

He closed his eyes to stop the tears but it was too late and they flowed hot on his cheeks. 'My legs? Why my legs?' But no voice came out of him. His mind screamed to be let back into the void of sleep, where at least the pain in his head was bearable. So he let himself be dragged back down into the dark.

* * *

Shelley stood in the schoolyard sneering at him. Walking in the streets of the town, oblivious to his stare. Her face in the back of his car, smiling, fuming—but always bold. Wild red curls around green eyes, flecked black and gold, she loomed in every corner of his mind.

He'd been watching her for twenty years, and longer. Since even before the day she spoke her first clear words to him in the corner of the bicycle shed.

'What are you looking at—Freak?' Her breath, sweet as sherbet in his face.

'You look like the Mona Lisa in red.'

Had he said it? Had it come out right? God knows he'd practiced it enough. It had occurred to him in art class a week earlier, and the image had haunted his dreams.

'Quickly class, compose one sentence that captures the atmosphere of Da Vinci's timeless masterpiece. You—Thomas!' The teacher eyeballed him from behind thick-framed glasses.

'Michelle Kelly's puberty,' he announced, confirming his conclusion with another glance at the portrait smirking from his open book. The room exploded in laughter and the youngest McNally brother hit him with a loosely wrapped sandwich in the back of his head.

A phone call was made to his home that night, when the art teacher conveyed her concerns to the woman on the line and was met with the most unanticipated of responses.

'I am deeply impressed by my son's mature approach to both the works of the masters and the complexities of blossoming womanhood.' Toady's babysitter hung up the phone then winked at him from the hall. His mother was on a foreign holiday, her only one ever, and he was in a strange place—halfway through a crash course in the female anatomy, courtesy of his opportunistic minder.

But his first advances on the young Miss Kelly took an abrupt downward turn that day in the bicycle shed, because the wrong words came out.

'Does the carpet match the curtains?'

It's a phrase that rolls from the tongue and his babysitter had loosened up his tongue the night before. The young girls conferred and reached a consensus on its meaning, resulting in a stinging blow to his face and a swollen toe.

Two years later, on the day before he left school to start his new job, he approached her, racked with nerves and stumbling through the fog of early manhood. He listened helplessly as his mouth did the talking once again.

'If nobody else wants to marry you, I will—no matter how old you are.'

By that stage, he had grown taller and she had slowed down and now he was looking her in the nose. Her nostrils were flaring in and out like a bellows, feeding the furnace of flames that burst through her head in those fiery curls and cracked her pale skin in a hundred golden chinks.

'I'll marry ye when ye give me a million quid and die in a pit of dog shite. How's that?'

If that's what it takes, he thought. He stared at her lips moving, just inches from his, then he bridged the gap and kissed her—in a moment of blissful fantasy.

He didn't see much of her in the immediate years after he left school. Their lives diverged only within the environs of the ramshackle streets and urban clatter of the pokey town. He spent most of his time driving a van, delivering boxes of Feta cheese to supermarkets. Gone from six in the morning, up and down the east and west coasts, he was the sole driver for the only Greek cheese company importing to the island. Five years he did that, coming home to just his mother and the quiet roast dinners at the kitchen table in the evenings.

'That redhead you were so fond of, Thomas?' she said one night. 'The one you were obsessed with in school. The one that went to work in Doherty's Supermarket. The one—'

'Yes Mammy, I know the one you're talking about.'

'She's getting married to some chap from up North. He manages the wholesale outlet. Drives a Mercedes, so I hear.'

'You were better off before you retired,' he noted between mouthfuls. 'The gossip is gonna rot your brain.'

She regarded him for a moment chewing on his sprouts and drinking his milk. His balding head gone brown from the summer sun. His thick neck and angular skull on squat, meaty shoulders and his arms solid from loading boxes and driving the truck.

'That comb-over makes you look twice your age,' she said, and not for the first time.

He sighed then looked her in the face. 'I'm not ready to be bald.'

'You couldn't be any balder. You'd better start thinking about getting ready.'

'D'ye think a haircut might change her mind about the wedding, is that why you're nagging?'

'Arra, she was never good enough for you anyway, Thomas. Redheads—' She leaned into him across the table and put her hand on his arm. 'Liars and thieves, I tell you. They only have tempers to distract you from their schemes when they get caught at whatever it is they're really up to.'

'Christ mum, that doesn't even make sense. Besides, I wouldn't care if she robbed me blind and broke a chair over my head every night.'

'What way did I raise you at all?' She tut-tutted him.

He stood up and brought his plate to the sink, cleaned it off, then kissed her on the forehead. 'If I could get her to love me, I'd be happy.'

'Love won't make you happy, Thomas. Nobody else can fill in the missing piece for you.' She put her hand on his chest. 'You have to do that yourself.'

'Okay then, I'll do that over a pint—while I see can I figure out a way to break up this wedding.' He winked at her as he slipped his jacket on. At the door she called to him and he stopped, looking back into the darkness of their home as she came from the kitchen.

'Put out your hands, Thomas,' she commanded.

She tipped a drum of salt and filled them while she spoke. A science and history teacher for forty years in the tiny Protestant school, she had a lesson for even the most arbitrary of things.

'After water and air, salt is the most precious necessity of life,' she said.

'Yeh?' He watched her stony, white face and wished she would smile more. 'Who said that then?'

'A very wise Indian man.' She stopped pouring and snapped the drum shut.

'Sitting Bull.' He smirked and watched her expression for any hint of weakness.

'That's how much salt there is in any man. If you're worth half of that by the time you die, you'll have made me proud.'

He went to walk away then stopped. 'What am I supposed to do with this?'

'Earn it,' she said, and closed the door in his face.

Down in The Ship Tavern he drank pints and dipped peanuts in a pile of salt on the counter.

'Mercedes,' he said and threw his pint back. 'Wanker!'

He didn't start fights but with a gut full of beer he was much less likely to pretend he wasn't there if one broke out. Just before closing time the McNally brothers started to poke fun at the local halfwit.

Danny Redmond, with the heinous purple bald patches on his head, or Fishfood as they always called him, was minding his own business at his end of the bar. But they just couldn't leave him be. Years this had been going on, and while Toady was an expert at looking the other way, this was one of the few things that he just could not abide. Apart from the McNally brothers and Danny, there was only one other person in the world who knew the story behind those bald patches and the reason why Danny was brain-damaged.

He got into the fight without a single utterance and let his temper rampage until the bar was silenced. Outside he crossed the road and threw himself into the river which is less than four feet deep when the tide is in. The tide was out that night and though he survived his lame suicide attempt, he never did get his shoes back from the mud. When he climbed barefoot to the wharf the McNally boys were waiting for him and they proceeded to kick him senseless. Toady was great at taking a hammering.

* * *

'Painkillers,' he said through gritted teeth and she brought him a couple with a pint of fresh water. He drank deeply and watched her face in the darkening room.

'Where are we?'

'Safe,' she whispered.

'Shelley,' he grunted, 'it is you—isn't it?'

'Nah, it's the angel Gabriel. You're dyin, so ye are.'

He looked at her through a squinted eye and the sheer physical pain of trying to imagine what possible reason there could be for the circumstances in which he found himself was nauseating and overpowering. He let go of consciousness again.

* * *

As things turned out, Shelley hadn't married the guy with the Merc from the wholesale outlet after all, and not long after that, Toady's truck driving days ended when the small company he worked for was sold to a UK distributor. He was offered a new job under the terms stipulated by the owner of the company as a condition of the sale.

'Mr. Zatakis has stipulated that you will be made transport manager of the Irish operation,' he was told by phone, and the promise was kept. But within a few weeks Toady missed the roads and the grip of the swirling wheel and he decided that if his cheese driving days were over, then his people driving days should commence, without delay.

'Hello?—Tell Mr. Zatakis I said thanks.' He put down the phone and walked out the door before the voice on the other end had time to even ask him who he was.

To say he liked driving the taxi might have been an exaggeration but it was different than sitting in the truck on his own, and better than sitting at home watching his mother go through two packs of Navy Cut a day at the kitchen table.

'Mammy, you're gonna give yourself cancer.'

'Please God,' she droned.

'What the hell is that supposed to mean?'

'It means I won't have to listen to that eejit on the radio in the morning and you can sell this place and start up a company of your own. Find a wife to take care of you.'

'I don't want a company of my own,' he protested, 'and the radio has an off-switch.'

On his days off he took her for a drive around the lake and they'd stop to have a glass of Guinness in one of the villages along the way. Each time they went she seemed a little thinner, her hands a little colder, and the pauses in her sentences a little longer.

'If I go senile that sister of mine will change the will quicker than she can get on the boat to get over here. Then you'll have nothing. You and that house, Thomas, that's all I have.'

'Don't talk rubbish, Mammy, you're too young to be carrying on like that.'

'I'm old as a goat,' she said, pointing at her chest, 'and the damage is done.'

Ten years in a taxi can take a toll on a man, on his friends and family, on his social life. But Tom Brody didn't have any of those things to worry about, so it suited him just fine. One hour after they had buried his mother he burned his brand new suit in the kitchen stove while he stood staring across the street at the river. He had paid the local publican to make sandwiches and soup for the handful of mourners while he slipped away to get back to work. She'd died suddenly, so the sister never got the chance to interfere and didn't even bother coming back from England for the funeral. The will was executed as per his mother's wishes.

The big upside to driving the cab was that he got to see Shelley more often. She became a regular passenger with the company he drove for. She used to ask for him by name, late at night, when she had no money left and needed to go home for free.

'I'll pay ye back—Tommy Brody,' she'd sing, her face

grinning with watery eyes and wet lips.

'I know you will, Michelle, don't worry about it.'

She'd go into the house and sometimes he'd hear the crashing and screaming start before he drove away.

'You deserve better,' he told her once.

She laughed out loud, spluttering the back of his neck with alcohol spit. 'No I don't, ye big eejit and anyway, what are you gonna do about it? Any girl would rather get punched than have a comb-over dangling in her face.'

'I'm not ready to be bald.'

'Well ye better get ready.' She snipped her fingers beside his face. 'Cos I'm gonna cut that thing off if I ever get a chance.'

One Saturday evening Toady was doing a circuit of the town and came across Shelley and her best friend getting into trouble with a gang of Brits on a stag party. As he cruised up to the kerbside her raucous voice was battering off the high facades of O'Connell Street. 'Touch me again and I'll make earrings outa your balls.' The girls were clutching each other for stability.

'Aww, cmon Red, we only wanna cop a look at your bush.'

She swung her handbag and clocked him across the face. He pushed her hard and she somersaulted backwards over the bin, to a chorus of cheers and laughter. They advanced on her, but Toady stepped in between them.

'Get her in the car,' he said to her friend, then he waded into the Brits like they were nothing more than long grass. But when one of them smashed a bottle over the back of his head, he went down and got a right kicking—which he took in excellent style.

* * *

He woke in the dark and the searing hot pain was now a dull hammer smashing on the back of his skull. He put his cold hands to the burning flesh of his face and moaned at the relief it gave him. He felt movement beside him and a light came on. He turned his eyes and Shelley was there, lying on the bed, smiling.

'Open up.' She held her hand over his mouth and dropped two more tablets in, then another drink of water.

'More.' He gulped and she lay there, pouring glasses of water into him as he sipped and spluttered and tried to fix her with his eyes.

'Are you still there?' he asked, and the words tore at his swollen throat as she faded out of sight.

'Yes,' her voice came back.

'Am I dreaming?'

'No.'

'What about my legs? I can still feel them.'

'Doctor said that's normal. Just sleep, you'll feel better tomorrow.'

He reached down with his fingertips and felt the tops of his legs, but when he went to lift his head his vision went white and nausea overcame him. He tried to wretch but his stomach was empty. He couldn't remember the last time he ate. He was losing consciousness again.

'Are you sure this isn't a dream?' he mumbled into the descending blackness.

'Not really,' came a reply.

* * *

He dreamt of memories he had lost along the way and in his fevered sleep they became memories again. He was in the forest and it was night. It was the same Sunday he'd brought Shelley into town. Nicky had caught up with him and secrets were unraveling. Jackie, the boss, was shoulder to shoulder with Nicky, and silhouetted pine trees surrounded the scene. The thin light from the moon made the pair of them seem as skeletons, with pale white faces and dark sockets. Their mouths moving, words were coming out from the darkness within.

'What are ye gonna do, Brody? We need an answer.'

In the dream he couldn't remember the question, so he had to play for time.

'Just let her go and I'll do whatever ye want.' He looked to Nicky's taxi and could see Shelley in it, too drunk to care that her fate was being decided for her. Steel glinted in the darkness between the two men and a smile spread across Nicky's ghoulish face.

'I have an answer.' Nicky glanced at Jackie and flashed the blade. 'Headline! Taxi driver gets stabbed in the heart for molestin drunk passenger in forest.'

The two ghouls split and started to circle Toady on either side while he backed away.

'No one's gonna believe that,' said Toady. 'Dave knows what you pair have been up to, I told him. He knows that I came out here too.'

'Fat Dave?' laughed Jackie. 'That cancer-bag? He'll do what he's told. No, Tommy boy—one way or the other you're goin away.' Jackie flicked his wrist and the telescopic baton extended with a snap. 'Preferably, the other.' They continued to circle him.

'Okay then!' Toady tried a different tack. 'I'll leave and you won't hear from me again.' He glanced over at Shelley. 'I'll take her home, then I'll disappear.'

'You'll disappear alright and nobody's gonna care about ye—just like that wee Flora tramp ye liked so much. No one gave a shite about her either.' Jackie spread his hands out, ready to make his move, then nodded towards Shelley. 'If it makes ye feel any better, we only needed her to get ye out here, ye soft bastard. We'll drop her back in a gutter somewhere when we're finished.'

'Don't worry,' Nicky added, 'she won't even know what the funny taste in her mouth is when she wakes up.'

'Shut your hole and concentrate on what you're doin.' Jackie only turned to him for an instant, but that was Toady's cue. He reached out with his left hand and grabbed the end of Jackie's baton and ripped it clean out of his fist. In the same motion he swung it hard in Nicky's face, cracking him straight across the jaw and sending him stumbling sideways. Jackie was lunging at him, so he thrust the butt of the baton straight back into the middle of his face. The contact split his nose, sending bloody streaks from his chin to his eye sockets. Jackie howled and screamed like a dog in a fire as he walked away down the forest track, blood pouring black through his fingers. Nicky let out a roar and took a wild swipe, then he held up the knife and waved it in the space between them. Toady smashed him across the wrist and the knife fell to the ground, then he swung a blow to the side of his head and knocked him out cold, toppling him over like a tree trunk. Jackie was still howling his way down the forest track when Toady picked up the knife and flung it after him in a moment of madness. He couldn't have done it if he'd tried, but the knife hit him with a solid thump and Jackie shut up with the howling. He kept walking in silence, with the knife sticking out of his back.

Toady grabbed his stuff from his own cab then climbed into Nicky's seat. The engine roared to life and he floored the pedal, shooting down the track to the road with Shelley out cold beside him. Jackie turned at the last minute and his mouth fell open in the glare of the headlights, then he took off, clattering up the bonnet and over the roof.

'That's my taxi-driver days over with,' Toady whispered to himself. Something like a smile was tugging at the corner of his mouth.

He drove thirty miles until he crossed the River Shannon and stopped the car in a lay-by. 'Wake up, Shelley.' He reached over and shook her shoulder. Her mouth fell open and she snorted, stirring herself enough to open her eyes and turn her head towards him. Her blank stare faded and her eyes closed again. He reached out and wiped the spit from her cheek with the back of his hand and she mumbled something about breakfast cereal. He pulled out onto dark the road and drove south.

EMERGENCY SURGERY

Shelley put her hand on Toady's head and it was cooler than it had been through the night and his eyes weren't screwed up tight anymore, he seemed comfortable. She lifted the light sheet and let it fall. The rank air of his stale sweat wafted up and hit her in the face.

'Lord Jesus, rotten so ye are.' She pinched her nose.

She pushed his head to the side and the red and brown stain on the pillow was dry. In the middle of the dressing she had put on the previous day, a rusty rose of dried blood had blossomed and died. Strands of loose hair had gotten stuck to it and tufts were matted in hardened swirls with dirt and grass dried into them. But the bleeding had stopped. She regarded the mess with her hand now covering her mouth as well and gagged.

Men's voices came from outside the window, shouting gibberish to each other and then a heinous racket commenced, as though someone had started a motorbike and was driving it around in circles. Then another one, and it sounded as though the two were having a race.

'What the fuck?' She reached over Toady and pulled the curtain back a twitch and saw two young men—boys, in blue overalls going up and down the railing outside with leaf blowers.

She glanced at her phone. 'Nine o' clock? Are ye well in the head?'

Toady stirred.

'Fuck this!' she declared and stormed out slamming the door, waking Toady from yet another nightmare.

'Fuck what?' he blurted and his lids snapped open and now he really was awake. His eyes flicked from one thing to the next, trying to make sense of what he was seeing. His ears strained and broke through the ceaseless ringing that had prevailed until that moment. He heard voices shouting on the far side of the window. Lifting his head from the pillow with a grunt he could see her gesticulating wildly as the two juveniles stared back. One had short, spiky, blonde hair and dark rings around intense eyes that followed her lips as her mouth moved. The engines died off. Two men in dark glasses and black tracksuits approached and she turned her attention to them. They smiled at her as she continued to rant. Then they directed the boys to the top of a set of steps that would take them out of sight. Half way to the steps the blond-haired boy turned on his heels and came after her, but one of the men caught hold of the back of his overalls and spun him around again. The engines restarted, but more faintly.

When she came back in the room he was sitting on the side of the bed with his head in his hands.

'Good news,' she cheered. 'Your legs grew back—Yay!'

'Ha-ha,' he mumbled at the floor.

'Oh well excuse me, but I thought you'd be—'

'I'm going to piss myself if I don't get to a toilet in the next twenty seconds.'

She dived out the door and came back with a bucket and placed it between his legs. He freed himself from his boxers and let fly a river before he even thought to check had Shelley left the room, but she was gone and the door was closed. Through swirling double vision he could see that he was in the smallest room ever built. He reached out with his free hand and touched the door.

'Midget Hospital,' he whispered as he finished off.

He knocked and Shelley reappeared.

'How do you feel?' she asked, sliding the bucket away with her fingertips.

'Don't they have nurses here?'

'Cutbacks.' She handed him two painkillers and a glass of water. 'Do you want to try standing up?'

He walked through the narrow door with his hand on her shoulder, watching his feet move as they changed shape, ten-toed flippers—then back to feet.

'Mind yourself on the stairs.'

His legs trembled as he negotiated each step, one by one. Hot flushes burned his ears, then the blood rushed away, leaving his head cold and his vision blank.

'I can't see.' He reached out and found her arm as he stumbled on the last step and his feet hit the ground. Gravel bit into his soles. She led him a few steps and he felt warm sunlight strike his face and the blur in his eyes turned bright white, tinged with gold.

'Sit here.'

He was guided into a cool plastic chair with the sun beating down on the back of his head and bare shoulders. He bent over and dry-retched and the pain in his head boomed for an instant then faded and he sat back in the chair and passed out.

* * *

The night he left the town, after the confrontation in the woods, it had taken five hours before Shelley woke beside him in the taxi.

'You missed your stop,' he said to her, gazing ahead.

She blinked out the window at grey clouds over a black sea, striped with thin waves. A ball of seagulls whirled at the water's edge fighting over something they'd found. A distant figure in a grey tracksuit used a scoop to fire a tennis ball into the sea and two German Shepherds were bounding over the foam to get it.

'My fuckin head is wrecked here', she groaned. 'What am I supposed to be looking at?'

He reached into the glove box and pulled out a bottle of 7-UP. She took it and drank until the bubbles stung her tongue and made her eyes water.

'Saint George's Channel,' he said. 'In about six hours I'm going over it on a boat, and I'm not coming back.'

'Sounds like some shite Country song.' She reached into her bag and took out her fags.

'No smoking in the cab.'

'Fuck off!' She lit up and sucked deep. Toady turned the ignition and let the two windows down. The salty breeze swept in.

She pointed across at the dash. 'Is that right? Eight o' clock? I have to be in work in two hours.'

'You may ring in sick,' he said to the windscreen. 'You're three hundred and eighty kilometres away,' he said and looked at her for a second with just the trace of a smile, 'so ye are.'

'Shut up!' she spat back.

She burst out of the car and stomped in high boots through the sand to a gap in the dunes behind and took stock of the blue and white ferry looming larger than life against a grey sky. Toady arrived standing beside her, arms folded across his chest against the breeze.

'Where does that go?' she asked.

'France.'

'Alright so—enough of this shit. Can ye get me home before ye take off please—like a good little man? You do know that there's laws against stuff like kidnapping?'

'Okay, I did a few dodgy things last night, and they'll be lookin for me surely, but kidnapping isn't one of them. I'm not making you go any further than here.' He looked at the boat then back at her. 'But you can come if you want.'

Her eyes bore into him as she smoked and took another mouthful of lemonade. 'If you weren't you, and if whoever you were was loaded, I might be tempted to think about that. But as it stands, ye can eat me—and I mean that in the nastiest possible way.'

He went back to the car and when he returned he had a large children's pencil case in his hand. 'Money?' He unzipped it and held it open in front of her. A thick brick of fifties sat snugly inside.

'Holy shit!'

'That's over three and a half grand. I've got more in the bank—plenty more.'

She looked at him, then down at his cheap plastic shoes, his shapeless jeans and the plain maroon jumper. Then with her revulsion apparent, she regarded the strands of hair standing upright in the wind, four inches over his bald patch.

'Money? Christ but ye wouldn't think it,' she scoffed.

'What's that supposed to mean?'

'It means you're a freak. Ye look like ye came out of a lucky-bag.' She held up her wedding finger in his face. 'Sorry, didn't I mention? I'm a little indisposed for fucking off to France with a circus clown today.'

'Oh right.' He gestured to the marks on her face. 'When I picked you up yesterday he was smashing you and your house up, but I suppose he's gonna have your dinner ready when you get back.'

She looked down her nose at him. 'That'd be none of your business.'

'And what about Nicky? Supposin he comes gunnin for ye?'

She stared at him a moment then shook her head. 'Who the fuck is Nicky?'

'Him and the other fella, they took you for a spin up to the forest last night, remember? They're gonna want to know what you know about me—just saying.'

'Know?' She shook her head and turned for the car. 'You're after dropping me in the shit, that's all I know.'

'It's not like I expect you to be a prostitute,' he said.

She turned back. 'What did you say?'

'Wait—that's not what I meant. I mean an escort.' He shook his head in a panic. 'Shit. Not that either. You can just do it for the money if you want. I don't mind.'

'Shut up!' She struck him across the face.

* * *

He gasped a deep breath and lifted his head. The warm sun felt so good on his back, the sound of chirping was everywhere and in the distance motors were buzzing in circles.

'You're back.' Her voice was soft and close. He opened his eyes and he could see his feet. A little brown sparrow was perched on his toe, while others were hopping around under the white plastic table pecking for crumbs. His head was propped up straight with a thick towel wrapped around his neck. He turned a little to the right to see an impressive looking campervan parked ten feet way.

'Hold still—nearly finished.'

He could feel her putting pressure on the back of his head and the pain was dull, like a deep bruise. His headache was a background rhythm now, rather than the deafening clatter it had been earlier, and his vision stayed mainly clear. His eyes hurt him when he looked up at the bright blue sky.

'Finished,' she announced, then came and stood in front of him. She looked him over then lifted a square mirror and held it in front of his face. His head was completely bald and his stubble had been shaved into a goatee.

'Medicinal purposes,' she said.

'A medicinal skinhead?'

'Yeh—well I couldn't dress the wound without surgically removing the twat flap. And ye know what, boy?'

'What?'

'You actually look like something.'

'I wasn't ready to be bald,' he moaned putting his hand to his face and then his head, rubbing the smoothness.

'Shelley?'

'What?'

'Would you mind telling me what the hell is going on?'

'How much do you remember?'

He took the mirror out of her hand and moved it around in an effort to see the wound on the back of his head.

'Start by telling me what happened to my head.'

'I don't know, but you have a concussion, and that's why you can't remember anything.'

'What else did they say? Will I get my memory back?'

'Who's they?' she laughed.

'Doctors.'

'Does this look like a hospital to you?' She gestured to the trees and the long row of dusty camping spots separated by hedges, each one numbered, all of them empty, save for the gangs of sparrows marauding back and forth. She put her hand in her pocket and pulled out her phone. 'Doctor Yahoo Kelly,' she announced and waved it in his face, 'says you'll be okay in a few days—probably. You're already a lot better than when I got you back.'

'Back?'

'From them.' She sat down in a chair and got a cigarette out. 'The gyppos.'

'On the boat?' he asked after straining his head to the point of snapping.

'Eh—yeh,' she replied. 'The ones on the boat and the gyppos in general.' She waved her hand as though there were gypsies in the trees.

'I think I can remember the boat.' He felt pathetic and lost as he rummaged in the empty space where a week's worth of memories was supposed to be. 'Hurts too much to think.'

'Maybe you should take a break.'

'Why did you get on the boat with me?'

She lit up and sat back, pulling her knees up to her chest. She was lovely in her pink tracksuit and her silver-sequined sandals showing scarlet, painted toenails.

'I made a mature decision based on my array of options.' She flicked her ash.

'And you chose me?'

'No, I chose the boat—and the money'. Her lips formed a dry smile.

'Right,' he said, nodding, then stopped. 'But the money—you lost it.'

Now she had a sheepish grin on her face and was half hiding behind her hand and the thin wisps of smoke. 'Theoretically. Doubles or quits adds up quicker than ye think. Besides—the gyppos were cheatin.'

'How much—theoretically?'

'I believe it was six thousand and something.' She dismissed it with a wave.

'Six what?' He lunged forward then froze in pain and hissed through clenched teeth, eyes screwed shut.

She put her fag in the corner of her mouth. 'Is that all you're worried about; the money?' She reached into her bag and pulled out a thick brown envelope fastened with a metal clip. She placed it on the table in front of him. 'Problem solved. I got it all back for ye, so I did.' She tapped it. 'Twenty-three grand.'

He felt a wave of nausea come over him.

'Ye don't look well, Thomas, ye just turned yellow.'

'They're after us, aren't they?'

'What do you think?'

'That's his campervan, isn't it?'

There was an evil grin tugging at her red lips. 'And everything in it.' She gestured to her clothes. 'This is all his wife's gear. All brand new—best designer shit.' She pulled off a sandal and waved it in front of him. 'Rene Caovilla, straight out of the box. This sandal's worth about three hundred quid—and there's two of them.'

The effort of thought was exhausting, especially when he wasn't sure he wanted to remember. 'There's the big fella with the beard, he's the one you were bettin with, right?' He rubbed his brow.

'Yeh, that's Mossy, him and the other pair of eejits. But it turns out they have a lot of friends over here too, and they're not that friendly either.'

'And where's here exactly?'

She flourished her arms in a grand gesture. 'Vive la France!'

She stood up and held out her hand. He took it and she helped him up out of the chair and walked him slowly to the railings. Down below, at the bottom of the bank, was a red-roofed building where a work detail of young men was busy scrubbing and sweeping and blowing. Three men in black tracksuits sat smoking on the fence, watching them work. Beyond them again, another steep bank, as the hill fell away in two more terraces of vacant camping sites, also shrouded with foliage and delineated in hedges.

'Look over the trees.' She pointed past a carpet of red roofs in the middle-distance, and beyond them, the shimmering line where the sea met the sky. 'The Mediterranean.'

Then she turned and pointed towards the end of the track. Through the railings there were more red roofs nestled in the trees and behind them were hills and behind them again, loomed larger mountains.

'Far side of them lads and you're in Spain.' She smiled and her eyes sparkled. It was clear to him that she was delighted with herself, and her smile spread to his face.

'Impressive,' he said, then looked down at himself. He was in his underpants, his body was white and his chest and legs were covered in welts and bruises. He pressed on one and pain melted deep into his ribs. He saw the unfamiliar sight of pity in her eyes and felt a warm tingle inside.

'I'm sorry for getting you into this trouble,' she whispered, 'but you started it.'

'Bit off more than I can chew, didn't I?'

'Maybe—is that a bad thing?'

He looked back to the glistening horizon.

'I'm starving. I can't remember ever eating food in my life. Is there anything here?'

THE GREY MAN

He was lingering at the edge of a dream when Shelley arrived back with breakfast and startled him upright at the table. The sun was warmer and she had thrown a towel across his lap for the sake of his modesty. His head throbbed from where it had been hanging over the back of the chair while he dozed.

'Is it too soon to take more painkillers?'

'Better wait.' She put a plate with three sausages, mushrooms and an egg in front of him, then a large mug of tea.

'Get that in ye, tough guy, don't mind your painkillers. I put sugar in your tea.'

He picked it up and sipped it, his senses devouring the beautiful sweetness and heat of the mixture. Sudden music in his sore brain and the warm sensation was a prayer for his half-dead soul. He closed his eyes and drank half the cup without saying a word. She watched in silence. He picked up a sausage with his fingers and bit half of it off and then shoved the other half in with a moan. He dispatched the other two without ceremony.

'Jesus Christ Almighty,' he said, and swilled his tea. Then he closed his eyes again and turned his face to heaven. The sparrows chirped, the leaves overhead rustled in the warm breeze and over the bank the men and the boys were laughing and shouting banter back and forth and, at last, Toady could hear their words. He had no idea what they were saying, but he felt as though he was being gradually teleported onto a brand new Earth from a cold and distant planet. The egg went on the fork and in his mouth in one go. While that was being processed he stabbed the mushrooms, one, two, three, four, five and then they were gone with the rest of the tea.

'More tea?' she asked him.

'Orange juice, have they got any?'

She came with a pint glass and a big smile spread across his face and she laughed to see him come to life. He drank half of it down and sat back in his chair. She peered at him over folded, slender fingers with the sun shining on her face.

'I nearly died,' he said. 'They almost drowned me. Horses—standing around, laughin at me, in the bottom of a well, or something. I was dying.'

She was smirking. 'Horses tried to drown you?'

'That's how I remember it.'

'I know where that was.' She pointed back over her head and he wasn't at all sure if it was supposed to be a reference to time or direction. 'Up in the hills, at a place called Quillan. A horse festival. That's where they took you. That's where I caught up with you.'

He shook his head. 'I don't even remember getting off the boat, or splitting up.'

'They took us off the boat in that camper. Then you did your Butch Cassidy impression and busted me out.' She stuck her two hands out like six shooters. 'If you hadn't done it then I'd probably have been with you in your well—gettin drowned by horses.'

He looked at her as though she was the one speaking French.

'Do you want me to remind you? See can that brain work again?'

He checked his imaginary wristwatch, turned his face to the big blue sky and shrugged.

* * *

In a town called Saintes, thirty miles inland from

Bordeaux, the day after they had arrived in France, their captors had tried for the first time to extort the six thousand and four hundred they claimed they were owed out of Toady. That's how quickly doubles or quits spirals away from you when you're cutting cards over a bottle of vodka. He had woken on the campsite that morning to the big, bearded face of Mossy Walsh smiling from across the table.

'Sleep well, Sonny?'

'You drugged us—the coffee.'

'Jaysus, it's an awful boring drive down, so it is. I saved ye the bother.'

They'd all been introduced abruptly the day before and outside he could hear his wife Ellen giving out hell to his son, a chubby fourteen year old called Arno. He knew there were at least two others knocking around who'd also been on the boat. His nephews, Pawdie and Geno, a brawny pair of idiots, could be heard yawping somewhere in the background. They were the ones with the machetes that had persuaded them to get in the campervan. Mossy stood up and fetched him a mug of coffee from the stove.

'Milk and sugar, boss?' He got no answer from Toady so he put them in anyway then placed it on the table before sitting down again. 'Sup up now chief, there's no drugs. I'm juss waitin on some fellas to get here to help out with the proceedins. Won't be long.'

Toady drank the coffee and looked out the window at a line of poplars swaying in a strong breeze. He could see Shelley standing by a fence on the far side of an empty field and he went to stand up. Mossy banged the table.

'Sweet Jesus son, ye better start listenin. Dem fellas coming up here aren't like me—ya hear?' He had big white teeth and two gold crowns on one side of his mouth. 'Me? I'm juss a Traveler, a Pavvy, a harmless tinker if ye like. Ye have the likes of me wherever you're from.'

'Don't know much about the Travelers, but there are thievin cunts like you everywhere for sure,' Toady said. He was still gazing out the window at Shelley smoking her fag by the fence.

Mossy sighed and squeezed his giant fist on the table.

'Look—dah missus o yours lost a bet.' He poked a thick finger into the table making the mug hop and Toady flinch. 'Ax the lads.' He pointed out the door. 'I told her to stop it. I told her to go to bed—but no. So I put me money on the table and if the cards had been kinder to her, ye'd be six grand richer today. She's a grown woman and I'm a fair man.' He banged the table again. 'Even if she'd won, I'd still be givin ye a lift down the road—cos ye axed me nice like.' Toady looked in his eyes, wide with either a deep sincerity or a calm insanity.

'Asked ye? To kidnap us?'

Mossy sat back and stroked his orange and grey beard then raised a finger. 'If I'm such a robbin bollox, then why didn't I go through your bag yessterday when yez were snoring like babies all the way down here. Go ahead, Sonny, check your pockets. Tell Missy to go check her bag too. Nobody touched nauthin.' He leaned forward right into Toady's face. 'Coz I want to give ye a chance to put dis right and take responsibility for your woman. That's the Traveler way.' He tapped the table lightly three times with a thick brown finger then sat back.

Toady considered saying something about loaded decks, marked cards, or filling her with vodka while he was asleep, but Mossy was talking again.

'Now—havin said all dah. I'm gonna tell ye somethin straight. See that missus o mine? She's not a Traveler.' He shook his head and tapped his gold watch on his thick, tattooed forearm. 'She's a gypsy and dem boys about to be here in a minute, well—dems her family. They don't even know what century we're spose to be in.' He looked around with a vacant expression and shrugged his shoulders. 'France? No such place. That's juss a name some fella thunk up for where they live.'

His fat finger popped up between them and he started

again. 'Now! They're only comin to help out, but if they decide to concern themselves with you—?' He spat in the palm of his hand then clapped the two of them together in Toady's face causing his hair flap to lift. 'You're fucked.'

He got up, then bent over and leaned on the table and spoke to the top of Toady's head. 'When I say fucked, I mean you're fucked. Her?—Big mouth?—Ginger Rogers over there? She's gonna wish that fucked is all she was. With the Virgin Mary as me witness, I swear, I'd cut me own daughter's throat before I'd let dem cruel bassards take her back down there.'

Mossy was leaving when he turned and spoke over his shoulder. 'Now, I had a word with her. I know about the joint accounts and I know you're not short a few bob. So let's just get the shenanigans behind us and get you and your missus back on your holidays.'

Toady arrived at the fence beside her.

'Are we beside the sea?' He was watching the kids carrying canoes into the trees.

'River.' She pointed through a crack in the foliage to the slow brown water snaking through dense undergrowth where other kids could be seen drifting past. Songs and chants were emanating from within the hulk of a big barn.

'School looks like more fun in France.' She peered through the wire fence, arms folded across her chest. 'You gonna pay them the rest or what?'

'I dunno, can we make a run for it?'

'I dunno, can you climb a seven foot fence and swim a river?' She kicked the mesh in front of them.

'It's not so bad, Shell, least you were thinking fast with that story about the joint account. Now they can't keep you hostage here.'

'Yeh—and you can't do a runner on me either'. She turned and looked at his creased jumper and sagging jeans and shook her head. 'God knows—I would.'

'If I wanted to do that, I'd have done it on the boat and

left you to face your own music.'

'Oh I wish you had,' she scoffed and threw her head back. 'At least my troubles would be over. Such a fuckin round. I'm supposed to be paddling my toes in the Med by now. I wish I never got on that shaggin boat.'

He looked at her baffled. A faint holler came on the breeze and her glare shifted from his face to the distance over his shoulder. They were being beckoned back to camp.

'Ye can't get blood from a stone,' she said. 'You're the cash cow here, not me. I should bid them farewell and be on my way.'

'This is nice,' he said and raised an eyebrow. 'You get off your face on drink, hand over a couple of grand of my money to that lot, then blame me for having it in the first place? It wouldn't occur to you that none of this was actually necessary?' He held his hands up as though he expected an answer, but as soon as she opened her mouth he was off again. 'A nice meal and a cabaret to pass the time—no? Ye couldn't have just passed out with your knickers round your ankles in the toilets like a proper drunk? Oh no, not you. Lemme see now. I've got a few hours to kill. I know—I'll drink a bottle of vodka and go and lose a couple of grand to some nutters. Oh great—lads with machetes—perfect!'

'First off, you gave me the money—remember?' She stuck one finger in his face. 'So don't look at me like I stole it. Secondly, I don't do singsongs and cocktails round the piano. Why didn't you just pay some brazzer to suck you off? It would have been cheaper and you could have just wiped her off afterwards and dressed her up like Kate Winslet—done the scene from Titanic up the front of your epic fucking romance.'

'I didn't ask for romance,' Toady sneered. 'I'd have settled for any scenario that didn't involve kidnapping and death by jungle swords.'

'Ah sure why didn't ye tell me that before ye asked me

along?' She turned her eyes to heaven. 'Aren't you the silly bollox?'

'Listen to me.' He took her by the arm but she pulled it away.

'Don't fuckin touch me,' she snapped. 'There's no money in the world you can pay to put your hands on me.'

'Sorry, I didn't mean it.' He held his two hands up. 'But please—listen to me.' Another cry reached them from the camp.

'Fuck off,' she roared a foot from Toady's ear. She waved two fingers to the distant gathering before folding her arms in anticipation of what he had to say..

'Ye really think that because there's a woman and a kid with them they'll go easy on us? Or even you?' He shook his head. 'It's business as usual over there. Mossy Junior is learning the skills of the trade. Today's lesson is how to take candy from a baby.' He pointed at the ground. 'This here is not about a card game. This is an abduction. Shit—it might even be a murder and we just don't know it yet. Cutting cards was just the bait.' He studied her with a dry smile. 'I bet he even let you win a couple before he reeled you in—didn't he?' She was silent as he pointed back at the camp. 'This right here, is what they call a shakedown. It's an open-ended invitation to ride with them while they figure out just how much candy we have and the best way to take it.'

He watched her swallow the bitter pill. Then she pinched his cheek and shook it noisily. 'Okay, so I fucked up with the candy—but you're still the baby.'

Back at the camp it was like a staging zone for a military operation. Four men stood around the rear of a red Hiace van that had reversed into the assembly area. Inside they could see plain wooden benches fixed to the side panels. Outside, Mossy was the man of the moment.

'Meet the brother in law,' he announced. He gestured to one of the men, a tall, dark-skinned man, with features lean to the bone. He seemed somewhere in his late thirties, though the sun could possibly have already aged him by a decade. His hair was greased with a long flick hanging on his bony cheek. His sinewy arms were woven with the vines and leaves of tattoos. Another small tattoo of a cross nestled under his bottom lip. His eyes were black and cold.

'Ca va, Bruno.' Mossy clapped him on the shoulder. 'How is Caesar?'

'Fashay!' Bruno looked Shelley up and down unreservedly.

'Quelle surprise, mon frere, ay vous?'

'Fam.'

'Man o few words.' Mossy nodded sagely.

He shooed the pair into the van and the suspension groaned and descended a foot as the goons bundled into their places behind them. The door was pulled down and with a wild roar and a puff of smoke, the van jumped into motion. The smell of body odour and aftershave mingled with the exhaust fumes leaking in through the floor as the van tossed and swung them about the roundabouts and hairpin turns of the narrow streets. Not a word was spoken in the dark climb up through the town, illuminated only by the light coming through the grill on the grimy rear window.

'I'm gonna puke,' Shelley groaned out of the corner of her mouth, just before the van bounced to a halt. The door burst open and they all bailed out. Mossy was waiting for them in the narrow street outside and he led them through a stone archway opening into a spacious garden. White buildings stood on all sides with lines of windows overlooking perfectly preened hedges, smooth lawns and white gravel tracks. Golden sunshine poured in from a glorious sky over terracotta roofs.

Mossy led them to a bench beside a fishpond and sat down, spreading his arms and legs to the sun. 'I'm gonna wait here and warm de bones while you do de business. It'll be nice and quiet here for ye when ye get back, and then ye can be on your way.'

'This supposed to be a bank?' Shelley looked around.

'No Luvvie, this is the Public Library.' He gestured to the old facades as though he'd built them himself. 'Not much of a reader, but I like the feeling of wisdom oozin outa de place. I can soak up a bit o that too. Bank's round the corner—the boys'll walk ye down. You're nearly there, Ginger, juss keep dah fella sweet.'

When they got to the bank the men deployed quietly. One on the corner, Bruno at the door and two stood at the kerb. As soon as the door swung shut Shelley's nails dug into Toady's arm. She dragged him over to the red leather sofa in the corner where they sat under a giant fern. Her arm linked tight around his, her eyes darting from side to side, she spoke from the corner of her mouth. 'Okay, bullshit aside—I believe ye, we're in big trouble.' She smiled like a demented clown at the security guard before her mouth shot to the side of her face again. 'Look, I'm sorry for getting us into it, but now—I'm beggin ye—just get the money and pay them. What do you care? You said you've got plenty, so invest a bit in your future—our future.'

'Our future?' He glanced at the side of her face with amusement. 'Now I know you're scared.'

'Of course I'm fucking scared. I appreciate it's your mother's legacy and all that, but I think she'd approve of a worthy cause.'

His shoulders relaxed and a calm silence hung between them as the smile drip-dried on his face. She scrutinised his expression for a hint of what he was thinking. 'Say something, boy.'

At the top of Toady's short list of impressive personal skills, and vying for first place with his ability to endlessly endure the mundane, was eighteen years of Shotokan Karate. Practiced most days, whilst he recited lengthy excerpts of an ancient Chinese Manuscript, written by a thirteenth century warlord called Sun Tzu. On the rare occasions that he admitted to being religious, this is was what he was referring to.

'This is the last time we'll have the element of surprise on our side.' He spoke to the empty space in front of his face. 'If we pay them today and they don't let us go, then we will never have surprise in our favour again. Are you prepared to waste this opportunity?'

'Surprise?' she muttered to herself. 'In a bank with Yoda—I am. Wait! Are you supposed to be talkin to me?' She stuck her face in front of his. 'You don't know any of that for sure, they might let us go if you just pay them.'

'Maybe—but what I do know is that this is the last time our objective will be so close.'

'Objective?'

He glanced towards the door. 'This might be our last chance—ever.'

She grabbed his face with one hand around his chin and squeezed his cheeks, her nails bit his flesh. 'Wake up Glasshoppah, there's three of them outside the door.' She turned his puckered face towards it. 'There's another one just around the corner.' Her nails slid through his stubble. 'You can't beat all those guys.'

'Imbalance of power,' he declared, 'they'd never expect me to attack them.'

'No shit!'

'Hit them hard—make them angry.'

'They're already angry.'

'They'll forget about you for a minute.' He turned to face her. 'You run. Get down a side street, then duck into a café. Hide.'

'What?' She sat back a little and searched his eyes. 'You're gonna let me get away? Why would you do that?'

'Once you're gone it'll be easier for me to make a break for it, when I get my chance.'

'But I haven't got a penny to my name.'

He pulled out his wallet and took his last bunch of

fifties and gave it to her.

She leafed through it and stuck it in her bag. 'You're actually gonna let me go?' He turned to her with an offended expression and she put her hand on his leg. 'I'm sorry. I didn't mean that, I just meant—what about you?'

Out the door he could see Bruno glancing impatiently over his shoulder trying to see through the darkened glass.

'I'll see ye later.'

She looked him up and down. 'Christ, boy, ye look like a bleedin schoolteacher or something. They're gonna murder ye.'

He winked. 'War is deception.'

'You're nuts.' She grabbed him by the salmon pink shirt collar and after hesitating momentarily, planted a kiss on his forehead.

'I'm sorry for getting you into this.'

'Don't worry,' he smiled, 'victory is assured.' He stood up.

'Wait,' she said, before he turned away. 'I heard them say Bordeaux is near here. There's a giant sand dune over there somewhere. If I have to leave the town, that's where I'll go. I'll wait for you.'

He nodded slowly and stared into the distance. 'Okay, Shell, I like the sound of that.'

Wars start with explosions and two seconds after he walked out the door the first one came laden with a sharp, bursting crack. She could feel the air pressure change inside the small bank when a thousand diamonds of glass exploded inwards. Bruno came twirling in the door like a drunken man chasing a waltz. He grabbed a giant Yucca tree for balance and took it with him. As he went down, his arms shot out and he slapped the corner of a large tray of business cards, sending it cart-wheeling sideways over his head. A thousand cards sprayed in every direction like a firework exploding and the screams that erupted from all around sounded like rockets taking off.

He hit the ground with a howl and Shelley felt the vibration of his head on the marble tiles through the rubber soles of her boots. An alarm bell rang out overhead and a siren came whining from behind the counter. Steel shutters were slamming on the cashier's desks and the few people inside were now scrambling for the door. Shelley watched the man peel himself up. He paid no attention to her, but stumbled straight out the door again, holding his face and pushing people out of his way on the footpath beyond. She pulled her scarf over her hair and tied it off, stuffing any lose ends down her jacket and zipping it up to her chin. Her shades went on.

Over the din came the next explosion as she heard metal smash into metal outside when two cars collided in the street. The deep stutter of bouncing rubber punctuated an eerie silence as a delivery truck ploughed into the cars. In the middle of the street she could see Toady trading blows with two men, turning and ducking as he stepped deftly through the traffic, choosing his spot, then calmly launching his attacks in flurries of two and three blows. She pulled her bag strap over her head and swung it behind her

A man's voice shouted, 'Ay vous, Madame—Arretay!' and she saw that the security guard was pointing at her. She had no idea what he had said, but another voice inside her head let out a roar—'Run bitch!'

She burst into a sprint. Skidding across the broken glass at the foyer, she arrived onto the footpath hopping sideways. People stood in ones and twos, in shallow concrete recesses, peering from behind tree trunks, transfixed by the mayhem behind her as it progressed up the main street. She took off in the opposite direction, careening through a pair of men in suits, knocking them apart. Across the road she saw a side street between two tall, brown buildings and cut out through the stalled traffic. Horns were blowing, men were shouting, then two loud cracks rang out and people's heads went down with another collective scream. She reached the path stumbling and managed to stop herself hitting the ground. Her arms flailing wildly in front of her, she burst through the crowd that had flocked to the gap in the buildings seeking safety in numbers.

The long side street stretched out before her and she had momentum. Her legs remembered what they were for and found their rhythm. Her arms pumping like pistons and her head up, she opened out her stride and felt her heart pounding hot blood in her chest. Some people saw her coming and ducked out of her way. A young couple didn't and stepped into her path only to get blown apart like a pair of saloon doors hit by a freight train. She came to a little green area and wheeled left across it into pedestrian street with a long downhill incline. Two hundred metres flat out, expecting to be grabbed at any second, she was running on fear as her lungs were bereft of air.

The lane was coming to an end with a main road looming in front of her and beyond that, a wide river. The last thing on her left was a blue canopy projecting over the path with the word BAR written on the side of it. Her left arm lunged out like a mechanical device and she stopped her flight by grabbing the wall as she passed and swung herself into the doorway with a loud crash. She fumbled with the handle then squeezed inside into the darkness. Barging through the wooden stools and struggling to get her balance in the dark, she breathed like a knackered, old donkey stumbling into its stall. She made her way to the farthest end of the bar where she stopped and spun around, then slid down the wall to her hunkers, then onto the floor. And there she sat, with her head down. Listening to her braying turn to wheezing and eventually back to breathing. She never looked up, she dared not. She could hear, away in the distance, the wailing of distant sirens. Then closer, whizzing past on the road beside the river, two more sirens and then—silence.

***

'Wake up, Toad.' She tapped him on the cheek and he sat up in the plastic armchair. The same sparrows were chirping at his feet as earlier. 'Ye goofed off for the last bit.'

He rubbed his face. 'Yeh, I remember. We bust out of the bank. Where did you hide?'

'In a bar. How bout you, can you remember?'

He drank the last of his orange juice. 'Yeh, sort of. They caught me. One of them had a gun, crazy bastard was actually gonna shoot me. Then the van pulled up, threw me in the back. I remember being back at the campsite. That Bruno guy was pissed off. Cut his pretty face when he went through the door.' Toady smiled vaguely, then he looked down at the scrapes, welts and bruises up and down his torso. 'I got the shit kicked out of me, didn't I?'

'Not in the face,' she noted, pointing, and that made him laugh a little. 'What's funny?'

'Now I remember. Mossy, leppin around, shitehawkin, then shouting at me "Not in the face, you have to go to the bank again, watch the face—" The smile melted and he shook his head. 'Like I had a choice in the matter.'

'Well you obviously went to the bank again, in Quillan, at the horse festival.' She motioned towards the table. 'It's written on the envelope and the bands around the money. And they obviously upped the stakes.'

He was thinking hard and it was showing in his eyes. 'All I can remember is sitting by a river, must have been that night. Big—like the Mississippi, steam rising off it in the evening. His missus gave me sandwiches and he gave me a half-box of beer. It was kinda nice. I remember the crickets and the lights twinkling in the trees, way over the far side and me sat right on the water's edge. There was a ferry goin over and back and I remember thinking if I could just get on it. Not a chance, they were watching me like hawks, and his missus barkin non-stop like a demented bitch, I knew there had to be more to it than just a couple of grand. Fucker was afraid, I could see it.'

Shelley poured him what was left in the carton of orange juice and Toady sat forward with his elbows on his knees.

'I remember—he comes and sits down. Tells me that the matter is slipping out of his hands. Said if I didn't pay him I was as good as dead and there was nothing he could do about it. Some shit about a queer fella he owed the money to. Said if I ended up in Perpignan, the divil himself wouldn't be able to get me out.'

'Well he was wrong,' Shelley announced. 'You ended up in Perpignan the day before yesterday, drove straight through it in rush hour—no divils or queer fellas. About twenty miles back up the road. I was following an English couple out of the mountains. Headed for Spain they were, on the coast road. I didn't like the idea of it with you half dead in the back, so I stopped here.'

'We're only twenty miles from Perpignan?'

'Less.'

'Wonderful—the lion's den. I need to lie down.'

She shook her head. 'Uh-uhhh, I just changed all the sheets on that bed and you're not goin back in it smelling like that. We're gonna have to share until you're better, cos I'm not sleeping on my own if all those nutters come in the night.'

'And what exactly do you think I'm gonna be able to do to save you?'

She smiled and winked. 'Tough guy. I've seen ye in action.'

She stood up. 'Now, I'm pretty sure you're not gonna make it to the shower, so it's an old-fashioned scrubbing for you.'

She came back with a basin, a big sponge, a towel and a pink floral shower cap that she placed on his head, then helped him to his feet.

'How do I look?' He stood with his arms by his side.

She put her hands to her mouth to hide her smirk.

'Like someone's putting a jonnie on a giant—' she gestured her two hands up and down.

'Okay, I get the picture.'

'Stand out from the table. I'll do it for ye.'

Embarrassment was futile. She soaked the sponge in warm water and squirted a load of shower gel onto it, then started with his face and all around the line of the shower cap. The water cooled on his skin and felt so refreshing that he groaned and dropped his head and closed his eyes. She did his neck then rinsed the sponge out.

'Give me a look at ye,' she whispered. She turned him a little more towards her and stood in front of him. With her boots off she was only an inch or two taller than him. She did his shoulders and the tops of his arms, then his chest.

'You're strong,' she said. 'Where did a fella like you get these muscles?'

'What's a fella like me?'

'A comb-over rehab in lucky bag shoes.' She waited for him to protest, but he didn't. 'What's that all about? Ye have all this money but you're wearin stuff the charity shop threw out.'

'Danny Redmond,' he said quietly.

'Who?'

'Fishfood they call him. I owe him.'

'Jesus, ye must owe him a lot.'

'It comes down to two survival principles,' he said on a deep breath as she washed his back with copious amounts of warm water. 'Don't draw attention to yourself.'

'Is this that Japanese bloke you were on about in the bank?'

'Chinese, and no, it's called grey man theory.'

'Go on.' She turned her eyes up to heaven.

'D'ye wanna know or what?'

'Go on, I said.' This time she waited until he started to

speak, before her eyes went up again.

'A bloke is an extrovert, fancy clothes, hair—loud. He walks into a room and all of a sudden everyone is on edge, watching him.'

'And that's supposed to—aid survival, is it?'

'No, that's the opposite of the grey man. When I walk into a room nobody pays any attention. Nobody gets edgy, everyone just says, well—nothin.'

'And that's the look you're goin' for? Nothin? Well ye nailed it, so ye did. Lift up your arms.'

He lifted his arms to shoulder height and she stuffed a soaking, warm sponge into his armpit and let a flood of water run out and down his bruised and swollen ribs. He flinched as she pressed the sponge to each of the welts. Then she came round to do the other one.

'What's the other principle? Black and blue man theory, is it?' She rubbed the sponge the length of his arm to his fingertips.

'Point Break,' he mumbled.

'That's the point where ye break, and say fuck the grey man, and kill everyone I suppose?'

'No.' He smiled and closed his eyes again, yielding his senses to the glorious streams of perfumed water. 'It's the calm bit of sea, just beyond where the waves break. The place where a surfer has to make the decision, possibly his last one ever, to take the biggest wave that comes along.'

'Or what?'

'Or try to sneak back to safety.'

'So you're a surfer now?'

'No—it's a movie.'

'Wait a minute—I know that one.' She pointed in his face. 'Keanu Reeves.'

'And Patrick Swayze,' he said with a grin.

'That's a great film. They never show the good ones anymore.' She dropped the sponge in the basin. 'That's the end of the road for me. I'm not goin any further south coz Patrick Swayze you ain't, boy.'

'Huh?' He opened his eyes and she nodded down towards his waist where the water had soaked through his shorts and an indecent scene was emerging. 'Oh right.'

She soaked the sponge in the basin then squirted more gel onto it. 'Knock yourself out, tough guy,' she said. 'I'm gonna get ye some clean jocks.'

He waited until she was gone then pulled his cheap, blue boxers off and set to work below the belt. He lathered up. Then with his hand on the back of the chair for support, he dunked the sponge in the basin, rinsing it out. He dunked again then turned to face away from the camper. Spreading his legs wide, he let a waterfall cascade down his front with a loud satisfying moan. Then he dropped the sponge and looked up for the towel, only to find that all the workers were sitting twenty metres away along the wooden railing. Rolls, wraps and bottles in hand, they relaxed in subdued conversation watching the spectacle. He stared at each of them a moment, then turned his hands up. 'What the fuck?'

A mumble and a laugh went from one to the other as one of the men in the tracksuits watching from the shade of a steep bank smiled and saluted. 'Bonjour.'

Toady picked up the towel and dried himself off.

'So which one is this?' Shelley was beside him with a hand up to the side of her face, shielding her modesty and looking at the workmen. 'Is this the grey man or the surfer?' She held out a pair of briefs. 'Calvin Klein's boy. Brand new, out of the pack. Even that Arno bollox has better taste than you.'

He took them off her. 'What's with the audience? I thought you were being nice to me.'

'Ay, I'm hurt,' she protested. 'How many grown men d'ye think I've washed?'

Toady stood firm, refusing to give her the satisfaction of his embarrassment. 'This one is Point Break,' he declared. 'Patrick Swayze said, project strength to avoid conflict.'

She glanced from man to man, calmly eating or smoking, none of them showing any signs of anxiety.
'It's workin, so it is. Either that—or they're all gay.'

THE POSSE

Nicky clattered a plastic chair over to the side of the bed. He noticed a six-pack of Lucozade on the floor beside the locker and pried one out and guzzled half of it down then smacked his lips.

'Is that what you came up here for?' a voice mumbled. 'To rob me drinks? On top of everything else I'm not even safe from gettin robbed in me hospital bed?'

'I didn't think ye wanted them.'

'I can't fuckin reach them, ya cunt.'

Jackie's head was wrapped in a bandage. His right hand was in a sling, both his legs in plaster and he wore a whiplash collar. Nicky grabbed a bottle and ripped open the bag of straws, sending them flying everywhere. He then got the end of one into the bottle and offered it to Jackie who was watching him from the corner of his black and bloodshot eye. He got his busted lip around it and sucked like a big, helpless baby on a tit.

'She's not in the town,' Nicky reported. 'She was supposed to be in work but she never turned up. She's not in any of the bars and I asked that clown of a husband. He knows nauthin—literally. He's a fuckin rehab.'

'They're in France,' Jackie muttered around his straw.

'France? How d'ye know that?'

'Cops were just here, they found your taxi at the ferry port. Looking to tow it back, so they were. I told them no, that you'd go get it.'

'Why would I go get it?'

Jackie huffed. 'Cos ye don't know what's in it, there

could be anything.'

'Ye think I'm stupid.' Nicky was picking through the box of Maltesers. 'There's nauthin in the car neither.'

Jackie was getting worked up and spoke in a strangled growl, trying to shout and whisper at the same time. 'How the fuck do you know? He might have a bag of fuckin heroin in the glove box and a typed fuckin statement on the Mc Carthy girl stuck to the wheel—signed by you, or me for that matter.'

Nicky sat with his mouth open. 'I never thought of that.'

'No shit, Einstein.'

Nicky gawped. 'But that's the far end of the country.'

'You're a driver for fuck's sake! Bring someone with ye. Get it back and park it up in the depot. They'll be back sooner or later. He won't last a week in this town. I know scumbags who'll knife him for drink money.'

Nicky offered him a Malteser, Jackie couldn't reach, Nicky went on eating.

'Tell the cops fuck all about anything that happened last night. I told them a bunch o kids on drugs tried to mug us, hit and run, didn't see nauthin. No faces, no numbers, all that shit—right?'

Nicky nodded. 'Who's gonna pay for the petrol? One car down, two cars back, that's a thousand miles easy, so it is.'

'Fuck's sake, ye'd swear I didn't pay you cunts.' Jackie huffed and puffed but Nicky wasn't offering. 'My bus—they towed it out of the forest. The day's takings are still in it, under the panel at the heating vent, ye know it. Take three hundred and put the rest in the safe.' He stuck a bandaged finger in Nicky's face. 'Don't get fuckin stupid, I know exactly what's in it.'

As soon as Nicky saw the money he started to get stupid. Two-thousand, eight hundred and seventy, most of the day's takings from seven cars and a minibus. Jackie didn't like the drivers going around with all the cash, so he took it off them every few hours. Usually he put it in the safe straight away. But with all the commotion of that day, it was all still in the bus. Nicky put it in his pocket as part of a plan he would surely think up later.

He drove to Shelley's house that evening and found Barry just leaving.

'Where are you going?'

'What's it to you?' Barry was big and brawny. That was one of the reasons Shelley had gone out with him in the start. He was big enough to make her seem slight and that wasn't easy. Being big made him think he could get away with acting tough.

'I found out where your wife went.'

'I don't care, she'll be back, now fuck off.'

'No she won't,' he scoffed, leaning back on the door of his Black BMW. 'She's run away with that Toady buck. Gone to France, so she is.'

Barry looked stunned then shook his head. 'That fuckin rehab? She wouldn't go anywhere with him. She only goes in his taxi cos he's a soft touch. She never pays him.. He even gave her money a few times.'

'That's the thing, isn't it?' Nicky winked. 'He has the money to give, and let's face it, your wife's a bit of a brazzer.'

It took a moment for the insult to bustle its way through Barry's thought process, but by the time he reached out to poke him in the chest, Nicky already had a blade to his chin.

'She's on a boat to France right now. Later, he's gonna be slippin the snake in and out of her for the price of a few vodkas. He'll be getting his money's worth out of all the free taxi rides then, so he will—ye big gobshite.'

Barry backed away.

Nicky looked around then put the knife back in his pocket. 'So the way I see it, he owes me money and he has your wife and I'm goin after him. I could use some muscle.

He's a tricky hoor when he's cornered.'

Barry's brain was crunching behind his upturned eyeballs.

'How much money has he got? I could lose me job again, it needs to be worth it.'

'What are ye sayin? The wife's not worth it, no?' Nicky looked him up and down and shook his head. 'I'll knock a couple extra grand out of him for ye, howzat?'

'When are ye goin?'

'Ten in the morning.'

'I'll think about it.' He started to walk off.

'Ay—that friend of hers, what's her name?'

Barry turned, walking away backwards. 'Maeve.'

'We have to go see her before we leave. Does she work?'

'No, she's at home all the time.'

'What about the husband? Will he be there in the morning?'

Barry shook his head and turned away.

That night, after Barry came back from the pub, carrying his curry chips in a soggy brown bag, he was angry. The thoughts of a short, bald taxi-man screwing his wife made him envious. It wasn't her touch or her love that he coveted, only her happiness. Happiness was a zero-sum competition for Barry and 'till death do us part' was just one of the rules that came with admittance to a game. Somehow he had himself convinced that Shelley should know this.

In truth, he wasn't worried about his job. The only decent job he was ever likely to have, he'd already lost. A job for life at the American medical plant, with a pension and redundancy packages and a family-health insurance plan. Security was the other main reason Shelley had been attracted to him.

Two years previous, a coworker had caught him slipping something in her drink at the Christmas party. In true corporate fashion it was sorted out quietly. She got a free holiday that summer, with spending money, and a promotion when she returned. He was given one chance to quit, without legal complications, and for all his passionate protestation of innocence to Shelley, he took it. No redundancy, no benefits, no questions.

He wasn't a bad looking man, with his dark hair and square features, but five years into a deflated marriage and his looks were starting to melt into fat, and the secure job was gone. By now, even Barry suspected that he was a busted flush.

He found his moldy sports bag and threw a couple of crumpled t-shirts into it. A pair of jeans, some socks and jocks, a porno mag and a bottle of baby oil. Then he went to the kitchen and opened the press where Shelley kept the breakfast cereal. In a Tupperware container, inside an old biscuit tin, he found her savings. She couldn't put it in the bank because he read all her mail. She'd been saving for two years, twenty a week whenever she could. She had over one and a half-thousand squirreled away with the stale muesli. He checked it monthly and had always intended to take it at the right time. He was in no doubt that the time had just arrived.

The only thing left to pack was the small envelope inside a sock with the Rohypnol tablets inside. People call them the date rape drug, Rufies for short. He called them his Open Sesame Seeds. Just knowing he had them made his heart beat a little faster when he saw a vulnerable girl, and there was no harm in that.

He went to bed in Shelley's room that night after watching girls doing squat thrusts and leg spreads on the Tele-Sales channel. In her clean, fragrant sheets he found the underwear she'd taken off on the morning of her departure and inhaled the stale fragrance of her sex. It gave him a throbbing hard-on, which he relieved into the soft cotton with a grunt and a curry-sauce fart. Then he threw them on the floor and passed out.

Ten-twenty the following morning found Barry knocking on a pretty, painted door in a damp housing estate. After a minute, it opened and a woman's face appeared in the gap.

'What do you want?'

'Need to talk to ye, Maeve. Lemme in.' He stepped forward.

'Fuck off, I'm not in the mood.'

'It's Shelley,' he said.

'What have you done to her now?'

'Nothin, she ran away.'

'Good for her, now piss off before I call Derek.'

Barry was nudged to the side and Nicky breezed past and hit the door with his two hands, sending the woman reeling back down the hallway and the door crashing into the table behind it.

'Don't have time for this shite, just find out what she knows, will ye?'

Down the hall Maeve ducked into the living room, Barry followed and Nicky was right behind. She was standing in the middle of the floor clutching the poker to her chest when they entered.

'Fuck off, bastards!' she shouted.

'Calm down, Maeve,' Barry said. 'No one's goin to hurt ye, I just want to know did ye hear from her, that's all. She tells you everything.'

'I heard nauthin, now get out or I'll call the cops.'

Barry felt Nicky at his shoulder as he lunged forward and punched her with a loud crack in the face causing her to tumble backwards over the coffee table, sending debris scattering. The poker flew out of her hand and hit the window behind her with a bang and she landed on the ground in a heap. Nicky pushed Barry aside and reached down pulling her from the floor then shoved her back into an armchair. Sporadic trails of blood fell from her nose as she looked around to get her bearings.

'We're playin bad cunt worse cunt here so where is she

before I break your fuckin nose all over your ugly head?'

Maeve was trembling like a leaf. Tears poured down her face, diluting the thick blood and causing it to flow freely around her mouth.

'Where's your phone, ya pig?'

She searched around then pointed at the floor where it had landed. Nicky picked it up and sorted his way through the menus for a minute. A smile spread across his face.

'Oh Jesus, Maeve,' he said with a high pitched voice, then winked and continued reading. 'I'm really goin to France with this tool. On the boat. He says he's loaded. Nothing to lose, I spose, cept that shit job. Fuck it. Seeya in a week. Question mark, question mark.' He scrolled. 'That's all there is from her,' he concluded and put the phone in his pocket. 'Listen, Maeve, luv, don't tell a word to anyone about this and if ye hear anything from her, ye ring us. Got it?'

She nodded without looking up.

'Don't try and warn her, and don't make me come back here and show ye what your arsehole is for. Ye hear me?'

She nodded again with her eyes fixed on the floor where the blood was starting to make a little pool on the cream carpet.

'Good stuff so.' Nicky clapped. 'Let's go, boy, we got a boat to catch.'

Barry looked at her a moment then turned to leave and walked straight into a young boy standing in the doorway.

'Tommy—what are you doing here? Why aren't you in school?'

'It's my birthday,' the boy said with his face down. 'Me and Mam are going to the cinema in the afternoon?'

'Happy Birthday, Tommy,' he stuttered. 'I'm gonna get a card for ye.'

'Thanks, Daddy,' the boy mumbled back.

'Daddy?' cried Nicky. 'Well that's cosy.' He laughed and slapped him on the back. The little boy pushed his way into the room past the two men and looked over to where his mother held a cushion to her face and peered at him with teary eyes. Barry walked to the front door.

'Ay,' called Nicky, 'ya mean cunt. It's your son's birthday.' He reached into his pocket and pulled out a wad of cash. He peeled twenty off the top and put it in the boy's pocket.

'You take Mammy down to the cinema like a good little boy,' he said and patted him on the head. The boy stared at her and she stared back slowly shaking her head.

'Don't forget now, Maeve, I'll be back in a day or two to find out how you got on at the pictures if I don't hear from ye.' The front door slammed.

Half way down the country Nicky turned off the motorway and snaked a couple of country roads before arriving into the main street of a dirty market town, pissed black and grey from the drizzle. Its boarded up windows and graffiti-covered doors defied anyone to stop. He turned into a side street that revealed an L-shaped lane of council houses around an overgrown wasteland that might have been a green area in a previous lifetime. He pulled up and went into the last house for fifteen minutes then came out carrying a supermarket bag rolled up in a ball under his arm. The BMW crawled out of the deserted main street as the drizzle turned to rain.

'What's in the bag?'

'Answers to all your questions, boy.'

MEETING THE STROKERS

Toady woke up in the campervan later in the afternoon feeling infinitely better for the earlier feed and smelling like a toiletries commercial. He sat up in bed and there were two painkillers and a bottle of water beside him. He took the tablets and brought the water with him. He wasn't dizzy as the food had fortified his head, but his legs were still shaking.

Outside, the first thing he noticed was the breeze. The leaves and branches swayed, then stopped abruptly. A few seconds later another gust would push everything the opposite way. It was like the wind was just mooching around with no particular plan. It was cooler and he had nothing but his new designer briefs on. He looked over the fences and down through the terraces; not a sinner in sight.

He went to the rear of the camper to find that Shelley had moved the table and chairs into a sheltered suntrap. She was reclined in a scarlet bikini, smoke in hand and a cocktail on the table. Her sequined sandals rested on the chair in front and her scarlet toenails gleamed.

'Darlings, if it isn't the grey man himself,' she drawled. 'Do come and join us, Mr. Swayze, it's just dreamy on the veranda.'

He sat down on a free seat, hands covering his package, he ogled her without reservation. 'Wow, you look nice.'

'Thank you, thank you.' She dipped her sunglasses and regarded him over the rims. 'Hmm, and you look—better. How do you feel?'

'Middlin,' he said with a shrug. 'I have a savage burning sensation in me head, but it's a lot better than it was.'

'I see.' She reached over and pulled the pink shower cap off him and dropped it on the seat between them. 'You have a purple ring around your nut from that thing. I'm seeing a whole new meaning to the phrase—knobhead.'

He moaned as the blood ran back into the purple skin on his crown. 'Lemme guess,' he mused, 'you're pissed.'

'Oh, not by a long shot, Thomas, but our good friend Mossy has laid on a free bar for the evening and I do intend to make the most of it. God knows—I earned it.'

She sat for a minute with a big satisfied smile on her face. 'Have one yourself, there's a load of beer in there.'

'Uh, no thanks, not tonight.' He rubbed his face and stood up. 'I'm only starting to feel better.' He walked to the fence. 'The lads are gone.'

'That's right, they packed up around three. Lovely guys, pure sound.'

'Is that so?'

'Yeh, they came up and said hello, the three big bucks in the tracksuits. Lemme think—' She sucked on her fag. 'Bernard, he can speak pretty good English—and then Theo and Jean-Luc, cousins. They don't have much English at all but they were smiling a lot.'

'No shit, what did they say?'

'The wind,' she sighed. 'Bernard said that it comes every day at the same time and that it will stop when the sun starts to go down. He says it comes from the sea, through the mountains. The Tramontane, he called it. Said it will bring thunder—per'aps.'

Toady walked the length of the fence to see the building they'd been working on. The slopes where covered in debris, cut bushes and branches. Not much else was evident in the way of progress.

'I must say, Thomas,' she called after him, 'there aren't many men who can get away with walking around in their underwear, even if they are Cee Kays.'

'And?'

'And I feel I really must say that.'

He shook his head and walked on. 'Well I don't know where my clothes are.'

'Try the bin.'

He arrived back at the table. 'You're funny with a few drinks, aren't ye?'

'Of course,' she beamed. 'It's my job to warm up the crowd before the circus starts.'

'I've seen your circus before.' He sat down. 'Any chance of some dinner?'

'Not a problem,' she said, pulling her feet down from the seat in front. 'I have the matter already in hand. I took two steaks from the freezer and we have mushrooms, onions and green beans to go with it.'

That made him smile. 'You're good at this.'

'Good? I am made for this shit, Thomas.' He watched her strong thighs as she walked away. Her ass was pink from the sun.

After ten minutes he started to smell food and his stomach groaned like a waking lion. She returned wearing a floral sarong and the pink tracksuit top, open to her cleavage. He couldn't help but stare at her as she approached.

'It's like a fashion show.'

She had her shades over her head and her long red curls poured onto her shoulders.

'I'm actually starting to like that evil bitch,' she said. 'She has taste. Well—some of the shit was heinous, but I dumped that.'

'Ye dumped her stuff?'

'Yeh, the heinous shit. The Louis Vuitton shades went in my handbag.'

'Ye mean you stole them?'

'Yeh—well lemme think. All the stuff kinda got stole in a bulk package when I drove off in their fucking house, ye know?' She gestured to the campervan then put a cup of tea in front of him and took some clothes from under her arm and dropped them on the chair beside him.

'I suppose,' he conceded. 'Just doesn't seem right to be chuckin their stuff out.'

'Ye know what your problem is, Toady?'

'I have no clothes?'

'Stockholm syndrome,' she stated.

'What brings you to that conclusion, Professor Kelly?'

'The fact that you're carrying on like Mother Theresa about the rights and wrongs of us putting clothes on our backs and food in our bellies. Two days ago they were knocking you around a field with your cock hangin out, after stealing twenty grand from ye. Did they give a flyin fuck about you, boy?' She covered her eyes. 'Jesus—I thought they were gonna ass rape ye for one horrible minute—I really did.'

Toady stared at the ground and strained to remember. 'I thought that was a dream. You were there for that?'

'I was hiding. That bastard Pawdie hit you hard enough to kill you.'

'Yeh.' He flinched at the thought. 'I think that's where my marbles went.'

'Listen—those scumbags kidnapped us, pure and simple. And if it wasn't for bustin outa that bank, I might have been raped by now. I might be dead—we both might be. And you're here worrying about their stuff?' She put her hand on his cheek. 'Stockholm syndrome, baby. Fuck those bastards straight to hell. You and the Chinaman were dead right back in that bank. They had no intention of letting us go. So they reaped exactly what they sowed.'

'Jesus,' he moaned with his head bowed, 'you're right.'

'Mmm-hmm,' she nodded. 'Besides, they've a lot more on their minds than Louis Vuitton or Juicy Couture.'

'Why?' He looked at her. 'Did you do something else?'

'You might say that.' She looked back with a mouth full of words but then turned away. 'You don't want burnt steaks. Put them clothes on, it's getting cool.'

The grungy ensemble, comprising a U2 T-shirt and three quarter length combat style shorts, was obviously Arno's.

The Tramontane died down after a while and the sudden gusts became less frequent. Toady was enjoying the loose warmth of his new clothes while savouring the smell of fried onions when their privacy was interrupted. A man and woman came by, walking a dog. Toady saluted them and they said, 'Bon Swoh.' It seemed as though they were going to pass by, heading for the stairs, when at the last minute they stopped and asked him where he was from. Then it became evident that they weren't going anywhere at all. Within two minutes of chitchat they were sitting down. Shelley heard the voices and stuck her head out the door and did a happy housewife routine, offering them wine and to Toady's horror, the man accepted.

They were German and they had been staying for the previous week in their caravan in the populated space around the offices. The weather had been bad and now that the forecast was good, they planned to tour a little. They both had good English though he was the vocal one. She spent exactly half the time looking deeply interested in what was being said and the other half beaming a beautiful smile from person to person in a kind of slow, inexorable spell she wove. She had short black wavy hair that licked her pointed chin when she spoke and her smooth skin was a pale brown, like creamed coffee. Three tiny moles formed a small triangle on her cheek and her thick, glassy lips were smooth and black.

On the other hand, the husband was all German, with his stiff, fair hair and a pointy beard to match. Bright, blue eyes squinted behind the wiry frames of his small, round spectacles. He told them they were from Frankfurt and they lived in an apartment in the outskirts. He drove a taxi by day and studied psychology at night and she worked in a huge bookstore.

'I'm actually a librarian,' she said, 'but I didn't imagine

how depressing those places were until I worked in one. Mien Gott—' she sighed, 'it is like working at a graveyard, surrounded by the words of dead people. I want action, give me the happy stories—make me laugh.'

Her husband seemed bored every time she spoke.

'I am the book locator and I know where every title we stock is to be found.' She tapped her head. 'No computer necessary. Oh—and this beautiful lady here, is my Bichon Frise.' She tickled the dog's chin. 'And her name is Sukie.'

'Well I made my money in cheese,' Toady professed proudly.

'Really?' she gushed. 'How interesting. Is there money in cheese?'

'Greek Feta—me and my Dad.' He swept his hand across the grand vista of some imagined empire. 'We set up the distribution lines for the importation and distribution of Feta cheese—throughout the entire land.'

Oddly enough, that was actually true and this pair of strangers were now the only people in the world ever to have been told that wondrous fact. The one and only thing his father had ever done for him was to set up a business for him to walk into when he left school. It gave him an unprecedented surge of pride to speak the words, buoyed up by the gratifying realization that he could no longer think of any reason to call himself a taxi driver. He sat back with his fingers linked across his chest and radiated a smug satisfaction that brought a smirk to the woman's face.

The steaks were ready and Shelley wasn't going to allow them to burn or go cold so she put them on plates and dumped the steaming mushrooms and onions on top and went outside. The librarian radiated impossible smiles and gushed with enthusiasm at Shelley's arrival.

'I'm sorry,' the man said. 'My name is Dirk Krazenstein, and this is my wife, Anna.'

'Oh how perfectly lovely,' Shelley cooed putting down her vodka and reaching out her hand. 'We're the Strokers,

Mickey and Fanny.' They all shook hands and the little dog barked approval. 'I hope Mickey here hasn't been boring you with his cheese stories.' She'd been listening at the door while she smoked a small joint she had made from a stash she had found in the caravan. 'Back home they call him Mickey Cheese. Never shuts up about it.'

'She's drunk,' Toady said, straightening in his chair, 'don't mind her.' He cut himself a big lump of steak. It was barely showing a little pink in the middle and that was just the way he liked it. 'Fanny, Fanny, Fanny.' He shook his head as he chewed the tender morsel. Anna glanced excitedly from one to the other and sipped her wine. 'My lovely Fanny.'

Shelley pulled out the scarf she'd tied into her hair as she sat down and her red tresses tumbled down her shoulders and Anna sighed. Her English was simple and perfect, moving rhythmically from word to word, the hard German edges softened by her thick lips.

'My god, this beautiful red hair.' She reached out and took hold of a few curls. Shelley just batted her eyelids at them both.

'My fiery-haired Fanny,' concluded Toady.

'Please, please,' Anna cried with glee and a smile that could have illuminated a small town. 'You must let me draw you. I have pencils. I study art you know? You are so pretty, you must let me.' The little dog yelped with excitement and Toady thought Shelley was going to take off vertically, her eyelids were fluttering so wildly.

'You are so kind,' she gushed, 'I'd be absolutely delighted.'

'Fantastic!' Anna squeaked. 'I will come by tomorrow—at noon? Bring my things?'

'That will be positively splendid,' Shelley agreed. She beamed across at Toady who grinned back before stuffing his mouth with succulent mushrooms.

The two ate and drank while Dirk told them of some of the tourist highlights in the area. Shelley said they were going to take it easy for a couple of days till the knock on Toady's head got better.

'Ooh—a knock. How did you do this?' Anna's perfect features transmuted to grave concern as her irresistible gaze alighted upon him.

'He got into a fight at a horse festival. Some rude men made a pass at me and my Mickey went in hard.' Shelley's fist came up from the table and Toady shook his head.

A new expression appeared on Anna's face as the corner of her glossy lip crept up. 'Hmm, I hope you gave him as good as you got?' She took Toady's hand and turned it over, then ran her thumb across his scuffed knuckles. 'Oooh, I see you can throw a punch.' Her dark eyes were hard to break away from. 'You know—I may seem harmless, but I was in the army and I have a nice pair of balls too.'

'Just balls is what you have,' Toady said and winked. 'You don't have a nice pair. Trust me.'

She was about to object when Dirk interrupted. 'Hey—he's Irish, he drinks, he fights, he sells cheese to Leprechauns—isn't that right, Mickey? You're a cliché.'

Toady tried to discern the humour in Dirk's squinting eyes as he pushed his spectacles up his twitching nose.

'I suppose so, and you burn books and practice marching on the weekends—sing catchy songs.'

'Correct,' agreed Dirk without hesitation.

Anna gave Shelley her concerned expression, but as soon as Shelley looked back at her, a beautiful smile exploded across her face. 'Men—' she stated and shrugged her slight shoulders, 'all the same.'

When Shelley went to clear the table, Dirk grabbed and drained the bottle into his glass then stood up causing Anna to lose balance on the arm of the chair and spill some wine on her lap.

'Oops, silly me,' he muttered. 'I will get a rag to clean it.' And off he went to the campervan behind Shelley. Anna smiled more awkwardly and sat into the seat. She had a thin glaze in her eyes that suggested she was already a little tipsy.

'I cannot wait to draw her,' she gushed. 'I want to open a little reading café in the town next year. Then I will sell my art on the walls. I am making a collection of sketches for now.'

'Sounds like you have a plan,' Toady said. 'You are the intelligent one, I take it?' She tittered and Toady could see a hint of modesty and felt pleased to have teased it out. Dirk eventually arrived back and dabbed at Anna's vaginal area with the tea towel in a slow ritual. Shelley returned and leaned against the camper, watching the show while she sipped her cocktail.

'There we have it,' Dirk announced and placed the cloth on the table. 'All dry, and now we had better go, my dear. Get you out of those underpants, it is getting cool.'

Anna declared that she would be by at twelve-noon to begin the portrait, the little dog barked with excitement, and they disappeared down the concrete steps.

'Well that went banana-shaped at the end.' Shelley drained her glass.

'Yeh, I have a feeling I don't like him,' Toady added. 'She's cute though.'

'Oh goody, let's have a foursome?' she chirped. 'I know Dirk is game.'

'How so?'

'I've known him for an hour and I've had more contact with his cock in that time than in the last three years with my own husband. You'd swear it was a phone booth and not a campervan, the way he was squeezing past me, with a banana stuck in his pocket. I hid in the bedroom till he went.'

He cringed as he finished his glass. 'It's been a great day, Shelley. But I think I've reached my limit of excitement for now. Thanks for taking care of me.'

She waved dismissively. 'Not like I don't owe you a bit of nice-time.'

'That's for sure.' He nodded. 'Okay, so what's the plan here again?'

'Sit tight—get better—take a break from the shit in life.'

'Okay.' He was still nodding. 'So are you happy?'

Her eyes betrayed a smile. 'Yeh, this is okay, I can live with it. Just keep your clothes on and stay over your own side of the bed.'

'Never thought I'd hear those words come out of your mouth,' he said, delighted.

She shook her head. 'Christ boy, but you're easily pleased.'

CONFESSIONAL

In the morning he found that the throbbing in his head had faded into the background and his vision was clear. He sat up in bed feeling refreshed and pulled back the curtain to look out. Sparrows, trees and sunshine. Shelley was curled up in a roll beside him, hermetically wrapped in a light green duvet. Her hair sprang from the top giving her the appearance of a giant carrot—reversed. Skirting past her out of bed, he found the painkillers and poured a pint of orange juice.

He sat in the plastic chair, warm from the sun. He could hear the voices of the work crew out of sight on the terrace below. Overhead a thousand swallows swirled and dived in a clear, blue sky. The sun was still climbing towards its zenith. He guessed at ten o'clock, then took a little pleasure from realising that he didn't care what time it was.

He'd been dreaming about dogs again. Teeth snapping, jowls drooling pink and red—that incessant howling, he could still hear it. A swathe of his recent past remained impenetrable, with distorted faces leering from the ragged edges of nightmares and no way of knowing which were actual memories. He felt an unfamiliar pang as he listened for any sound of movement within the campervan and realized it was the feint stir of loneliness.

After a while, he became impatient to see Shelley, so he made coffee and wafted the rich aroma into her dreams with the aid of a tea-towel at the bedroom door, enticing her to wake. She appeared in the crack, one smudged eye peeping out.

'Coast clear?' she whispered.

Toady beckoned her outside carrying two mugs and the coffee pot. 'Bring milk and sugar.'

She had a smoke with her coffee.

'Don't forget you're modeling in an hour,' he reminded her.

She was using a hand mirror while she wiped at her features. 'I'm sunbathing—she can do what she likes. I'm on holidays and I plan on getting a tan on these freckles.' She cast a sideways glance at him. 'How's your head? Any more memories?'

'I don't know. So many dreams, I just can't seem to separate the two.' His gaze went blank for a minute. 'I can't figure out how you came to be down here. That horse festival in the hills, how did you get there? I know the gyppos took me, but how did you track them down?'

Now she had her eyes closed, enjoying the sun on her naked face. 'It's early, are you sure you want to hear all that?'

He sat forward in his seat. 'There's a shit storm out there somewhere, and I need to start figuring out what to do next and I can't do that if I don't know what happened before.'

She took her phone from her pocket and checked the time. 'Right so, we have an hour, but I need time to make myself into a goddess, so let's make it quick.' She poured herself more coffee and took him straight back to the bar she had escaped to after fleeing the bank.

She had eventually caught her breath while sitting on the floor, when a voice came out of the far corner of the bar. Blinded by the golden corona of sunlight coming through the blinds, she could only hear the shuffling of footsteps approach.

* * *

'Bonjour Madame.'

She slid up the wall, then dipped and squinted, shielding her eyes, as out of the light approached the slight figure of an elderly man. An unruly mop of yellow hair and two tired eyes waddled along the counter until he stood in front of her, smiling. He placed a round tissue on the counter and sighed, 'Ca va.'

She pulled her jacket straight and brushed her arms and sat sideways onto the last stool at the bar. 'Hi.'

'Troopluh dong la veel, non?' he said with a chuckle, pointing out the window at the far end. Her expression was blank. He made a pistol with his fingers and pointed at her face. 'Boom, Boom,' he said. 'Gherr manoosh—Gypsy war.'

'Hmm.' She looked to the door, expecting the arrival of the war at any minute but the room was a well of stillness, except for the occasional rattle of the ice machine.

'No worries, please. You are safe, Mademoiselle.'

She fumbled for her cigarettes and produced them for the man to see. He waved his finger and pointed at the NO-SMOKING sign over her head, then took note of the brand and produced an ashtray from under the counter. 'Ahh way—lay blonde.'

She gave him one and they lit up. He inhaled sharply before coughing and choking then bending over and banging the counter. 'Smooth,' he said.

'Beer?' she suggested. He put his fag in the ashtray and scuttled up the bar returning with a stemmed glass of lager. She checked her phone for the first time since the boat. Thirty-seven missed calls from Maeve's house phone, right through the night. Also there was a recent text message from Maeve's mobile.

- - WTF IS GOIN ON? WHR R U NOW?

She threw back the beer in one guzzle and replied.

- - TOWN CALLED SAINTES, EVRYTHNG GN 2 FUCK.

It was only one-thirty, as the sunlight came around and started to shine directly in the window. She had the whole day ahead of her, hiding, waiting for news. Toady had been right; he'd taken Mossy and his men by surprise, and the rest of the town too it seemed.

The door opened and she froze as light streamed down the bar as far as her knees. A man stood in the doorway and regarded her bathed in sunlight. Then a big welcome from the little barman as the newcomer jostled onto a seat. Dimness returned to her hideaway as the door inched closed on the spring. After a while her little friend returned with a small plate of olives.

'Ze trouble is finished.' He pointed to the window again. 'Lay Gitanos are—Vamoose.' He waved his hands. He was walking away when she piped up.

'Hello, scoozay mwoh?' The little man turned and now she made the shape of a gun with her hand. 'Dead people?' She put her hand on her heart and played dead.

His mouth flapped noisily up the bar to the other end and then he shook his head. 'No Madam, nobody is shot.' Not long after, a small plate with cheese arrived and another beer..

- - WHERE TOADY GONE? WHR R U?

She regarded her surroundings while texting with one hand and nibbling with the other.

- - IN A BAR, VICTOR HUGO SMTHN. TOADY DUN A RUNR.

She sat there for an hour, like a lone gorilla might sit against a tree, with her jungle of half-thoughts surrounding her and shafts of afternoon sunlight probing the canopy. The two men muttered and laughed in an endless exchange of tumbling phrases. Maybe it was time to go home, she thought. She could not imagine what purpose she could possibly play in Toady's fortunes. If they had him, she was no use to him, and if he was free, she had no business with him. A voice in her head reminded her, 'He just saved your ass, you thankless bitch.'

- - WHERE U STAYIN? U GOT MONEY?
- - OKAY FOR MONEY, STAYIN NOWHR YET.

The bell rang and the door burst open and light streamed in to the foot of her stool. The silhouette stood in the doorway and bid his farewell to the old man, then left.

'You okay, Mademoiselle?'

She gave him a thumbs-up. Later he brought her a plate with a thickly sliced lump of cured ham. She asked him for a glass of red wine. Kidnapping and gunshots aside, she was finding her first afternoon in France quite pleasant.

- - **WHR R U NOW?**

She turned her eyes up to heaven. 'Jaysus—what difference does it make?'

- - **SAME PLACE. GETN PISSD. DUNNO WHT 2 DO.**

Time eased by and it was pushing four o'clock and a half pack of cigarettes when her phone rang. She grabbed it up and the screen said, *Toady Taxi Calling.*

'Toady!' she gasped into the phone.

'It's me, Ginger,' Mossy's gruff voice returned. 'We have him up here in the Camping, if ye come up we won't kill him.'

'Shut up, ye daft bollox,' she spat back. 'You're not going to kill anyone, not until you get your blood money anyway. And if I go down there it's only gonna make your job easier.' In the background her phone peeped twice meaning someone was trying to ring through.

'So you're just gonna leave him here?'

'Listen, ya muppet, he's not my husband, he's nobody—a fuckin taxi man, ye hear? I lied about the money, that two grand was all he had—I'm a prostitute. He's been saving all his life for this trip and I stole it from him.'

'He already told us all that.'

'What—that I'm a prostitute?'

'No, that he's a taxi-man and he's got no money and all that shite. But ye know what, Ginger? I already seen into your soul and I know all I need to know, so I'll be takin him along for the ride until ye paid your debts. I've got plenty of work for a good prostitute—or even a bad one. So lemme know when you're ready to take responsibility for your actions, instead of lettin an innocent man take the drop for ye.'

'Ye think I'm afraid of the likes of you—a bully? Maybe I will come down there and bring a load of cops with me. Maybe I'll just come down and dance on your fuckin face for ya.'

'Wastin your time with the cops, darlin. They don't want nauthin to do with us. But you're welcome to sit on me face, ceppin ye better hurry, cos we're leavin in five minutes. Anything you want to say to this poor bassard?'

'Yeh—tell him I hope he kicks your cunt in.' She hung up and dropped the phone to the bar. 'Jesus, Brody, why didn't you run when you had the chance?'

Her phone was buzzing around the countertop again, another message from Maeve.

- - DON'T GO ANYWHR YET.

'Where does she think I'm gonna go?'

- - WHAT U RINGN ME ALL NIGHT 4?

She put her head in her hands. 'Thomas shaggin Brody,' she exhaled, long and slow. 'I didn't ask you to get yourself into this for me.' She kicked the bar and hurt her toe and that brought a tear to her eye.

The door opened and another tall silhouette appeared in the golden sunlight, wearing a cap. He turned in the doorway and spoke to the old man who pointed down the bar at Shelley and rattled out a machine gun sentence. The tall figure started to approach her as the door swung closed and she saw a policeman emerge out of the light. He was right in front of her before she could see his lean dark face and roguish smile.

'Ca va,' he said.

The only thing moving was her jaw, chewing on a bit of salty ham.

'My father said you are frightened, but I think he might be taking advantage. He is old, but he is still French. Are you okay, Madame?'

She nodded like a schoolgirl eating at the back of the class, caught by the sudden attention of her teacher.

'The trouble is over.' His perfect words and soft accent

rolled over her. 'You can go in the town—it is safe, you have my word.' He bowed his head a little. His strong fist rested on the end of a baton and the dark grip of a pistol protruded above his belt. It occurred to her for a moment to tell him about Toady, but considering he was the one who'd smashed up the town, she wasn't sure how that might go. Her phone rang again and she tilted it up to see that it was Maeve ringing from her house phone again, then cancelled it.

'Are you alone in the town?' he asked. He reached inside his pocket and pulled out a pen and wrote a number on her napkin. 'In case you have no dinner plans later, I know some splendid places.' He kissed his fingertips.

'Jesus. I mean wow.' She shook her head giddily. 'Shit, I mean thanks.' She slid the napkin from his fingers. 'Sorry—I'm not me,' she concluded.

He seemed confused. Her phone buzzed in yet another text message.

'Well, I see you are busy, Mademoiselle.' He smiled. 'I hope you enjoy your time here and please call me for any reason—Au-revoir.'

She nodded and batted her eyelids but couldn't think of an intelligent word to say, no more than she could figure out what to do. The old man called something gaily to the handsome cop and gave a big salute.

'Bon sworay, Papa.' He tipped his hat and the door swung open and the light flooded in once again, then faded.

- - IF I RING AGAIN DON'T ANSWER ME.

That was the first message. The second message was telling her that Maeve had left her a voice mail but before she had a chance to listen to it, another message buzzed in.

- - JUST STAY WHERE U R FOR FIVE MINUTES

She texted back frowning and muttering while stowing the policeman's number.

- - WTF ?

'Vodka,' she called out to the old man. 'Sill vous play, avec lemonade.'

She thumbed away at her phone getting her voice message up and put the phone to her ear. She lit a fag and offered one to the old man. He accepted and just as he was about to say something, the door opened. Two large shadows stood in the light making it impossible to see their faces. Maeve's panicky message came rattling in her ear.

- Shelley, answer your phone will ye? For fucks sake. I've been trying to get ye since yesterday. Did you get my messages? Look—I don't know what's goin on, but Barry was here with that Nicky bastard from the town.

The familiar guffaw was blunt and nauseating as the men approached her with their faces coming into focus as they drew near, the door closing behind them. An ice cube fell from her open mouth.

- They took me phone. I couldn't help it, he punched me in the face. Just don't fuckin send any text messages to my phone—understand?

'Hey Shell!' Barry's face loomed into her and he kissed her on the cheek, her mouth still agape. 'Don't look so happy to see me.'

- Gimme a call on this phone when you get this. Love ya Shells. Please-please—be careful Babes.

She looked at the faces leering in at either shoulder; two sides of a bent penny. Emissaries from the banana republic of the day before yesterday. She picked up her glass and downed the vodka in one go.

* * *

'I nearly passed out when I saw that pair standing in front of me, I thought I was dreaming. I'd have done a runner except I just hadn't got it in me at that stage.' She shook her head. 'Before they left, Nicky pulled a knife on that poor old man and took all his money. Then Barry knocked him out cold with a punch—killed him for all I know. After that we went up to the campsite and you lot were all gone. The guy in the office rang Mossy and told him we were looking for him.' She clicked her fingers. 'Mossy just told him to tell us exactly where he was going. Drew us a fucking map, so he did.'

'And you went straight down after us?'

'More or less. Spent the night trying to keep Barry out of my room in a shitty hotel somewhere.' She put down her coffee cup and retrieved her cigarette box from the tabletop. 'I caught him trying to put something in my drink at the bar. I had to get a bottle of wine and lock myself in the room, him outside, bangin like a mad yoke for half an hour.'

Toady was watching her from under his brow. 'You know, it's kinda funny, you laughing at me for being a lucky bag man, and there's you—married to a psychopath.'

For just a split second her face began to purse up in defense, then she slumped forward with her elbows on her knees. 'Aw fuck it, sure who am I kiddin?' She jammed a fag in her mouth and lit it.

Her voice was soft, her tone formulaic. 'All started off as a joke. Said he'd gotten some drugs off some buck at work, never tried them before. Did himself one night, then he did me. No big deal. Makes ye really dopey.'

'Is that what people do for fun?'

'Next thing I know he's sacked. Best job in the town—gone! Then he gets into a fight in the local boozer. Same thing—all a big misunderstanding. One day I remember asking myself, who is this guy?

She whispered something and Toady leaned in a little until he felt the tickle of her stray curls on his cheek.

'The whole time this shitehawkin is goin on and I'm thinking back to when Maeve got pregnant—out of the blue.' She made inverted commas with her fingers, either side of his face. 'Apparently, Barry arrived on her doorstep one night after the pub. Me and him were having some big fight, I'd thrown him out. So she let him in. He had a bottle of vodka with him and he was always good at the sob story. She never knew what hit her. She says he hugged her at some stage and it was like he squeezed all the air out of her lungs—until she remembered nauthin.'

Toady raised his eyes and saw the sky through the light haze of her hair.

'So you're saying your husband raped your best friend,' he mumbled.

'Yeh—,' she cast a glance sideways at his cheek. '—sounds rank, doesn't it?'

He abandoned logic and gripped the crown of his boiling head. He felt dizzy and when he breathed deep, sprigs of her hair teased his lips and made him shudder.

'In the movies, Maeve would have told me what happened and we'd have put two and two together and cut his balls off or something.'

'Of course.'

'But, it's not like that, is it? So I didn't know a thing about it—and it gets worse.'

'Jaysus.'

'So—he still had this great job then, good money, security—and that's all I wanted, in case one day I could have a kid.' She patted her chest and said, 'My kid—my own child, can you understand?'

He nodded, but then shook his head, eyes closed. 'Not really.'

'He came back to me all romantic and proposed and we had a quickie wedding, down in the registry office. Still didn't have a clue that Maeve was up the pole and she was too terrified to say anything, you know—denial?'

He was lost in the fragrance of her hair. 'Sort of.'

'Besides—' she slapped Toady on the side of his shoulder, 'how do you break news like that to your best friend? Oh Shelley—FYI—I think I mighta rode your new husband a while back. I'll be havin his kid by the time you get back from your honeymoon. Couldn't say for sure, but he might have raped me.'

She went to get another fag and he could see her hands were shaking.

'Well—somewhere in a blur of drink and bullshit I had a miscarriage, but Maeve—she had a little boy, alright.' She drew smoke from her new cigarette, then blew it out noisily and tossed her hair with her hand. 'He was a year old before she eventually told me about the night Barry stopped by. We couldn't keep secrets. She never even liked Barry much, so it didn't make a bit of sense for her to be with him like that. I was just too tired to be angry anymore. She got a son and I got a dildo for a husband. Barry never wanted to have a thing to do with Tommy. Imagine what it would have been like for my baby. Sometimes—I thank God he died.'

Toady had been listening intently with his hands on his head. 'So did you ever tell her about the pills?'

'Started to one night, but as soon as she saw where it was going, she just got up and walked off. We just don't talk about it now. Me and Maeve and little Tommy—we're like a survivors group. The two of them are the only reason I can stick my fucking life.'

'But you're still married to that bollox.'

'Guilt is good glue. I thought that if he stayed married to me, then he wouldn't do it to someone else. Kinda like—penance. One day ye look out the window and another five years is gone and ye can't remember what the fuck it is you're supposed to be angry at anymore. You're just angry all the time, but it's a lifeless anger.'

'I'm sorry about your baby, Shelley, I wasn't being nosy, I didn't mean for you to tell me all that.'

'It's okay.' She wiped her eyes then looked him in the face. 'I don't have anyone else to tell.'

She sat back and breathed deep, then said she had to get ready for Anna. Toady decided he was going to try a shower, even though his legs were still a little shaky. So it was on with the shower cap again and he walked like a geriatric, away through the trees with his towel under his arm and Shelley laughing.

'You look like Homer Simpson's dad,' she shouted after him.

Upon returning from the longest shower in the history of sanitation, he stumbled upon a peculiar sight. Shelley was laid out on her side on a sun lounger in just a red bikini, her hair tossed over the top of her head. She was sucking from a straw in a cocktail that she occasionally lifted from the ground in front of her. Behind the camper, Toady found Anna sitting in a deck chair, one foot up on the seat and a large pad resting on her knee in front of her. She was swiping and scratching at it in spurts and stops. She had a pencil in her hand, another in her mouth and one more tucked behind her ear for good measure.

'Hellooo, Mickey,' Shelley cooed.

'Fanny,' he replied flatly, surveying the spectacle.

Off to the side, less than twenty meters from where she lay, was a line of eight teenage boys sitting on the fence eating lunch. An intense air of concentration pervaded the group. They conferred among each other in murmurs as though they might be asked for marks out of ten at the end. The kid with the short blond hair and the dark rings around his eyes stood alone in the middle of the track, staring, with his hands by his side. At the end of the track, resting in the shadow of the stony bank, were the three men in black tracksuits and shades, each one puffing smoke, mug in hand. 'Henri,' one of the men calmly called to the blond boy. 'Assayay vous, tronkeeyay.'

It was like some flash Hollywood movie star had arrived impromptu along with her entourage and security detail.

'Wow,' he gasped. He stood in a pair of Crocs and shorts with towel and toiletries under his arm and a floral, plastic shower cap on his head. He crossed to where Anna was vigorously applying lead to paper. He could see straight away that she had talent.

Anna had come dressed casually for the occasion. She wore a loose cut off T-shirt, which was designed for minimal functionality. From his aerial vantage point it was serving no purpose at all and he had complete view of her two little handfuls. They were tipped with large black nipples, smooth and shiny, dark as chocolate with a small gold piercing in each.

'Very nice,' he mumbled.

'You like it?' She leaned back and tipped the drawing forward slightly to give him a better view. The loose waste on her denim shorts relaxed and now he could see straight down into them as well. She was wearing a pair of white cotton briefs with pink frills and a little yellow ribbon. A few curls of black hair were escaping from the top. It surely was an exotic and unexpected sight on a Tuesday afternoon and immediately he felt stirring in his shorts. Her long lashes blinked up at him. 'Well?' she asked, her mouth barely open between thick, glossy lips. 'Can you see it?'

'Nearly.' He dragged his gaze away and walked towards Shelley who was sucking on her straw.

'You're lookin better,' she offered between gulps.

'I feel it,' he said, and walked past her to see the eight heads in a line, chewing and vigorously pulling at their baguettes. The vacant stare of the blond boy in the middle drew Toady in, silent and close to his unflinching eyes and a murmur stirred among the three men close by.

He turned and stood beside him and glanced back to see what kind of view they were all enjoying. Shelley's generous hip protruded upward and the roundness of her soft pink behind was cleanly bisected by the tight red elastic of her bikini. The sun shone golden on her back and the groove of her spine and the dimples at the base trapped just enough shadow to show them off.

'Yeh, I can see the attraction here,' he said, then turned back to the row of silent faces.

'What the fuck, lads?' he called out with his two hands upturned. 'Is this some kind of a piss take? The whole campsite is empty.'

'Bonjour,' they chimed back in unison. He turned to the three men close by, eyes invisible behind their shades. Their dark skin and stubble made them appear more Arabic than French. They all saluted quietly as they continued with their smokes and coffee. Nobody was going anywhere as a result of anything he might say. That much was clear.

'Did you notice you have a fan club?' he remarked to Shelley taking the water bottle from the table.

'I take no notice of such things.' She sucked noisily as she emptied her drink. With her other hand she lifted the mirror at her waist, as though to check her hair. She turned it slowly, then put it down. 'Only eleven of them—I'm wasted out here'.

He took her in from her painted toenails to her mischievous eyes. 'You officially have everyone's attention,' he said with a wave of his hand. 'What more do you want?'

'At this point in time—nauthin. Wait!' she called as he turned for the camper. 'Vodka and coke. What about you, Anna?'

'I would just love—' her black lips cracked open like a slow kiss, 'some ice cold water.'

He fetched it and placed it beside her, taking another glance at the sketch and the tiny beads of sweat that rolled into each other in the shallow cleft of her breasts.

'How is it?' Shelley asked him.

'Sweet.'

'Yeh, I'll bet,' she sneered. 'Listen, I have another problem. I'm almost out of smokes.'

'—kay,' he said. Anna had started doing Shelley's bosom and she was sketching her naked. 'She's gonna do ye topless, Sweetheart.'

'Focus now, Michael—smokes,' she repeated. 'You don't want me going into town, do ye?'

He shook his head.

'So you'll have to go for me.' She picked up her box and shook it. 'Soon.'

He was still a little light headed but his legs had steadied up in the shower and the water had refreshed his outlook on their situation. Staying there with two half-naked women and an erection wasn't going to help his headache, or his frame of mind. He took two painkillers and went.

'Ay—back to work,' he shouted up when he reached the bottom of the steps. The small crowd gathered at the end of the track were otherwise engaged.

'Au revoir,' they replied with a wave.

THE NEW MAN

He stuffed his hands in his pockets and breathed in the air of freedom on that fine May afternoon. At the gate he surveyed the sprawling façade of a supermarket across the road and was seduced by a charming idea. 'Jesus, I'd love a new shirt,' he said to himself, as only a free man can. He crossed the road, then the wide expanse of car park and into the cool interior of the supermarket.

As luck would have it, there were many aisles of lifestyle paraphernalia and among them clothes to suit all tastes. He soon found the shirts and one in particular: an appealing dark blue affair with short sleeves and a faint leaf-pattern in gold thread stitched in one vertical line down the left side. He tried it on and it was perfect. On his way out of the shirt section he passed by the trousers rail and the sight of the faded denim made him long for the reassuring weight of a nice pair of new jeans. Not the crap he was used to wearing day in and day out in the cab. He found his size 32, 32 in a casual cut, but damn they were expensive.

At the end of the line of jeans a thick, dark-brown, leather belt with a brushed brass buckle seemed to fall right into his hand as he passed and that didn't come cheap either. 'Fuck it—shoes,' he said, looking at the miserable khaki crocks. He sauntered along until he came to the moccasins and the very pair that matched the colour of his new belt as though they had been cut from the ass of the same cow. He slipped them on and the snug warmth of the fit assured him he was right in the groove of a divinely preordained sequence of events, and that burgundy T-shirt just threw itself in his arms.

This was an experience he had denied himself for most of his adult life. Only on a couple of extraordinary occasions had he ventured to buy proper clothes. The comfortable suit he'd bought for his mother's funeral that he'd paid top price for and worn only once, then burnt.

More recently he had treated himself to a new outfit of jeans and sports jacket when he went to Amsterdam for a weekend to screw some prostitutes for his thirtieth birthday. On the evening of his return they sported an array of foodstuffs along with a selection of DNA that would have made an orgy in a kebab shop seem evident. He arrived beside the bin at the back of the rank at eleven that night with the ensemble in a plastic bag. They terminated their working life after barely twelve hours service. But the truth was, he liked clothes. He liked to admire them on other people, especially men.

'Vanity is like a faulty shotgun,' his mother had once told him. 'It's tricky to put it down once you've loaded it up, and it can easily go off in your face.'

'What's seldom is wonderful, Mother,' he whispered.

He was in and out in fifteen minutes with a full new set of clobber and no cigarettes. It transpired that they don't sell them in supermarkets.

'Dong la veel, dong la veel,' the woman said. A young man tapped him on the shoulder. 'Go in the town, Missyuh. Tabac shop.'

He found himself in the car park with forty quid left out of four-hundred. He stopped and put down his bag and stripped down to his Calvin Kleins. Some people making their way to their cars altered their course to give him a wider berth. Others just laughed. A car horn beeped as he pulled the T-shirt out. He turned and a man and woman were sitting in their car behind him.

'Sorry,' he called out and gathered his stuff and shuffled to the side to allow them to pass. The man said something as he passed and Toady smiled and responded with three or four 'wees'.

The T-shirt was cool and smooth on his lightly sunburned skin and he sighed with pleasure. The jeans were a perfect fit and the light pressure they applied to his package was instantly gratifying. He slipped in the belt and buckled it up and squared off the brass with his fly. But the moccasins were the real deal-clincher: soft, yet firm support to all his sole and a snug interior lining that was at once soothing and cool. He pulled the labels from his new shirt and swung it over his shoulders and slid in his arms in one fluid movement and it came to rest with a gentle breath, and the man was complete. He transferred the old clothes to the bag, Mossy's Ray Bans to his face and the last forty quid to his new pocket, then hit the road again.

'Thomas, your new clothes are absolutely smashing and I cannot say how happy I am to see that you got rid of that ridiculous hairstyle. You look like a handsome young man.'

'Thanks Mammy.'

When he arrived at the edge of the car park and flung the bag in a skip he was happy, and it was a kind of happiness that he wasn't familiar with. It existed outside of him and he was walking into it, which was the opposite of what he was used to, skulking in emotional silence on the fringes of his own life.

He followed the main street and a wide dry riverbed under a railway bridge then turned left onto a side street where he was less likely to bump into anyone searching for him. He wasn't exactly sure by which route he arrived at the seafront having passed through narrow residential roads, hardly big enough for a car to pass him.

Shuttered windows, two, three, and four storeys above. Balcony railings strewn with laundry and trellises thick with scarlet and purple blossoms. The sea breeze couldn't find its way through the maze and the air was much stiller and laden with heat and the smells of the town. The heady fragrance of flowers transformed seamlessly to onions and garlic wafting from a half open door. The shouting of kids echoed around corners and a seagull called from a red tiled roof. Radio music was dropping like leaves from overhead windows with louvered shutters ajar.

A pretty, middle-aged woman approached. As he was coming to suspect was surely an obligatory part of French culture, she was veiled in a mild scowl. He lifted his glasses onto the top of his head and offered a smile as she approached and as though he had learned how to break the spell of solemnity that bound her, the frown melted and her eyes dropped bashfully. The warm, sweet expression of the younger girl inside burst across her face and the blue of her eyes sparkled from beneath her lashes as she passed by.

'Bonjour, Madame,' he said to her in passing.

'Missyuh,' she replied in a low soft tone. He resisted the urge to look after her but he inhaled deeply in the moment of their passing and was left with the fragrant bouquet of the sun in her rich, black, wavy hair, so strong, that he tasted it on his tongue.

At the seafront he was chilled by a cooler breeze rushing in across the road from the beach. As luck would have it, fifty metres to his left a small boutique jutted out onto the footpath with the word TABAC in big letters.

It was a small shop cluttered with gifts of tiny shell and stone creatures, key rings, post cards and glass cases, a myriad of trinkets for tourists that hadn't arrived yet. They had every cigarette ever made. He got change for his tenner and another flirty smile from the young woman behind the counter and now he was starting to wonder where he'd been all his life.

He walked back down the promenade and could see that this place was geared up for tourism. Every other door was a bar, restaurant or café, each with its own set of parasols, seats and tables. Across the road most places had a veranda on the sea front, decked out in the same colours and motifs as the restaurant. He could visualise the waiters crossing back and forth with trays through the traffic, tea towels flung over their arms, the car horns hooting. The whistling and shouting and the music would make for quite a spectacle.

He pondered the notion of sitting outside and having a beer, but it was too cool in the breeze and the locals were all dressed in sweaters and jackets. He knew he'd feel out of place, and he was only starting to feel in place for the first time since the shock of being told he'd lost his legs.

Just then he noticed the black car with the tinted windows advancing slowly in traffic on the far side of the road and he spun on his heels, slipping inside the nearest doorway. He watched it go by then stuck his head out. It had an Irish registration plate. Not too many Black BMWs with tinted windows and Irish plates in that neck of the woods, he reckoned. A terrible notion occurred to him as his thoughts shot back to the campsite. He started into a run but within ten paces the jarring of his brain was agonizing. He settled into a fast walk with the beating of his heart throbbing in the top of his skull.

When he got back to the camp he advanced up through the terraces, sticking close to the hedges and banks. Staying low on the flights of concrete steps as he drew near, he could see that the work detail was gone. The ground and banks were strewn with the day's debris of piled, dead leaves and newly severed branches. He could see the roof of the camper come into view over the bank as he climbed the last flight of steps. The campsite was quiet and the women were nowhere to be seen. He stood motionless on the top step before walking to where he could see into the cabin. It was empty. He pulled the door handle and it swung open. He climbed into the living quarters. The bedroom door was closed, so he put his ear to it and tapped.

'Shelley—are you in there?'

The wind gathered outside buffeting the trees and massaging the camper on its wheels as he took a hold of the handle and cracked open the door. It was darker inside with the blinds pulled, the air a little stuffy. The smell of woman was heavy and sweet, a heady mixture of perfume and hair, tinged with sweat. He let the light enter the room a little more until he could see her unruly nest of hair on the pillow, her nose and lips protruding.

'Shelley,' he whispered, 'are ye okay?' Not a flinch or a twitch from a single curl on her forehead. A little louder, just above a whisper, he called her name and watched the ringlet that rested on her lip to see would her breath stir it. He opened the door wider and let light in across the bed.
The covers only came to her waist. She was wearing her red bikini top and her gold speckled breasts filled the cups roundly. Her nipples were pointed, their shape clearly visible through the thin fabric.

'Shelley,' he said softly, 'are ye asleep?' He watched her breasts closely to see would they rise on her breath, but he could discern no movement. Further down the bed, the covers started just below her tummy and were tucked in between her bare thighs. One knee pointed at the roof, the other lolled to the side. In the space under the cover he could see her bare hip and the smooth side of her cheek. She wasn't wearing anything down there.

'Shelley, are ye okay?' Her breasts heaved upwards as she breathed deep like she'd been holding her breath in whatever dream she was having. He froze to the spot as she shifted her back in the bed, then her arms came up and she stretched a little with her hands behind her head and her moist armpits showed just the beginning of stubble. She shifted on to her side and turned her back on him exposing to him the full roundness of her ass with the two lines crossing diagonally where the sun had made it pink against white. He stood dead still for a moment as she exhaled and came to a rest. His gaze lingered on her soft curves and the dimples at the base of her back. Her skin had a light tan and the freckles across her shoulder were like tiny golden leaves on honey. He could see the pale side of her breast under her arm, just above where the red strap bit across the round puckers of flesh.

He came into the room and took two quiet steps down the bed, then slowly eased down to his hunkers until his face was level with the pale skin of her ass. He was close enough to feel the heat emanating from her pink waist and to see the feint glow of sweat in the groove between her cheeks. He closed the gap between his mouth and her skin until he thought he felt the light fuzz touch his lip. He was breathing as softly as he could, but his mouth was so close to her that he could feel his own warm breath come back to him, scented with her perfume. He moved his face closer to the shadows and took a deeper breath, the smell of sex and sweat that permeated the air beneath the covers made his head swim. His nose accidentally brushed off her, sending the tiniest shudder into her as her skin rose in goose pimples. 'I'm sorry,' he whispered and slid up the wall behind him with a hand over his face, his eyes closed.

Shelley's eyes were open as she gazed into the corner, her face shielded from his view by her tossed hair. She trembled on her breath and the silence in the room forbade her to sigh or to make a sound as Toady retreated. The door latch clicked home as the breeze buffeted the camper to the sound of tinkling glasses.

'Jesus!' Toady yelped. A hand landed on his shoulder and he spun to face the dark figure behind him. The light from the door made it hard to see her face until she backed away, then down the steps. It was the dark-haired woman from the office with a smirk on her face.

'You watch over the sleeping lady. So kind.'

'Tucking her in,' he said.

'Of course you were,' she said in a thick, soft accent. 'Well I am from the office and I want to give the lady some news.'

He stuttered as he came down from the camper and felt the breeze chill the sweat on his body. 'You can tell me.'

'Okay,' she said, then slowly picked a careful path through her words.

'Earlier—men came. Three of them.' She held up three fingers.

He helped her a little. 'One big lad, with a beard?' He inflated himself up and stroked his chin. 'The other lad, thin, with dark, short hair, yes?'

She nodded all the while then added, 'Ze man with ze beard, he speaks good French. He searches for you, he has your number.' She pointed at the camper. 'He searches for La Roo—ehhh—ze redhead. I told them, you did not come here. Your Sweetheart—she asked me to say this.' She smiled and paused. 'Then I told them that all campers are down there, I told them to see for themselves. So—they walk about, they find nothing, and they leave.'

Toady put a hand on her arm and squeezed her gently. 'Thank you, Madame, Merci beaucoup. You don't know how much you have helped.'

'Mm-mmm.' She was shaking her head with her eyes closed and her long lean finger wagging in his face. 'Non, Missyuh, I sink it is you who don't know. Zis two men, I don't know, but the other man—I know him. Many people do.' Her expression became even more solemn. 'Caesar Perpignan, Luh Rwoh Manoosh.'

Toady was trying to gauge the severity of the crisis from the intensity of her frown.

'King of Gypsies,' she announced with gusto. 'Zis man, brings only one thing where he goes.' She drew her finger across her throat then made a cross on her heart. 'If zis man knows that I lie to him today, then even I cannot feel safe. Please Missyuh, make your stay short and be very careful.' She spun on her heels and left.

He went to the railings and watched her as she descended and disappeared into the shifting leaves. He scanned the eerie solitude of the deserted terraces, then back and forth over the lonely tracks. Nothing stirred but the trees and the gangs of tiny birds raiding back and forth from level to level. Then the cool breeze exhaled slowly with the rushing of the leaves on the Tramontane. He waited and watched and felt the unfamiliar twist in his chest of a man that had something precious to lose. The leaves stopped again and he watched everything, until the incessant chirping of the sparrows prevailed over the silence.

THE KILLER ORPHANS

It was getting dark when Shelley's head swung around the door of the campervan and she peered over to where he was sitting with his feet up on the table and a beer in his hand.

'Cocktails!' she gushed and vanished. Her voice came from within. 'Oh, well if you insist.' When she arrived she was in her tracksuit again, her scarf wrapped around her head for warmth against the cool of the evening breeze. She was toting a glass of ice, a bottle of Vodka and two litres of Coke under her arm.

'So this is where the party's at.' She plonked herself down and put her collection on the table before immediately popping up again. 'Well sniff me sideways, Thomas Brody!' She walked around to Toady's chair and held out her hand. He took the tips of her fingers and stood up like a kid in a clothes shop.

'Oh come on now and let's see the cut of ye, ye big baby.' She lifted his chin up and straightened his shirt off. She pulled at the hem and stroked his jeans and tugged on his belt, then took note of his shoes as she spun him around by his waist and lifted his shirt again. She slapped her palm into his ass and shook it firmly. 'Not too shoddy, Thomas, I wouldn't be as embarrassed to be seen with you now. You have an ass and a pair of shoulders on ye, boy.'

'Thanks,' he muttered then sat back down. She stood over him a moment then rubbed the stubble on his crown, 'Your hair's gettin long.' She stroked the back of his head making him shiver down his spine. He squirmed.

'Tough guy has tickles,' she mused and scratched her fingernails lightly on the back of his neck just below his collar line. 'Your head's healing well. How's it feel?'

'Still middlin,' he muttered.

She went back to her chair and poured herself a large Vodka and Coke. They sat in silence for a while and it grew darker and the crickets took over from the sparrows. The rustling in the leaves was gone as the breeze had retreated out to sea once again for the night. From her relaxed appearance and easy tone he gathered he had gotten away with his earlier indiscretion at her bedside and he dared to breathe easily.

'What did that woman want earlier?' she said out of the blue.

'You were awake?' He hid behind his can, taking a sip.

'Yeh,' she sighed, staring into the night and slipping the last fag from the box.

'Were you awake when I got back from town?'

'Oh, I don't know. The sun and the drinks knocked me out after Anna left.'

'When I got back I peeped into the room,' he ventured. 'Do you remember that?'

'You peeped in?' She was indignant. 'But I was naked in there.'

'It was dark,' he stammered, 'the covers were on you, honest. There was nothing to see.'

'Are you sure? When I woke up my ass was in the air.'

He swallowed his beer like it was gravel, then held up a hand. 'No way Shelley, you were all covered up, I swear.'

'Well okay then—if you say so.' She drank a long draft of her cocktail. 'So?'

'So nothin,' he insisted, putting his beer down.

'Okay, I believe you,' she sneered, 'but what did the woman say? I heard you talking.'

He paused a minute while he rearranged his thoughts.

'They were here, Shell. Mossy, Nicky and this Caesar Perpignan fella, a real bastard apparently.'

'Shit—here? Today?' She sat up. 'What're we gonna do?'

'Not a lot we can do, but we better start thinking straight.'

'Make a break for Spain.' She pointed at the darkening hills.

'Maybe—but not yet.' He sat forward. 'There's got to be a load of campsites around here and they'll be checking in all of those as well. We may have bought some time today, thanks to your friend in the office.' He went inside and brought out the Road Atlas from the shelf and leafed through it.

'Here we are, Banyuls-Sur-Mer. There's only one way in and out of this place. One road, up and down the coast. It's a bottleneck and they're probably hedging their bets on us going to Spain.' He tapped the page. 'I bet they have someone up there right now.' He chugged a half can of beer to dampen his unease at the sight of the dark mountains looming to the south. 'When you stole the campervan you must have left them a clue to which road you took. They know we came this way.'

Shelley's expression was trying hard to say nothing. Toady waited but whatever was on her mind was staying put.

'So—do you think we're okay here for now?' she asked.

'For a couple of days, as long as we keep the camper off the road and you and your hair out of sight. I just need time for my head to clear up a little more, then we'll figure a way out of here.'

'So—on a panic scale of one to ten—' she poured more vodka into her vodka, 'where d'ye think we are?'

'I dunno—maybe five-point-nine?'

She sat back again and sighed. 'Well okay then, so we can go for a drive tomorrow.'

He scratched his head and pointed at the camper. 'Are we having the same conversation here? We're not budging for now.'

'Yeh I got that, but our buddies want to take us

somewhere special.'

'We have buddies?'

'Yeh,' she replied with a grin. 'The Banannasteins. Apparently there's some fabulous town just up the coast, "prettiest town in the world" she called it. I think she had an orgasm when I told her we'd never been there.'

He rubbed his creased brow then shook his head and he was the old familiar Toady again, beset with worry. 'I dunno, it's a risk we don't need to be taking if you ask me.'

'Thomas, you're like someone's granny. Just think about it. We'll be in their car, I'll keep the mop out of sight and we'll both keep a low profile. Besides—I swear—she isn't taking no for an answer and if we don't go, we're gonna be stuck here. Lord knows I don't want to be sat here again and a gang of horny teenagers drooling over me all day.'

'You'll tolerate it.' He raised an eyebrow.

'You'll only get bored.'

'I like bored.'

She leaned forward and put her two hands down on the table and, if nothing else, he was delighted to have her attention. 'Toady, darling, I don't know about you, but I'm having a nice time here. I feel good and I don't see why those bastards should ruin everything for us. We're sitting up here hiding like mice when it's them who should be worried about us going to the cops, not the other way round.'

He watched her moist lips moving and her long lashes dancing. He polished off his beer. 'They're not one bit worried.'

As they got drunker they talked of lighter things and their troubles drifted further away. The stale crust that encases the mind of a cab driver over years and years steeped in the malignant gossip of a stagnant town was cracking away. He told stories of childhood games in cobbled streets that he'd never had the chance to tell anyone, he rambled on and she laughed.

The dank interior of Shelley's council house looking out

on Barry's rubbish piled high in the yard, was burning in the dancing flame of a candle she had placed on the table between them. Her life sentence in the supermarket had been suspended and she remembered, in streams of words, accounts of a disco-dancer and a singer who roamed the streets, hand in hand, in search of their next audience. Her and Maeve, sisters by chance, in a time when choices were ripe berries and not bitter pills.

Her wandering eyes landed on Toady, her new friend, a smile clinging to the corners of his mouth, humming quietly to the night. His eyes were kind and warm and in that moment she felt safe, even though she knew she'd never been closer to true danger in her life. She remembered thinking once in her pokey kitchen that she'd never make a new friend again and it pained her now to think how easily she had accepted such an ill fate.

'Why did you kill your mother?'

It seemed as though he was going to ignore her at first, the smile fading to a vacant stare.

'Now that we're friends and all, I thought it might help to clear it up.'

'Help what? Who said I did it anyway?' He emptied his can and opened another.

'Come on,' she scoffed, 'tell me you didn't kill her if you like, but don't pretend it's not a rumour.'

'Everyone said I was gay at some stage too.'

'Gay? Ye need some fashion sense to be gay.'

He couldn't help but smirk.

'Well I can only presume you heard the rumour that I had something to do with that Mc Carthy girl going missing too?'

'Don't be daft, I never thought you were like that. A freak, sure, but not bad.'

He threw back his head to swill from his can and moaned loudly at the sudden pain. He pulled the blister pack from his pocket and dispatched two tablets with a mouthful of beer and sighed deeply into his clenched fist.

'She asked me to.'

Shelley waited, but nothing else was forthcoming. 'Why would she do that?'

'She was dying, losing her mind, bit by bit. She was afraid her sister would change her will and get the house off me. She used to see monsters in the corner of her bedroom and scream the house down. I'd come running in and find an old vampire, blood streaks around her mouth from that fucking tumour. "Don't let me die on my own", she used to say, "make it easy for me". So I took her into the river on Christmas Eve and the cold water washed what was left of her away in less than ten minutes. The cops couldn't prove any foul play when they found her in the bath. Hypothermia—open and closed. She made me promise to sell the house as soon as she was buried, in case her ghost came back to haunt me. So I did, and then she decided to haunt me everywhere else instead.'

'So that's where you got the money?' she asked and he nodded. 'Where's your dad?'

'Greece.'

'Why?'

'He's Greek.'

'Did he not live with you and your mum?'

'No, he already had a family in Greece, kids 'n all. He met my mother when he came to Ireland selling cheese to supermarkets. Greece was joining Europe, he was setting up the contacts. She put him up in lodgings and had a momentary lapse in character. She claimed that he plied her with Metaxa Brandy and Feta cheese—I'm a product of European integration in more ways than one, she used to tell me. She didn't allow herself many sins, just that one. She seemed almost proud of it.'

'She was,' Shelley sighed.

'What would you know?'

'She told me so. The day she came into the supermarket and asked me to marry you.'

He wiped beer from his cheek. 'Would ye go way outa

that.'

'She did too. About two weeks before I nearly got married to that wanker with the Merc from up North. She said she overheard me and the girls one day talking about dresses. Said you were a good boy and she couldn't bear to see you broken-hearted.'

'Nah—don't believe it.'

She shook her head and sat up straighter. 'I'm deadly serious. She cornered me in the frozen section and me with an arm full of Brussels sprouts, gob-smacked, and me tits turning blue with the cold. She told me that I didn't look like a happy fiancée. She said that I'd be making a huge mistake to marry a man I didn't love.' She held up a finger and closed her eyes. 'I remember her words, "My boy Thomas is an honest man with a strong back and a kind heart". She said that no matter what happened, you'd never go behind my back with—' she paused as she conjured up the past, "—scandalisers!". Toady's mouth fell open as he knew Shelley was telling the truth. His mother was the only person in the world he had ever heard use that term.

'Dear Jesus,' he groaned, 'I'm officially mortified to death. Ground—' he commanded, 'swallow me now.' He emptied two thirds of a can down his throat and slung the empty over his shoulder and called out to the stars, 'Mammy—you're crazy.'

'It's probably the sweetest thing that ever happened to me.' She reached over and put her hand firmly on his. 'Don't be embarrassed, your mum was lovely and she gave me the push I needed to wake up and get rid of that guy. She just couldn't push me hard enough to marry you.'

'Thanks.' He groaned again, then lifted his head, and she could see an innocence in his face as he remembered his mother with renewed fondness.

'That's what I don't have.'

'What?'

'A way to see my mother that makes me feel like that.'

She pointed at his face and this time there was a tear in his eye and she glanced away to spare him. 'Me and you have one thing in common, Thomas Brody. We're a pair of orphans,' she said softly, 'with no one to love us just for who we are.'

He lifted a fresh beer and toasted her. Then they sat for a moment, taking a break from the rawness of the words while the crickets played a familiar tune from the darkness.

'Well—you've embarrassed the hell out of me, so you may as well tell me all about your folks. Did you kill your mam too?'

She took a deep puff of smoke then blew it into the air. 'Yeh—I sure did. And my dad for that matter, killed him too.'

'Ritual killings no doubt.' He raised his glass for another toast.

'Me mam—she jumped out a hospital window because of me.' She was staring at the night and he froze, mesmerized by her perfect silence while she smoked and took sips of her drink. He watched her lips on the edge of the glass and the shudder of her lashes in the golden light and time was obliterated.

He whispered, eventually, 'I'm sorry I asked, it's none of my business.'

'She was ridin my dad's brothers,' she said.

Toady coughed and spat beer out onto the ground. 'Sorry, did you say brothers?'

'Two of em,' she said, nodding slowly. 'Coming around when he was at work, in his big important job at the box factory, and stickin it to her.'

He grunted and used a tissue to dry his lips.

'I was about twenty. Came home from work one day, not feeling well. Went to my room. Before long the front door opened, there was a racket and I heard them all piling into the house. The drinks cabinet was going, but that wasn't anything unusual for mum, then laughing and more racket. So down I went, like an eejit, to see what the party was about. By the time I got down and opened the door she had uncle Brendan's cock in her mouth and Uncle Joseph was banging her doggy style.'

Toady found something deeply interesting printed on the can and studied it in intense silence.

'That's why she killed herself,' she said, after a minute. 'She was afraid that someday I'd tell Dad and that made her go even more off the deep end. They put her on drugs in St. Jude's and she started hallucinating that everyone knew, that I'd told them all, the doctors even. She dived out a fourth-storey window right in front of me. Stone-cold-fuckin-dead on the footpath. Then my dad went to his bedroom and died of the shame—only took him a year.'

Toady wanted to crawl under the table, but she started again.

'Not because his wife was fucking his brothers—oh no!' She shook her head. 'Poor bastard didn't even know that. He died because he thought that even his own wife would rather jump to her death than live out her years with him. I couldn't tell him what she'd done because the truth would have killed him for sure.'

She was quiet again, swirling ice cubes around her glass. Ghostly shadows shifted at the fringes of their bubble of light, shuffling in close to feed on the intimacy of the living. Toady shuddered as Shelley spoke softly to him. 'What you did to your mum in the river is a happier memory than I can ever find of mine, can you believe that?'

He bowed his head and let the weight of his crime settle on him for the thousandth time, and though it felt no lighter, it felt a little warmer.

'So nobody ever knew about your uncles?'

'Everything comes out sooner or later, so I announced it at his funeral.'

Toady choked on his beer again.

'Ladies and gentlemen—Father Driscoll.' She lifted her

head and nodded to whatever was lurking beyond the light, to the darkness hunching between the trees and posts that seemed to shift uncomfortably at being addressed so formally by the voices of the past. 'I'd like to thank my two uncles, Joseph—', she gestured to the right as though she was back in the pulpit, 'and Brendan, for filling my mother with family love while my dad was at work. I just want to say that if either of you happen to be my real father, then thanks for killing this fake man I've called Dad for the last twenty-four years and reuniting him with the drunken slut that I called Mum for twenty-three years.'

Toady sat stunned and watched her for a minute as she drew on her fag. A cold breeze stirred the leaves and another shiver ran the length of his body. 'I think they're listening,' he whispered.

'Good. I've never told that story to anyone before, not even Maeve. I forbid her to come to the funeral and never told her why.'

'What happened at the church?'

'What do you think happened? It went off like a riot at a football match. Everyone in the front dishin out slaps in two seconds flat.'

'And what did you do?'

'I left, phoned a taxi. They sent you. Half way down the hill we saw each other in the mirror and you told me to cheer up. Said I looked like I was going to a funeral or something and I told you to—'

'—eat shit!' Toady finished it for her and shook his head. 'Christ, I'm sorry.'

'That's ten years ago, boy, d'ye think I care at this stage?'

'Surprised I didn't hear about it,' he wondered, 'in the taxi.'

'I heard the priest made a special plea at the graveside to let sleeping dogs lie—and that's exactly how my dad got buried.' She stamped her butt out. 'Like a sleeping dog. A couple of people heard the rumour, nobody believed it, and that's the only mercy he got.'

She swilled her glass empty again. 'That's why I haven't got a sinner in the world to call family.' She paused and gestured into the endless night. 'Except that useless tosser of a husband, I suppose.' And right then Toady remembered that he was supposed to know something about that, but as he tried to bend his mind to it, the shadows leaned in closer and thwarted him.

'Okay,' he proclaimed. 'So that makes two of us. The killer orphans—fuckin great name for a band.' She burst out laughing in the sweetest music he had ever heard, and right then he wanted to kiss her. But more than that, he wanted everything to stay just like that forever.

Soon after, he gave up and went to bed with his head spinning and his vision going blurry in bouts. She went to bed an hour later and crawled in after him. She checked her phone and couldn't believe that it was only midnight. The silence was complete in the small room and her face rested lightly against his shoulder softened by a pillow of curls. For the first time ever, Toady dreamed of flowers.

Shelley wasn't there when he woke in the morning with a dull throb in his head. He took the two painkillers she'd left for him beside the bed. He thought he could hear voices outside, so he sat up and shifted the blind until he could see her, sitting at the table with the three men in black tracksuits and shades. The sun was bright and he could see she was in her bikini-sarong combo as she reclined in her seat, fag in hand, shades on top of her head talking expressively about who knew what.

He groaned and rubbed his face. The thoughts of joining that mob for breakfast didn't appeal to him much. He was too warm in his T-shirt so he took it off and slid on his new shirt from the back of the door. He pulled off his jeans and folded them and held up Arno's shorts. 'Fuck it!' He dropped them back on the seat.

In the fridge he spotted a large bottle of water then

pulled Mossy's shades from the shelf and stepped out into the warm day. He passed his lovely new shoes on the way and slipped them on.

Shelley was in the middle of describing the house by the sea where she lived with her three Dalmatians when she noticed she had lost the attention of her audience. Toady passed by and took the only free chair from the table and kept walking. The only reason for the free chair was the man sitting strategically on the fence, with an excellent view down Shelley's cleavage. Toady said nothing and the three men said nothing back.

'Ay, Tommy, that thing about men in their underpants didn't change overnight, ye know?' she called after him. 'Those shoes aren't helping either—au contraire, mon cheri.' She smiled to her company who winked approval at her use of the vernacular.

Toady placed his chair in the full glare of the sunlight in the open area at the top of the steps. The trees in front of him were full of teenagers in blue overalls. They were chatting and laughing and shouting to each other as they sawed, chopped and snipped at the branches with an array of tools. An enclosure of giant blue monkeys at the zoo came to mind and he watched as he soaked up the warm rays and drank deeply from the cold, refreshing water. One of the boys bounced on a branch that his companion was busily sawing. Toady glanced back to the three men who were paying no attention whatsoever.

'What the fuck?' he called up to the boys.

They all stopped and looked at him for a moment, then gave a collective, 'Bonjour,' before getting back to it. The boy with the blond hair and the dark rings around his eyes leaned on a rake and watched him, then gazed off to where the men sat with Shelley.

Toady got up and walked to the edge and peered down the steps. Men in painter's overalls were busy lining up the internal doors of the toilet block against the walls. An eerie but melodious whistling was emanating from the darkness inside. 'Bonjour!' the two painters called up, and he acknowledged them. Two vans were parked below and the drivers leaned on their doors and chatted to each other.

Past the industrious scene he could see the empty terraces below. He scanned down the long tracks of deserted camping spaces and could see no other sign of human life anywhere.

'Someone's rippin the piss here.'

He crossed back to his seat and sat down and breathed deeply the clean air of the sea. He poured a little water in his hand and rubbed it on his face and shoulders, in his eyes, under his shades. It felt wonderfully cool and served to wake him up. An unbridled eruption of laughter from Shelley and her friends snapped his attention to the fact that they were all watching him. Of course his noticing that instigated another hilarious bout of laughter.

'Brilliant,' he sighed and closed his eyes. When he opened them again the bouncing boy was dangling silently, the branch beneath him having fallen away. The three men in black tracksuits were paying no attention again. One of them was up, doing an imitation of a guy with a machine gun, or maybe it was a guitar. Whatever it was, he just knew it was going to be hilarious, and sure enough, it was. The hanging lad had disappeared when he turned back. He tried to resist the temptation but found he couldn't. He crossed to the fence and peered down the steep slope. The painters were holding him up against the van, brushing him off and they too laughed to each other as the dazed young man looked back and forth between them. Something infectiously stupid had invaded this far-flung hill, completely validating his presence there in his underpants, and that observation brought a smug smile to his face.

Of all seventeen people gathered tightly in this deserted end of the world, it was he who was the true lord of all he surveyed. All the others were here by decree, by necessity, or even against their will, but he was the only truly free man there that morning. Master of his own destiny, having arrived from far away in his luxury carriage with his beautiful bride, Toady was experiencing another first. He'd never been the object of other men's envy before, and though he was sure his mother would disapprove of his vain pride, he decided a banquet was in order.

When he passed by the table the three men all gave a smile. He asked them through mime did they want something to eat. They all declined in a loud mumble with shaking hands and heads.

'Toady, Love,' she called after him, and he stopped without turning, 'no cooking in your underpants. You know what happened last time.' A rash of sniggers ensued for whatever she mimed to the men, but he kept going.

Bacon, sausage, pudding, egg, mushrooms and tomatoes arrived as the men were departing,. 'Seeya,' he called after them and popped down a pot of tea. To their credit, Mossy and the missus had brought a freezer full of traditional butcher's products and a cabinet full of teabags, bringing Toady to the conclusion that the French didn't do fry-ups and their tea was piss. Shelley was tucking in as he poured from the fresh pot.

'So I suppose I get the last laugh,' he said. 'King of the hill with the pretty girl, and they're all back at work.'

'That's not how they see it.' She was being equally smug, holding up a sausage.

'Oh yeh? How's that then?'

'The way they see it is that I'm getting paid to bring my retarded cousin on a holiday—get him out of the home for a couple of weeks.'

He cocked an eyebrow.

'Oh, you think that's a hard one to sell? You strutting around in your togs, getting afternoon sponge baths—your highness?'

He thought about it for a moment then conceded the point with a smirk and a nod of deferral. 'Can you not just let me be king for a day, no?'

'Man will never be free until the last king is strangled with the last priest's cock.' She growled at her sausage then bit off the end. 'Some French bloke said that, by the way. About the only thing my mum ever told me worth remembering.'

'So that's a no then?'

'You be what you like, Thomas, and when the Gypsy King comes lookin for his hill back, the two of ye can strangle each other for it. Any chance you can make it Friday, cos I won't be here? Jean Luc asked me to go out with him to some game everyone plays in a shed around here. Boules, they call it. Says ye can bring beer and wine.'

'We won't be here.'

'Arra now, Thomas, ye don't have to be jealous, it's just a bunch of lads trying to get their balls as close to each other as possible. I can be judge, they said.'

'And there's me thinking the French were romantic. Shed, booze, balls. Not wastin any time, is he?'

'It's culture, you wouldn't understand.'

'I'm not planning on hanging around if Mossy and company figure out where we are.'

'Well maybe you can loan me your balls if you're not using them?'

He put his head in his hands. 'For the love of Jaysus— if we're here ye can go and judge as many balls as you like. Now can we just get through today first? What time does that start at?'

'We have to present ourselves at their caravan at midday.' She checked her phone. 'It's only ten now, loads of time.'

'Grand, so can I be king for the next two hours?'

'Okay, but the grey man's gonna be awful disappointed when he finds out you've been showing off.' She flourished her hand and dipped her head in acquiescence.

They relaxed a while and once his food settled, Toady was in his underpants doing his Karate movements, which he had been deprived of for over a week. The men below pointed at him and gesticulated to each other. He attempted his usual fifty press-ups but conceded defeat on twenty-three and just sat in the dust and closed his eyes and let the wondrous heat soak into him. The team of juveniles passed back and forth carrying severed branches to be dumped along the fence line separating the campsite from the sprawling vineyard above. The one who fell down the hill had been taken to hospital with a broken finger. The one with the blond hair and the dark rings around his eyes always seemed to be on the verge of saying something each time he passed, slowing down to study what Toady was doing and then staring off to where Shelley languished in her bikini.

'Henri,' one of the men shouted and the boy started. 'Tronkeeyay vous.'

'What exactly is your problem, kid?' The boy's head went down on Toady's words and he got back to work.

Twelve o'clock loomed and Shelley disappeared into the van and reappeared with her hair tied under a fuchsia and gold patterned scarf. Her eyes were heavy with mascara and her lips the darkest scarlet. She wore a pair of tight black pants and a red T-shirt under her own short denim jacket. Toady went inside then emerged bedecked in his new ensemble and they appraised each other with mutual satisfaction.

'Shelley.' He stopped her as she walked down the track.

She spun dramatically. 'What?'

'What's the key phrase for today?'

She pointed at him and clicked her fingers. 'Low profile, baby, Operation Grey Man.' She spun back.

'Outstanding, now you're gettin it. Shelley—' he called her again.

'What?' She stopped and turned and he stepped in close in a moment of brashness to kiss her, but her hand went on his mouth. 'Lipstick,' she whispered.

Her eyes were cool and green, like the calm sea with sunlight trapped over the white sand.

'Kissing cousins,' she breathed onto his cheek.

Toady checked over his shoulder, but none of the work crew was paying any attention and when he turned back she had walked away.

TWENTY PILES OF SHITE

Shelley's glorious day at the horse festival in the mountain town of Quillan, in the Midi-Pyrenees, was definitely one to remember. She had woken in the Municipal Campsite, just above the town, in a cabin she had rented the previous night upon her arrival. They had initially driven up there thinking that Mossy and his crew would be there. To her delight they weren't and the other pair had refused to sleep on a campsite when there were perfectly good hotels in town, and bars, and food.

'And women,' sneered Nicky from the car.

'Shut up, ye dickhead,' Barry grunted. He was standing beside his wife as she pulled her new shoulder bag from the car.

On the drive down she had taken a break from the incessant French pop tunes when they had chanced across a shopping centre. She lost them for an hour while she picked up some toiletries then ate lunch in a Bistro and watched them run back and forward outside the window like the Keystone Cops. If she'd had enough money in her purse just then she might have gone missing for good. But the few hundred she had left wouldn't cut it and the thought of spending time with Toady didn't disgust her anymore, so she had surrendered herself back at the car to see how things might pan out.

'Honey,' Barry pleaded as she pulled her bag from the backseat at the campsite, 'I know I made a complete tool of myself in the hotel last night. I'm sorry, but I just wanted to have fun, like in the old days, like we were on holidays. Let me make it up to ye, I'll buy dinner.'

'Get away from me, Barry, you're not well.' She slammed the car door.

'C'mon now, Honey, just let me and Nicky get set up down below and we'll come back up and bring ye down the town—get a bite to eat. Looks like there's a good crowd around.'

'I will in my shite have dinner with a pair of minkers like you. I've had enough.'

'Last chance, Love,' he said with pathetic eyes.

'Go rape each other, ye dirty cunts.' She cleared her throat and spat a large ball of phlegm into his face. Barry fell away in shock.

'Ay, Red, don't you go anywhere, or you'll be the one getting raped, ye dry hoor.' Nicky was leaning out his window. 'I might need ye again, so I'll be checkin on ye. We're only goin down the road.' She snorted at the back of her nose for some snot for Nicky. He took off with Barry falling into the car beside him, using his sweatshirt to wipe his face.

After settling into her cabin she set off down the track to the only other campers in the site—two elderly Dutch couples, brothers, with their respective wives, dining al fresco. She was inquiring if she could buy a bottle of wine from them, but they set her a place at the table, then fed her cold meats and cheeses with beef ravioli and French bread.

They gave her peach Schnapps from time to time. The ladies stroked her hair while the gents tried out Irishman jokes, smoked Cuban cigars and plied her with ice-cold bottles of expensive Belgian beer. She was in paradise.

When their gentle soiree came to an end, they gave her a bottle of chilled Zinfandel and the men walked her to her cabin. Dark forests surrounded them on brooding hills hunched in somber contemplation over the lights of the town below.

'Are there wolves in the Pyrenees?' she asked them

before they left.

'No Goldilocks—just bears.' They laughed as they plodded away down the track puffing smoke into the clear night sky.

The threat of bears didn't stop her from sitting on her decking and getting quietly drunk as she listened to crickets and night birds sing. The hollow sounds of the town rose up from the streets below and drummed on the bottom of the painted sky.

Friday morning, she checked through her door then exited to her decking in her mismatched underwear to find that her Dutch friends had left her a flask of coffee and two croissants, freshly baked and delivered from the local Boulangerie that morning, while she slept.

Out across the neatly preened divisions of the campsite, the shape of the large valley was like nothing she had seen before. The dark mountains were now rendered verdant green in golden sunshine beneath a deep blue sky. She had imagined them further away in the dim light of the previous night, but they communed closely above the town, close enough for her to see the detail in the forests. In front of her, a big mound of land rose up from the valley floor to a summit high over the red roofs of the town. Jagged claws of rock clung to the steep hillsides that sprouted above the treetops. The town below was a jumble of clay roofs stretched along a meandering river, hemmed in by the hills and bursting upwards with the hum of cars and the blowing of horns.

She passed the morning in her underwear on the decking, smoking fags, drinking water and getting a light sunburn on her delicate skin. Scents of Coco and Aloe Vera creams she had bought the previous day brought back memories of her and Maeve on the beach as teenagers. How long had it been since she had really felt the sun on her body? Beer garden afternoons, descending into the abyss of forgotten nights, had replaced the sand dunes and straw hats of their adolescence.

The men hadn't shown all morning and as the afternoon wore on she started to sense that an arrival was imminent, so she dressed and put on her makeup, tying her hair into her scarf. Finally, she stowed her new shoulder bag under the bed and headed for town. She found the humble town centre and secreted herself to a table in a tree-sheltered square and ordered pancakes with ham and cheese and spring onions, followed by another with chocolate and whipped cream, all washed down with sweet, chilled Rose.

She sat and smoked as she watched the traffic slowly building and the components of the horse festival filtering through the streets, approaching the time and location of its launch. Horse boxes, trucks, and, of course, horses, being both ridden and led, passed by in the evening traffic. A couple of streets over, the P.A. system was being tested, echoing voices and bursts of music arced over the rooftops and battered occasionally through the narrow alleyways.

'So Mr. Brody, what to do about you?' With a couple of drinks and a warm belly, she sighed, and she rationalised. If he wouldn't give them the money, then he was a fool and deserved what he got for being such a stubborn ass. If he had already paid then he'd probably gotten a clip around the ear and been sent packing. She might see him around the town later, have a beer and maybe even laugh it off and hang out together for a day or two. He had the finances and she was wide open to suggestions on such a glorious day.

She checked her money, well under a thousand and the fare home would have to come out of that. She sure as hell wasn't going back in Nicky's car. Then she thought about what that meant—going home—walking back in the door of that little box with Barry behind her, blocking out the light. Then the door slamming, like the lid on her tomb. A dread panic turned her stomach over and she had an epiphany of sorts. 'That's it Brody, you owe me a dip in the Med, boy.'

Upon her arrival on Boulevard Charles de Gaulle it was obvious that the horse festival was about to kick off at any minute. People were walking in groups up the road towards the makeshift arena. It had been constructed in a huge area of waste ground bordering an abandoned section of railway line. The marquee was up and the stage was finished and a sound test was underway. A village of striped stalls on the far side of the arena constituted a market where all items equine could be bought, from tan leather saddles to pretty pink ribbons for a pony's mane.

The crowds were forming into a large thin rectangle around the periphery of the arena, demarcated by temporary steel fencing. Between the arena and the Boulevard a podium and viewing area had been constructed. A number of half-glamorous dignitaries were arranging themselves into their plastic seats. A man in a large-brimmed hat and checkered shirt was greeted with a loud cheer and sporadic clapping. Shelley took her place as discreetly as possible behind a group of noisy kids.

Presently, over the muffled P.A., came the sound of a drum roll and a fanfare of trumpets and the man in the hat commenced to count down the final seconds. The crowd joined in and clapped in time to the count and Shelley found herself smiling in sympathy. A shot rang out, cracking the warm air overhead and piercing the pale blue evening sky. The starting pistol burst the music to life and instantly the crowd roared with delight at the spectacle they had created.

From a gap at the far end of the arena issued horses and riders in a straight line. Starting with a giant black beast, tossing its mane, thudding hooves on the fresh golden sand. The line of horses descended in size to the small white pony at the rear. Its rider, a little girl no older than ten, had a bright red flag flying from her back. As they approached the spot where Shelley stood, she could see that each rider was decorated in the motif of a different animal. The first young girl, an exotic beauty with long, black, flowing hair and dark olive skin, had the stripes of a zebra painted on her bare arms and cheeks. Following her were a tiger and a lion, and then what appeared to be an eagle with brown, silken wings rolling behind her on the breeze. The girl on the smallest pony was a panda and her long, honey curls bounced around her beaming face as she approached.

When the black stallion reached the end of the arena it wheeled left and Shelley felt the ground beneath her vibrate with the rhythm of its graceful turn, then the canter slowed to an easy trot. The rider's head was held high and her own shiny mane of hair lifted and fell on the breeze as she drifted past. The others followed in a perfect line. The pony at the back was still cantering in order to keep apace as they turned again and headed back up the arena in a perfect straight line, now side by side. The people showed their appreciation and the folk music rolled over their heads on banks of warm air. The riders crisscrossed and looped their way to every corner of the rectangle in perfect synchronicity, each rider simultaneously producing a blue or white flag from her saddle and circling it overhead.

The music faded and the riders trotted in single file again out the same gap in the fence through which they had arrived. The MC warbled into his mic and the crowd responded. Then the music burst forth again and the men issued into the arena on their mounts from the same gap.

Shelley was really starting to enjoy the buzz when she noticed, second from the back of the line, the unmistakable round face and greasy, flattened fringe of Mossy's son, Arno. She pulled her scarf tight around her face and put her hand over her eyes as though shielding them from the bright sunlight as they approached. But Arno would never have noticed her, so deeply was he ensconced in his moment, the effort etched in his furrowed brow. It occurred to Shelley that his proud, doting mother would have to be close by, if not Mossy himself. She faded back into the crowd and fixed her sunglasses then made her way back to the road and crossed.

Continuing up the Boulevard, she cleared the arena and the staging area and kept walking until the music echoed in a jumble across a scrubby wasteland. And then she saw them, tucked in the far corner of the waste ground, some two hundred metres away. Twenty or more campers parked in rows, one behind the other. Vans and horseboxes were parked randomly around and a slow stream of people and horses walked in a line defining the shortest distance between the camp and the arena.

She crossed back over the road and sat on the low wall, in between the trunk of a tree and a bush. She watched, then waited, as patiently as she could, with fingers fiddling and cigarettes flapping, hoping to catch sight of Toady.

After half an hour of sitting in the softening rays of the evening sun, her pink forearms glowing and the tip of her nose growing hot, a black car with tinted windows emerged from a gap in the hedge to her left. It followed a dry track around a grassy area where horses were tethered between her and the camp, raising a thin dust-cloud like an angry snake crawling into a desert town.

Nicky parked up beside the corner camper and knocked on the door. Mossy appeared, bare-chested, with a ten-gallon hat on his head and they went back to Nicky's car. From the back seat, he produced Shelley's leather shoulder bag from the chalet.

'Assholes!' She stamped her foot. All her new possessions were in there. Everything she had just bought for herself. Fresh underwear, makeup, socks and toiletries. Mossy pulled at the zip and rummaged inside and she saw her stuff fall out on the ground.

'Oy!' she protested and sprang up, then sat back down and covered her head with her hands. 'Fucks sake Shelley, ye twat.'

She dared to sneak a peek at them between her fingers but they were paying no attention to her. Mossy was pulling her stuff from the ground and shoving it back in the bag, then he pointed out over Nicky's head and shouted. The words barely reached her on the dry air. 'Fuck off and find her, lad.'

'I'm in demand,' she muttered to herself.

Like a scolded dog she could see Nicky's head going down and he made his way back around to his car door and Shelley stepped back over the wall and crouched down behind the solitary bush. A large cloud of dust arose where Nicky spun the car around and came back across the waste ground towards her. Mossy returned to his lair with her bag.

Earlier, while Shelley had been digesting hand-baked croissants in her mismatched underwear, Nicky had spotted Toady while eating brunch outside the Hotel Terminus just before midday. Surveying the area opposite with his binoculars he had noted the caravans and knew that it had to be the gypsy's base of operations. There had been enough of them in the pub the previous night to tell him that they were somewhere close by.

'I think we have our man,' Nicky muttered, squinting hard into the morning sun. He identified the shape and gait of his fellow taxi driver flanked by men, crossing the dusty halting site. Toady was pushed out in front, stumbling to his knees, then falling face down in the dirt with his hands bound.

'Oooh, I felt that,' Nicky said with relish.

They pulled him up by the collar and spun him around and a big lad landed a punch in his stomach and doubled him over again.

'Jesus lads, don't kill him yet.'

Nicky was up from the table and crossed the road to where his car was parked. He dumped the binoculars and jogged across the waste ground, straightening his black beanie cap and donning his shades as he went.

Toady squinted up at the glaring sky and felt the heat of the shimmering sun on his face. It certainly was a beautiful day and there didn't seem to be a cloud in sight. He wondered if Shelley was getting to enjoy the heat wherever she was, and had she managed to get to the seaside after all.

'Enough o this shit,' Mossy's voice boomed. 'Juss kill the cunt.'

Toady felt himself levitate from the ground and then he was enveloped in cold darkness as he sank to the bottom of a horse trough. The horses' heads were nodding with approval in the undulating rectangle of blue light. 'This sure is a funny place to die,' he thought.

'What are you doing in here, Thomas? And look at the cut of you,' his mother gently scolded him.

'Ah, it's nothing, Mammy, just a couple of bruises. I got a few slaps off them fellas. They're trying to get a few quid outa me.'

'Thomas Brody, you're an eejit and I'm telling you now—for your own good, to pay those evil men and be done with it, or they're going to kill you for sure.'

'But I owe them nauthin, and I'll be damned if I'm handing over your money to a shower of knackers.'

'And tell me, what use can that type of language, or the money, serve either of us at the bottom of a horse trough? I didn't give it to you so it could be a weight around your neck. Just stay alive, Thomas, help is coming.'

'Shelley? Is she okay? Don't let her come down here Mammy, they'll kill us both.'

'She's fine, but you're not. Your face is turning blue.'

'Jesus, don't I know it. There's an awful burnin in me lungs and I can't see the horses anymore, are they still there?'

'They are, Thomas, but you're leaving now and I won't tell you again to pay those men or I'll be very angry. I don't want to see you back here.'

'Alright, Mammy, I'll try. But I've a feelin they're gonna kill me anyway—so I'm not promisin anything.'

He hit the ground like he had fallen from forty feet, not four. With no air in his lungs left to exhale, he struggled to get his throat around the corner of his first breath, twisting and writhing in the dirt. Then a raucous cry burst from his chest as he dragged life back from the cold fringe at the end of the world. The black gave way to white and the bubbles burst into blue as the sky and the heat of the world seeped back into his senses.

'You were nearly done for that time,' snorted the giant Mossy, towering a mile above him. 'What's that, Sonny? Ye wanna say somethin? Are ye with us lad?' Mossy clattered him across the face, then two big shovel hands came out of the sky and grabbed him by the collar, dragging him upright. He brushed the straw from Toady's chest and looked him in the eye. 'C'mon, Thomas lad, enough's enough. The bank's only down the street, ye'll be on your way by teatime. What d'ye say?'

Toady coughed wildly and thought he was going to puke on the stale water in his guts and the smell of horseshit thick in the air. 'Me mother—' he gasped. 'She says I should pay ye.'

'Does she now?' Mossy smiled bitterly. 'Smart woman, so she is. Loves her son, no doubt.' He blessed himself. 'God keep the dead.' He waved a hand around at the beautiful day. 'So what's it to be? Happy ever after, for you and Ginger Rogers, or a table for two with your Mammy—this evenin?'

Toady shook his head, a vague expression of amusement playing across his features. Mossy stood holding him upright with a mangled fistful of shirt and jumper.

'Shelley's a thousand miles away from here and she doesn't give a shite about me. So if it's all the same with you, ye may send me to hell. God knows, you'll be comin soon enough—and I'll be waitin for ye. There's another pair of bastards I'm supposed to be meetin down there too.'

Mossy gritted his teeth. 'Jesus wept but you're a fuckin curse.' Searching Toady's eyes, back and forth, he tried to find a bit of him he could reason with. 'I'm wastin me time, amn't I?'

The last few scraps of humanity drained out of Toady's face as he locked stares with Mossy and saw into his twisted soul.

'Alright so, have it your way.' Mossy pushed him to arm's length then pulled his other fist back level with his head and Toady straightened himself up to it, like staring into the breech of a loaded cannon. 'Enough o your shit, boy, I'll see ye down below.' Mossy's gold teeth sparkled.

'Ye will,' Toady grunted back.

Just then a cry went out like the call to ceasefire on a bloody afternoon in no man's land.

'Stop!'

Toady heard the birds twittering high overhead and the sound of horses neighing gently close by. The grip on his chest was released and he went down on his ass in the dust, the searing pain in his ribs bringing tears to his eyes.

'Jesus lads, hold up before ye kill the cunt,' came a voice from somewhere. The group turned to see a young man approaching and Mossy immediately recognised him from the bar the night before.

'Listen!' Nicky shouted with his hands in the air. 'It's money you're after and ye can't get it from a dead man. I can help ye—I know this stubborn bollox.'

'Go on,' grunted Mossy.

'His girlfriend,' Nicky grinned, 'I can get her for ye. He'll give you what you want once ye have her, I guarantee it.'

'And what do you want?'

Nicky held his hands up. 'Justice.'

'You're gonna get justice alright,' Toady grumbled.

Unsure if he was hallucinating or not, he was trying to focus on Nicky. 'Where the hell did you come from?'

He got a loud wet slap on the back of the head as Mossy passed behind him, then walked around Nicky, sizing him up and down. 'I'm glad you showed up, so I am. Tell me—where's that big arsehole ye had with ye in the pub last night? A good friend of mine wants to have a word with him.'

'I can get him for ye too, so I can,' Nicky offered. 'I can get them both, man and wife.'

'And what kinda justice is it ye want?' Mossy completed his circle then snorted and spat into the dust.

'The only kind. The money he owes me—and a guarantee.' Nicky dropped his shades to the end of his nose and eyeballed Mossy.' I just want to be sure that Mr. Brody here never makes it home, that's all. You've half done the job, I just want to be sure you finish it. I wanna see it.'

'Alright, sonny, I'll think about that,' said Mossy, stroking his chin. 'But first off, go get that big fella ye had in the bar last night and bring him over here.' He gestured to his two nephews to go with him.

On what was to be the shortest day of his life, Barry awoke in his hotel bed beside a prostitute, both still drunk from the night before. He had slipped her one of his Open Sesame Seeds so that he might get some extra value for one of Shelley's hard earned fifties. He got his money's worth learning the gentler side of what his fists were for, with the help of a half bottle of baby oil.

For all Barry's trying, he hadn't ever had much success with his pills, Maeve being the most notable exception. They say that the worst thing that can happen to a gambling addict is to win big in the beginning, then they spend everything they have, and ever will have, trying to get back to that initial high. Well that was Barry, always trying to relive that moment of realization; the sheer ecstasy of grasping something truly extraordinary from the ether of an unsuspecting day. To him it was more about the thrill of the chase, the irresistible danger of slipping in close and delivering the package, and then the tension of watching the victim as they became overpowered. Like a spider that injects its quarry, then waits in the shadows for the moment to feed.

He had spotted a real exotic beauty early in the night. Jet black, silky, straight hair and dark, olive skin with zebra stripes on her arms—young and bubbling with noise and laughter. He got the powder into her drink while he bullshitted around her, bumping into people at the bar, making highfalutin efforts to string French words together into idiot phrases. That part was about distracting her while he delivered the magic potion. She wasn't impressed and she shooed him away and turned her back on him. He watched her for a while, through the crowd, as she became louder, her actions more chaotic and darkness descended outside. He guessed it wouldn't be long before she had to head for home and his heart quickened.

But that is not how the gypsies conduct themselves. A young girl in that state would never be allowed to walk alone into the night. Gypsies are not like townsfolk who admit their daughters into the streets like meat in pretty ribbons. Her father came in the door and the men handed her over. He took hold of her by the arms and he stared into her rolling eyes and slapped her face lightly, then threw her over his shoulder. He stood in the middle of the bar, music playing in the background, as everyone fell silent. His black eyes went from man to man as he scanned the faces in the darker corners of the room. Then he spun on his heels and left.

'You-fuckin-gobshite!' Nicky had whispered in Barry's ear as he passed him on the way to the bar. Barry just sniggered nervously, then turned his attention to the rough blonde who had been giving him the eye.

'Wake up, ye degenerate.'

Barry blinked and found Nicky standing in the middle of the room with sunlight pouring in the windows.

'C'mon, ye rehab. I found Toady. We're in business.' Nicky threw Barry's bag on the bed. 'Get all your shit up, we won't be comin back here. I'll see ye in the car park—and get that fuckin minger outa here too.'

Barry crossed the car park, the heat and light making him feel nauseous as he approached Nicky standing by his car. 'I need a cup of coffee to get me started,' he groaned and reached for the door handle. The dull ring of metal on bone jarred his skull and all light was extinguished as though he'd been shot in the head with midnight. Before long he'd live to wish he had been shot in the head with something.

Back in the camp, where Nicky's intervention had saved him from a fatal beating, Toady was seated at a wooden table. He was beginning to see that his stubborn attitude was having the desired effect on a frustrated Mossy. The only problem with convincing Mossy that he wasn't going to get paid was that it only left a couple more options, none of them pleasant. Toady had decided he was in a lose-lose situation and he was just clinging to the hope that he could still drag Mossy down with him.

Mossy paced up and down and his wife Ellen was perched in the driver's seat of the camper supping tea as she checked her watch again. Then Mossy stormed over to the table and put his two fists down, knuckles to the wood. 'ELLEN' tattooed down one arm and intertwined with roses. A foot-long likeness of the Virgin Mary on the other, with the words 'Pray to Thee' in fine writing at her feet.

'I'm comin clean with ye, boy,' he grunted and eyed Toady from under thick eyebrows. 'I need the money and I need it quick. It's twenty grand, we're talkin about, that's what it's always been about. Now, I'm sorry for hijackin ye and for gettin your missus into a game she wasn't gonna ever win.' Then he shook his finger in Toady's face. 'But she had it comin—with that big shaggin mouth of hers runnin amok.' He drew his arm across his mouth and sighed. 'Now—I know ye have it and ye can afford it, and that's why I picked ye. I'm axin ye to do the right thing—the easy thing. Give me the money and I swear, with Christ as me witness, you'll walk away from it—with Ginger. Ye have me word.' Mossy straightened up and spit in his palm and held it to his chest. 'That Nicky Bassard? I'll even take care of him for ye. Whad'ya say, Thomas lad?'

'Who do you owe it to?' Toady watched him from under a grimy, matted flap of hair.

'The missus is waitin for her brother, the lad ye busted in the face.' Mossy slapped the table and shook his head. 'Bent fucker, I never liked em.' He winked and squeezed Toady's shoulder. 'He's comin up from Perpignan in the evenin and if I don't have the money in me hand, for him to see—with dem beady fuckin eyes o his—then I better might as well get in me van and fuck off over dem hills. You and me both, kid.'

'Your own wife's brother's gonna kill ye.' Toady said with satisfaction.

'No Sonny, not him.' Mossy shook his head and pointed over the hills. 'Caesar—the King.' He bowed his head solemnly. 'King of the bum boys, that is. He's a different species o lunatic that I wouldn't normally associate with, ceppin I owe the cunt—see?' A car horn blew and startled Mossy from his story. 'Alright Chief, let's go. I want to show ye somethin that might put all your conflictin interests in perspective for ye.' Mossy reached over and grabbed him up from the table.

The smell of stale cowshit and animal bones was suffocating as Nicky was pulled from the back of the van and marched barefoot over concrete. The bag was whipped off his head and an exotic young girl with long, black, silky hair and dark, olive skin stood before him. She nodded once and the bag went back on as he was dragged, then pushed, another distance. Then the clanking of chains on the steel door opening and he was pushed inside to the deafening eruption of barking dogs—just for a moment—then silence.

Toady stood with hands tied behind his back to the forefront of a degenerate crew on the far side of the metal hayshed with light coming in through a thousand cracks and a flickering set of fluorescent tubes swinging in a breeze overhead. Not far away a steel cage beckoned. He squirmed at his bonds. 'Jesus Christ, don't do it,' he begged on a dry whisper. 'Just take the money, ye can have it.'

'Hold up now, Sonny, it's not always about money,' Mossy assured him calmly. He pointed to the tall, dark-skinned man stood still, watching Barry being led to the door of the cage where the bag was pulled from his head. The dogs went wild again, jumping chest height at the metal chain link fence, setting it rattling against the bars. Barry put his feet up against the gate to stop them opening it, his back arched against the two men holding his arms. He whined and grunted through his nose as the duct tape plastered across his mouth stopped him from screaming.

Mossy picked Barry's travel bag from the hay and rooted inside as he crossed the floor, then dumped the contents onto the ground at Barry's feet. He knelt down and fingered through the things then pulled out an envelope and stood as he opened it. He turned and showed it to the dark-skinned man, whose facial expression remained dead. Nicky was sucking on a cigarette by the door and he glanced over to Toady with a nervous smile then pointed at Barry and mouthed the words, 'You're next.'

'This man here's a Copt,' Mossy announced, then chuckled. 'Not a cop now, laddie, cos he'd be fuck all use to ye here. No—an Egyptian Christian, a rare enough thing in Egypt these days, don't mind these parts. That beautiful lassie you were putting drugs in last night is his one and only daughter. She's all he has, but you were fixin to do something terrible to her.' The Egyptian seemed strangely serene, blissful almost, but the cold emptiness of his gaze hypnotised Barry with a paralysing fear.

'Her mother was a Muslim and she was killed by the Muslims—her own brothers no less. Burned alive in the street in front of the wee one, cos she married a Christian.' Mossy pointed at the silent man. 'Him—by Christ!' Then he blessed himself and kissed his fingertips. He clenched his big fist in Barry's face and squeezed it till it shook and he grunted with the effort. 'That's what I call a nugget. It's tight, it makes sense, and it's all in there. The start, the middle and the end. Now—do ye wanna know what you're nugget is?'

Barry shook his head wildly.

'Tough,' he laughed. 'Mousa here is a very religious man, which means, he's taught to hate the sin, but not the sinner. Which is unfortunate for you, because he doesn't see any difference between you trying to do what ye did, and actually doin it.' Mossy tapped Barry on the chest. 'The sin is still in there and he has to open ye up to get it out, or ye can't go to heaven and that's not what he wants. He wants to make an angel out of ye.' Mossy clenched his fist in Barry's face again till it trembled and a tear ran down Barry's cheek.

'There ye go son, let it out.' He turned to the Egyptian. 'Allay, mon frere.'

Quiet terror gripped Barry's eyes as the man stepped into him with the blade and buried it in his guts. He tugged it upward to open him up, then pulled it out, letting blood and stomach contents spill onto the floor and purple and white entrails slither through the hole in his shirt. Mossy opened the gate and the dogs that had been watching eagerly went into a frenzy and Barry was shoved inside. The gate closed behind him.

Mossy watched for a minute as Barry writhed to fend

off the dogs as he lay on the ground, but four hungry pit bulls weren't going to be fought off by a tied and wounded man. They had his guts out across the floor in a flash, then one of them started tearing at his neck and Toady didn't see him move again, except to be pulled and jerked back and forth as the dogs rattled their heads violently to pull lumps of meat free. Mossy came over and stood in front of Toady's bloodless face.

'This time tomorrow there'll be nothing left of him but twenty piles of dog shite. There'll be no body, and no body means no murder. No one's ever even gonna look for that poor cunt, d'ye hear me? Okay, now listen up—next it's Ginger, then it's you, and that's the lass time I'm axin ye nice.' He pushed Toady to the door then turned to Nicky. 'Are ye right?'

Nicky watched on at the cage. 'I'll follow ye down, I just want to watch this craic for a bit.'

'Go get Ginger when you're finished.' Mossy shoved Toady out the door.

Toady was quietly cleaned up. He went to the bank and he got twenty grand out for Mossy without any more fuss. The five-percent penalty he incurred for an emergency cash withdrawal didn't seem important in the overall scope of the things he was learning about himself and his fellow man. Toady went quietly back in the van and was returned to the campsite to find that Bruno had arrived from Perpignan. Bruno counted the money then made a phone call. After a couple of whiskeys with Mossy, he went to work on Toady for a bit, with his bare fists.

'Pah luh visage,' roared Mossy with glee. 'We're gonna milk the little bassard like an old bitches tit, so we are.'

Bruno knew not to mark his face and was working on his ribs and guts, putting in well aimed shots like blunt knives. The bandage across his nose screwed up in concentration below his beady black eyes. Toady had himself clenched tight and could take the shots, but he lost his footing and stumbled backwards over the tow-bar of a caravan. His head hopped off a rock and he passed out.

He was left there till dark and Arno was tasked with the job of keeping an eye on him as he went back and forward, stealing drink from the camper. Every now and then the boy would get a bucket of water and throw it over him for a laugh, but to little or no effect. Then the bonfires were lit and the party started. Toady was dragged into Mossy's camper and left on the floor.

'Thomas, my love.' His mother's voice was soft in his ear as he floated in black cotton clouds, soaked in acrid horse piss.

'I'm sorry Mammy, I gave them your money. I had to.'

'Nothing comes from nothing, my beautiful boy. Don't worry, she's coming for you. Be strong.'

* * *

He lifted his head from the glass of the window and looked across the back seat to find Shelley's green eyes smiling through long dark lashes and her velvet red lips puckered like an opening rose.

'Twenty piles of shite.' The words murmured hollow in his head.

'I think I zoned out for a minute,' he said. 'Where are we goin again?'

'Prettiest town in the world,' she replied. 'Isn't that right, Anna?'

'Yah!' Anna pointed out Dirk's window. They were crossing a bridge over a deep gorge and down at the coast, less than a mile away, a collection of red roofs projected from the leafy hillside.

'Collioure,' she announced, 'the jewel in the Vermilion Coast.'

'Shelley,' he whispered and she smiled again, 'I remember where Barry is.'

She raised her finger to his lips and shook her head.

He felt a crushing sympathy for her right then and

hoped that maybe in Barry's evil passing another one of Mossy's nuggets had earned the right to exist. Maybe her constant despair could pass tidily into twenty piles of shite, a suitably logical conclusion to their foolish marriage.

He lay his head back against the glass and let the country roll by and spared her more sadness by making it his own, and he cherished the intimacy of it.

SWITZERLAND

A low wall skirts the edge of Collioure's middle beach, the one most central to all the streets and cafes. Toady was sitting on the wall with his back to the town. Eclectic groups of tourists strolled back and forward behind him. Relaxed families with beautifully behaved children shared cobbled pathways with designer-clad Italian men more exquisitely appointed than their enchanting ladies, all strolling by each other beneath a symphony of language and laughter.

Anna and Shelley were sitting in the sand, down near the water's edge. Dirk was nowhere to be seen, having taken responsibility for parking the car. Toady found himself suspended in an unprecedented moment of clarity as he watched the women talk to each other in short refrains. They traded smiles and gestures freely and the outlines of their short sentences reached him faintly over the shimmering sand. Anna reached over, putting her hand on Shelley's shoulder, then threw her head back laughing.

It seemed that they must have known each other for years. Shelley with her broad shoulders, freckle-sprayed and honey-coloured, her strong form tapering into soft round hips, coppery curls peeping from her scarf to the middle of her back. Anna, small and slight at her side, her lithe waist hovering gracefully above chiseled, square hips, her short, ebony hair curled at the ends from the moist sea air, sat on smooth, coffee skin.

Like women from two different planets they shared no physical attributes bar the basic human form. Yet still he could see that they shared their womanhood so readily in smiles and touches and soft words. Anna had brought it out of Shelley so easily, when Toady didn't even know where to look. Hell, he wasn't even sure what he was supposed to be looking for.

There weren't many people on the beach, it being so early in the season. A boy and a young teenage girl were trying to acclimatise themselves to the cold water.

'I thought the Med was supposed to be waum, Mummy.' Her gentle British accent was music to Shelley's ears.

'It's wuss than back home,' the boy called out.

A mature man with grey hair and an athletic physique emerged from under the water not far away and spoke to his golden-haired wife in a hushed American drawl. 'It's cold enough that I don't feel safe, Honey.' He came ashore and toweled himself off in front of her.

Anna had gone to find Dirk with the dog and Toady came and sat beside Shelley as she soaked in the hushed reverence hanging over the water.

'I'm starting to go brown,' he said to her.

Head leaning sideways on her arm, she pulled up her shades then popped them down again. 'It suits you. You look a bit—Greek.'

'I'm starting to remember more stuff as well. Bits and pieces of everything are starting to line up and make sense.'

'Good,' she smiled, then frowned, 'or maybe not.'

'Switzerland,' he whispered and laughed quietly.

'Shut up.' She punched him on his shoulder and hurt her own hand and blushed. 'I got excited, I was trying to inspire you to live, with the grand imagery of it all. Besides, you should be worshipping the ground I walk on, I saved your life.'

'I do.' There was no sign of the other pair returning, so he shuffled a little closer. 'Tell me then, it's the only bit that I can't remember.'

'That doesn't surprise me,' she said. 'You were out cold,

I really thought you were dead. You were lucky I got there when I did. I was only going to check on you, half expecting you to be alright, feet up on a table, playing cards with that asshole, trying to get your money back.'

'No.' She shook her head, her gaze lost somewhere across the sun-kissed bay. 'Fuckin desperate, so it was.'

* * *

Mossy's nephews stared out into the darkness, muttering to each other. Behind them, back in the camp, the flames from the two steel barrels leapt high into the air. The sound of singing and clapping wafted over the night breeze and reached Shelley where she was sitting in the darkened stalls, not more than thirty meters away from the two men. Behind her the thumping of the band on the stage competed with the gypsy music for the thick air beneath the canopies.

She had seen them coming through the grass from the camp and had instantly recognised the shape of Toady, though his gait was reduced to a stumble, his hands bound together, his head bowed and lolled with his steps.

'What did they do to you?' she sighed into the cup of her hand shielding the tip of her cigarette. She shifted her weight and knocked the beer can she had just emptied onto the dusty ground with a rattle. Pawdie stepped forward and peered into the darkness and Shelley watched on. 'Can ye see me, fucker?' She lifted the two-foot long, steel bar from beside her leg, part of a table she'd found as she'd picked her way through the market. The flames and sparks of the camp leapt twenty feet into the air, outlining the two nephews in stark silhouette. Toady squatted, his head just visible. Pawdie took a few steps closer to where she sat motionless and cocked his head to one side for a moment. 'C'mon over, ye bad bastard, and I'll break your face for ya,' she whispered.

But Pawdie had no inkling that he was being watched

from the blackest of the shadows before him. 'That's U2 they're playing over there,' he brayed.

He stomped back to where Toady was now standing with his trousers around his ankles. Shelley could see the orange light shine on his bare ass as he held his hand out to Geno, perhaps hoping for a piece of paper to wipe himself with. He took a punch to the head instead. With his trousers down he was unable to adjust for balance and went straight over. She heard a faint thump and a moan as he hit the ground.

The two cousins stood over him joking and Shelley came to the edge of the light and had they turned then they would have seen her there, hair blazing in reflected firelight, denim jacket buttoned up to her chin and her handbag strap slung across her front. Her weapon of choice was hefted in two hands across her heaving chest. A fag dangled from the corner of her mouth.

'Motherfuckers!' she cursed on a slow, smoky exhale.

Toady was hauled upright from the grass, barely able to stand on his own feet as one held him and the other pulled his trousers up.

'A lil cunt with a big cock, so ye are,' wailed Geno, and Pawdie hooted like a baboon. 'There's a couple of knife-slingin, arse bandits waitin for ye in Perpignan.'

They got his trousers closed and started to walk when Pawdie spun fast on his heels. The chaos of the deserted market and the loose tarpaulins hanging in every direction pitched shape and form into the dark. A loud peel of laughter rose from the far side of the stalls to where Shelley stood. A bunch of teenagers sat in the shadows smoking and drinking beer from plastic cups. When she looked back the trio was walking back to the camp. Toady's legs were struggling to stay under him, stumbling and tripping, then yanked aloft again, the pair dragged him along, eager to get back to the party.

She emerged from the shadows again and watched them take him to the nearest camper, which she recognised as Mossy's, with the sticker in the window—'Is Feidir Linn!' Geno hauled him up the steps and after a few seconds he returned and slammed the door behind him.

She waded out into the waist high lake of grass, weeds and bushes, alive with the singing of a million crickets. The low bass drum of the band was beating on the night air like the heart of the festival in the open chest of the town. The ribs rising up all around in the form of the big, black hills ever present against the sky.

'I can't live, with or without you,' she sang to herself, then went down on her hunkers. The door of Mossy's camper opened and the man himself descended the steps in a bright green shirt and black jeans, spruced up for the event. He donned his cowboy hat and headed straight for the fires.

She advanced again on the noisy party and the music of two acoustic guitars became audible. She scanned back and forth for signs of any outlying stragglers. The campervans and the tables and the multitude of clotheslines were deserted as any and all, from young to old, were in attendance at their own private festival. The pop music behind her faded as every sensor in her body now pointed forward and the gypsy incantations came into sharp focus.

Two men were singing, more in contest than in harmony, their voices rising and wrestling each other upward on the sparks. The dueling guitars attacked each other in crashing waves. Shelley turned right and skirted the fringe of deeper shadow just beyond the light from the camp. She passed over a disused train track with bushes bursting through rail and sleeper. She circumnavigated the camp, step by rhythmic step, one hand out flat, skimming the grass tops, the steel bar in the other, resting from fist to shoulder.

The hum of a petrol generator emanating from between two trees explained where the power for the strings of lights that crisscrossed the gathering was coming from. The music came to her clearly now, the entwined voices of the two men, each strumming and beating his guitar passionately as the crowd hooted and cheered.

A young woman spun in circles around the clearing, her hands writhing and clapping one side of her face then the other. Jet black hair whirling back and forth over the dark-brown skin of her bare shoulders. Her arms rising and falling, breathing to the rhythm of the guitars. A loud roar went up as a huge billowing mushroom of sparks leapt into the air above all their heads and the voices of many women joined in with a shrill, high-pitched lament.

Shelley passed close enough to feel the faintest heat on the very edge of the light before arcing out into the pitch dark on the far side of the camp. Two dogs came barreling out from under a campervan; she froze. A Jack Russell and a black and white mongrel scrambled right up to her shins, barking. The mongrel with his wet nose sniffed her hand, the terrier circled her feet. She cast a glance over at the camp. They were deep in the throes of revelry as another young woman joined the dance. This one with long blonde waves cascading to her shoulders, catching firelight as she circled the flames on the far side. A tall, dark figure entered the dance, clapping his hands over his head. The blonde waited motionless for him to reach her then commenced to spin circles around him.

Shelley resumed her steady gait to the farthest corner of the camp where she melted into the waist high grass and the mayhem of abandoned horseboxes. Beyond that, towards the rear of the encampment, she could see the outlines of the scattered horses against the streetlights of the town. They sensed her presence arriving at the rear of the campers and flicked their manes, then pulled and whinnied at their tethers. She stopped at the corner of the last campervan and watched for any signs of humans among the horses. Nothing stirred but the tops of the long grass and further away, over the wasteland, other horses lifted their heads and snorted. The music was still ringing out from the camp as she started along the back of the campers on the final leg of her circuit. The steel bar in her hand, sweeping over the long grass, awaited the unsuspecting.

Through the gaps between each van she could see the blazing fires and the milling crowd as more couples joined the dance in ever increasing circles. Each time, the music coming in loud and crystal clear then fading as she passed behind the next caravan.

She arrived at the last camper having circumnavigated the makeshift town without meeting anyone. Down at her feet the two dogs smiled, tongues lolling—if anyone was lurking nearby, they gave no indication. She peeped her head around the corner and saw that the coast was clear, then paced along the length of the camper and tried the handle. It yielded and the door cracked open. Her heart fluttered and her breath trembled hot over her bottom lip. She pulled open the door and set a chain of tiny bells ringing that hung from the inside handle to act as a warning device. She grabbed them and froze in silence. The fires were too far away and the frenzy too passionate for anyone to have heard. She climbed the last step into the darkness, pulling the door shut behind her, and knelt in the stairwell. Toady's head was illuminated in the stripes of light coming through the blinds.

'Toady,' she said and stroked his cheek, 'it's Shelley.'

He groaned and moved a little and the light caught the sticky mess of blood caked to the back of his head and down his T-shirt.

'We're gettin out of here,' she whispered. 'Hang in there, boy.'

She went to the driver's seat and sat in. She took three deep breaths and watched the revelers in the distance as she reached to the ashtray where she had twice seen Ellen stow the key. She pushed it once with her index finger. It clicked, then slid open, projecting a shiny drawer. Inside was the black stallion key-ring with two keys attached. She slipped it into the ignition and checked the gear stick for reverse. She'd also seen Ellen apply the hand-break lever under the dash. She pulled and with a deep clunk the van rolled back from its spot a little and rested on the gears.

Four failed driving tests, twenty-two professional lessons, along with a few Sunday afternoon screaming matches around the town with Barry had to count for something.

Her heart threatened to beat its way out through her ribs as she depressed the clutch and turned the ignition. The engine whirred into life and the vehicle started to roll backward on the incline. A robotic hum and another clunk as the external steps retracted. She eased off the clutch and let the engine engage a little, creeping over small bumps, then bigger ones, as the camp slowly receded in the front windscreen. She checked the rearview mirror to see the silver light of the moon burst from clouds over the wasteland, illuminating the grass and the horses in her path.

Backwards she crept, as the rear of the vehicle climbed over the bedding of the disused railway. Then the front of the van, rising and falling violently with Ellen's faithful packing ensuring that nothing tipped out of the presses.

'Enough,' she grunted.

She stood on the brake and opened her mouth and gasped air like a swimmer breaking the water and she realized she hadn't breathed since she'd started the engine and now her lungs and throat were burning. She found first gear with a grind and a clunk and she swung the campervan into a slow arc to the left, towards the gap she'd seen Nicky use earlier, where the disused railway alignment exited the wasteland onto the side road.

The van crept around jostling from side to side as it lumbered to the hedge, then through it. She wheeled hard left again to bring the van around onto the narrow road, gouging the hedges on the far side with crunching twigs and snapping branches. Nonetheless, the arc delivered her to the junction with Boulevard Charles de Gaulle. To the left the festival and streetlights illuminated the street's facades and bunting a couple of hundred yards away. To the right, the road faded to the edge of town where it was engulfed by the night. This was as far as she had contemplated her plan and without ever wondering why, she just wheeled left again. Putting the camper into second gear she headed into the chaos of the town. A car was coming at her, and as it drew close it flashed its lights repeatedly.

'Fuck it—lights.' She fumbled with the stick ends. Her hands crawled and flicked at the buttons and dials on the dash. Windscreen wipers, hazard lights and blowers all sprang to life before she found the lights with the demented laugh of an evil genius.

'Let there be light,' she roared at the windscreen.

With that, the car swerved out to the right, just missing her and blowing its horn.

'Roadhog!' she shouted across the passenger seat then glared out the side window and across the moonlit grassland. She could see no sign that the gypsies had been alerted to their escape, just the silhouettes of horses and the orange ball of light in the distance. Another car was approaching flashing its lights.

'What's your problem? I have me lights—Fuckin France!' she roared and hung right on the wheel. With a shriek the van shunted on its tyres to the right side of the road, out of the way of the oncoming traffic. The car passed by blowing its horn and again she scanned the wasteland for trouble, but still it was clear and she laughed like a maniac. She was passing through the town now. On her left, the stage lights flashed and the loud music thumped through the window and crowds of people were jumping around the car park to the theme of Bruce Springsteen.

'Baby, we were born to run.'

She progressed through the clusters of people walking back and forth on the road and glanced over her shoulder.

Toady was motionless. They reached the traffic lights at the end of the street and straight through the junction, then another hundred yards in a line of traffic to the next set of lights.

'Shit!' They turned red, but just then the left side feeder arrow turned green and that was enough for her to decide her next move. She swerved out into the lane and the camper whooshed around with squealing tyres as she accelerated onto the incline. She had it moving nicely now in third gear, up a slow hill and into the darkness where the streetlights ended. She swiped and jabbed at the controls again until she found the full beams and the road lit up wide in front of her, striped white and gold far into the distance. She checked the mirror and nothing was behind her but the receding light that marked the edge of town. The engine took the hill on with a reassuring purr as she slid it into fourth gear with shivers rolling up and down her spine.

'Toady,' she called over her shoulder, 'd'ye hear me? We did it, baby.'

She whooped and shouted, glancing in the wing mirrors as she bounced in her seat and slapped the steering wheel. 'C'mon you fuckers, catch me now.' She pressed harder on the pedal and up they climbed, taking twists and turns with growing confidence. Out to her left some scattered lights lay below, twinkling in the valley floor.

'Jesus,' she gasped, shocked at how quickly they had ascended the unseen heights. So flushed with adrenaline were her veins, the sheer size of the mountain she had set out upon was a concept that had never occurred to her. There hadn't been a thought in her head until then but snatching victory and glory from the gates of hell. 'You big bastard of a mountain,' she called, 'I'm comin through!'

On they charged, up another straight stretch, then gearing down for a tight bend to the right. Her chest heaved at the sight of the town nestled far below in the dark abyss.

'Toady, are ye alive at all?' she called over her shoulder. Her head snapped backwards with such force that her neck might have broken had it not been for the headrest. She let out a blood-curdling screech as the pain in her locks stung deeply into her cheeks and again her head slammed back against the headrest.

'What the fuck—Toady? It's me,' she grunted through gritted teeth, trying to keep her eyes on the road. The camper careered along another straight section.

'Pull over, ya fuckin hoor ya.'

She twisted her head round just enough to see Arno's contorted sweaty face and greasy fringe, his eyes stained bloodshot evil and his breath reeking of beer and garlic.

'Pull over or I'll kill ye,' he shouted. He yanked hard and landed a clatter to her ear with his open palm. Shelley howled in pain and strained to keep control as another bend came into sight and she took her foot off the pedal. She lashed out sideways and got him in the balls with the back of her fist and he doubled over blowing a loud windy moan in the side of her face. She grabbed hold of his ear and sunk her nails into it and tore at it while he squealed. He stumbled back into the passenger seat with streaks of blood rolling down his cheek. Shelley struggled to steady their approach to the hairpin bend that hung in the empty blackness ahead. It was too tight, she had no choice but to step on the brake at the exact same time as Arno reached out and caught the wheel. He pulled it out of her hand causing them to veer off the road into a lay-by, brakes squealing until they hit the grass verge then grinding over the dry soil.

'Bastard!' She managed to yank the wheel back out of Arno's hands, but that only had the effect of sending them out over the kerb and onto the road, straight for the low wall that was suspended before them in the void of the night. She pulled hard on the wheel, slamming her two feet onto the brake pedal at once. The wheels locked and they arced sideways across the road in a deafening chorus of screeching rubber and screams, then slammed sideways into the wall with a loud crash. The engine jumped to a halt. As Shelley rallied her senses, Arno was hauling himself out of the passenger seat with a mixture of rage and terror etched into his pale face.

'Fuck you!' he roared hot in her eyeballs. He shuffled past her seat and made for the door, tripping flat on his face over Toady. He rose up and spun around, pointing a finger at Shelley. 'You're dead—Mossy's gonna murder you, ya mad bitch.' And with that he flung open the door and stepped out, toppling straight into the black of night. The last thing he grabbed was the chain of bells from the handle before he flipped over the low wall and tinkled his way into the treetops below.

'Holy God!' She clambered out of her seat to the door. Her head spun above the dizzy heights as she reached out and took hold of the door handle and slammed it shut. She stepped over Toady in a chastened silence and slid sideways back into her seat. Panic was all around her, urging her to abandon herself to a helpless scream and dash into the night. But she put her head down and wrestled for control, breathing in through flaring nostrils, then out, seething through clenched teeth. She shunted the camper into motion and started wheeling it around to face the black mountain, grinding metal along the low wall to break free with a clatter. She found a mantra to steady her trembling arms in long abandoned Catholic prayers.

'Holy Mary, Mother of God, pray for us now and at the hour of our death.'

She arced out across the road, the wheels slowly lumbering over the verge and back down until she was on the right side of the road with a jarring crash.

'Hail Mary, full of Grace—the Lord is with thee,' she called to the night. The engine screamed at the top of the gear as she rounded the tight bend, hitting the climb once again, just in time to see headlights coming down the hill on the other side of the road. 'Blessed be the fruit of thy womb, Jesus.' She jammed it into third and spoke aloud to the darkness all around. 'Toady—wake up for Christ Sake, it's just me and you, boy.'

'Heavenly father—I am truly sorry for having offended thee,' she wailed, gouging the pedal to the floor. 'For fuck's sake, Toady,' she roared, 'are you alive or what? In the name of God, will ye say somethin?'

She drove until she saw a turn to the left and wheeled into it with a clatter, burying the gear stick in second and jamming her leg rigid to the floor. The engine snarled and spat smoke across the road before the wheels bit into the incline and shoved them onwards and upwards. On they went into the night, with her checking the rear view mirrors for headlights and intermittently calling out to Toady over her shoulder. He lay in silence, dead as Arno surely was. Now it was just her, alone in the mountains, headed for who knew where. Her knuckles were white on the wheel, her nails biting deep into her flesh, while her prayers issued over a dwindling stream of curses.

One last time she caught sight of a distant valley through the trees, far below in the dark bosom of the land, spread beneath a pale moonlit sky. The tall hills that she had seen poised above Quillan were arranged around the horizon below her as she climbed on into the night.

The valley was long gone when the road eventually leveled and she drove past flat, silver fields high in the mountains. The shadows of cows standing motionless on either side of the road gave a notion of scale to the expansive landscape. In the distance, all around the plateau, were the jagged points of pine trees and behind them, the smooth, dark flanks of further-off hills looming ever higher into the night sky. She wished Toady could see it. She wished anyone could see it, just so they would believe her when she told them she had been here.

'Thomas.' She called his name gently, again and again, as they crept on through small villages with little to suggest they were inhabited, save for a dog sitting still here or a dim light behind a curtain on the side of the hill there. Silence within and without, like spacemen they traversed the silvery reaches of a fertile moon. Her headlights illuminating huge rosebushes on whitewashed walls or brightly-coloured shutters in neat rows, she wheeled left or right following the road, wherever it took her.

Then climbing again, away from the plateau and the sleeping villages, into the trees and around the tight climbing bends, her arms starting to burn with effort and her wrists threatening to crack with the strain. She puffed and sighed and once again called for Toady as loneliness took over the cold empty space inside where the glory of the escape had seeped away.

Eventually, in the darkest recess of the early morning, she arrived at the ski-station on top of Col de Chioula. The trees and the darkness of the road fell away to reveal open hillsides all around. The road widened and leveled off as she allowed the camper to slow. Then turning into the car park she allowed it to squeal to a gentle stop before turning off the ignition and plunging them into complete silence. She gazed out the windscreen at the moonlit panorama. Icy white clouds hung like lace over the jagged teeth of the mountain range. Shelley had never seen snow-peaked mountains before and now that was all she could see, across the entire width of the front window. Row after row, under a star-studded and moonlit sky.

'Toady,' she whispered, 'you need to see this—quick.'

She sat in awe of the timeless vista and somehow worried that it might disappear before she had time to drink it all up with her eyes.

'I'm sorry, Toady, please don't die.' Rivers of hot tears poured down her cheeks and her nose leaked salt water over her lips, but she didn't take her eyes off the mountain range for a second.

'Wake up Toady and see where we are, look where I've brought you. It's the top of the world and we're on it.' She sniffed and wiped her hand across her mouth like a sloppy child.

'Toady, I promise I'll love you if you wake up. I promise I'll be nice to you, I'll do anything you want, please don't leave me here on my own.' And with that, she was sure she heard a breath stir. She spun in the seat, then scrambled to his side. She put her hand to his cheek to find that he wasn't completely cold. She lowered her wet face to his and pressed against the bristles and felt his warm breath on her chin and then a long moan escaped his lips.

'Toady, ye bastard,' she whispered, planting a kiss on his forehead as his eyes flicked open weakly.

'Shelley?' his voice cracking in his dry throat. 'Where are we?'

'Switzerland,' she sighed in his ear. 'We made it to Switzerland.'

Toady closed his eyes and groaned as his memory evaporated in a perfumed mist. She could see the smile trying to break out across his lips.

'Switzerland,' he croaked, 'is it nice?'

'It's beautiful. There's snowy mountains as far as the eye can see, I swear it.'

'Yeh—that'll be Switzerland alright.'

RED MIST

Toady dug his hands into the warm sand as he listened to the story, then sat in silence a moment. 'Wow, that's some story for the boozer. You've got some balls on you, girl.'

'Oh, ye know me, just gimme a call.' She waved a nonchalant hand towards him.

'Well—now we know how they figured out which way we came.' He found a little pebble and threw it into the sea. 'Arno.'

'Yeh, with bells on.' Her frown turned to a grimace. 'Jesus—he was just a kid.'

'Ay,' he chided her, 'fuck em all, Shell. Remember? Reap and sow.'

She tried to smile for him before turning back to the incredible vista. Her eyes could never get tired, sitting in a place like this. The hills surrounded the town and on top of the final outcrop, over the sea, a big castle commanded a complete view from its vantage point on the far side of the bay. It sat above the rows of red-tiled roofs that climbed up the slope to its feet from the water's edge.

To her right was another castle sitting with stout shins planted in the water. Flags snapping in the breeze above its ramparts, strong buttressed walls entered the sea with small boats moored to the ancient stone. To her left the pointed, red roof of a bell tower loomed overhead, where a church rose straight out of the water. The two British kids had swum out to it and were holding on to steel rings bedded in the seaweed and stone. Beyond that, the harbour wall extended hundreds of metres across the wide bay to where yachts were passing each other in and out on bright sails.

'It's a different world,' she sighed. 'Did you ever imagine a place like this even existed? I'd happily sit here for the rest of my life.'

'Okay, but you know what you have to do now.' He gestured towards the water lapping at the sand close by. 'This is why you came here, remember? Paddle in the Med? This is what it all comes down to. All this violence and madness—you and your toes.'

She smirked back like a kid being dared. 'Buh it's cold mummy,' she said a soft British accent.

Toady lay back on his elbows and the warm sand poured over his arms. Each time she glanced back at him he nodded toward the water. 'Well? Go on. I nearly got killed trying to get you here, don't make me drag you in screaming.'

She wagged her finger. 'Low profile, Thomas. The grey man wouldn't approve.'

Dirk and Anna were back, sitting on the low concrete wall with the dog on her lead. When Anna noticed Shelley watching, her smile immediately exploded onto her face and she waved with a green poop bag on her hand. Shelley gave a wiggle of her fingers. Anna nudged Dirk with her shoulder and he waved too, but without a smile.

Shelley stood up and took off her T-shirt. She slipped off her bottoms, then folded them and placed her designer sandals on top of her little pile.

'Don't take your eyes off that, not for a second,' she warned him over her shoulder.

'Never,' he replied, taking in every curve of her body.

'Am I gorgeous?' she asked him without looking back. He gave her a quiet wolf whistle in reply. She pulled the elastics from both her cheeks then snapped them back with a quiver. At the water's edge she waded in up to her knees and he watched her buttocks clench up when the cold water hit her inner thighs. He sat up to get a better view just as Dirk pounded by in the sand and crashed into the water, sending splashes everywhere, causing her to squeal and go rigid.

'Fuckin dickhead,' Toady seethed.

Dirk was barking like a seal, not far from where she stood.

'Don't be afraid,' he called to her in his Germanic drone, 'it's not cold.'

'Of course it's cold, ye silly bollox,' Toady grunted onto his arm. Then Dirk was wading waist deep back towards her with obvious intent in his beady, blue eyes. Toady lifted his head to shout a warning but stopped himself from drawing the unwanted attention and disrupting the peaceful decorum of the scene. But Dirk didn't do decorum when it came to getting himself up against a pretty girl and he grabbed her around the waist and started to pull her slowly into the deeper water. She put her hands to his chest and pushed, but she couldn't get enough balance on the tumbling shingle under her feet to force him away. Blood boiled in Toady's head and it was all he could do to stop himself going berserk into the sea to kill him there and then. Fists and teeth clenched, he moaned.

'That poor girl doesn't want that, George,' he heard the American lady say to her husband.

'Naw, Honey, she sure doesn't,' he said, shaking his head. 'That idiot needs his ass kicked.'

Toady stood up and watched as Dirk crushed his waist into hers and she compounded the matter by pushing harder on his torso, giving him the excuse to thrust his lower half forward. Just before the red mist descended, something told Toady to look at Anna. She was standing at the wall, wringing her hands with the last scraps of a desperate smile falling from her face. A wretched pleading in her eyes searched for empathy in him and he felt a grinding pity for her. He was unexpectedly partaking of that miserable communion he had sometimes heard others refer to as the human condition. For the sake of Anna's timid soul he swallowed just enough sympathy to slow his rage.

'Aw Jesus,' he whimpered. Slumping down into the sand, he exhaled raw heat all the way through gritted teeth. Dirk wasn't pulling so hard on her now, but hanging his weight back and wiggling from side to side.

'Come have fun with me, Fanny,' he said. She pushed and squirmed till he let go.

The American man who had sat down beside his wife was indignant. 'What did that son of a gun just say about her fanny?'

His wife put her hand on his shoulder. 'It's her name, dear. Calm down now, George, it's not your business anyhow.'

Toady was feeling deeply inadequate as Shelley stormed out of the water and rummaged in her bag till she found the towel and sat down. 'Asshole just rubbed his thing all over me.'

Toady bowed his head and let the words flow over him. 'I'm sorry,' he groaned.

'Wasn't your fault.' She was pulling on her bottoms and wiggling her hips into them. Dirk was coming towards them and he passed them by, still grinning. Toady glanced over at the American, now glaring back at him and shaking his head as though he had just stormed the beach at Normandy to find Toady sucking Frankfurters in the shade.

'That was fun,' Anna chirped, flashing her winning smile again. Shelley was dressed and back at the wall where the two Germans sat. 'Are you hungry?' she asked. Shelley nodded and Toady had to admit that he could feel hunger pangs somewhere beneath the knot in his stomach.

Numerous restaurants fronted onto the beach just beside them, with plenty of empty tables. They found a nice table for four in the sun and the underemployed waiter had water, bread and menus in front of them before they were even settled in their seats properly, with Dirk managing to get himself in on the other side of Shelley.

'Big beer,' Toady called without delay.

'Get me one too,' Shelley begged.

'Duh siryuh,' Anna piped up for them. 'Ay un bootay du maison blanc.'

He came back with two huge, frosted glass mugs of lager and a bottle of white wine. Dirk ordered for both him and Anna in fluent French before the waiter came to Shelley who was licking her lips at the picture of a rack of lamb.

'Voila!' she exclaimed, pointing.

He looked at Toady. 'Ay Missyuh?'

He held up two fingers. 'With chips.'

'Avec freet,' Anna interjected and the waiter smiled and left.

They sat in silence for a while with Anna beaming over her glass of wine as she fed little corners of bread and butter to the dog and spoke to it in German. They made a bit of small talk about the scenery and Anna explained what she knew about the town in her finest English accent with Dirk assisting her vocabulary from time to time.

'It's okay, Dirk,' Toady assured him, 'she speaks beautifully.'

'Why thank you, Mickey,' she said beaming.

'Yes, but I can make her better,' Dirk said, sitting forward and Shelley jumped in her seat. Toady looked at her, but her eyes went down to his clenched fists on the table and the veins bulging on his forearms.

'I better go to the toilet,' she said.

'I better help.' Anna jumped out of her seat, gripping Shelley's arm as they walked through the tables to the restaurant door. That left Toady looking miserably across the table at Dirk's head craning after the girls.

'Well, Dirkhead, you having fun?' Toady's disposition hovered somewhere in limbo as he slouched back in his chair, submerging to his eyeballs in open disgust.

'Yes,' he replied. 'Anna really likes you two, she is so excited to be here. We don't have many friends.'

'Yeh, she's such a nice girl and you're a complete cunt—can't be easy.' He was staring across the table at him and Dirk was rearranging the bread in the basket avoiding eye contact.

'Oh now, Mickey,' he laughed a little, 'there's no need to be rude, I'm just trying to be friendly.'

'Try being a little less friendly with my wife and we'll get on much better.'

'Oh come now, I'm just playing and anyway, we all know she's not your wife. She has a ring, but you have never worn one—ah?'

Toady was caught a little by surprise and started to sit back up.

'Mickey and Fanny Stroker, that was funny, but my English is quite good, yah? She is somebody's wife certainly, but not yours, Mr. Brody.'

Now he had Toady's undivided attention.

'Ah yes, I saw your wallet in your campervan—what am I saying, it's not even your campervan, is it?'

Toady was leaning forward on his elbows now, his nose lodged between his palms and his eyes fixed.

'Yes, camping receipts in the drawer, Ellen and Mossy Walsh? You see, Thomas, I know what people are like. Five years driving in a taxi, I meet many people, I see things, I notice things. Your redhead, I like her game, it's exciting to me. Does her husband even know where she is? What's her name—Michelle?'

Toady regarded him for a minute and could see that his body language was now betraying his true character as he came out of himself. The way his weight lay to one side and the tiny angle he held his head at—he was starting to see him afresh now. He wasn't a big guy, but he wasn't weak either. His shoulders were broad and he carried a bit of weight high up. Toady pegged him for a swimmer or possibly a martial artist of some discipline or other. 'Oh please,' said Toady, 'don't stop now or you won't get your Gestapo badge.'

'Well—I'm only saying that we can all relax and be friends.' He smiled and needled Toady with the sharpness in his bright blue eyes. 'Anna likes you, she told me so. You could have some fun with that—you know?' He sipped from his white wine and raised an eyebrow to compliment his pinkie salute.

'Not really,' Toady replied. 'Do elaborate.'

'She is of African descent.' He counted on his fingers. 'Her great-great-great-great grandfather was an American slave, his ancestors were taken from the Ivory Coast—' he waved his hands in the air nonchalantly, 'I don't know, seventeen hundred and something. Think about that for a minute—an actual slave.'

Toady didn't move a muscle or say a word. Dirk was coming in loud and clear.

'Her great grandfather fought in the war and when the nasty, evil German Reich was defeated, he stayed in Germany. Then he left the army and opened a supermarket in Dusseldorf and married a beautiful, blue-eyed Bavarian girl and they made little brown German babies.' There was no trace of the meek and proper Dirk to be found in the sneering face pointed across the table at him.

'Unth zis, my friend, is zee irony of zee legacy of our dear Herr Chancellor.' He snapped his back straight, clicked his heels and gave a Nazi salute across the table staring into the distance.

'Goddam it, that's it,' came a voice from a few tables away and the sound of plates rattling and a glass falling over.

'Now, George, Honey, calm down,' said the woman. The American couple was sitting not far away from them, waiting on lunch also.

'Son of a gun,' he said over the sound of more rattling.

A Fistful of Salt

Dirk was slowly lowering his hand, still staring into the distance. When their eyes met again, Toady wondered if he had finally met the real man or was he being introduced to some sophisticated brand of European sarcasm.

'Ever fuck a slave? It's empowering.' Dirk clenched his fist and sighed in satisfaction.

Toady put his beer down and wiped his mouth and glanced across to where the American and his wife were in negotiations at their table, with her stroking his arms while he shook his head.

'So you want me to screw your wife, Krapstein?'

He shrugged his shoulders. 'If I give her to you for a night, it's not my business what you do to her.'

'Lemme guess—you want to swap.'

He sipped wine through his teeth. 'Yah, Mick—I do.'

'You're a special case, Dirk. We're gonna talk later.' Toady straightened up as he saw the girls approach.

Anna was linking Shelley's arm again and practically skipping out of her sandals with the exuberance of the moment. It seemed to be rubbing off on Shelley, who was smiling like a Cheshire cat and bouncing on the fragrant air.

Shelley had redone her hair in a lose plait at the back and tied the scarf lazily around it leaving much of it visible.

'That's nice,' Toady muttered. The mayhem in his head was precluding him from worrying about her hair at this stage.

'Thanks—Anna did it for me while I was peeing—she's mad. We did a line of coke in the toilet, she's pretty wired now. So am I.' She put her lips down to the edge of the glass and sucked froth from the head in little sips while that gem sunk into Toady's creaking brain. Anna had the little dog up on her knee again and she sang a tune to it, and the pooch whined back.

'Such a beautiful singer, you are.'

Shelley giggled and Dirk drank deeply, emptying his glass with a sigh of satisfaction.

The food came and they ate and passed remarks about themselves and their trips and their plans. Dirk and Anna were going to Spain but hadn't quite decided when. Dirk was watching Shelley's lips move when she spoke and Shelley was trying not to notice. Toady was watching Dirk watch Shelley sucking lamb off the bone and he could see Dirk sucking on some fantasy he was conjuring. Each time Toady picked a bit of fat from his lamb and put it on the side-plate, Anna's fingers walked across the table, picked it up and brought it back to the little dog with the tiny pink tongue, panting on her lap.

'Another special present from Mickey to Sukie,' she sang.

Whenever he glanced at Anna she was waiting for him with mischievous eyes peeking from under her fringe, biting a smile on her lower lip. She was infectious, the more she caught him looking at her, the more giddy her smile appeared and the more he wanted to check her again. He couldn't put the pair together. Dirk was like her vampire master, sucking in all her selfless light and exuding an ultra-violet narcissistic darkness.

The table was cleared and coffee was brought and just as they had it finished and Toady imagined that all the potential mayhem gathered around the table might come to nothing, Anna asked Shelley why she kept her beautiful hair covered up all the time.

'Modesty,' she said with a straight face. 'He wants to be a Muslim when he grows up.' And she pointed at Toady's solemn brown face, her finger two inches from his nose. Anna's head went down in an uncontrollable snigger and Shelley's shoulders lurched into silent convulsions and tears came out of her eyes.

Dirk took that as his cue to pull the scarf from her hair and when her hands shot up to grab it, he slid his hand up her leg causing her to squeal and the whole table jumped in the air with a rattle. Her arm shot out and she backhanded him with a loud slap in the face. He said something in

German and Anna's jaw dropped, which left Toady no option but to assume it was an insult. Dirk started to rise from his seat but it didn't matter anymore what he had in mind because the switch in Toady's head had flipped.

Before Dirk was even half upright the table and all its contents were arcing sideways out of the space between them. Past Dirk's face: cups, saucers, sachets of sugar and milk trails were taking off as Toady stood up and cast everything from his line of fire. With the same rising momentum that he used to fling the table away, he thrust his foot into the middle of Dirk's chest, catapulting him out of their company, as though an invisible car he was tied to had sped away. It happened so fast that the table and Dirk landed at the same time with a crash that made every woman within twenty metres let out a scream.

'No,' cried Shelley, reaching out to grab Toady as he passed by. He bent over and rooted in the debris of tables and chairs and came out with a stiff and terrified Dirk. He stood him up straight then landed a punch that sent him reeling into the last row of tables, taking one to the ground with him as he went down.

Toady went and stood over him, seething with violence. 'Now that's empowering.'

A loud whistle was heard across the plaza and two cops that had been standing on the street corner were now charging towards them.

'Dammit son, that's more like it,' came a shout. Toady glanced over to see the American pointing proudly at him.

'Shit,' he whispered. The cop smashed into him taking him straight to the ground.

He was cuffed and taken across the street. A car was called and a crowd gathered around to watch events unfold. Dirk was standing close by being interviewed by the other cop while they waited and Anna stood on the other side of the road stroking the little dog in her arms with mascara smeared across her pretty face.

The policeman came to Shelley. 'Parlay vous Fronsay?'

She shook her head.

'Ziss man—says your usband—attacked is wife. Is zis correct, Madame?'

'What?' She gasped. Over the cop's shoulder Dirk was standing like a bullied kid with a tissue held to his nose. The sight of him made her demented. She reached past the cop and latched her nails into his scalp, dragging him out and down. He screamed like a schoolgirl, flailing his arms, and she swung her foot up and managed to kick him in the face before the cops could pry her off. She was shoved to the ground and cuffed then dragged away kicking and cursing like a fishwife to the car that had just arrived.

'Low profile,' Toady said staring out the window at the crowd. The car sped off with the blue lights flashing and the sirens howling up through the town. She snorted and growled beside him, her hair completely loosed around her face, vicious eyes glaring through her locks.

'That's more like it, Shelley. I was wondering where you'd gone.' He sat back in the car to watch the pretty painted windows and doors of the town whiz by.

GUCCI TO THE RESCUE

A grumpy officer put them in a cell, took their handcuffs off and pointed at a bottle of mineral water with two plastic cups on a table in the corner, then slammed the door behind him. The hatch opened and a woman's voice grated. 'Vous parlay Fronsay, no?'

'No,' Shelley replied. The hatch shut. The two of them sat on the side of the single bed. An hour passed before they spoke.

'It's hard to believe that a sweet girl like Anna would stay with a prick like him,' Shelley said to the wall. 'She deserves better.'

'No she doesn't,' he mumbled. 'She could leave him, same as you could have left—'

Shelley's ice cold glare shut him up. He sat forward, recalling the manner in which Barry had departed, the images more clear each time they flashed before him. 'Well at least it's over now,' he said.

'I'll be the judge of that,' she objected.

'Events can pass you out sometimes,' he mumbled. 'That's all I'm saying.'

'Well, Thomas Brody, a whole load of stuff passed you out, living under your Mammy's apron all your life, in your little grey world. Try living in the real world. Try being a woman. You go from being daddy's little girl to havin every dirty bastard in town trying to stick his lad up your arse in the space of a couple of years. It's a fucking war out there and women are losing. I'd like to see you do any better than me—or Anna.'

He stared at the floor. 'Or Melanie.' Then he shook his head. 'Or Flora.'

He couldn't look at her. He wasn't used to adult conversations. She was right, what did he know? Grey man, fake man, sitting in his car, watching the parade of pretty asses going past the rank every day and picturing them naked. It had always been easier just to presume he had nothing women needed and steal little pieces of their dignity in secret. Never wondering if they might be struggling to hold onto the few scraps they had left. He'd spent so long trying so hard to be nobody that it never occurred to him to just be human.

'I could have saved her.'

'Who?'

'Flora. They say good men only need do nothing for evil to win, but a good man wouldn't do nothing.'

'I think that's the point of the phrase.' She rolled her eyes.

'But nobody ever does anything.'

'Because there's no good men. Duhhh!'

He turned to face her. 'I should have tried to make you happy, Shell.'

'You? Make me happy?' She put her hand on his cheek and sighed. 'That's the most retarded thing anyone's ever said to me. Thanks, Thomas.'

The door rattled. A middle-aged man walked in with a chair, put it down in front of them and sat on it. A handsome, tanned character with a jaunty smile and a swaggering composure, he put a foot up on his knee and an arm over the back of his chair. He dipped his hand into his pocket and retrieved their identification and threw them onto the bed.

'Welcome to France,' he said and flourished his hand in a whirl then tipped his head in a little bow.

'Thanks,' they both said together, sitting up straighter.

'Ze fighting Irish are in town,' he said with a grandiose grin across his supple face. 'Roll up, roll up and see them smash up the ancient streets of our quaint Mediterranean resort.'

Shelley couldn't help but let the amusement flit across her face. Toady wasn't smiling. He just reclined again with his back against the wall and folded his arms, unmoved by the performance.

'Okay Sir, I can see you are a busy man with a lot to do, so I will get to the point. You have committed what we quaint French folk like to call a Class A dayleet, or misdemeanour in English. Assault and battery, destruction of private property, breaching the peace and resisting arrest.' He was talking to Toady while pointing at Shelley.

'Who? Me or him?' she demanded.

'You,' he said, still looking at Toady. 'The penalty for such charges, in this little make-believe kingdom we call France, is imprisonment, or maybe some thousands in fines and perhaps a bit of both, if the judge decides that he doesn't like you. I can tell you now that you are not his type.' He smiled at both of them. Shelley opened her mouth and lifted a finger to speak.

'—You will be charged, you will be held here and you will be tried and found guilty and punished if the law so wishes.' He slapped his knee making Shelley jump. 'My town is a spectacular cultural landmark, if it were up to me I would make tourists shit in a bag and take it home. But alas.'

The detective got out of the chair and went to the corner and poured himself a cup of water and held the other cup up to Shelley. She shook her head. He knocked the water back then straightened his suit a little and sat back down again. 'But this matter here *is* up to me.' He pulled a small notebook out of his pocket and flipped through it.

'Madame Anna Krazenstein,' he announced grandly, closing the pad and slipping it inside his jacket again. 'The wife of ze—victim, has asked that charges not be pressed in relation to the assault.' He shook his head and stroked his chin. 'Such a beautiful smile and a perfectly lovely lady.'

Shelley beamed before Toady interjected, 'But…?'

'But,' he said with a shrug, 'this is a public order offence and as such requires a public prosecution, not to mention Missyuh Gagnard and the damage you have caused to his restaurant.' He put both his hands in a point to his chin and squinted at Toady, then with his two index fingers still joined, he pointed at him. 'But…you have a special patron who has made approaches on your behalf. The consular attaché at the American offices in Toulouse, a Missyuh George Beaumont and his lovely wife, were dining close by and witnessed ze—event, shall we call it? He has reliably informed me that you were defending ze honour of ze—lady.'

'That's true,' Shelley burst in, 'he grabbed me by the—'

'Contrary to what you may have been led to believe,' the detective said, raising a finger to silence her, 'we French like our Americans, especially here in Collioure, and Missyuh Beaumont in particular. He is a regular patron of zis restaurant and he has also spoken with Missyuh Gagnard and convinced him to drop all charges.'

Shelley clapped her hands and this time even Toady dared a smirk.

'Bof!' The cop threw his hands up. 'What can I say? You are free to go.'

'Great!' Shelley bolted upright. 'It's been nice. Love your accent, by the way.'

'Thank you Madame, but wait—please.' He put up his finger again and held it there until Shelley sat down, then took out his notebook and leafed through it.

'Missyuh Gagnard has provided a list of damaged items and has agreed to accept your offer to reimburse him the full cost of the damages.' A pregnant silence preceded the next obvious question.

'So what's the damage?' Toady muttered, putting his hand out to take the notebook. But the cop just folded it and slipped it back in his pocket. He opened his two hands, looked at the ceiling, humming to himself as though the number was going to fall from the sky. Then his head went down and he wiggled a bit, as though it was going to fall out of his ass.

'Three!' He held up a single finger of enlightenment and stared into space as inspiration arrived and two more fingers popped up. 'Yes—three thousand.'

'Three-fucking-thousand-quid,' gasped Toady, 'for a couple of tables and chairs?'

The notebook was out again in a flash. 'Ten chairs, three tables, five table cloths and two vases,' he corrected him calmly. 'And the loss of business, let us not forget that this was a traumatic experience for the customers. Mon Dieu—frightening.'

'Ask my crack,' Toady brayed and sat back.

The cop laughed then slapped his legs and got up. 'Madame, Missyuh, thank you and enjoy your stay.'

He knocked on the door and it rattled and clanked outside.

'Where are you going?' Shelley asked.

He checked his watch. 'Home, Madame, for my dinner.'

'But we can't stay here,' she objected, gesturing around. 'It's disgusting.'

'Ask his crack, Madame.'

'You want us to give you three thousand quid—here and now?'

'Not at all, I want you to go to jail, Madame. But Missyuh Gagnard wants you to pay for his damages. Personally, I don't care, but I can't sign your release forms unless you do.' He checked his watch again. 'Oh, quelle damage, ze banks have just closed for ze day, so—I bid you good night.'

'Wait!' Shelley jumped up and grabbed the detective's arm. 'Please, Sir, let me talk to him alone for one minute.'

He checked his watch and tapped it. 'Madame, be quick. Zis is France, my dinner is waiting.' He left the cell.

'Do you want to get out of here?' She rounded on

Toady.

'No,' he scoffed, 'I love this shit.'

'Will you pay the money?'

'Will I have a choice? But you heard the man, zis is France, land of ze dinner and ze fucking bank is closed. We are screwed—Madame.'

'But will you pay it?' she persisted.

'Yes, I'll fucking pay it.' He threw his arms in the air. 'Do you really think I'm gonna go to jail for that neo-Nazi arsehole?'

She went to the corner and sat down at the table, pulled open her denim jacket and lifted her top. Beneath, strapped diagonally across her chest, was a small beige leather satchel.

'Gucci baby!' She popped open the top, reached in and pulled out the entire wad of hundreds.

'What?' His mouth fell open. 'You've been carrying twenty grand around all day?'

'Ye didn't think I was going to leave it in the camper, did ye? Supposin the mob found out where we are and drove off with it?'

He was still standing with his mouth open when she started counting. He rubbed his head and slumped onto the edge of the bed. 'You're right—you're absolutely right.'

She counted out thirty hundreds, then closed her bag, buttoned up her jacket and told Toady to get him back.

'Sit down Mister—sorry?' she said. I didn't get your name last time.'

'Lieutenant Pascal.' He smiled and sat down on a stool beside her. She had the money in her hand and his eyes lit up when he saw it.

'Okay, Mr. Pascal,' she said. 'We are grateful that you have managed to get a deal on our behalves. Me and Thomas Brody here, are happy to pay the money to the restaurant owner, Mr. Granddad. Aren't we Thomas?'

'Yes, yes, for fuck's sake, get on with it, Shelley,' he said and walked off to kick the wall.

'Missyuh Gagnard,' the cop corrected her.

'So three thousand cash in your hand and we are free to go, Lieutenant Pascal?' She held up the money.

'Yes, that is correct.' He could barely contain his glee at the unexpected bonanza.

'Voila!' She banged it down on the table.

It went in his inside pocket in a flash.

'Aren't you going to count it?'

'No.'

'Do I need a receipt?' she asked pleasantly.

'No.'

'Well that is just craptastic. Can we go now?'

'Absolutely.' He stood up and showed her the way. 'I will pass on your gratitude to Missyuh Gagnard.'

'Sure ya might give him a few quid while your at it and tell him we're sorry.' She gathered her stuff from the table, put her bag on her shoulder and before they knew it they were standing on the steps outside in the cool breeze of the late afternoon. Toady stood on the path checking up and down the street then came back to her side.

'Better put your scarf on.'

'Fuck the scarf. Do you really think it matters a shite at this stage?' She stuck a fag in her mouth and sucked hard, then took her phone out of her bag to hold it up in front of them. A man's voice came back.

'Lieutenant Pascal.'

Then Shelley's voice. *'Okay, Mr. Pascal. We are grateful that you have managed to get a deal on our behalves. Me and Thomas Brody here...'*

She knocked it off and stuck it in her bag. 'That's him fucked, innit?'

'What're you gonna do with that?'

'Dunno,' she said, 'can't do any harm though, can it? Now, how are we gonna get home? Don't suppose Dirk and Anna waited for us.'

'Good one, Shelley. Funny,' Toady muttered.

'We'll get a train—I like trains.'

'I don't think so.' He was barely audible.

'What's wrong with you?'

'What do they look like to you?' he asked, nodding at the two scruffy kids on the far side of the street staring back.

'Gyppos?'

CAESAR PERPIGNAN

It took two taxi rides to get back to their secluded paradise on the deserted hill over Banyuls-sur-Mer. The first took them to Port Vendres, the next town down the coast, where they got out and made a show of walking purposefully up a side street before diving into a lane and finding an empty shed to hide in until two kids jogged past. Then Shelley tucked her hair away and they flagged down another taxi that brought them back to the campsite, dropping them half way up the hill. The driver's face lit up when Toady held up a hundred.

'You don't see us,' Toady repeated, covering first his eyes, then the drivers, until Shelley shoved him aside.

'Jesus—are ye playin peek-a-boo? How fuckin gay are you?' She stuck her face in front of the driver's and pulled an invisible zip across her mouth. The driver laughed and the taxi wheeled a circle and slipped down to the front barrier and onto the road.

Down through the trees and past the office, they could see Dirk and Anna's caravan with their jeep parked outside. Once again, darkness was spreading from shadowy corners outwards and from the leafy canopies downwards. Some lights were on and the crickets were firing up their tiny whirring engines for the night. They walked up to the start of their terrace, where he told Shelley to wait in the shadows and he continued on. All was quiet as he drew close to the campervan. He tried the door and it was still locked. He rounded the end of the camper to where the empty table sat in a ghostly light, then jumped at the sight of the solitary shadow tucked in the corner.

'Hello Tomas,' she said.

'Anna—you frightened the shit out of me.'

'Sorry. I was hiding.'

'From what?'

'Everything. It took you such a long time to make it back. Is Michelle okay?'

'Yeh, she's fine, she'll be up in a minute.' He sat down beside her. 'I see you know our names.'

'Dirk explained it to me—your joke,' she said with a dry smile, 'very funny.'

'I'm sorry, we were just playing. And about the—' he raised his fists, '—I just lost my temper.'

'Yah, I understand. This is Dirk we are talking about. He tries to claim that each nasty thing he does is a psychology experiment. Trying to provoke the ego, he claims. His problem is that he became Sigmund Freud's asshole along the way, but hasn't managed to diagnose that yet.'

'You know—' Toady shook his head as he wrestled with Dirk's notion of Anna, the sex slave. 'He said some pretty awful things. I don't think he—'

While he struggled to find the words, she came and sat on his knee and wrapped her two arms around his head and gently squeezed her tiny bosom into his cheek.

'Respects me?'

He was taken completely by surprise and he put his hands loosely around her waist. Her weight was almost imperceptible, as though a little night bird had landed on him.

'She told me she has never been in love before, Tomas,' she whispered in his ear. 'Can't you feel it—so perfect and fragile?'

'Not really.' His muffled voice came from her armpit. Her fragrance permeated his head, a mixture of skin, sweat and spicy perfume. It was an unfamiliar combination that stirred his heart to beat faster.

'Be careful—she's not as strong as she pretends.' She put her hand on his cheek and pulled his face up to hers and planted a moist, waxy kiss on his lips.

'So much energy between you pair, it makes me dizzy.' She kissed him on the forehead and stood up. 'I'm sorry I am not more normal.' She spoke like a little girl with her hands behind her back and her head down. 'I only wanted to be your friend—I have so few.' Her eyes peeped out from under her fringe. 'People say my heart is on my sleeve, and maybe that's how Dirk tricked me into marrying him, but I think life is too short for trying to reverse. You're better off to just hit the gas and see what falls off.'

'You don't have to be sorry, Anna,' he said, taking her hand, 'you're probably the nicest person I've ever met.'

'Danka, Tomas, please tell Michelle that I said goodbye. Give her a kiss for me too, I am ashamed to look her in the face.'

'She'll be here in a minute, you can do it yourself.'

She reached down and picked up a stiff sheet of paper from the side of the seat she had been sitting in and placed it on the table.

'Don't worry, we won't be here tomorrow, we are leaving first thing.' She went to the top of the stairs where she gave him a flash of her beautiful smile, then disappeared into the dusk.

He picked up Shelley's portrait. The green eyes were seductive in the dim light. The golden hair seemed luminescent, with a life of its own. He could see her in the cheeky smirk, the curl of her lips and the dimple in her cheek. The glimmer in her eye seemed to say that even her portrait knew more than him about something or other.

'Did you enjoy that?'

'Jesus!' He jumped out of the seat. Shelley was standing at the corner of the camper grinning. He went to rub his mouth, then decided to leave the cooling moisture of

Anna's kiss there a little longer.

'I told ye, she's mad. Wow—that's amazing.' Shelley had come around to view the portrait. 'Phwaor! What a hottie. Look at the baps on me.' She scanned the terrace below, but Anna was gone. 'Damn, I was starting to like her.'

'Yeh, me too.' Toady shook his head like he was coming out of a spell.

Shelley threw her hands in the air. 'Alrighty so, what's done is done, Ay? No regrets and all that shit.' She opened the door of the camper. 'So—what do you think the panic meter is at now? Twenty? Time to go maybe?'

'Go where? How?' He rolled up the drawing and slumped into the seat. 'I'm not gonna get caught like some dog in the street, or pulled off some train by a lynch mob.' He shook his head with resolve. 'If I have to have it out with that lot, it'll be on my terms.'

She was studying his expressions, checking for any hint of self-doubt and when she saw none, a smile tugged at her lips. 'Alright then, I second that stupidity.'

Toady banged the table and stood up. 'They don't know we're here, so we stay for now and I'll think it through tomorrow. How's that for decisiveness?' He pointed upwards, like a dictator. 'And no more fucking day trips.'

'Sound!' She clapped her hands. 'Now, I don't know about you, but I'm parched.'

She went inside while he paced the fence, breathing the night air, occasionally stopping to strain his ears for the sound of the sea. She produced beer, vodka, coke and ice and a long three-skin joint. Toady came over and partook of the smoke. His frown eased as he stood, leaning on the fence. He stretched his back and soon the pacing subsided, then he slipped himself into the chair opposite her, coughing a little. 'Where are you getting these drugs from anyway?' he asked. 'Don't tell me that our innocent little Anna is travelling around Europe laden down with narcotics?'

'Innocent me arse—she's passive aggressive, same as

you—give me that.' She whipped the joint out of his hand and pointed at the camper. 'Anyway, it's not hers, it's Mossy's. Amazing what you find when you go rooting through people's houses.'

'Like what?'

'Oh well now,' she said as she rose, 'you're gonna love this.' She went inside and reemerged with a box and dropped it on the table in front of him. She started by putting down blue movies. Chinese, Japanese, Lebanese lesbians, Hairy Insertions, Strap-on Nuns, Raiders of the Lost Arse. A couple of canisters of pills and a small bag of white powder. A big bag of grass. Then came a huge black dildo, handcuffs and some small white doorknobs.

'Butt Plugs,' she said.

'Jesus!' He had just picked one up and he threw it back in the box and rubbed his hands on the table.

'Get a load of this.' She put down a long hunting knife in an ornate sheath. 'And what about this?' It was a meat cleaver with a polished wooden handle, the blade so sharp it stuck in the table falling under its own weight.

'Where was all this hidden?'

'Everywhere,' she laughed. 'I ransacked the place while you were unconscious. In behind lockers, underneath the cabinets, ye haven't seen the best bit yet. Secret panel—back of the wardrobe.' She pulled up her top and showed him the waistband of her tracksuit. The shiny black handle of a gun protruded. 'Stick em up, Muthafuckaaahh!' She pulled it out and pointed it out sideways in her best gangster pose, lips pouting. 'You talkin to me?'

'Holy fuck! Is it loaded?'

'How would I know?'

'Pull the trigger.'

'Sure thing, Denzel,' she laughed, 'and ten minutes later the cops arrive and find us up here with hash, coke, dildos, knives and guns—and let's not forget the stolen tinker's caravan.' She was poking around with the muzzle of the gun. 'Oh yeah! Cos that's what I want my friends to remember me for back home—when I go to jail for kiddie murder.'

He reached over and gingerly took it from her. He'd never held a handgun before and the instant he felt the weight of it in his hand, his blood ran cold. He pointed it in front of him and tried to imagine a difference between shooting Nicky and not shooting him, but he couldn't. Hatred oozed out of the darkness.

'To forgive is human,' Shelley murmured by his ear and her hair brushed his face. He held the gun straight out and closed an eye, taking aim on a distant light. 'But to kill is divine,' she whispered in his other ear.

'Who said that?'

'Pope Alexander—The Great.'

"Yeh? What about turning the other cheek?'

'That's for Buddhists and hippies.' Her breath was warm on his neck. 'You look good with a gun.'

He lingered in the potency of the moment then spun back to the table and put the gun in the bottom of the box and piled the rest of the stuff on top of it. 'I can't go to jail.' He shook his head. 'I wouldn't last a week. Better off dead.'

'What are you gonna do if they all arrive up here? Throw butt plugs at them? Slap em in the lugs with a dildo maybe?' He pulled the box from the table and stowed it back in the bottom of the wardrobe then threw some clothes over it and shut the door.

'Spoilsport.' She was sitting with her feet up on the chair when he returned.

He refused to discuss it further, so they proceeded to get drunk and stoned, but at some stage Toady knew he would soon pass out in the chair and be immovable.

'Give us a kiss, tough guy,' she said, as he was getting up, mumbling excuses. He leaned over her, resting on the arm of her chair.

'I'm sorry for what I said about men,' she said. 'I was angry.'

'I'm sorry I didn't try to make you happy,' he replied.

'Ay—' she grabbed his face, 'at least ye didn't make me sad.' She kissed his lips. 'Thanks for defending my honour.'

'Sure what's three thousand between friends?'

'That's not what I'm talking about.' She kissed him again.

'I'm kidding, I know what you mean, but my mother used to always say—' She slid her hand around the back of his neck and pulled him down to her open mouth and kissed him more deeply with her sweet flavoured tongue. When she let him go his eyes were closed and he teetered back and forward. 'My mother used to say, ehhh—discretion is the better part of—something.'

'Sex?'

'No, that wasn't it,' he said, shaking his head. 'My mother wouldn't talk like that.'

'No, ya tool,' she whispered, 'do you want to do it?'

'Sex?' He straightened up and stumbled with an idiot smile on his face and she had to grab him by the belt before he went backwards. 'Oh God yes, but I'm not sure if I can stand up much longer.' His head was spinning. Some of it was panic but mostly it was the marihuana. 'Shit, I have to lie down.'

At some stage during the night he had a dream that he woke up and Shelley was in her underwear beside him on the bed. She was on her knees with her legs spread wide, her breasts were bare and soaked with sweat. Her face glowed in the moonlight coming through the window.

'Fuck yeh, Baby,' she whispered and closed her eyes. He turned his head and could see she had her hand down the elastic of her pants. His cock ached in her other hand and he groaned at the tightness of her grip, working it back and forward in her long oily fingers.

'C'mon, ye cunt,' she grunted as she bent forward and pressed her tits into his face. Her nipples, long and hard, shuddered on his lips as her breathing died into a gasp and he felt his cock burn as she worked it rapidly to climax.

They rose early the next morning and decided the best thing to do was to hit the road. Things were packed away in a frigid silence and neither was in the mood for making breakfast. She had nothing to say to him, perhaps he was a little embarrassed but she doubted it, he probably wouldn't even give it a second thought. After coffee and croissants in the town they headed for the hills.

Spain was the easiest route of all to watch. With only one coastal pass across the border, the gypsies had it covered since the day after Shelley had made her getaway at the horse festival. Almost without exception, all who toured down that road would stop at the car park on the border and take a photo for posterity, and in spite of the prevailing mood, this pair were no different. She handed him the camera and stood with her back to the winding, rocky coastline with her little, white dog held up beside her face. Dirk took the snapshot.

Not far away, sitting on top of a picnic bench, a man in a duffel coat was watching. The kid beside him had spent three days riding up and down the coast, hitching lifts and jumping on the back of the garbage trucks that went back and forth, searching for La Roux in the cafes and bars, scouring the streets and beaches with his cousins. And now it was payday. He held up a mobile phone on which he had a picture of the people that had been spotted in Collioure the previous day in the company of the redhead. The man in the grey coat looked from the photo to the couple standing before him and a thin smile crossed his lips. He directed the kid to commence the operation that would make these people disappear from the face of the earth. The gusting wind from the sea tossed his greasy fringe as he made the phone call and watched the unfortunate pair switch position for photos.

'Keep them there for half an hour,' he was told.

'Already done,' he assured the voice on the line.

Caesar let the prostitute finish with the blowjob as he emptied his bottle of wine by the neck and barely flinched as both were drained simultaneously into their respective open mouths. He patted the young man on the head like a friendly dog as he swallowed the last drop. Caesar owned the establishment and everything in it and he always conducted job interviews in person.

'Give him Room 20.'

Bruno nodded.

'I have to go to Banyuls. The Irish just surfaced.'

Bruno nodded again.

Caesar Perpignan cut an unexpected figure on the Spanish border at eleven in the morning in his tight jeans and pointed boots, his hands jammed in the pockets of his thick brown leather jacket. A cigarette hung from the side of his mouth as he crossed the car park. His mean composure and complete lack of interest in his surroundings ensured that he couldn't be mistaken for a tourist. He sat at the table beside the man and the boy who had raised the alarm. The young man tipped his head in the direction of the caravan, where an enraged tourist danced frantically under the sullen sky with his wheel brace, shouting German obscenities. A woman sat on the table close by facing the sea with a little dog by her side watching forks of lightning crack the dull horizon.

Caesar peeled two fifties from a money clip and gave them to the eager kid. With the leftovers of a smile clinging to his leathery face, he sent him on his way. Sunlight caught the tips of his golden teeth where he had lost his own during a phase of bare knuckle fighting he pursued in his thirties. His half ear strangely cocked outwards under his greasy locks, a souvenir of blade fighting in his twenties. A pale star-shaped scar on his cheek was a more recent testament to carelessness while dog fighting in Marseille in his early forties. The salty breeze whipped strands of hair around his face having escaped from a tight bun just above the skull tattoo on the back of his neck.

In Caesar's philosophy, money could be made from anything that could be fucked or fought and Mossy had found himself utterly fucked the year before when Caesar proved he had an uncanny ability to back the winner in most fights. With a twenty-grand debt and a dead dog Mossy had managed to escape back to Quillan after going missing for a week after the horse festival. The dog he had borrowed cost him two thousand, which he had paid promptly. But the twenty was a different matter—he didn't have it. Had he not been married to Bruno's sister he'd have been fed to the dogs himself the very same day, but that was one privilege a disowned Irish traveler had gained when he married into the Roussillon gypsies.

Fifteen years earlier at the wedding, in the wee small hours, a younger Caesar had held Mossy at knifepoint and offered, right there, to cut him open before he defiled the blood of Bruno's family—just to find out what particular part of him was supposed to be Gypsy. Caesar declared for the record, and to all gathered that night, that he'd rather exterminate an Irish tramp than ever pretend he was a gypsy. Grudgingly, he'd learned to drink with him over the years and gradually found a muted respect for the spontaneous brutality he had witnessed Mossy unleash at times. He had eventually accepted Mossy as a member of Bruno's extended family.

Mossy had been given the intervening year to come up with the money or forfeit his belongings and whatever respect he had garnered. Toady was Mossy's last desperate chance to save it all. Shelley's casual propensity for chaos was the instrument of their converging fates.

Dirk and Anna were discreetly moved into the caravan at knifepoint once the puncture was fixed and then driven to a quieter stretch of coast overlooking the sea. Dirk was gagged, tied and made sit quietly at the table while Anna was shown the picture of the redhead and her friend and asked where they were. She shrugged her shoulders before being dragged from the caravan to the edge of the cliff. Large drops of rain were starting to hit the ground around them and the sun was gone. She said she knew nothing as a low rumble of thunder shook the cloud-covered mountains behind. The dog was retrieved and handed to Caesar, then shown briefly to her before being flung over the edge. She fell to her knees and wailed her anguish at the thunderclouds. Her husband was brought to the edge of the cliff and she only glanced up, then her head went quietly down again. This brought an uproarious peal of laughter to Caesar's contorted face as he slapped his legs and punched Dirk in the arm. A flash of lightning illuminated the gathering.

'I should have thrown you first, she cares more about the dog.'

More thunder rolled down the hill as though a giant tomb had opened in the mountainside and something evil was emerging from within. The gag was taken off Dirk and he spoke in fluent French like a man possessed, blathering in tongues. He told them of the pair in the campervan in Banyuls Municipal Campsite, pitch number 185—their hair colour, approximate ages, heights and nationality as well as full names and emotional dispositions.

'She is a little crazy and will lose her temper, but he is dangerous, especially when he appears most calm. He can handle himself, that one.'

The black belly of the sky cracked and rain poured down on them. The two were taken back down the coast to a silent house in Banyuls-sur-Mer. Their luxury caravan went back to Perpignan and was stripped of all identifying numbers and was in position on the gypsy camp in the north of the city, before dark that evening. A cousin of Caesar's had recently married and had been promised a new home and that night his dream came true.

The huge SUV, which was less than six months old, was sold that night in Marseille for less than six thousand, which Caesar deemed to be his call-out fee. This is how the remnants of a life are scattered to the wind and disposed of for cash and favour, as real people are made to vanish like errant stitches from the fabric of their own lives—for good.

Later that morning when Mossy was told that they were closing in on his campervan, and the money, he spoke with Caesar, respectfully requesting that nothing be done until he got there in person. Arno was in Toulouse hospital and had just had a plate put into his head. He wanted to be there by the bed, because the missus had gone off the deep end for the time being. Mossy promised he'd be in Banyuls the following evening. Caesar spat at the ground and cursed Ireland. Mossy thanked him.

None of that mattered for Dirk who had no monetary, social or recreational value. He had his throat cut the first night when he made a break for the stairs out of the basement, knocking over a kid. Caesar offered the boy the opportunity to do it as a terrified Dirk lay trembling on the cold concrete, a puddle of piss spreading beneath him and the smell of fresh shit wafting freely. The boy made a promising start with a plume of hot blood spraying him in the face, but hadn't the stomach for finishing it.

'Ay, you better learn to get tough or you will be getting fucked by bastards like him for the rest of your life.' Caesar finished the slicing and the gurgling subsided.

Anna watched in silence, nostrils flaring over her taped mouth. It wasn't the time for crying or panicking, it was the time for survival. She delved into her two years army training and found the rat inside. She breathed the iron flavour of her husband's blood on the humid basement air and retreated to her primeval brain to await her moment. It always came, but sometimes it was so brief that only a rat would recognise it and chew its own foot off to seize it. She got lucky when Caesar groped between her legs to see how tight she was.

'Nice,' he said. 'I like it like a boy's asshole, not a camel's face.'

He took a shine to her glossy, black hair and pert lips and for the time being decided not to send her to the brothel, where she might get stretched out. They stayed quietly in the house on the edge of town where Caesar, and later Bruno, were afforded bottles of wine, warm pheasant and fresh bread as they played cards. Others came to mop and scrape Dirk off the floor.

Anna sat so calmly gagged and tied in the corner that they forgot about her from time to time as they got drunk and smoked a little heroin to pass the hours till the Irish tramp arrived.

The kid who couldn't finish cutting Dirk's neck open had been given a chance to redeem his position as Caesar's favourite and was dispatched to the campsite to verify if the redhead was where Dirk had said she'd be.

The phone text confirmed that things were exactly so. He was instructed to stay until he was relieved and to warn of any movement, whatsoever.

They could be at the camp in three minutes flat, if need be.

THROUGH THE LOOKING GLASS

First thing he noted was the sparrows chirping through the open window. Then Shelley's voice, couched in the low murmurs and occasional laughs of the men. He was pleasantly surprised to find that the pain in his head of previous days had largely dissipated. He pulled up the edge of the curtain and at the end of the track a row of teenagers sat on the fence in blue boiler suits. That meant it was probably elevenses, which in turn meant it was anytime between ten and lunchtime. The kid with the blond hair and the dark eyes stood in the middle of the track, arms by his side, staring in their direction.

'Deja vous.'

He pulled his jeans from a chair and slipped them on, then his blue shirt. He took a half carton of orange juice from Mossy's fridge and went to the window. The table had been moved out into the middle of the track where it basked in the morning sun.

'Missyuh,' they greeted him with smiles.

The third man started to pour the coffee. 'Assayay vous, sill vous play.' He gestured to the chair. A cup was put in front of Toady and one of the men filled it for him.

'Ay voila!' Bernard took the carving knife to the half loaf of bread in front of him and cut a slice.

Shelley explained that it had been freshly baked by Jean Luc himself, as a gift. The man with the coffee pot bowed his head a little. 'I told you, Jean Luc wants me to go to these games with him tomorrow night. What's it called?' she asked Bernard.

'Boules,' he responded.

'Brioche,' chimed in Jean Luc simultaneously.

'The game is Boules—the bread is brioche,' Bernard explained in a deep accent, rich and slow. His black eyes moved lazily and a grin played at the corner of his big mouth. 'Bread, made with butter and sugar, very light, try some, Missyuh.' He held up the plate and Toady took a slice and when the bread melted over his tongue and the butter dissolved in the coffee he grunted with satisfaction.

'Say bon, no?' said Jean Luc and they all agreed .

It wasn't hard for Toady to see the irresistible charm the trio held for her. They were no movie stars, but they were easy on the eye. Their dark complexions and their smooth sallow skin highlighted the whiteness of their eyeballs and their teeth. The slowness of their movements and the fluidity of their banter rolled on the bubbling music of their language. It was enchanting, even for Toady, to be part of their boisterous fellowship, which he could see had obviously been well founded over time.

'You win, I give up.' Toady put his hands up in surrender. 'Why are we all here every morning with that mob, like we're best buddies? Is it a TV gag?' He pointed and glared into the trees. 'Hidden camera—Big Brother, no?'

Bernard's mouth fell open then he riddled a few sentences to his friends who burst into laughter. 'Apologies, but not quite so glamorous, I'm afraid. No— they are prisoners.'

That earned a minute's silence and as they enjoyed their brioche, Toady formulated his next question.

'So what did they do? What type of crimes are we talking about here?'

'Not supposed to say, ah?' He could see that his comrades didn't fully understand what was being discussed and he released a stream of words. They exchanged glances and waved dismissively.

He held out his hand and started counting on his

fingers. 'Car theft, two of them. Assault with weapons for three.' He picked up the knife and waved it in Toady's face. 'A man had his throat cut, he almost die.'

'Nice.'

'The little guy, he took the school bus and drove his class half way to Italy before he ran out of gas. Everybody had a great time but, ehh, how you say, kidnapping? Uhh—that guy on the end—they call him Shit Happens.' He turned to his friends and said something that raised a few sniggers. 'He makes a hole through the loft to watch the neighbour's daughter in the bathroom then falls through the ceiling while the wife is taking a shit.' He turned to Shelley. 'Pardon.'

'And he got prison for that?'

'He landed on top of her. Broke both her arms, then tries to wipe her ass for her before the ambulance arrives. Merde non!' He shook his head. 'We cannot allow this in France.' The other men laughed between sips of coffee.

Toady was studying Bernard's face and could find nothing to imply he was making it up, just a vague hint of pleasure in the telling. Shelley was beaming like the cat that got the cream with Jean Luc winking in her direction from time to time.

'What about the blond one, with the eyes?'

'Oh, mon Dieu—Henri? He rape his girlfriend—not violent, you know? She is fifteen and Henri is seventeen. Her parents are rich, so they get him locked up for two years to keep him away from her. But this went, uhhh—not so good in the end. He's not a bad boy, intelligent, good English, but his family is—how you say—wrong side of the track?'

'What's with the eyes?' asked Toady, tracing rings around his own.

'Aww oui, poor bastard. He received bad news last week. So now—he cries a lot.' Bernard shook his head. 'Very sad. I don't want to say more, Missyuh, you are on your vacation.'

A whistle sounded from below and they checked their watches.

'Ah la vache, is nearly time to go.' All three stood up brushing brioche crumbs from their laps. 'Half-day Thursday.' Bernard winked. 'A bientot, mes amis.'

Jean Luc was gesticulating to Shelley as he backed away. She wiggled her fingertips and gave him a wink. When she recognized the look in Toady's face as envy, she blew them all a kiss for good measure.

'Tough job, guys,' Toady called out after them as they walked away chatting. 'How do you possibly stick it?'

Bernard grabbed hold of the blond kid and turned him around then called something over his shoulder and pointed upwards. The sky was growing angry, with bruised clouds muscling in from every direction. The sunlight was failing.

'Everything's kind of the same, but different,' Shelley mused as she watched them go. 'That's why I love it here. I feel French after talking to those guys for a while. Don't you?'

'I feel scared—car thieves, knife thugs, rapists. We come to a deserted campsite and look who we get for neighbours—you're a trouble magnet.' And with that a huge drop of rain landed right in the middle of the table. An apocalyptic sky was turning inside out, revealing its black heart. The trees had become still and the air was calm around them. The sparrows worked in around their feet, brazenly collecting the crumbs of sweet homemade bread before the imminent deluge.

'Looks bad.' The words were just out of his mouth when another drop fell and hit him right in the forehead, then another and then the sound of rustling erupted throughout the canopy and torrential rain poured down. Shelley shrieked and jumped up grabbing her clothes and scarf from the table and ran for the camper. Toady sat, wet through in an instant. He finished the brioche in his hand before the rain could dissolve it, as it was doing to the half-loaf on the table. A brilliant flicker of white light electrified the scene and roused a loud cheer from the terrace below, the end of which was drowned out by thunder. A cold, hollow darkness rushed in beneath the trees as the sky was obliterated to premature dusk.

Toady heard a high-pitched scream from the campervan and laughed to himself then turned his face up to let the rain pummel his skin. Through his tightly shut eyelids he saw pink lightning electrify the shapes around him like an x-ray. Before the shuddering light extinguished, an ear-rending clap of thunder fell from a thousand feet overhead, to land just above the treetops in an explosion that set the ground itself shaking. Another wild scream came from the camper.

The rain had encircled all things with a wall of noise, coming down in straight rods, and he was already sitting in a deep pool in the well of his plastic seat. His coffee danced and overflowed and the remains of the brioche flowed laterally from the tabletop.

He stood up and walked away toward the top of the stairs, shedding his soaked jeans in the mud along the way. The ground beneath his feet dissolved instantly to shifting, gritty mud that oozed between his toes. He draped his shirt over the fence. Puddles formed in the depressions and started to flow in little streams, crisscrossing each other on his path. Rain pounded him on the bare head and shoulders as another blinding electrification liquefied the substance of the world, sending waves of thunder reverberating over the trees. Toady could feel the static bristling in everything around him. Between the thrashing of the rain and the rumbling sky came the faint sound of singing from the lower terrace.

'Is that you, Mother?'

He reached the top of the stairs. Tepid water streamed through the grooves and crevices of his body, trailing in waterfalls from his fingertips, pouring down his legs to form little rivers on the steps below. In the shifting darkness under the canopy, he could make out Bernard, standing in the doorway of the toilet block, with his back to the outside. Arms dancing, he conducted the music emanating from the murky interior. Weaving its way upwards, the embattled chorus came in waves, suddenly clear, then enveloped again in the noise of the storm.

'No, Thomas, this is chaos.'

Crooked fingers of lightning cracked the sky over the town and thunder pounded between the clouds and the red roofs. The human world had been overwhelmed by sound.

'I've never heard anything like it before, it's beautiful.'

Waterfalls had sprung from the rocks and spouted arcs of water down onto the terraces below and he could hear each one individually add its voice to the tumult. Another flash turned the world white and thunder rolled down from the mountains now shrouded in the rushing clouds.

'What are they singing about?'

The men's voices grew bolder for the chorus.

'They want justice.'

Streams of white paint were snaking down the hill from the toilet block that now seemed more like an artillery bunker under an enemy barrage. The concrete storm-drains at the sides of the road, which had seemed absurdly large, were now bubbling and frothing white. A sudden gust of wind rushed up the hillside like a tidal wave hitting land and struck him where he stood, rocking him on his feet and setting the trees in motion in an instant. He gasped and the words were snatched straight out of his lungs and carried into the sky.

'Chaos and justice.'

Under a tree on the far side of the toilet block stood a young man with blond hair and dark rings around his eyes. Henri Duval, seventeen years old and sent to prison for two years for making love to his young girlfriend. Although it had been his first time too, he'd received no mercy from the court.

By the time Toady recognised his ghostly features peering at him from the twilight they were already locked together in the moment. No hint of recognition was conveyed between them. Thunder grinded the heavens overhead and another violent gust struck the hill. Toady was overwhelmed by the misery of the boy's predicament and found himself cast into the familiar shadows of his own past.

He had also lost his virginity when he was a child, to the woman who had been left to mind him, while his mother went on the one and only foreign holiday of her life. Laura Bennet had been his baby-sitter since he was five and now she was twenty-one to his fifteen years. She was about to have the boy to herself for a whole week.

Each day he came home from school and sat patiently waiting for her to arrive with her swinging leather satchel of college books, brimming with the promises of the future. The deconstruction of the present was more painful than he anticipated.

She made him shower on the first night, while she was supposedly cooking his dinner, though Toady had no recollection of eating for that entire week. His hunger consumed his innards and became his companion.

'Make sure you wash your penis and show me how clean it is. Oh look, Thomas—such a gift you have been entrusted with.'

He was naked as she taught him everything he needed to know to ignite the passion of a woman. The first night she instructed him in due procedure, having him practice slipping his hand inside her blouse as they kissed again and again until he had it right. She showed him how to kiss with his tongue and corrected him when he became sloppy. He learned how to take her bra off from behind, and then in front. And finally, the different ways to fondle her breasts and for just how long to squeeze her nipples.

The next night he learned how to suck them properly,

then how to flick them with his tongue when they stood up hard. Then the sweetest way to kiss her neck and ears and mouth, while she sighed and moaned and praised his efforts, occasionally repositioning his hands.

Each night she finished the lesson by pulling up her skirt and letting him masturbate onto her underwear, her legs wide open, the black, shiny curls licking around the elastic, while she lay there smiling for as long as it took.

'Good boy, you'll be ready soon.'

Then she showed him how to rub her pussy in the ways that mattered, then how to go down on it. 'Hunger is passion,' she explained, and he was weak and dizzy with both.

On their penultimate night together she guided him to her spot inside, the trigger that shot a bullet into her soul. She moaned like a cow as he drew spurts of juice from her. She opened her mouth and let him slide it in and out till he fainted and struck his head on the fireplace. She left him there to awaken in the cold dead of the night when he crept into a freezing bed.

The last night she came and took off her black stockings. She tied one around her eyes then held her hands together until he eventually realised he was supposed to tie them with the other. Then she lay back on the armchair, placing her bound hands behind the headrest and did nothing else. Toady exercised all his new skills, pushing her clothes up, till buttons popped and stitching ripped, then tearing at the fabric that refused to budge with his hands and teeth. He sucked at her milky flesh for as long as he could before he ripped off her underwear and lined himself up with aching intent to penetrate her. He felt her lips begin to swallow him.

'You're such a strong young man, Thomas, please don't hurt me.'

He was as careful and slow as he could be, though all he wanted was to devour her body completely.

'No,' she moaned, with her mouth open wide and her

tongue licking her scarlet lips. He buried it in her and left it there for as long as he could, then sliding slowly back and forth while she whispered his name on hot curses in his ear. His vision turned blank as he stretched taut. His skin ripping at the neck and his teeth crumbling into powder to the rhythm of wet slapping, he could barely control his rage. Then, as though his blood had turned to acid, he simply dissolved from the inside out and crumpled to nothing on top of her.

She pushed him off, then pulled her hands from her stocking and took off her blindfold. She stood up and straightened her torn clothes and put on her coat. All the while, the boy lay lifeless on the rough carpet at her feet.

'What happens if I get pregnant? Will you tell your mother you raped me?'

She was dressed and going out the door while he still struggled to lift his head from the stale floor. He clutched his guts to still the abject hunger in his stomach that was trying to kill him. 'Don't cry,' she said, standing in the crack of the closing door, 'you're a man now.'

After his mother came back he spent most nights awake in bed, waiting for the police to arrive. He was ashamed of how much he wanted to rape her again—the woman who had taken care of him as a little boy. Night after night the crime was recommitted in a sweaty rage, while he prayed for her to come back and take him away to some corner in hell, where at least they could be together. He listened for sirens in the town and each time he heard them he dreaded his mother's scorn, disowning him, as they took him away.

It was right then that he had begun to see Shelley differently. Whenever he saw her he imagined her on his couch just like Laura Bennet, legs spread and he showing her the expert things he knew. But the terrible guilt turned him around in ever decreasing circles. Shelley was only thirteen, and he was a man now.

How quickly it had all vanished, all the childish dreams

he used to have of her in which he would ask her to the cinema, or send her a secret Valentine's card. It had all somehow been swept away in an instant. Michelle Kelly surely knew what he was and what he had on his mind—what he'd done to his babysitter. She could see through him and, that day in the bicycle shed, she'd made it clear.

'What are you looking at—Freak?'

Toady snapped out of it and the blond kid was gone from under the tree. The branches overhead shifted and swayed as the rain began to ease a little. A light flicker painted the leaves and the ensuing rumble seemed distant, having slid down the far side of the mountains into Spain.

The camper was rocking on its wheels. Was it the wind, or was Shelley still cavorting inside, terrified. The sound of singing came wafting up from below once again, this time putting him in mind of a ship at sea. Having made it through the worst of the storm, they were headed for the thin light on the horizon. The noise of the waves came crashing through the branches overhead.

He turned and made his way to the camper with the rain drifting sideways and upwards in his face. The wind was cool, raising goose bumps on his soaked flesh. There before him, standing outside the camper, was Henri Duval, staring at the window as though he was surveying an oil painting in a gallery.

'What are you doing, Henri?'

The boy didn't acknowledge him when he came to stand close by, but after a moment he responded in a low voice and heavy French accent, though his English was clear.

'I only ever wanted to be like you, Missyuh.'

Shelley was static in the window frame, hands by her side.

'You can be—someday. You are young.' Toady came closer. 'It's not as wonderful as it looks, believe me, I have problems.'

'You have no problems,' Henri replied. Toady was glistening wet in his Calvin Klein underpants, his skin tanned, stubble on his head delineating in shadow where his hair used to be before Shelley had shorn him. The boy looked him up and down without a trace of emotion.

'You are free, Missyuh, and I remain a prisoner.'

Henri reached into his pocket and Toady stepped back, shifting his weight and raising his hand a little. 'Easy now boy, I'm on your side.'

'I will never be free. My crime is permanent, there is no escape.'

'Nothing is permanent, believe me. You and me are the same.'

'More than you imagine.' Henri drew his hand from his pocket and extended it, but Toady's reaction was lightning fast and he had his wrist in an iron grip before the boy could react. He turned his hand over to find a folded card clutched in his fingers. The boy's hand opened and Toady released him and picked the card from his palm, opening it out. It was just a photograph. The trees were falling calm as the boy turned his face back to Shelley.

In the picture Henri was smiling and had no rings around his eyes. He was defiant and proud in the way a young man asserts his early manhood. With him was a pretty young girl with full red lips and freckles across her cheeks. Red, curly hair to her shoulders framed the cheeky smile that sat easily on her round face. It was Shelley, exactly as Toady remembered her from the bicycle shed that day when she stamped on his toe for what he had said to her. Her, a child reaching for womanhood, and him, a newly made man.

'She is beautiful,' Toady said.

'She is dead.'

Face to face, eye to eye, Toady only now noticed they were the same height and past the dirty grey rings of his sockets, his eyes were the same brown as his.

'She hanged herself.'

Toady's stomach heaved as he remembered the insanity that had plagued him from the day he lost his innocence and the loneliness that had filled his soul as he walked the earth a criminal. He could see it in the boy's eyes now—ten times more virulent, a thousand times darker.

'Life is never fair, Henri. Sometimes a man must pay a great price and still not get what he wants. I can't tell you why, I don't understand it either.'

Henri's eyes filled with tears. 'But I wasn't ready to be a man.' Toady went to hand back the photo but Henri shook his head. 'There is no way back.'

Jean Luc came running out of the drizzle. Whatever he was shouting was smothered under a low rumble of thunder.

'I've reached the end, I can go no further.' Henri cast his eyes down as though he was contemplating an abyss. His hand proffered a small red rose. Then Jean Luc had him by the collar and tore him away as Toady clutched the blossom from him.

'What do you want me to do, Henri?'

Henri fixed him with a stare as he stumbled away backwards and appeared to smile. 'Keep her for me.'

CARPETS AND CURTAINS

Before long the sky cleared and the heat returned to the air. The angry gusts of wind subsided and the Tramontane prevailed and was gentler through the afternoon as though remorseful for the earlier violent tantrum. The sparrows returned and found rich pickings in the dried puddle beds beneath the table. Steam rose from the hillside in columns and the fragrance of flowers and foliage was dizzying. Toady sat at the table staring into the distance, the photo still clutched in his hand when Shelley emerged from hiding.

'Holy shit, I thought we were all gonna die in that storm. Then I thought that kid was gonna go postal on me.'

She slammed her vodka and coke on the table and dried a seat off with a towel and sat down with a smoke.

'What's up with you?' she asked. He shook his head. 'What did that kid say to you?' He shook his head again then put his arms on the table and lay his forehead down on them.

'Suit yourself—be like that.'

She put her feet up on the seat in front of her and said no more to him.

An hour passed in which Shelley drank two cocktails, rolled a joint and smoked it and Toady got up and went to the far end of the track above the steps and did his Karate, grey mud dried up to his knees, streaks across his chest.

She stood up from the table, disappearing inside the

camper and returning a moment later to where he stood. 'I have an idea.' She put her drink on the post then swung a leg over, straddling the rail, and started carving with a steak knife.

'What are you doing?'

'Oh, it speaks.' She bent over, redoubling her efforts with a grunt. 'If you must know, I'm immortalising us.'

The late afternoon drifted by over the treetops on steam-laden pockets of air painted gold in the occasional sunshine. Toady soon finished and pulled his shirt from the fence and his jeans from the mud and walked over to where she was still working.

Etched into the wood—**SHELLEY WAS**

'I thought you said you were immortalizing—us. Shouldn't I get a mention?'

She pointed at the space she had left. 'No room for you, sorry.'

He was turning away when she reached out and took his hand and stopped him.

'Where are you going?'

'Laundry.'

'What's that?' She pointed to the photo sticking from the waistband of his pants. 'I saw that headbanger give it to ye.'

'Don't call him that, the kid has problems, that's all.' He pulled the photo out and placed it in her hand.

When he returned he found that she had made new potatoes fried in garlic butter with shreds of bacon and green beans on the side. She opened a cold beer for him while he threw Arno's shorts on the ground and put on his jeans. His disposition had improved over the course of a hot shower and the melancholy had receded.

'This is mighty, Shelley.'

She played soft music on the stereo and they talked about life as they drank the last bottle of white wine.

'The food is nearly all gone,' she said, 'and the drink too. Only the hard stuff left.'

'That's okay, we're leaving tomorrow. I organised transport.'

Earlier, while his jeans rattled alone inside the tumble drier, he had gone from caravan to campervan below until he found an elderly Spanish couple who were happy to take them, once Toady had offered to pay two hundred for fuel.

'So where are the old farts goin?'

'Bordeaux.'

'What about Spain?'

The border hills were shrouded in mist. 'Not this time, not on that road.'

'You're wreckin me buzz, I'll think about it tomorrow.'

They got drunk as the night descended and they became cocooned in a private bubble of candle light in the gathering darkness.

'What about the photo?' he asked her during a protracted silence.

She took it from her tracksuit top and put it back on the table face down. 'Ye can burn it, it's not even funny. What did he say to you?'

He leaned forward and rubbed his brow then looked at her. 'Guard her for me?'

'Who?'

'Who do ye think?'

She took the rose from the edge of the table and sniffed it, then put it down again. 'To be clear here, this isn't for me, is it?' She nodded at the photo. 'And she's dead, isn't she?'

'Killed herself.' Toady replied. 'He said he wished he was me. I feel like I know the kid at this stage. I should have said something back—something optimistic.'

'Like what?' she scoffed.

'Every dog has his day—I dunno.'

'Is that what this is, Mr Brody?' She gestured around. 'Is this your day?'

He closed his eyes and breathed deep the air. 'Yes—I

A Fistful of Salt

do believe it is.'

She held up her drink and they toasted, then she watched him for a while over her glass before pointing a finger at his face. 'Now you're starting to look like a king.'

An hour rolled past and Toady's occasional smirks grew contagious.

'What's got into ye? Spit it out, boy.'

He had his head down when he mumbled the words, 'Carpets and curtains.' The second time he caught her smiling inside her glass, he asked, 'Were you afraid of me in school?'

'Afraid?'

'Like a pervert, ye know? You called me Freak.'

'The world is full of freaks,' she said with a shameless grin. 'You just nailed first prize in the bicycle shed that day.'

'It was one of those—' He clicked his fingers, 'Freudian slips. I read it in a porno mag after having sex with my babysitter and I couldn't stop thinking about you. I had a much better line thought up, I swear.'

Shelley's frown turned to a grimace. 'Whoah, boy, way too much.'

'She said I was a man.' He scratched his head trying to find the words. 'She showed me things—and then I was stuck in the middle, like the French kid; too scared to go forward, too ashamed to go back.'

'It's called life, we all did it.'

'I was trying to tell you that day, that I could see you— in here.' He tapped his skull. 'Like a classical painting— waiting to be finished.'

Shelley searched his eyes. 'And a porno mag one-liner was the best way to express that?'

'No.' He shook his head. 'That's just what came out. I was more shocked than you were, believe me. Spent years wishing I could take it back. Confusing times.'

She threw a mouthful of vodka back and sniggered. 'Babysitter? You were some hairy baby at fifteen, I can tell ye.'

And just like that, twenty years of Toady's adolescent paranoia dissipated in a drunken slur. He smiled stupidly at her hurtful laughter, till it didn't hurt at all, then his head went down and he gripped it with both his hands.

'Aw Jesus, now he's cryin—get the babysitter!' she called into the night with a hand cupped to her mouth.

He didn't know if he was laughing or crying, truth was, it didn't matter. 'I didn't do anything wrong,' he said. 'I know exactly what that kid feels like and I want to help him—but I can't.'

'Arra, just do like the lad said and be my personal bodyguard.' She was pouring another drink. 'And try not to get killed yourself, please.'

'I've always been nice to you Shelley, haven't I? A gentleman—more or less?'

'The only one ever, boy.' She took his hand then sniffed down her nose at him. 'You want a medal for that now, I suppose?'

He shook his head then took the rose from the table and slipped it behind her ear. 'It's all for you now, Shell.'

They sat like that for a while, until she felt silly holding his hand and he felt stupid for having dried tears on his face.

'C'mon, ye maudlin bastard, it's too cold out here. I don't want to remember my last night freezing my ass off.'

They went inside and pulled the curtains and she turned on the stereo and found some old-time French crooner on the radio and let him serenade in the background. Toady's head was drifting when Shelley came and stood a foot from his face.

'Okay Brody, for one night only, it's your big chance if you still wanna know.' She glanced downward and slid the waist of her top up to her navel. 'Carpet inspection.'

He put his beer on the table then ran his hands up her outer thighs taking hold of her waistband. Her face was peering down from her mop of red curls, sucking on a fag with a wry smile and a scarlet blossom resting on her cheekbone. Then he inched them down over her hips, to the tops of her thighs. That's where he came across the little red ribbons that hemmed the elastic on the top of her black lace knickers. He slipped his fingers into them too and pulled downwards again, revealing the final dip of her tummy. He slid his hand around and took hold of her soft cheeks and squeezed them, then pulled the elastic down to the backs of her legs. She watched him and exhaled smoke slowly through moist puckered lips.

He edged the lot down her long smooth thighs until they landed loosely around her knees. Then she opened her legs a little and ran her fingers down through her curls and grabbed a handful and pulled it.

'Well?—Is it a match?'

He buried his nose in the bouquet and filled his lungs. 'Close enough.'

She put her hand round the back of his head and felt his tongue flick in and out of her. She pulled one foot out of her clothes and put it up on the chair beside him and pressed her hips forward. He licked and sucked her until her body trembled each time she exhaled and her whimpers turned to loud moans. He slid his fingers into her and found her trigger inside and stroked it until he felt wetness cool his wrist.

'Don't stop now,' she gasped, 'go faster.'

She braced herself on the wall and grabbed a handle overhead and he stroked and pulled inside her just the way he'd been taught and applied a wet tongue to her exactly as he knew she'd like it. Her knees turned inwards and her thighs crushed his face as she squeaked and shuddered to a halt. She let go of the handle and eased back from his face, her thighs trembling and wet. She pulled her other foot out of her clothes then walked to the bedroom door and pulled it open and sat into the semi darkness on the edge of the bed. She breathed heavily and glared at him from under her fringe, an angry smirk at the corner of her mouth. She unzipped her top and slipped it off, then lay back on her elbows and unclipped her bra and let it lie lose on her chest. She spread her legs wide.

'Okay boy—good and hard.'

'Ohh yeh.' He sat back and picked up his beer. 'Gimme a minute, I wanna savour this.' The butt of a joint sat balanced on the edge of a full ashtray. He lit it up then threw her a fag and the lighter.

She regarded him with a curious mixture of mirth and disdain and she was glorious to behold. 'Look at you,' he said smiling, with curls of smoke leaking from the corners of his mouth. 'Mona Lisa in red.' He took a long draft of beer.

'And who does that make you? Leonardo Da Caprio?

PEEPING TOM

The next morning Toady made coffee and rooted through the fridge and then the cupboards. He found a packet of digestives and had a brainwave. He sat outside and buttered the biscuits then smeared them with blackcurrant jam and ate a combination he hadn't tasted for decades. It brought him back to his kitchen table, steeped in the half-light of early morning before school. He closed his eyes, took a big mouthful of warm coffee and let the combination dissolve in his head along with the happy thoughts. A hand gripped his shoulder causing him to swallow down the wrong pipe. He choked as he jumped up and spun around.

'What the fuck?' he rasped. Bernard standing there apologetically, hands held up. Toady shook his head as he sat back down in a chair facing the man and gestured for him to take a seat, but Bernard politely refused.

'No no Missyuh, merci. We are trying to get finished here, so we have no time for coffee today, I am afraid.' His face became serious. 'I just want to warn you that you must be careful. You are being watched.'

Toady was up again, brushing crumbs off his lap, scanning the trees.

'My friend Theo, when he came this morning, he caught a boy, standing on the fence, peeking in the window of your—' He pointed to the camper. 'Little bastard wouldn't speak, but we know him, he is Gitano kid, from the camp.'

'Gitano?' Toady shook his head.

Bernard rooted in his brain for the word. 'Uh—gypsies.

I think probably that he is waiting for you to go out and then to steal your things. We kicked him in the ass and he ran, but I tell you, these are tough little sons of putahs. He will be hanging around. Be careful, Missyuh.'

Toady's brain was racing for he knew in his heart that the kid wasn't there to steal, but to watch and report and that the noose was now about to snap around their necks.

'Thanks, Bernard.' He gestured again to the seat and the coffee but Bernard was backing away, pulling his shades down from his head over his eyes.

'Non merci.' He made two fists and shook them. 'Very busy today—nearly finished.'

'Merci beaucoup,' Toady shouted after him. The man gave him a thumbs-up without looking back.

He tried to go back to his coffee but his hackles were up. He went inside and replaced the coffee pot in the machine. He closed the door of the camper and walked down the terrace checking methodically, from side to side, up and down, peering through the trees for a trace of furtive movement. He froze when something stirred at the toilet block ahead. An old man appeared in a pair of shorts with a towel over his arm and sauntered on down the hill. Toady watched him until he was gone, then carried on. He slipped on the shirt he was carrying in his hand and took the shades from the breast pocket.

He looped his way right around the bottom, into the area were the campers and caravans were huddled together and communal life bustled in technicolour. Old folks sat chewing and chatting at tables—mats of grey hair on mahogany chests beside colourful blouses and big sunglasses. Younger folks with tin music rattling from earphones reclined in space age sun-chairs. Smiles, toasts and salutations came from each table. This was camping for many people—being corralled in with a hundred fellow humans, surrounded by a clutter of paraphernalia, fitting in with a seamless efficiency, whilst keeping up with the Joneses, the Schmidths and the Van Dijks. He came to the

Delgados. She was sitting at her table reading and he was polishing the windscreen.

'Buenos Dias!' Toady offered and they waved back. 'We are still okay for tonight, yes?'

'Si si,' the man assured him. 'No problema—Eight o'clock—Vamanos!'

Toady smiled and gave him a solid salute. 'Mucho gracias.' He carried on with his loop of the site.

There were few kids to be seen, bar a couple hanging around the offices. One was lying on the ground with his hand stretched under the vending machines, searching for errant coins. Toady noted that his clothes were grubby and his hair was lank as he watched him sifting through the coins in his hand. When he became aware of Toady the boy slipped his hand in his pocket and stared back, then gave him the finger. Toady had no idea if he was a spy or just someone's scruffy kid.

He stuck his head in the office door and the woman smiled at him. 'Anyone looking?' he asked. She shook her head.

Back up at the camp Shelley had arisen and was sitting at the table in her tracksuit bottoms and bikini, a large mug of coffee and a cigarette in hand. The three guards were sitting enjoying their own coffee and the cultural fusion that is Mc Vities digestives with French butter and Belgian jam as he came to their side.

'Mmm, tres bon,' they agreed.

'I thought you guys were busy, busy, busy.' He copied Bernard's fist gesture from earlier.

'Ay, what can I say?' Bernard announced to his comrades. 'Is elevenses.' He rattled something off in French and they laughed out loud.

'Brilliant,' Toady conceded and he walked off impatiently to do his Karate until elevenses were deemed finished.

'Need to talk to you, Shell,' he called back.

'Need to wake up, Tom.'

Elevenses ended around lunchtime as they headed off down the steps, giving a passing nod to Toady who was finishing his press-ups.

'Ay Bernard.' He caught up with him at the top step.

'Missyuh?'

'Where's Henri? I wanted to say something to him.'

'Ahh merde, too late for talking I am afraid!' He scratched his head. 'He had—uhhh, accident last night.'

'Is he okay?'

Bernard smacked his lips and started down the steps before stopping again to gaze over the treetops and the town. 'Life is short and sweet, my friend.' He breathed the air then shook his head. 'No—Henri is definitely—not okay.'

Toady sat down at the table with his trademark frown and told her about the spy.

'So what do we do?'

'It's game over—we pack and we leave.'

'When?'

'Now.' He banged the table top.

'Fuck it,' she spat and threw her fag down. 'I hate them all. I hope the bastards die.' She gouged the butt into the dirt with her foot then picked her mug up and flung it across the path and it smashed on the rocky bank. She was looking around for some other futile gesture to make when Toady reached over and put his hand on her leg. She grabbed the knife lying on the table and brandished it at the world. 'It's not fair.'

'Fair doesn't come into it.' He sat back to a safer distance again. 'We adapt and compromise. Find another place, beside another sea, where bastards don't exist.'

'But I found this place,' she grumbled. 'I stole my very own campervan and discovered those French men—for me.' She pointed at her chest before gesturing about. 'I built this reality out of nothing.'

'And made me king,' he proclaimed, rising regally from his chair with a teaspoon held aloft while she struggled to begrudge him a smirk.

'Bollox, Brody, I'm happy here,' she moaned. 'I don't want to go back to that miserable shit. I have a right to be happy, don't I?'

'There's no going back to that shit, trust me on that one. But right now, we really do have to go somewhere, or dead is going to be the new happy.'

She resigned herself and stood up silently and turned to the camper. He snapped his fingers to get her attention then shook his head. 'Don't make it look as though we're leaving.'

'I'm takin all that shit,' she said, pointing at the camper. 'It's mine, and I fucking earned it.'

'Good for you. If it fits in your bag then bring it.'

'Right,' she said .

'Not the ass plugs,' he called after her.

She found her new leather shoulder bag and laid it on the bed. She sifted through the inventory and arranged her loot in descending order of monetary value, from bottom to top. Toady stuffed his few personal items into the corners when she slung it on the table.

'We can't leave here like this.' He pointed out the window. 'The little fucker will have us ratted out before we get to the front gate.'

'What are you gonna do about it?' She slumped down on the sofa. 'You don't even know where he is.'

'He'll be close, we just need to lure him out.'

'Okay,' she said, tying her hair up in the mirror and checking her mascara, 'what's the bait?'

'Boobies,' he replied.

He took a towel and his wash bag and went outside and called Shelley out. She came to the door in her tracksuit, zipped down to her cleavage, bikini on show.

'I go to shower now,' he stated loudly. He tapped his wrist. 'One hour—in shower.'

'Great,' she called after him from the door, 'I go to bed.'

'Okay.' He walked backwards down the track. 'No

hanky panky!'

'Yes,' she called out and pulled a large cucumber from behind her back. She descended the stairs and watched Toady disappear over the brow of the hill and down to the toilet block in the distance.

'Great, that short, baldy bastard is gone,' she called after him, then brandished her phallus. She unzipped her top and then slid it up and down between her breasts. 'Cucumber sandwiches,' she announced. She placed the cucumber down the front of her pants and pulled the string around her neck releasing her freckled boobs to the warm sunshine.

'Hello tits,' she said and stretched her arms overhead while gyrating her hips and body in a circle. She pulled the cucumber from her waistband and held it up. 'Hello fucker!' Then she headed for the camper and at the last minute turned and moaned loudly, then slammed the door behind her.

Toady had entered the toilet block and could hear Shelley's performance faintly on the breeze. As soon as he got in he ducked and scuttled to the far end and out the other door. Then on his hunkers he doubled around the back and peered out from behind the corner of the block, keeping dead low. For a minute, nothing happened. The trees gently swayed in the warm breeze, their leaves swishing back and forth like the waves breathing at the edge of the sea. The gangs of sparrows chirped in from all directions and not a soul was to be seen.

Eight o'clock that morning had seen the shift change, when the new boy came up from the town to relieve his cousin who had been on lookout duty all night. The boy laughed and slapped his back when he arrived.

'You missed it last night, you little shitsucker.'

'What are you on about, you dickless retard?'

'I saw it all, in the window, the pussy shot of the century. He licked her slit and it was gushing and spraying stuff everywhere. He finger banged her and licked her ass, fuckin, splattering and pissing like a horse, all over his baldy head, whoooshhh!'

'Fuck off, you lying faggot, you fell asleep and dreamt about screwing your baby sister?'

'Eat my balls—I saw everything. She pulled off her knickers and sucked on her own titties and he stuck his big purple horn in her and then he splattered the walls with ten litres of jizz, I swear on my life.'

'Swear on your mother's life, and that your sister will be blinded with scabby dog pox when you go home if you lie?'

'Well shit, okay, he didn't splatter the walls with jizz, he fell asleep at the table, but I splattered the walls with jizz cos she was passed out on the bed for two-fucking-hours with her big red fanny dripping honey all over the place. Her tits up in the air and her rock hard nipples sticking up like Russian nukes waiting to blast off and—Kabooom!—blow my man-size balls to pieces. I nearly tore my own knob off, it was an all night wank fest.'

'Manhandled balls, you mean.'

'Haha, fuck you and your girlie tits, it happened, and you missed it. Best night ever!—and now I am going to get paid.'

He threw him the mobile phone and walked down the track making masturbating actions and grand spraying gestures over the whole world in general.

'That lucky little ass banger,' he growled and began to climb up the tree but then wondered if he shouldn't go and check the scene in the camper first. Not long after that Theo had found him and kicked his ass, a full hour before the pair had arisen from their barbiturate coma.

Toady lay low at the toilet block and knew in his bones he was there, somewhere. He could feel him watching. First it was a shuffle that drew his eye, then a foot dangling, and then two. From the lowest bow of a tree, across from their camp, two legs appeared then lowered down until the chubby body of a boy dangled from the branch. Then down he dropped. He glanced around before creeping over to the camper to listen carefully at the door. A stupendous amount of moaning emanated from within, precisely compatible with what one would expect from a sex-crazed redhead with a cucumber. He tiptoed to the front windscreen and peered over the dashboard carefully. In the dim light within he could see two feet up on the table spread widely apart, but the owner of the feet couldn't be seen from that angle.

'Merde!' he grunted and stole back around to the side window to find an opportune crack between the drawn curtains. He came in low and showed great self-control, slowly ascending towards the window with the sound of sighing and moaning in his ears.

'Oh sweet Jesus, be good to me,' he whispered.

There she was, legs on the table, swirling a cucumber in one hand and a cigarette in the other. She gave him a little wave just before Toady hit him hard enough to knock him out cold. Shelley flinched as the kid's head thudded off the window. A second later the door flew open and Toady dragged the wretch up the steps and inside.

'Jesus!' she cried, 'did ye kill him?'

'Don't think so.' He dropped him on the floor like a sack of turf. 'You ready to go?'

'Yeh, I suppose.' She checked her bag then her pockets and looked around one last time. Toady rooted the duct tape from the drawer with one hand and held the boy's collar in the other then dragged him through the door to the edge of the bed. A long moan escaped while Toady ran the tape a few times around his wrists, then his ankles, then taped ankles and wrists together. 'It ain't pretty, but he's not goin anywhere.'

Shelley was standing in the door with her hair tied up and her shades on. 'Better gag him or he'll be screaming blue murder before we get to the road.'

Toady pulled out a length of tape and bit it off then slapped it across his mouth.

'Wait,' she said and felt the boy's pockets, then pulled out a mobile phone.

The crew was still on lunch and while they both agreed that it felt wrong to leave without saying goodbye, Shelley admitted that she wasn't one for goodbyes at the best of times.

'Never gonna see those fellas again,' she moped. 'Never gonna use these lovely toilets, all swanky and new.' She stopped dead. 'Shite! Never gonna get to judge a load of French men's balls.'

'Never say never,' said Toady, taking her arm. 'Now will ye c'mon before some fucker jumps out of a bush.'

At the reception block Shelley decided to avail of the services while Toady entered the office and told the lady they were leaving early the next morning and that they wanted to fix up. When the account was settled he slid two fifties over the counter and winked at her. She smiled coolly back and slipped it straight into her cleavage.

'Thanks for everything.' He asked her to order a taxi.

'Pah du problem.' She pouted her lips and batted her eyelashes and became ten years younger instantly. He reckoned that he had the dour French woman trick mastered.

'How's your father?' he said with his seductive smile.

'Dead.'

The taxi was there in less than five minutes and he had to go and root Shelley out of the toilets where she applied her makeup at the mirror, blinking and puckering, pouting and cursing the gypsies to hell. They both climbed in the back and Toady pointed out the front window in the direction of town.

'The town,' he said. 'The sea.'

'La mer,' the driver replied.

'Yes, la mer, la mer.'

They left and headed into the town and when they got

to the seafront Toady pointed left.

'Go up, over the hill.' He arced his hand. 'Follow the road.'

'Sweev luh coat.' The driver nodded.

'Oui oui, luh coat, sweev it.'

The driver followed the road up the hill away from the town centre. The rugged Vermilion coastline came into view, a pale blue and golden sky over the dark sea with red and green fingers of land jutting outwards into breaking waves.

'There is a beach,' Toady explained. 'Beach!' He pointed down towards the sea.

'How do you know?' Shelley asked him.

'We passed it the other day in the car, with Anna. A secluded cove—like a suntrap.'

'La plage,' Shelley called out to the driver. 'Petite plage.'

'Ah way!' said the driver. 'Les Elmes. Pah du problem, Madame.'

In another minute the driver pulled off the main road at a roundabout and made a sharp right in behind the Hotel Les Elmes, to a secluded car park.

The meter said Ten, Toady gave him twenty.

'Seven o'clock,' he said, pointing at his wrist, then held up seven fingers. 'Seven—here!' He pointed at the ground.

'Way, Byansur,' he agreed. 'Set err ici, no problem.'

They found a short tunnel that went under the road and led straight out onto the beach. It was early Friday afternoon and most people were at work. The beach was practically deserted, save for an elderly couple decked out at the far end against the rocks. They passed by a bar on the right where one man sat on a stool talking to the man on the other side of the bar. Shelley took off her sandals and dug her toes into the soft sand. 'Wow, this is nice.'

BEST LAID PLANS

'Well spotted, I like it.' She ambled down the beach a little then dropped down into the sand not too far from the water's edge. Toady was about to sit down beside her when she held her hand up. 'Bloody Mary.'

'Fair enough, your lushness.' He dropped the bag beside her.

'The word is luscious, ya flute.'

'We'd better move over behind the rocks, just in case.'

'Just in case what?' she spat over her shoulder. 'I'm sick of those bastards, let 'em come! I'll make such a scene I'll get us all arrested. We'll see who comes off better out of that. I might just play my recording back to the Three Thousand Dollar Man.' She waved the back of her hand at him. 'Not a chance—I'm stayin here.'

They sat in the heat and drank a couple of drinks and Shelley lit up the joint she had rolled earlier. When she started to feel too hot she went and paddled in the water with a cooling breeze drifting in from the Mediterranean. Later in the year it would have been unbearable to sit there in the dead heat of the mid afternoon sun, but right then it was perfect. She pulled a phone from her pocket and thumbed in a text then put it away. She took off her top and returned to drop it beside Toady, getting the attention of the men at the bar momentarily. Rolling up her bottoms, she then waded back into the water, up to her knees. She just stood there while Toady watched her, jealous of each ripple and shimmer that touched her. Soon she came back and lay down in the golden sand. He turned on his side and watched her breasts rise and fall, quivering each time she shuffled her bum in the sand. Her nipples were pink and soft and fair hairs on her body caught the golden sunlight.

'How do you know it's a topless beach?'

'Cos I'm on it with me tits out.'

'I wish I'd made love to you last night, I'm ragin now.'

'The less said about that the better—for both of us, don't ye think?'

He laughed. 'I bet it would have been nice though. Can I feel your tits now?'

She sniggered. 'Ask me crack boy, ye missed your big chance. Before you know it this will all be over and we'll be back home again.'

'Why?' he protested. 'Who said we have to go back at all?'

'Sooner or later, let's face it, we gotta go back.'

'But I don't gotta go anywhere.'

'I have to sell my house, get a divorce, sort my life out. I'd get over ten thousand if me and Barry split up and sold that house. I'm not lettin him just keep all that. I busted my arse in that hole for five years and I want my cut.' She sat up and pushed her shades up onto her head.

Toady was looking at her sideways as he rolled the ends of his jeans up his shins and buried his feet in the sand. 'I'll give ye twenty thousand not to go. Hell, I'll give ye fifty.'

She turned and checked his face for lies, but then shook her head. 'It's not about the money anymore. It's about doing what's right—Karma.'

'You do realise that I can't go back to Sligo,' he said, staring out to sea. 'I'll have Nicky searching for me on one hand and Mossy on the other. I'd need eyes in the back of my head just to go get a newspaper. The minute I sit back in a taxi, every wino and junky in that town's gonna want to put a knife through the seat for a couple of hundred quid. That's if Mossy doesn't get me first and cut my throat.'

'You don't have to go in a taxi. Ye have money, just keep a low profile until it's all forgotten about.'

'Go back there and hide in a bed-sit, peekin out curtains at the rain, waitin for a Hiace to pull up outside? No thanks.'

'Listen.' She leaned in against him. 'I don't want to go back either, but sooner or later reality is gonna come knocking. I'm a married woman and some things just don't go away.'

'You're not a married woman anymore, Shell.'

Her lips moved a few times and a noise came out of her open mouth, then she just closed her eyes and waited.

'Barry's dead.'

The words were lighter than he thought they'd be. He imagined they'd fall like giant crashing boulders in an earthquake, but instead they hung like balloons in the air between them.

'Barry's dead. I know he's dead because I saw them kill him.' Toady said the words slowly and clearly so he'd never have to say them again. 'Trust me, there's no chance that he's alive, or that you'll ever see any part of his body—ever again.'

'Where?'

'Back in Quillan—Mossy and the gypsies.'

'How?'

He held her stare for a moment then shook his head.

She reached out and dug her nails into his arm, but he didn't flinch. He looked at the sand then out to sea, but she kept squeezing.

'Oww—Christ, woman, I surrender.'

'I'm sorry.' She stopped and rubbed his arm where the deep marks were purple on his flesh.

He told her that it was fast, and painless, with a lethal injection that put him to sleep, like a Labrador, and that the gypsies had disposed of the body by dissolving it in acid. He added that they had killed him because he wouldn't tell them where she was hiding. He noted that he had taken the chance to mention how much he loved her and also he had regretted being bad to her, and hitting her—and all that other stuff.

'What a pile of shite,' she said, holding her head and staring at the sand. 'But you're right. I don't want to hear the truth, because I know that Barry would have sold his mother to save his own ass in the end, and I can't even bear to think about it right now.'

'That woman's about to have the slowest bit of bad news in her life.' The words popped out of his mouth before he could consider them.

'Jesus,' she gasped, 'that's horrible. We have to tell the cops.' She fumbled for her cigarettes. 'There has to be an investigation and all that.' Her hands were shaking as she pulled her lighter from the box.

'No way, Shell—we never tell the cops. No body, no murder. He's a missing person and that's all he's ever gonna be. The gyppos will never take any of this to the cops. Stealing the campervan, Arno going out the door, not Barry, the money, nauthin.' He was counting the calamities on his fingers. 'They never go to the cops about anything. Omerta, it's called. The mafia have it and the gypsies have it—nobody's gonna talk to anyone.'

She sucked on her fag and her lips trembled as though she was cold. 'Omerta—sounds nice.' She stared out to sea and blew smoke onto the breeze. 'Poor Barry,' she whispered. 'Last thing I did was spit in his face, now I can't even find a tear for him—my own husband like.'

'You reap what you sow Shelley, and he sowed himself some evil shit.'

He went and got two beers and brought them back and she was crying when he dropped into the sand beside her. She sniffed and a tear fell from her cheek. He put his arm around her back and pulled her into him a little.

'Okay then, he did get a tear.'

'It's not for him,' her voice trembled. 'It's for me—and you, and what we had to do just to get here. Life is so hard. So many bastards, it makes me tired just thinking about it.'

He put his hand on her long smooth neck, her hair tied up in some kind of a bun with wisps and spirals projecting at different angles from the unruly nest. He kissed her cheek and tasted the salty tears.

'It doesn't have to be hard,' he whispered. 'A little house somewhere, nobody will ever know where we went. I'll work on making you happy.'

'I'd be lying if I said I loved you, Toady.' Her voice wasn't trembling now. 'I like you, and right now I want to be with you. You're the biggest surprise of my life, I could never have believed it. You've changed everything.' She looked around his face for a moment then shook her head. 'But I don't love you.'

'That's fine—I don't need you to love me. What you just said is better than any love that I could ever think up. I don't care if it's a week or a year, so long as we have today. You see this?' He slapped himself on the side of the head then rubbed his thickening goatee. 'This is me in here. You actually found me. I'm not afraid of any of those bastards, and I'll do anything to keep you with me. Even if it's just for the rest of today. Hey Shelley, guess what? We're alive, both of us.'

She kissed him on the edge of his lips and he kissed her back and ran his hand up her neck to her hair.

'I'm afraid that I think I do love you, Michelle.'

'Is that right, Thomas? You're afraid that you think you love me? How overwhelmingly vague—yet sweet.'

'And what's more, I've got a present for you.' He pointed out to sea. 'Your very own part of France, named after you.'

She followed his finger out to sea, to the end of the rocks at the last tip of land on the northern side of the bay. A sea stack overlooked the waves rolling into the bay.

'It's you.' He was still pointing. 'Can you see her? Long neck, curly hair tied up, lovely cheek bones—she's you.'

She could see the rock, and sure enough, the bust of a woman just as he described, left there by time.

'Point Michelle,' he said. 'I told the gods to make if for you, ten million years ago, when I hatched a crazy plan to drag you here with wild tinkers on our tail. We are immortal.'

Shelley stared at it with her chin on the back of her hand, the breeze teasing the loose strands of hair back and forward across her face.

'It's beautiful, thanks. I'll treasure it all my immortal life. This is the nicest kidnapping ever.'

'I didn't kidnap you, I saved you. Remember?'

'Yep.' She looked at him from the corner of her eye. 'Out of the fryin pan, ay?'

There was a beep in her pocket and she was texting again.

'Who's that?'

'Caesar.'

'What?' Toady gasped in horror.

'He sends a question mark on the hour.'

'And what are you sending back?'

'French comprehension lessons.' She showed him.

- - **L'HOMME MANGE SA DINER.**

'Last time I told him that the woman is washing her hair. Next time he gets to find out that the dog jumps through the gate.'

He frowned then shook his head. 'Did I tell you you're good at this?'

'Throw me in the sea, boy, I'm on fire, so I am.' She pushed send.

When they got hungry they went to the hotel on the other side of the road and ordered dinner and as time wore on Toady became sullen. Staring out the window he gradually grew silent, yet more restless. He sighed and he puffed and put down his fork then picked it up again and coughed and put it down again.

She watched him for as long as she could before

cracking. 'What's up with you? You're like a junky over there.'

'Shit,' he spat the word out sideways and shook his head.

'Ahem.' She sipped from her drink. 'When you're ready.'

'Aw Shit,' he said. 'I'm not going to be able to come with you tonight.'

'Come again?'

'You said it earlier.' He put his knife and fork down neatly on the plate. 'Sooner or later, you're gonna want to go back for something and Nicky'll be waiting. He's seen what I've seen. Mossy knows that I can bring the cops up to that little zoo they're running up in the hills. I can bury them all, and they know that.'

She had a sour look on her face as she watched him shuffle and squirm in his seat then lift his knife only to put it back down.

'Truth is, when you think about it, we were never supposed to survive this. It was all supposed to be stitched up in the end, neat and tidy. Mossy calls it a nugget.' He clenched his fist with a bitter smirk. 'I was supposed to be a nugget by now—you too.'

'Okay, so call us chicken nuggets then. We run and we hide—but you're not pullin this shit on me.'

'Do ye think I want this? This is the hardest thing I've ever done in my life. But the way it is, I'd wind up dead, and one day you'd just go missing. It'll go on forever, lookin over your shoulder until—ye know?' He whipped his thumb across his throat. 'Ye wanna live like that?'

'Yeh!' She was getting louder. 'I'd rather live like that than for you to abandon me now and send me off to the arsehole of nowhere with a pair of geriatrics. Supposin something happens to you? How will I even know? I'll still have to go back and face all that shit on my own.'

'It's not the arsehole of nowhere, it's Bordeaux. I'll deal with these bastards and I'll meet you there.' He picked up his fork again, as if to say all was sorted.

'You'll deal with them?' she scoffed. 'How many of them exactly? There could be twenty, did ye think of that? They're not gonna come down here on their own. You just said it. They're coming down to finish us off. They're gonna be ready for anything, specially fucking you, boy—they got a taste of that already.'

'Nah,' he said and shook his head. 'The bottom line here is money. He wants the twenty grand—and probably the rest. The more people he brings, the more ways he has to split it. There'll be three or four of them, tops. I can handle three or four.'

She lashed out with the palm of her hand striking his forehead and a loud slap rang out through the empty restaurant.

'Did you see that comin, tough guy?' She had her chin stuck out and her eyes squinted and her brow was deeply furrowed. Toady's frown turned to a grin.

'You should see yourself.'

'Oh fuck off, Toady.' She threw her fork on the table. 'You're not leaving me on my own. First you tell me we have to leave the camp, then you tell me you'll do anything to keep me with you. Then you love me—now you tell me that we have to split up.' She put her face into her two palms. 'I can't take this shit anymore.'

He reached to take her hand but before he knew it she clattered him hard across the face. The two staff at the counter stood up this time as the loud slap reverberated around the room.

'Fuck you,' she growled, 'I'll kill ye myself, why should they have all the fun?' Her other hand came up and she got him clean on the other cheek, even better than the first time. An audible gasp rose from the staff.

'Three or four?' she scoffed. With no restraint she pulled her hand back and slung another blow at his face, but he caught it before it made contact.

'Ye can't even handle me. They're gonna kill ye, and I'm gonna be left on my own.' She swung the other hand but he grabbed it and held her by the wrists as the waiter came and stood beside them.

'Everything okay? Madame—Missyuh?'

'Couldn't be better.' They glared across the table at each other. 'Get Madame a vodka and Coke.'

'Byansur,' he replied. 'Ay vous, Missyuh?'

Toady shook his head and restrained her while she grunted and grimaced and the waiter left.

'Gimme back my hands.' She tore them out of his grip at the same time as he let go, almost causing her to tip out of her chair. The whole table jumped a foot from the ground and Toady let out a nervous laugh.

'Will ye calm down, ye crazy bitch?' With that she struck him clean across his face with her full force and he saw sparks.

'Crazy bitch!' she spat in his face. 'That's what the other cunt used to call me—the dead one.'

She stood up with misery and fear contorting her face then with all her fury she pulled her arm back and he lifted his chin to give her a clear shot. He wished it was Mossy who was swinging the blows. He wished the final fight was here and now, and that he could get it over with, one way or another, be done with it and know his future.

'Traitor!' She spun on her heels and stormed out the door.

'Madame's drink, Missyuh.' The waiter put it on the table.

Toady's hand came to his cheek and he wiped his face as tears flowed freely. 'Fuckin hell,' he uttered on his breath and the waiter gave him a pathetic smile.

'C'est l'amour, Missyuh,' he said. 'C'est la guerre.' He squeezed his shoulder. 'Lay mem shose.' He walked away.

Toady heard his mother's voice from the seat opposite.

'You cry, son,' she said. 'God knows you've earned it. But when tonight comes you'd better be finished with all this.'

'I'm not afraid,' he whispered and wiped tears from his

bowed face with the napkin.

'I've never seen you more afraid,' she sighed. 'You're afraid of losing her, and you will lose her if you don't do what you have to do.'

He glanced across the table at her in her powder blue suit and hat to match. Her large cameo broach decorated the wide collar and her silver hair gleamed in the light from the windows. Her pale eyes regarded him with so much love.

'You look nice today, Mother, what's the occasion?'

'It's my birthday, Thomas. You forgot it again.'

'I'm sorry, Mum. I have a lot on my mind at the moment.'

'Don't worry, Son,' her soothing words came on the faint sound of waves from across the road. 'I will be there when you need me. I'll make it easier.'

'Thanks mum,' he muttered and straightened himself up.

'And Thomas, whatever you do—never call a woman a crazy bitch.'

He pulled two fifties from his pocket and dropped them on the table then knocked back Shelly's drink in one go and went outside, but the street was empty. He ran down to the car park and passed under the tunnel to the soft sand. She was busy storming her way up the beach towards the far end. He pulled his shoes off and set out after her at a jog. She reached the far end and sat down in the hot sand, not far from the old couple who basked leathery-brown beneath matching straw hats in the late afternoon sun. He arrived beside her and sat down, taking her hand. She tried to pull it away, but he held it firmly and she stopped. He put her long fingers and ruby nails to his mouth and kissed them. He flattened her hand in his and pressed it to his cheek.

'Forgive me, Shelley. Please don't leave me.'

'But you're the one leaving me.' She stared stonily out to sea.

'I'm not leaving you.' He kissed the back of her hand. 'I'm gonna be there right after you, the day after tomorrow, I promise. All this will be over, we'll be free.'

'Where?'

'That big sand dune of yours, remember? You said it was there.' He squeezed her fingers gently. 'I'll meet you on top.'

She continued to stare out to sea then her head tipped onto his and she closed her eyes.

'Fine,' she whispered, 'but if you're not there I never want to see you again.'

'Okay.' He kissed her forehead.

'If you get caught and taken or killed or some shit,' she shook her head, 'I'm not coming back to save you.'

'You already saved me, Shell, now I'm gonna finish it.'

'Christ, I hope so, boy.'

The taxi driver arrived at exactly seven and took them back to the town and they had him drop them in the supermarket car park, opposite the campsite. They surveyed the scene for a while then slipped across the road and ducked in the pedestrian gate, skirting the trees to the side. They arrived in the Spanish camp as they were having some supper for the road. They exchanged greetings and were offered a place at the table, but declined and asked to sit inside. Toady boiled a kettle of water and found the bits and pieces to make a cup of tea and they waited at the table like it was the departures lounge in the airport.

'Just come with me, Toady,' she started pleading again. 'Just let's go and hide. We'll figure it out.' He shook his head.

She tried again. 'Okay, I'll stay with you, I'll hide. I'll only come out if you need me. Back up—I'm not afraid to fight.'

'I know you're not, Shell, but I can run quicker on my own.'

'I'm pretty good at runnin too.'

'I know ye are.' He kissed her. He squeezed her hand and the butterflies in his stomach made him dizzy. He thought he was going to faint as the heat of anticipation rose in waves from his neck to his head. Then he remembered something. 'Shit, shit, shit!'

'What?'

But he was gone out the door.

He scuttled past the offices and launched himself up the hill, his heart pounding. When he came to the newly painted toilet block he stopped dead and listened for voices. He advanced up the steps, fists clenched and teeth gritted, his mind's focus sharpening on a sphere of relentless violence that he was creating in the space before him. If he met them now he would destroy them utterly and be long gone before their bodies cooled.

He pulled the door open and the kid shuffled on the ground to see who it was, then squeaked as Toady stepped over him into the bedroom. When he returned he was carrying the portrait rolled tightly in one hand and the seven-inch blade in the other. The kid let out a muffled cry and his eyes were like saucers as Toady passed, grunting on his breath. The clock on the dashboard said it was quarter to eight.

'Come for me now, bastards,' he seethed as he stepped onto the dirt and squeezed the leather handle of the dagger tight in his sweaty palm. He looked from side to side with white heat bursting in his temples as he summoned all his hatred and tried to will his enemies into existence before him. The terrace remained deserted, the sparrows cheeping in the otherwise soundless void of his brain. He walked to the top of the steps and now he could see both approaches.

'Dear God,' he prayed, turning his eyes to heaven, 'I've never asked for anything, but send them to me now, and I will eat their souls.'

He slowed his breath to a whisper and the tension in his stomach bled cool into his guts like venom. He closed his eyes and cold tears of hatred ran down his face.

'Let me have victory at any price.'

'Stop it.' A voice spoke to him from below. He opened his eyes and at the bottom of the steps a grey haired woman stood alone, her gaze stern as only a mother's can be. 'That's enough of that.'

Sound and heat returned to him and he gasped air from above as though he had risen from the bottom of a cold dead pool and broken the surface. When he looked down she was gone and his blood pumped hot in his throbbing arm as he squeezed the knife and his tears were warm and salty again. Hatred yielded completely to the suffocating imminence of Shelley's departure.

His hand went to the fence beside him for support, his fingertips fumbling onto Shelley's message. Unfinished, half-carved in her childish enthusiasm, then abandoned and forgotten. The innocence of it brought him hope. He was overcome by the need to finish the sentence that recklessly flaunted so many endless possibilities to cruel fate. And like a child, he too carved his message in the wood.

As he did a horn blew three times below and he knew that the time had come to put childish things aside. He jammed the dagger into the rail and took off down the steps.

OF MICE AND MEN

The gentle swaying of the campervan and the low hum of the engine vibrating through the cushion caused her to wake. She lifted her head from the couch and looked out the window behind her to see her own dim reflection on the shivering window pane. A pair of headlights sped silently past in the darkness. She looked up the length of the sparsely lit cabin but could see nobody else. Her bag was on the table before her and she pulled it open and frowned with deep confusion as she pulled her portrait from the top of her things. She sat forward and looked around.

'Thomas?'

At the other end she could hear faint notes of music emanating from behind the checkered curtain that spanned the width of the vehicle. She fixed herself as best she could in the window's reflection, then worked her way up to the front.

'Hello?' she called and was reaching forward to open it when it was jerked back. She could see into the cab where the elderly couple sat in front of their array of lights and dials. The white lines whizzing past and a single pair of red taillights in the distance were the only features on the broad, black canvas of the night.

'Buenos Tardes, Senorita,' the lady sang. 'You sleep well?'

'Yeh thanks, what time is it?'

'Two-thirty.' She pointed at the clock. 'Nearly halfway already. Is beautiful, no?' She gestured out the window.

'Eh—no.' Shelley rubbed her face. 'Yes! I mean yes—truly beautiful. Where is the toad—the man, my husband?'

A maternal pity seeped into the woman's wrinkles, then she reached forward and took a piece of paper from the dashboard and handed it to her. Shelley retreated to the table.

Dear Shelley,

I hope you had a nice sleep. Sorry about the drugs but it was the only way to shut you up. You looked so beautiful when you were leaving that I almost could not let you go. I wish I didn't have to do this. But I do.

How can we justify anything we've done if you can't be yourself, too afraid to even show your hair? There is no room for people like us in a world where men like that have control.

I've never actually started anything to know if I'm able to finish it, but maybe this time.

I love you and I'm not afraid, so you shouldn't be either. I will see you on the top of your big dune in two days. If something goes wrong then go home and give this to the manager at the Bank. Leave the town immediately and don't ever go back. There is enough money to make a clean start somewhere else. No matter what happens, I'll always be glad you got on that boat. This is the only part of my life that matters to me now.

Love Thomas

P.T.O.

To Whom It May Concern.

Even if my death remains unverifiable at the time of delivery, Laura Bennet, Assistant Manager, is authorised to open and execute the instructions in the Letter of Consent in the Event of Untimely Demise or Disappearance which is already on file with the bank since the Dutch episode.
Michelle Kelly, the bearer of this letter will be the main benefactor instead of the Burmese Orangutan Orphan Sanctuary, but I want them to get the money that I had allowed for Red Squirrel Protection instead.
Whatever's left, split it 60/40 between the dogs and the donkeys.

The letter is lodged in Safety Deposit Box 721. Password on the box is Greyman.
Consider this my will, I have no next of kin. This is a legal document.

Signed : Thomas Zatakis Brody.
Witnessed : Maria Delagado Munez. 2105 Calle Davila, Santander, Cantabria, Espana.

*

Sitting among the vines and the wires, all the noises of the town drifted up to him on top of the hill. The sky was a dirty orange with the light from the town reflected on heavy clouds sweeping overhead. There it was again, the distant flash of lightning, far out to sea. He strained his ears, trying to make out the rumble, but he couldn't decide if the low breath he heard returning was thunder or the rolling of the waves.

Music rose up through the trees along with shouting and laughter and somehow it came to him in the clamour of his thoughts that it was Balls and Booze night close by. He stood up and peered down to the campsite and could see the roof of Mossy's campervan through the trees below.

After having left Shelley sleeping with the Delgados, he had spent a while hiding in the toilets, counting a half minute between each shiver until his breathing slowed and his conviction returned. Initially, he had considered going back to sit and wait in the camper for a head-on confrontation as they came through the door. But something about the deathly stillness of the scene had made him nervy as he watched on from the trees. He decided on an old-fashioned ambush instead.

He had skirted his way around the perimeter of the camping grounds in the growing shadows, finding a gap in the fence through which he clambered to the vineyard. He'd been sitting there an hour and had already survived one minor heart attack when a large animal came loafing along the fence line. What looked like a Rottweiler had come skulking in the dark and stopped in its tracks when it got wind of him sitting there. 'Good boy,' he whispered to the two luminous eyes staring from the shadows. He had tried to back away a little and stumbled over a dry tussock. The animal came bounding closer, screaming like a demented woman, stopping ten feet away with its big snout flaring and its beady eyes gleaming, two curled tusks champing at the whiskers on either side of its nose. 'Holy shit!' He crawled away on his hands and knees through the leaves. But the boar hadn't perceived him as a threat and just grunted before retreating to the shadows and stealing away into the night.

He'd stayed put for a while to let the commotion die down, watching the lightning draw closer while his heart found its rhythm again, and now, he tentatively advanced until he could see the camper properly. He dropped down when he saw a person standing at the door. Unable to make out who it was through the leaves, he crept closer. The sky flickered again and this time the low rumble of thunder rolled in on a stiffening breeze.

He came squatting on his hunkers to the fence until he could see the figure plainly. Pretty little German Anna in T-shirt and shorts glanced about nervously then tapped on the door again. Nothing stirred so she pulled the door open. Toady strained to look left, down the length of the terrace, but it was hard to see the track below. He tried to whisper to her but his throat was parched and nothing came out.

She entered the camper and a loud start came from within. Toady guessed she had found the boy. He was about to call her name when a man's voice came from right below him. He strained forward against the fence and could just see the top of a head and shoulders. Anna reappeared at the door and uttered something back to him in French. The voice came back, deep and grating, then from the left, another man could be heard talking. Mossy approached out of the darkness.

'A boy,' she said. 'There is a boy tied up in here.'

The man below stepped in a little and beckoned her out of the camper with his hand. She came down and crossed the track to him. A sudden lunge and he laid her out on the ground with a single punch, her two arms neatly by her side and her eyes closed. He stepped past her and entered the camper then reappeared dragging the bound boy by the feet. With one tug the kid's body cleared the steps and landed in the dirt. The man lifted the back of his jacket where a sheathed knife rested on his hip. He drew the long blade and with three cuts the boy was released and scuttled to his feet. He grumbled at the boy, who said nothing then took an open-handed blow to the back of his head.

'Juh say pah, Caesar,' he squealed. He took another meatier blow to his cheek which had him in tears and as he raised his arms to shield himself he was stuttering excuses.

'Juh mon fu, putah,' Caesar growled and kicked the wretched cur. He was coming at him again with the knife loose in his hand and Mossy stepped in.

'Tronkeeyay! He put his hands up to the man's chest. 'Vous luh tooay.'

'I fucking will kill him.' Caesar grinded the words like glass marbles stuck in his throat. 'Less than an hour ago, my money was here.'

'Save your energy, Patron.' Mossy was calm. 'Where could they be? The nephews have been sitting outside for longer than that. Not a sinner in or out.'

Caesar was going through the boy's pockets. 'Phone?' he growled. The kid cowered then took another slap. Mossy pulled him away from Caesar and tossed him into a run. The boy stumbled, then sprinted into the night.

Mossy went into the camper and came back with the roll of tape. He sat Anna up and rested her on his knees and slapped tape over her mouth and around her hands then dropped her head back in the dirt to tape her ankles. He pulled her up by the hair and stood her on her feet, letting her flop over his shoulder. He carried her inside and a bony thump came muffled out the door as he dumped her on the floor, then the sound of more taping before he came out and slammed the door.

'They're still here,' stated Mossy. 'I say we stake out the wagon.'

'Ah yes, you have your precious wagon,' Caesar raged, 'but what about my money?'

Toady could see violence building up in Caesar's agitated twisting. He was like a wild animal tugging at a chain as he put his phone to his ear. The French national anthem reverberated from Toady's pocket as the boy's phone sprang to life.

A short whistle drew everyone's attention to Nicky at the top of the steps. Sucking on a cigarette he pulled the dagger from the rail and pointed it up at the fence where Toady was pushing buttons to no avail. The other two spun around and caught sight of him peering through the fence. Toady stood up and realised that this was as far as his ambush plan went. He put the phone to his ear. 'Hello?'

Mossy burst out laughing and slapped his leg. 'Priceless!' he roared.

Toady tossed the phone over the fence and it landed at Caesar's feet.

Caesar's brown and ravaged face went from rage to calm as he scanned the fence for a way to get at his prey. He walked ahead towards the end of the terrace and Toady walked in time with him.

'Shelley-Was-Mine,' Nicky called out. 'That's really nice,' he said tapping the blade on the message carved into the handrail. 'Ay Toady, I swear to ye now boy, even if she makes it home, I'm gonna lift her outa that town some night when she's drunk.' He turned the knife and it flashed bright. 'I'm gonna cut the hair out of her head in dirty red lumps—with this, and then I'm gonna make her mine.'

'Whatever you say, Sham.' Toady didn't take his eyes off Caesar. 'But if you're still around after tonight I'll be surprised.'

Mossy was on his phone. 'Get up the road to the winery, quick.'

Toady hadn't brought a weapon as he knew they weren't going to kill him until they got the money, which meant they were here to capture him, and to do that, they would have to get in close and that's how Toady liked it.

What he wanted now was to get them out on the street where he had flatter ground to conduct the negotiations.

'So tell me, Mossy,' Toady called down. 'This fella here is the reason why my dream holiday is all gone to hell?' Caesar was sliding his knife back in the sheath. 'This greasy son of a bitch is your Gypsy King? To be fair—he looks more like a Fairy Queen to me.'

Caesar's face showed no emotion.

'C'mon so, your highness, I have your money just where you like it,' Toady sneered. 'Up my hole.'

Caesar launched himself up the slope and onto the fence as Toady took off stumbling over vines. He found a furrow and ran along it, watching Caesar teetering on top of the fence then drop into the darkness. He ran a hundred meters to the end of the vines and was delivered into a yard full of barrels behind a building. Automatic lights burst on and a dog on a long chain lunged out of a corner, barking rabidly and turning him a tight left. Caesar tried to take a shortcut by jumping across the rows of vines but his feet caught and he disappeared to the ground.

Out in front of the building Toady could see the road and ran straight for it but as he was about to vault over the low ditch Mossy's nephews arrived in front of him puffing wildly. He swung his foot and caught Pawdie straight in the mouth sending him stumbling back. Toady landed on his feet but the big lad went down heavy on his ass. As he spun to face Geno, he stamped his heel down on Pawdie's closed hand with a crunch. Pawdie curled up tight on his side and wailed uncontrollably, holding out four crooked fingers.

Geno came running at him and tried to swing a wild kick. Toady shifted his weight to the back foot and raised the other, blocking Geno's efforts at his shin. Geno's own momentum sent him stumbling forward and Toady lunged and met the centre of his face with the full force of his forehead. Blood sprayed down Geno's chest and Toady roared with satisfaction at the sight of it. Geno went down on his knees and vomited onto the tarmac.

Up on the hill, Caesar was coming around the end of the furrow and into the yard. Toady watched his advance as he walked around behind Geno and gave himself enough room for a short run. Puke and blood dribbled through Geno's fingers as he staggered to his feet in time to get the full swing of Toady's boot between his legs. He tipped forward into the road, going down on his forehead with a hollow thump. Toady took off down the hill.

When he got close to the campsite entrance Nicky and Mossy rounded the corner in front of him. He wheeled a tight left and arrived into the car park at the large corrugated shed where Boules night was in full swing. Cars were parked everywhere with kids playing football under floodlights. A group of men and women stood at the corner of the building, smoking and drinking from plastic cups. They looked him up and down as he arrived panting into their company, then at the two men standing outside the gate, now joined by another who charged into view down the hill. Toady grimaced an attempt at a smile and pushed past them into the strong white light and the wall of noise inside the building.

The shed was split in half with eight Boules courts on one side and seats and tables arranged on the other, all covered with bottles of wine and beer or soft drinks. A storm of plastic cups littered the ground. Cheering and shouting battered the corrugated steel and people jostled back and forth in laughter.

'Ay Irish!' he heard over the din. Coming towards him was none other than Bernard in his jeans and short-sleeved shirt, plastic cup and cigarette in hand. 'You come to play a little of our great sport, my friend'? he shouted across the hall. 'Ay, Jean Luc, voici layz earlonday.' Toady saw Jean Luc and waved then checked over his shoulder to the door. His pursuers hadn't followed him in. The two men came tiptoeing apologetically across the Boules courts.

'Oo ay Shelley?' Jean Luc searched the crowd.

'He wants to know where is your cousin.' Bernard's big lazy smile turned to a frown as he got close enough to see blood on Toady's forehead. 'Ay—quoi passay?' he gasped and put his hand on Toady's shoulder.

Toady pointed out the door. 'Gyppos—Gitanos—they're outside. We caught them robbing our camper and they went mad.'

'Mon Dieu!' Bernard dropped his cup and was already walking past Toady explaining in rapid fire over his shoulder to Jean Luc who then let another shout across the crowd and was joined by another man. 'Allay,' he said and they pushed Toady towards the door. They all arrived outside into the darkness and went to the roadside. Up the hill four figures stood on the path with another sitting on the roadside bank at the winery.

'Ay batarr!' Bernard called and started walking, his two friends jogging up either side. As they drew close, they recognized Caesar.

'Ay regarday Caesar, tay sal onkoolerr day putty garcon,' called Jean Luc.

Bernard turned to Toady. 'Caesar—King of Perpignan. He likes to pimp and fuck little boys in the ass.' He clapped his hands. 'Be careful with this shit-eater boys, he has a sting, ah? Show us your sting, Caesar.'

Caesar backed away and pulled his knife from his hip, holding it out sideways, level with Bernard's head. The other two fanned out around him.

'Juh vay tonkool avec su cootoh.' Bernard leered in close and Caesar swiped the blade at him. The three friends all shouted and spread out further, surrounding him on three sides as the fiend backed away.

Mossy made a lunge and grabbed Nicky's hand as he reached inside his jacket. 'Jesus, don't do that,' he said and pulled Nicky's hand out, diverting the trio's attention.

'Who's this fucking putah?' Bernard stopped. 'What have you got under there? Another blade—a pistol maybe?'

'Not at all, boss,' said Mossy, pulling Nicky back, 'he's a harmless bastard.'

'Have you any fucking idea how many cops are in that building?' Bernard pointed across the road at the noisy car park. 'You want to sit in a jail for ten years maybe? Let's see what you have.'

Jean Luc shouted and they turned to see Caesar jogging away up the road.

'Fuck you, your highness,' Bernard called after him then returned his attention to the group. Pawdie and Geno stood in the shadows moaning and nursing their injuries.

'Fuck off!' Bernard waved at them and they backed away down the road and that just left Nicky and Mossy, surrounded

'Okay,' Bernard said, zeroing in on Nicky, 'so who is this pair of fuckers? Maybe we search this one and see if he has a gun—maybe shoot his balls off? Ay Irish—you want to shoot this putah's balls off?'

Toady wanted to blast Nicky's balls off so much it ached. He wanted to put one in each of their faces right now and be done with it. But he knew that for all of Bernard's bravado, he wasn't about to let him execute two men on the side of the road and Toady needed to survive tonight a free man.

'You know this pair, my friend?' Bernard asked him.

'Not really, just some dog shit we stepped in earlier—fuck it, just let them go.'

'You sure?' Bernard asked, surprised. 'What about Shelley? She okay?'

'Yeh,' he said and pointed towards the town, 'she's—eh—dong la vill. I'll get the camper and pick her up.'

'I can get cops out here, man, make these bastards disappear, no?'

'No, it's okay, you've done enough,' Toady assured him.

'Okay, bitches, you hear the man, fuck off.'

Jean Luc cracked Nicky over the back of the head with his open hand as they started to walk and Bernard planted a boot up his arse as he passed. 'Boom-boom, big man. Must be a water pistol you have.' The friends laughed.

'I'm not finished with you, boy,' Mossy said from the corner of his mouth as he passed. Toady swung from the torso smashing his fist into the side of Mossy's face, sending him careening over the kerb and into the rough grass. He was standing over him before Mossy even knew what hit him.

'That's right, ye evil cunt—you're finished when I say so.' He spat in his face. 'I'd break your fuckin jaw right now if it wasn't for these fellas. But don't you worry, boss—cos you and me are gonna dance tonight.' And he buried his fist into his face with a lightning jab. Mossy's head was lying on the ground and had nowhere to go and something had to give. A ragged hole opened up in his top lip as the skin tore and teeth broke out of the gums.

'Ohhh meeerrrde!' The three French men shouted in unison at the grisly sight and the sound of the blow. Jean Luc and Bernard grabbed Toady, laughing nervously, and pulled him off.

'Whoa, Karate Kid, you don't want to go to prison for this piece of shit.'

'You too, ye rat,' Toady shouted down the street. Nicky was walking away leaving Mossy to pull himself off the ground. 'You're dead, Kid.'

Nicky turned and raised his empty hand to him like a gun and pulled the trigger. Mossy staggered away, spitting bits of teeth and gum into his hands.

Nicky's car and the Hiace van were parked in the car park at the supermarket and the four made an undignified exit.

Jean Luc grabbed Toady's shoulder and piped up in his face with an eager string of words.

'He wants to go get Shelley with you,' Bernard translated, 'he's worried about her.'

'I'll get her in the town and I'll have her back for you in the morning,' Toady stuttered. He patted Jean Luc on the arm.

Before they all parted Bernard called back to Toady, 'Ay, don't go back up on that hill. Come down the bottom with the other people, you'll be safer, no? I'll talk to some cops in here, maybe send a car to pick up that Caesar pig.'

Toady waved his gratitude as he backed away. He had no intention of staying up top, but Anna was up there and he had to get her out before the injured mob regrouped. Toady took off into the campsite as fast as he could.

A young couple at the toilet block let out a shriek as he raced past, appearing out of the night and vanishing into the shadows just as quickly. A pair of collared doves took flight on the second terrace as he galloped past their hiding place in a thick laurel bush. On the third terrace Toady stopped running and approached the newly painted toilet block with caution. The sky flickered and the sound of the crowd at the Boules night packing up and getting in their cars mingled with the rumble of thunder. The crickets were strangely silent. Toady reached the last step to find the lonely campervan sitting in darkness.

He approached it from behind and scanned the trees and fences as all was suddenly illuminated in a single lightning strike on the hills behind him. A rolling boom passed overhead followed by another prolonged illumination. He put his hand to the door and pulled the lever out and it swung towards him. Darkness hung inside.

'Hello?' he spoke softly and in return he heard Anna grunt from the shadows under the table.

'Anna?' He climbed the steps and strained his eyes to see into the dim interior. Another flicker of lightning threw long shadows around the cabin and on the floor he saw the two whites of Anna's frightened eyes and beside them a pair of dirty boots. The clunk of the metal pot in his face and a sudden clap of thunder drowned out the sound of his head hitting the floor.

Caesar dragged him to the seat and secured him. Then, for the first time in a week, the camper's engine turned slowly on its half-dead battery and sprang to life with a shudder.

He pulled the wheel sideways and set the camper lurching out from its snug emplacement onto the track, taking half the hedge with him. The table snagged on the edge of the bicycle rack and was dragged along before sundering with a loud snap. He negotiated the wide bend of the road past the shower block with the lights off, then down the slope of the hill towards the office. The front gate came into view at the bottom of the road.

A tall figure rounded the corner at the entrance, jogging. On seeing the approaching camper he waved his arms in the middle of the road. Jean Luc, unable to resist his enthusiasm to help save Shelley from the town, ran smiling at them. His face turned to horror when he caught the bitter sight of Caesar, snarling ecstatically behind the windscreen. The headlights burst on in Jean Luc's face as Caesar floored the pedal and mowed him to the ground. Caesar exhaled his passion as he anticipated and savoured the light hop in the rear wheel. 'Merci mon Dieu—you are too kind.'

SUKIE'S REVENGE

He lifted his face from the table with the taste of blood in his mouth and light piercing his lashes in hot splinters. He raised his cheek a few inches from the board and the tape on his hands pulled tight underneath. He was secured to the steel pole under the table. So was Anna; at a strain he could see the side of her head below him on the floor. He coughed and blood sprayed out of his aching nose and brought tears to his eyes. Then the camper screeched to a halt, the door flew open and Mossy jumped up the steps into the bright cabin light. Even with the mess around his mouth he beamed a triumphant grin and let loose a wild primal roar.

'Gimme me wagon—I'm home.'

Caesar obliged and Mossy climbed into his seat and revved the powerful engine a few times, hollering joyously at the top of his lungs. The camper lurched into motion again and Toady strained at his hands to lift his head higher as Caesar approached.

'Fee-fi-fo-fum,' he growled, 'I smell the blood of an Irish man.'

He pulled his knife from his belt as he approached then brandished the jagged blade in his face. It glinted razor sharp and the teeth on the back were stained black with slivers of skin and dried blood.

'Not feeling so brave anymore, I think.'

He crouched down behind the table then rose with his knife in one hand and Anna's arm in the other. He pulled her to her feet, her eyes wide with terror. He spun her around and with one stroke of his knife he split her t-shirt from the back of her neck down to her shorts. He pulled the front of her shirt down to her wrists exposing her slight torso, her skin covered in goose bumps. He cut her bra strap and it fell to her bound hands exposing her tiny breasts and black shiny nipples, hard with fear. He grabbed her hair and snapped her head back then slid the knife up her tummy to her nipple and tapped the stud lightly.

'I'm going to fuck the nigger out of you, cherie.' He shoved her and she tipped forward onto her face in the bedroom. He slammed the door then came back and sat on the seat opposite Toady, banging his knife down on the table.

'I would fuck you too—but you are ugly.'

'Thank God for that,' he mumbled through bubbles of spit and blood and earned himself a loud slap on the side of the head.

'Still with the jokes,' grinned Caesar through brown and golden teeth. 'You will make hilarious dog food. But only after you have begged me—then paid me, to put your nigger out of her misery. But you, my friend—I will kill for free, and I swear, it is going to take a very long time. I own you now and you have half an hour before you begin your new life.' He checked his watch and gestured around. 'Enjoy these simple things, my friend. Life is short and hell is an eternity.' He slipped his knife back in his belt as he stood up and pulled open the cabinets. He found a half bottle of whiskey and spun the lid off onto the floor. 'I should know, ugly toad, I grew up there.' He took a swig. 'Ay, Mossy,' he called, 'take your time. I want to teach this frog and his nigger the theory of relativity.'

'No problem, Patron,' Mossy shouted over his shoulder.

He tipped the bottle back again then spat the mouthful down onto Toady's face sending searing hot pain into his eyes and nose.

'Right now, she thinks she is scared and you think you

are angry, no?' Toady could only glare at him from under his brow. 'But the truth is that she doesn't comprehend fear. And your anger—' he held his hand flat and tilted it from side to side, '—let's just say, you still have a way to go.' He leaned on the table, his knuckles right in front of Toady's face—LULU—one letter tattooed on each bony promontory, his fingers bedecked with a collection of ladies engagement rings. 'Only when hope is gone, will you know true anger.' He pointed up in the air. 'When your god has deserted you and left you at the mercy of his devils.' He tapped him on the temple with a long sharp fingernail. 'Then, once the anger is extinguished, you will experience—pure fear.' He stood up straight and filled his lungs through his nose then stared up the cabin and out the front window as he swayed from side to side and tipped the bottle to his lips again, the excess whiskey streaming from his chin. 'Steady as she goes,' he shouted and Mossy howled with laughter. When his eyes alighted once again on Toady, Caesar was grinning and almost benevolent in appearance. 'Hope is a razor blade, little frog. Embrace it—and it will set you free.' He made a grand sweeping motion with the whiskey bottle. 'Welcome to my kingdom.' He dipped his head a little by way of a bow then turned and walked to the rear, and with his foot he pushed the door open on the darkness inside. A brilliant flash illuminated the doorway and a dull explosion shook the walls. Caesar flew back and landed on the floor, his brains and skull flew past and splattered the walls and windows in clumps. The tyres on the camper squealed with Mossy standing on the brakes and Toady fell from his seat to the floor, nearly dislocating his shoulder. Caesar's head was right there, sporting a jagged hole the size of a fist, and inside, he could see the slow glistening of his ruptured brain. Then Anna came hopping up the passage and fell down to her knees in front of Toady's face.

'He's dead.'

'No shit—get his knife,' he grunted. 'Cut me out, quick!'

She dropped the gun then hacked and tugged at the tape until his hands flew apart. He scrambled upright at the table then stumbled to the front. The door was open and Mossy had fled into the night and left the engine running. He pulled the door shut and revved, then crunched it into gear and set it to the road again.

'Where are we?' he shouted over his shoulder. 'We need to get off this road. They'll have people in Perpignan.'

She cut herself free and then calmly took the road atlas from the counter. She came up beside him and leafed through the pages. 'Listen!' she stated loud and clear, in a matter of fact tone. 'Thuir, Ile Sur tet and Prades, take the turn for these towns on the D612 at Elne, soon—very soon.' She pointed out the window at the passing signs. 'Elne approaching.'

'Fuck me, you're good.' He shook his head in disbelief.

'I have plenty of experience with Dirk, he calls me Satnav.'

'No, you crazy bitch, you just blew that fucker's head clean off.'

She drew the gun from her waistband and pulled the slider back and let it click forward with the muzzle pointed into the side of his face.

'Glock nineteen, best thing to ever come out of Austria—simple, safe and very light. I never thought I'd actually get to shoot somebody with one.' He heard a click at the side of his head. 'Don't call me a crazy bitch.'

She slumped into the seat beside him as he indicated to leave the motorway. He checked the mirror and saw headlights behind in the distance. 'We need these bastards to follow us.' Anna was stony-faced. 'Oh Jesus, Anna, are you okay? I'm so sorry we got you into this. You did what you had to do, you had no choice.'

She looked at him and smiled. 'Him? I'd shoot him again if there was any point. I'm thinking about my Sukie, I wish she could be here for this. I'm not worried about him—or me, but Sukie?—she was innocent.'

He checked his mirror and saw the headlights trailing off the motorway behind them and grunted satisfaction, before looking back at Anna. 'Huh—who?'

'Sukie, my dog. I miss her horribly.'

'Oh right, Sukie—what about Dirk?'

'He's also dead, but I think he was not so innocent.'

'What?'

'I told you already, Tomas.' She showed him a bare forearm and tapped the gun on her chest. 'My heart is on my sleeve. There's no point in pretending he didn't earn it. He nearly took me with him—as well as my Sukie.' She stuffed the Glock between her thighs and ran her hands through her hair sticking her bare chest out, her nipple studs sparkling green in the dashboard lights. She tied her hair back in a short ponytail, then ran a finger along the side of his chin. 'But you came back for me.'

'Forget your heart and your sleeve for a minute, if we get stopped by the cops it's gonna look bad, you sitting there with your tits out and a handgun on your lap.'

'Bad?' She pouted and feigned confusion. 'Worse than these brains on the window here, or that man on the floor with a hole in his head?'

'No,' he conceded. 'Probably not, but it won't help with the overall impression.'

'Ahh. Perhaps you expect me to wear the clothes of these bastards?'

'No—you can have my shirt.'

'I see,' she said, 'so my body offends you. Perhaps yours is nicer?'

'No.'

'Shut up, Tomas, and drive. Fate will decide what is to become of us tonight. I pray that my mother will watch over us.'

'Your mother?'

'Africa,' she sighed blissfully.

He shook his head then laughed and banged the steering wheel. 'Africa!' he cried. 'Do you hear that,

Mammy?' He blasted the horn and Anna beamed her fabulous smile, and on they rolled, like a bus escaped from a lunatic asylum.

On the D612 they drove defiantly into the darkness, all the time the headlights behind them never closer, never further away. She suggested they stop and simply wait for them to catch up and shoot them both in the face. Toady was somewhat taken by the wonderful German simplicity of the idea and mulled it over. The problem was that while the police weren't going to get overly excited about Caesar turning up dead in a ditch somewhere, two foreigners shot with the same gun, on the same night, gangland style—that would be a different matter.

'We couldn't get away with it.' He shook his head. 'Besides, I think Nicky has a gun and I'd hate for us to get shot in front of our mothers.'

They drove on into the emptiness of the night and after half an hour the road became twisty and steep in parts. Progress slowed, with the headlights behind keeping pace.

'We should head for Andorra,' she said, poking a finger at the map, 'then into Spain. We could disappear in the hills for a week, maybe more. I've been there. Throw this dead bastard off a cliff, let the wild dogs eat him. No wait—' She put her hand out on Toady's shoulder.' We can drive him off—in this thing. Yah! The cops will be looking for it anyhow. Ooh hey—let's blow it up, for good measure.'

'Jesus,' he said and shook his head. 'Settle down a minute—what about the other pair?'

'They are going to run out of gas.' She waved the back of her hand dismissively. 'We lure them out into the middle of nowhere and then we can do what we want to them in the middle of the night.'

'How do you know we won't run out first?'

'Come now and use that tiny Irish brain,' she said. 'Look at your tank. There is less than two hundred kilometers gone from that gas. There is a one hundred litre tank in this thing.' She was waving the pistol around like it was a TV remote and she was in her living room. 'That idiot—' she pointed over her shoulder, 'is driving a BMW 3 series—60-litre tank. Even if he filled it to the top before he left—which he didn't—he will run out of petrol climbing in these hills.' She wobbled her head in deliberation. 'I estimate he has less than five hundred kilometers.'

'They could have guys coming out from Perpignan—who knows? A whole busload. What then?'

She shook her head with a cool smile and pointed a thumb over her shoulder to the stiffening corpse in the rear. 'The king is dead, no new orders will be transmitted tonight. Now it's just two stupid Paddies in the mountains—no offense.'

'None taken. What about the other two arseholes in the Hiace van?'

Anna raspberried her pretty lips. 'Where we are going? Not a chance.'

'Great!' His eyes scanned the mirrors, then landed back at her. 'Wait—where are we going?'

She whistled and pointed upwards.

'Look, Tomas.' She put her hand on his leg. 'You drive and this pair will follow. They just want the money and the camper. They will kill you, for sure, then probably me—then each other. That's their plan.'

'Well they're shit out of luck,' Toady said with a grin, 'Shelley has all the money.'

Anna gasped then beamed with delight. 'She is okay? I was terrified to ask.'

He told her of his plan to meet her on the sand dune in two days.

'That's beautiful,' she whispered and squeezed his leg. 'It's like a movie. Lauren Bacall and Humphrey Bogart.' She swept her hand across the windscreen. 'The Sands of Destiny.'

'I like the sound of that. So who are you?'

She feigned offense. 'Who do you think? I'm Humphrey Bogart.'

'So who am I then?'

'You're that little guy who's always following him around. You know—with the big eyes and the funny voice.'

'Oooh, hey boss—whadya say we blow them up in the mountains?'

'Yah!' she cried in delight. 'That's the guy.'

On they drove, winding their way through hairpin bends and ever steeper gradients. They passed through small towns that lay asleep in wide valleys with the mountains sweeping dark flanks into the night sky. Occasionally the universe above lit up bright pink or blue with lightning, silhouetting the jagged peaks of the High Pyrenees.

After an hour they came to the little town of Bourg Madame, sitting right on the border with Spain. They slowed for the roundabout and the cogs in Toady's brain tightened his eyes to a squint as he pondered. 'Spain? No? Yes?—Shit.'

'Tomas!' she shouted, startling him. 'Shelley is your woman, go after her.'

He shook his head. 'She's the closest thing I have to a friend right now, but she's not my woman.'

'Surely I am the closest thing you have to a friend right now?'

'Of course, yes. You're my friend—she's not my woman.'

'Stop talking shit, Tomas.' She slapped him across the cheek with her open hand. 'You know that once you have decided your path, you should act decisively and without delay? Sun Tzu teaches us so. You have chosen your path, haven't you?'

'But this is love, not war.'

'Same thing, you idiot.'

Three and a quarter times he had driven around the

roundabout before he veered north, away from Spain.

'You're right, Anna, I should stick to the clear path,' he agreed, 'and now—I'm going to let you out.' She was staring out the window at the small streets going by, paying him no attention. 'It's time for you to go, you shouldn't even be here,' he insisted. 'They won't do anything in a town like this. Just take my shirt and go, I can give you some money.' He pulled over to the kerb and in the mirror he saw the BMW coming off the roundabout and pulling to the kerb a short distance behind.

'Drive,' she said. She pushed a button on the pistol and the clip fell out of the handle. She checked it for bullets then slapped it back in again. 'I go out this door and start blasting in three seconds, I swear it.' She pulled back the slider then let it slap home. 'Tonight, we live or die—together.'

He shunted it back into motion and headed for the dark edge of town.

'Did I tell you you're a crazy bitch?'

'More than you know.'

Deeper and higher into the dark shadows of the mountains they drove, the roads practically empty now bar them and the headlights behind. Intermittent trucks passed, headed for Spain coming out of the high pass ahead. The sky was as dark as the vaults of hell, lit by lightning that came in flashes and occasional white streaks that leapt from peak to peak.

'Mein Gott, it's so beautiful,' she whispered. 'Sukie, my darling, wake up.'

'Wait a minute. How did you know about Sun Tzu?'

'Ahh yes—well,' she hissed through a wicked grin. 'Shelley told me all about your adventure while I was doing her at your camp.'

'So you knew all that and still took us to the beach that day? Did it not occur to you for one second what might happen? The trouble we could get you into?'

She shot an evil glare from the corner of her eye. 'You surprise me, Tomas. You think I treat strangers like that? Like consequences? That I should fear the random destiny of my own life? Is this what you think—that I am so afraid of the monsters that I will turn my back on a chance friendship?'

'What? I'm just sorry you got dragged into it—that's all. You and Dirk.'

'Fuck Dirk.' She crossed her fingers and held up a blood spattered hand with a glistening gold band. 'Tonight me and you are married—in blood and revenge.' Then her eyes smiled and she burst into a long snigger that brought her head down to her chest. She reached out and took a gentle hold on his arm. 'Mickey Stroker—this is so funny.'

And with that, Toady's perspective was finally undone and he felt an immense and sudden joy at being relieved of the burden of reason. 'We're a law unto ourselves now, aren't we?' She patted his arm and nodded.

In the final couple of miles climbing to the pass at Cols de Puymorens, the road stretches out into long straight sections that double back on themselves in tight hairpins. There are few places to pull over or stop. In the summer the road is choked with busses, trucks, campers and cars. Gangs of motorcyclists will roar past marauding in and out of line, weaving up the column of traffic. This isn't a place to come if your car is not in the best of shape and many fools who have tried it have abandoned their smoking wrecks to the narrow verge as testament to that. The high passes of the Pyrenees are not for the faint-hearted. Not for those who get nervous peering down into dark, bottomless valleys in the night. Not for people who ride the clutch on grinding teeth. Toady, even with his ten years in a taxi and another five in a cheese truck, was sweating profusely. Hunched over the wheel, he laboured around the hairpins, biting and hissing as if he was sailing a galley around a chain of deadly whirlpools. Just then, on a particularly acute turn, the clutch pedal dropped flaccid to the floor and it was all he could do to swerve on to the patch of gravel and ram on the brake before they started to roll over the edge.

'What's wrong?' Anna asked. 'We're nearly there.'

'The clutch died.' He held up his hands. 'It's just lying on the floor.'

'You drove like an old lady, with your foot on it. Now it's overheated. Well done, Grandma.'

'Excuse me,' he protested, 'I did not.' But he knew he had.

'We all do it the first time, we just need five minutes.' Out the window and down the hill, the headlights of their pursuers were rounding the turn below. 'This is five minutes that we do not have.'

She opened the door and jumped down and walked out onto the road. A pale moon was peeping through a crack above, illuminating heavy grey clouds spread across an endless sky. The weak light made the road shimmer as though it were damp.

'What are you doing?' he shouted, the cold air nipping the back of his throat. 'Get back in.'

'We cannot let them catch us here, we have no advantage.'

'But supposin it's not them?'

The Glock came level with her shoulder and a dull report snapped out with a flash of light. A dreadful awe washed through him as he stared helplessly at the little woman in the road, her feet planted apart and her two hands clasped on the pistol. Her head leaned forward decisively against the gradient. The feint echo of the shot rolled up the mountain on the far side of the wide valley. Down the way, the headlights stopped.

Toady reached and yanked the pedal from the floor and it popped back up into position. He put his foot to it, but it fell limply to the floor again. Out the window he turned his attention to where the headlights idled below. A flash illuminated the side of the car and the camper vibrated with a loud wallop as glass flew from an exploding cupboard.

'Ay!' he shrieked, 'they're shooting at us.'

She laughed. 'Now we know it's them, yah?' She turned back and shouted something in German down the hill then raised the pistol again and steadied herself. A bright flash lit up her thin arms as they jumped on the recoil and another clap rang out across the black abyss of the valley. One of the headlights disappeared and she jumped up and cheered.

'Anna, get in,' Toady called. He pointed up the hill to where a pair of headlights was rounding the hairpin a few hundred yards above. The outline of an articulated truck could be seen against a flickering sky. Big spotlights swept out into the void of the night then came wheeling around and bore down on them like the eyes of a dragon descending from the mountain. The window in the rear of the camper exploded inwards and the door of a cabinet shattered in splinters.

'Jesus, Anna!' He covered his head and pumped the pedal until it resisted his foot. The engine of the truck was howling on the steep incline and the lights drew nearer as she turned sideways to her target. With one arm extended in line with her bare chest and her tiny frame exposed to the valley, she loosed another shot then turned on her heels. As she did, Toady saw another flash illuminating the side of the car below. A spray of dust shot up from the ground behind Anna and she yelped as a shower of debris clattered into the side of the van and she stumbled forward. She reached the door and climbed in as the truck snorted on its final approach into the bend. The brakes squealed and the road shuddered beneath the weight of the giant. The blazing eyes of the beast swept through the cabin, blinding them both. The truck's horn bellowed as another cabinet door flew into splinters.

Toady reached down and turned the ignition then pumped the clutch and slipped it into gear. He swung it out onto the road just as the last corner of the trailer was coming around the bend and the wing mirror beside him was ripped from the door like paper. The engine screamed to the top of first gear as it cleared the hairpin and he got up enough speed to get it into second. Jumping forward, it gained purchase on the steep road.

'You alright?' He turned to Anna who was twisted in her seat trying to get a look at the back of her calf.

'It's not a bullet,' she huffed, 'the road bit me.'

He clunked it into third gear and drove hard up the three hundred metres of straight road then jammed it into second as he spun into the bend making the tyres squeal on the tarmac. They tore away from a cloud of exhaust smoke and in the next moment saw a building rise up from the ground in front of them. Its roof shone silver in the sickly light and its angular form was dwarfed in the expansive void of the mountain landscape. The road leveled off and a huge empty car park lay prostrate beneath the sky, ringed by distant, jagged peaks of snow. He swerved off the tarmac and brought the camper to a violent stop in a giant ball of dust.

'Enough of this shit,' he growled and jumped up out of his seat. He lifted Anna's face and she was crying.

'I'm sorry, Tomas.' She tried to smile though her tears. 'It hurts.'

'Come on, soldier, it's me and you.' He slipped his arm behind her. 'Just get them in here and we can take them down.' He pulled her up from the seat and sat her on the couch opposite the door. He switched off the ignition and turned off all the lights inside and out. Through the rear window and the crack in the bedroom door, the headlights came peeking over the crest of the road and lit up the inside of the cabin briefly. Toady stumbled over Caesar's corpse as he drew the curtain and opened the door latch, then calmly turned to Anna. She was grinding her teeth against the pain and the effort was bringing beads of sweat out on her forehead against the cold mountain air.

'Tell them that they got me and I'm injured,' he whispered. 'Bring them in.'

She nodded and a car door could be heard shutting outside. Toady slipped back low into the shadows at the bedroom door. All was quiet but for the sound of crunching gravel.

'What's going on here?' Mossy's voice sifted through the new gap in his teeth. He got no response. Toady could see Anna's face bowed, eyes closed.

'You want me to burn this fucker out? Y'aren't getting away from here without payin the piper, lad.'

The deathly stillness was ruptured when a truck appeared over the brow of the hill. It passed in the darkness with a whistling blast of air before sounding its horn. The noise echoed outwards from peak to peak.

'Well? Are you fuckers comin out, or are we burnin it out? Nicky—get the petrol can from the back of the camper.'

Anna's head came up as her thumb worked the top of the clip, bullets falling to the floor. She snapped the slider once releasing the one in the chamber then slid the clip back in. The door on the back of the camper slammed shut.

'Last chance,' he warned.

Anna's eyes snapped open and she spoke. 'You're not going to do that.' She was wiping the pistol with a tea towel, grabbed from the counter beside her. 'You don't want to burn out your own camper and then have the cops up here wondering why there's a dead body inside. You want to take it back to Perpignan, get rid of this piece of shit, and collect your money.'

'Aww Jaysus, little girl,' he called out, 'you're too smart for me. I don't want you. I just want that fella ye have with ya.'

Toady nodded his head impatiently at her and she put a finger to her lips.

'Fair is fair, sweetheart. His missus lost a bet. She's a

grown lassie.' Another truck could be heard coming over the brow of the hill. Headlights illuminated the interior and through the lace curtain on the shattered window, Anna could see Mossy staring in. She slunk down lower into the shadows and winced at the pain in her calf. She gritted her teeth and wrung another tear from her lashes.

'She broke the deal. She insulted my family—my wife. She refused to pay me what's mine. Then they stole me home, everythin I ever worked for. They stole me wife's clothes, her very dreams. They tried to kill me son. They threw him from a cliff in the night and left him for dead. Did they tell ye all that? '

Anna's eyes fixed on Toady's across the dark space between them. His face betrayed no inkling of it, but he was guilty as charged.

'That laddie's only fourteen years old and he never hurted no one, now he's lyin in a bed with a steel plate in his head. His mother cryin—day and night. We have to wait till he wakes up to ever know if he's gonna walk again. I'm only axin for justice, that's all. If he's a man—let em stand up for his actions.'

Anna drew her thumbnail across her throat and Toady's heart skipped a beat with the malice in her glare.

'He won't be doing any standing, okay?' she answered. 'You got him in the side with your pistol. You got me in the leg too.'

'Fuck it!' he exclaimed and a muffled exchange ensued outside. 'Is he dead?'

'No'.

'Well what is he then?' cried Mossy impatiently.

'He's bad, but he's breathing'.

'Okay then, sweetheart, you come on out and I'll get him some help. There's a first aid kit in there. He doesn't have to bleed out. There's people in Perpignan that'll fix him up. I been shot meself, it's not the end of the world.'

'What about me?' Still staring Toady in the face, hatred and pain pulled the corners of her mouth into an evil grimace.

'I'm sorry what happened to ye, precious,' he said. 'I wanted none of it. Caesar? He's not like me—he's not like anyone. What he did to you and yours was wrong and he got what was comin. Do you want to spend time in prison for this? I'll make that body go away. Ye suffered enough, girlie. We can all go home outa this.'

She sat in a moment of silence, punctuated by a bright flash of lightning and surveyed the scene. Toady crouched beside the dirty boots of a dead man, a meat cleaver clinched in his fist, while two figures stood high in a mountain pass, talking to a campervan, lace curtains flapping gently in the breeze. She looked to Toady and he wrapped his fingers tighter around the wooden handle. 'Come in and take him before he dies—I can't walk.' A rumble of thunder rolled slowly across the sky.

'Throw out that shooter first, ya lunatic.'

She held up the gun by the barrel and Toady nodded then she tossed it sideways out the broken window. There was a quick exchange outside before the door creaked open. Another flash of lightning illuminated everything neon white.

'Where is he?' Mossy's voice was close as the muzzle of a gun came into sight in the doorway. She glanced toward the back of the camper. A loud clap of thunder drowned out all sound as Mossy stepped onto the stairs and his arm rounded the door. An unusual wet slap impacted an unfamiliar part of Mossy's senses, preceding a sudden and peculiar sensation of itching below the elbow. The lightning flashed again and in the light he saw his hand, with the gun still in it, falling away from his arm towards the floor. Anna lunged forward from her seat, her smooth skin and compact muscles rippling as she snatched Mossy's hand from the air, an arc of blood spraying her across the face. She snatched the gun upside down from his fingers and slung his severed hand aside. Then pitching the barrel into the air, the handle somersaulted backwards giving her time to get her right hand over and catch it correctly. By the time Mossy's dead appendage tumbled under the driver's seat, she was kneeling before him with the barrel of the Berretta in his face.

There was a sharp clatter of glass as Nicky rammed his arm through the remains of the window and, with his loudest war cry, pulled the trigger two feet from Anna's face—click. In a flash of lightning and through the spray of blood pluming from Mossy's stump, Nicky's bewildered face seemed childlike.

'No!' Toady's plea was drowned out by thunder as Anna's hand and the barrel of the Beretta came level with Nicky's mouth and snapped once, sending him and a fan of blood sprayed backwards in a thousand shining beads.

Toady jumped up from the floor and grabbed a wailing Mossy by the hair and pulled him up the steps. Stumbling over Caesar's shattered skull, Mossy was thrown onto the seat. Anna jammed the gun in his busted face.

'Don't fuckin shoot him,' pleaded Toady.

Outside Nicky was sitting on the ground with his back to the campervan. Toady took his chin and lifted his head. Nicky coughed a mouthful of blood into Toady's face.

'How the fuck are you still alive?' He wiped the blood from his eyes to see Nicky's cheek was hanging off in a flap, his teeth and gums exposed where the bullet had ripped through. He grabbed him by the collar and pulled him up from the patch of snow he was sitting in. He hauled him along the side of the camper then shoved him backwards up the steps and into the seat beside a sobbing Mossy who was trying to figure out the best way to hug his stump in order to slow the bleeding.

'How d'ye expect to get away with this shite?' Nicky huffed and chuffed with half made words escaping from his open face. 'You're fuckin doomed.'

'Oh I don't know about that,' Toady grunted, grabbing the tape and wrapping it around Nicky's wrists. 'You came up here selling guns or drugs, or whatever a shower of cunts like you get up to. This pair got a hold of ye—then there was a fight. This fella got his hand chopped off by that fella, before that fella got his brains blown out by some other fella. How does that shite sound?'

'Not very convincing,' Nicky gargled from his throat to his cheek, then spat a cupful of blood onto the floor. 'You can't get away with killin us, Brody, don't be fuckin stupid.'

'Not to mention the fact that when I get out of here, by Jaysus—' Mossy was talking in a low hateful voice as he lifted his face to Toady, 'I'm gonna hunt you down with every member of your family and cut all yez are fuckin throats—one by one, until your dead mother wishes she was never born.'

Toady stepped back, his bloodied face turning to stone. 'Family?' He cast a glance at Anna who grimaced an evil smile back through clenched teeth. 'What family?'

He lifted the cleaver above his head and brought it firmly down in the middle of his skull where it lodged two inches deep with a solid thump. Mossy's eyes widened and fixed on Toady's, then he sat back in the chair. He had the expression of a man caught by surprise, like he genuinely thought he was going to get a chance to change his ways before he saw his god standing before him.

'Is that convincing enough for ye?' Toady clenched his fists and surveyed the spectacle of his creation while Anna cackled and lunged forward, screaming like a wild animal in Nicky's blank face. The headlights of a truck blazed past outside and the horn bellowed its raucous note to the blackened sky before it disappeared over the brow again.

'Time to go.' Toady reached down and put an arm around Anna's bare, blood-streaked body and hauled her upright. 'Keys for your car, Nicky.'

'They're in it,' he mumbled.

'Get in the car, Anna. I'm gonna give this bastard one minute to save his life.'

'Fuck that,' she protested. 'You kill him now, or I will.' She went to stick the gun in Nicky's face but Toady clasped her wrist upwards and spun her away.

'Enough,' he shouted, bustling her around to the steps.

She gritted her teeth and struggled. 'I'll be the judge of enough.' She pulled the gun around to level it with Toady's face. 'It's my revenge,' she grunted. But he slapped it sideways and pushed her stumbling down the steps to the ground outside.

'Trust me, Anna,' he demanded before turning back to Nicky.

'You won't be sorry,' Nicky sobbed. 'I'll do whatever you want, boy. I'll disappear—I promise.'

'You have one minute.' He held up a finger in his face. 'Tell me exactly what ye did to Flora Mc Carthy. Own up to it. Then you can go—run away like a fuckin rat and hide your face from humanity.'

Nicky spluttered and coughed his way through sixty seconds of vile testimony while Toady waited for him to finish with a cold indifference, until there was nothing to hear but sniffling.

'Okay, kid, that'll do. And now I'm gonna set ye free.' Toady reached out to the gas stove as he retreated from the grisly scene. He turned on all the jets and took the lighter from the shelf and a mug from the press. Nicky's head was bowed and silent as Toady descended the steps, grabbing a tea towel from the hook before he shut the door. Outside he located the petrol canister on the ground and walked to where Anna stood. He handed her the lighter then poured some petrol into the cup and stuffed the towel in after it.

'What's the smell in here, Brody?' Nicky's muffled voice came from inside.

Toady watched her face as she sucked a ball of spit from her mouth then spat it on the ground. 'Yah,' she ordered, '—do it now.'

'What the fuck, boy?' came a pitiful cry.

'Game over, kid. This is for that little girl ye murdered. I promised her she'd see ye burnin while ye went down to hell.'

'Don't fuckin do it, man.'

The lights of a truck came over the brow of the hill illuminating the couple standing in the patch of snow outside their camper; her half-naked, him with his mug of tea. He gave two loud hoots on his horn. The headlights pierced the camper and inside they saw Mossy stand up and gaze out at them, the cleaver still buried in his head. He turned and went to his bedroom as the truck roared over the brow of the hill and out of sight. She clicked the lighter and presented it. A flame leapt to the mug, igniting a fireball in his hand.

'For Sukie,' she said.

'Okay, Anna—for Sukie.'

He flung it across the open space and straight through the broken window into the blue ball of light that appeared and rushed out to swallow it up. It exploded through the windows, blowing glass and flaming curtains straight out, then rolled upwards into the sky.

'Gimme the gun.' He wiped it off and tossed it in the window.

Twenty seconds later Nicky's car spat gravel through three-hundred and sixty degrees before taking a bite of smoking tarmac and catapulting over the mountain pass.

BRODY'S DESCENT

Driving a campervan up the side of a mountain, sweating fear and riding the clutch is not a memory Toady would ever be regarding fondly, but thundering down out of that mountain pass in Nicky's 3 litre BMW 325I is a different story altogether.

Less than a minute after they leave the high plateau they are doing seventy when they pass a truck lumbering up the slope. This means they have about four or five minutes before the alarm goes off in the nearest fire station.

'There is a town about twenty-five kilometres from here,' Anna says. 'There will be a roadblock once they learn of what has happened up there.'

She looks him in the face, then up and down at the bloody mess caked to each of them. 'Hurry Tomas, we must get to the far side of this town before they know, or we will spend the rest of our lives in jail.'

The stony walls of the valley are silent, curving up to the sweeping sky. The noise sounds at first like an insect flying in the dark overhead, high pitched and intense as it quickly builds. Out of the valley of death they ride, hurtling on one burning white headlight, spraying gravel into the ferns and sending wind whistling through ancient boulders as they tear by with nothing but melting rubber and the muttered scraps of a prayer holding them down. The sound of the engine drops two octaves as it passes a twisted oak in a swirl of dead leaves, then the valley is silent again.

Speeding onwards they meet a fire engine on a long sweeping bend with the red needle tapping at the heels of a hundred and twenty miles an hour, the steering wheel trying to burst free from Toady's iron grip and the tyres spitting out lumps of tarmac. The fire truck's steel mirror slaps the aerial against the roof like a gunshot and the wing mirror beside Anna explodes into dust as the blue lights and sirens pass in an instantaneous flash.

'That was close.' She smiles through the pain.

'It will all be for nothing if we die now.' A sadistic grin tugs at the corner of his mouth.

'Better than prison, Tomas, better than many things. Go faster. The town is near and there is a place where we can wash this shit off us if we hurry.'

He puts his foot to the floor.

They came into the resort town of Ax Les Thermes at two in the morning and pulled into a line of parked cars at the side of the road in the town centre and switched off the engine and lights. Anna pointed out the window. 'Over there, get this blood off us in case we meet cops.' She opened the door and grimaced as she swung her leg around. Toady watched her limping across the deserted road until sirens came pouring upward from the streets below. He swept her up in his arms and carried her to the far side of the road, to an open square under a formidable old building.

'Here, quickly,' she whispered in his ear, pointing to the large rectangular pool in the plaza. Steam rose from the silent ripples up to the orange streetlight. 'Get down, Tomas.'

He carried her in and sat down in the warm sulphuric water then peeped over the edge as a police car sped past, heading for the mountain pass.

'They couldn't know yet, we still have time.' She perched on his knee and took handfuls of water and rubbed the side of his head where small spits of Caesar's brains and skull had stuck to the stubble. She wiped the blood-streaks from his face with her forearm. 'Look, your shirt is a mess.'

He took it off and rinsed it, then used it to wipe the splatters of blood from her forehead and cheek. She leaned back and he dipped it in the water then wiped more dark smears from her breasts. She held out her arms and he wiped them clean and then her hands.

'Fix my leg.' She rolled over in his lap then floated her body on top of the water. The back of her calf had three lacerations. When he lifted the skin to wipe the grit and tarmac out, fresh blood clouded the water.

'One of these could use a couple of stitches.'

'Forget it,' she grunted, 'just get the dirt out.'

When he was finished he took her by the waist and helped her lift her torso out of the water. There were tears streaming down her cheeks as he pressed her close to his bare chest.

'It's okay, you can sleep soon, Anna.'

She leaned her head into his neck and he felt her kiss him. He held her close in his left arm and was about to climb out of the pool, when another siren wailed out from the streets close by. He lingered on the lip of the top step and watched the cops shoot past up the hill then climbed out and carried her back to the car, where he put her in the passenger seat. In the boot he found Nicky's bag of clothes. Unlike Barry, Nicky was clean and his clothes were freshly laundered and Toady donned a clean black T-shirt. He pulled out a fleece-lined hoodie and helped her get it on and zipped it up to her neck. In the boot he rummaged in the side compartment on a hunch.

'Good man, Nicky,' he whispered and pulled the first aid kit out from the niche. Jackie had put one in each taxi but it was an unwritten rule that a driver should award himself one from time to time and blame it on passengers taking luggage from the boot.

A Fistful of Salt

Headlights off, the car moved as a slow shadow through the empty streets and out the far side of town. They stopped after a mile, in the blackness under overhanging bows, on a deserted wasteland. He got out again and came around to her. He swung her legs out of the car and turned her injured calf to him.

'This is definitely going to hurt you more than me.'

'Do it, Tomas.' She rubbed the palm of her hand on his head then down his chin and gasped as he took hold of her wound. He poured and rubbed surgical spirits into the depth of each wound lifting the skin to let the blood and grit trickle out. He wiped at each wound mercilessly with soaking cotton wool. She groaned and grunted and squeaked and her eyes rolled in her head.

'Good girl, it's not too bad, we're nearly there.' He massaged antiseptic cream into it then took a bandage and wrapped it around and fastened it. He lifted her feet back into the car then popped open the glove box and found a bottle of water. 'Here, take these.' He handed her three painkillers.

Her eyes were dark with pain as she touched her fingertips to his lips and searched his face, but still it wasn't hard to see the tender smile within them.

'Hell of a team, Tomas.'

He kissed her forehead.

Thirty miles further, on the outskirts of a town called Pamiers, he turned off the main road and disappeared westward into the dark, endless countryside.

At that moment, the first roadblocks were being set up outside Ax Les Thermes after the discovery of charred remains at a grizzly double murder scene in the high pass at Cols de Puymorens.

KELLY FALLS

On an endless stream of time, mile after mile of motorway passed by as they crossed the sleeping heartland of rural France. If she pressed her face to the window and blocked out the dim light of the interior, she could sometimes see vaguely striped fields stretching into the murk of the landscape. But mainly there was only the night and red taillights passing over the persistent sigh of smooth tarmac.

At four in the morning she pulled her phone out and rang Toady's mobile. A buzzing came from her shoulder bag and she reached in and pulled out his phone.

'Perfect—it's official, if you're gone, you're gone. I'm never gonna hear another word, am I?'

The darkness turned grey outside as she employed herself rolling joints and lining them up in a tin case supposedly for the discreet carriage of a sanitary towel but infinitely better suited to this. The Delgados were unaware of the world as they sat in their cab, mesmerised by the silent passage of white and yellow lines. They were going to a campsite at the edge of Bordeaux and when the journey entered its closing stage and the city traffic started to gather around them in the weak morning light, they asked her exactly where she was going.

'Big sand dune.'

'But Senora, is forty miles.'

They didn't want to leave her on the motorway in the industrial belt at eight in the morning. 'Your husband has paid me well, I cannot leave you here.' Senor Delgado sucked on his moustache and shook his head. 'I will bring you to the centre and you will find autobus.'

Shelley stood in the central plaza and waved to the departing campervan at nine in the morning. She was tired and hungry and so very lonely. She missed her stolen campervan, the secluded terrace in the trees, the gangs of sparrows underfoot and most of all, her French men.

'Jean Luc!' She checked her watch. 'Maybe not, it's Saturday.'

The early morning sun hadn't yet topped the roofs of shaded city streets, sparsely populated with weekend workers and early shoppers. She found a café with tables outside and spent two hours drinking coffee, eating croissants and smoking. As the hours passed, the sunlight found its way into the narrow back streets and warmed the plaza. People arrived in ones and twos, then groups, and soon in busloads. She smoked a joint and if the waiter could smell it, he gave no indication of the fact, at least none that would have registered over his flirty smile.

'Jesus, eleven o clock and they're at it already.'

She was getting used to the men and had perfected an aloof arc of the eyebrow combined with a slow curl of the lip that served to keep their attention with minimal effort. So different from her hometown—the awkward mouthy advances of drunks typified what she hated about her claustrophobic life. She considered just how small her life must be, that a week on a deserted campsite should seem life altering—then she remembered Barry.

'Your life is altered,' she whispered to herself, feeling relief and remorse in an instant. How quickly people adapt, she mused. Who would have thought it possible that some warped part of her brain would come to look forward to Thomas Brody appearing in his underpants? She felt a grudging admiration for his impervious nature and the cool shrug of his shoulders as her snide remarks rolled off him with no apparent effect. Her brain was liquid, filling the cracks as it flowed over these improbable circumstances. How tiny the empty space left by Barry's departure felt in the warm light of day.

She went for a walk through the narrow streets of the centre and found the river. She sat there for a while as the sun grew warmer. She transferred half the contents of a small vodka bottle to an ice cold bottle of Coke, then enjoyed al fresco cocktails and became hypnotised by the dancing pools of golden light on the passing water.

It was possible that Toady could have made it to the sand dune already and it was also possible that he might not arrive for a week, or a year—or ever. At what time should she commit herself to going out there? Probably not today, give him some time.

'I don't love you.'

She remembered her words and regretted them. He hadn't even asked. He was perfectly happy just to take it as it came. Patience and a hard neck—two admirable qualities in any man.

'Maybe I do love you a bit,' she mumbled into her knuckles as she leaned on the steel fence beside the river. The small and easy parcels of affection she had noticed herself bestowing on him had appeared from nowhere. No enchantment, no sudden sexual compulsion. Her fondness for him had arrived without fanfare, in spite of her best efforts.

'You sneaky grey man—have you tricked me?'

She felt a sudden guilt at having left him to face their enemies alone and she recoiled inside at the thought of the confrontation. She never knew she had a limit for this kind of mayhem until now. But now she felt exhausted at the effort of trying to be tougher than everyone else. She just wanted it to be over.

In the one short night since she had escaped the ominous threat of the gypsies she had found herself breathing easier, her shoulders lighter. She was touched with humility in the face of Toady's modest bravery, the way he just assumed he was the man for the dirtiest jobs.

She tried to remember the last time she had cared so much about the outcome of events she could more easily have walked away from. She couldn't, and now she wondered at what point she'd lost that part of herself. Tenderness, warmth, empathy—without these qualities, was she even a real woman anymore?

'How long have I been so dead inside?'

She swilled from her cocktail and cursed herself for having been so hard on him for all those years. Simply because he would take her spiteful blows, she had methodically administered them. Brody only wanted a gentle word from time to time and she had made sure that he never got one.

'Jesus boy, what do you see in me?' She clenched her fist till her nails bit hard. 'I swear to God, I'll make it up to you. Just come back.'

She was beginning to realise that if he didn't come back, a much purer strain of loneliness awaited her. Panic stirred in her guts and a shiver ran down her back.

'You're a coward, Kelly.' She took another swig. 'And a bully.'

She had never acknowledged how much of an embarrassment she was to herself until then.

'Nah—that's bullshit.' She did it every time she got drunk and just couldn't remember. She turned away from the river sometime after midday.

'What's wrong with you?' Her head began to feel light with the familiar harmonies of self-destruction.

'You're one toxic bitch.' She lit a fag and wandered off down a side street. 'And you drink too much.'

She came to a bar where the noise of men shouting lured her in.

'Yeh?' She flicked the butt at her reflection in the glass door. 'Mind your own business, ye mouthy cunt.'

SNOW WHITE GETS GRUMPY

He'd been driving for four hours, skirting one small town after another, making decisions based on signs that pointed north and west. Nicky didn't have a Sat Nav. If he had, Toady wouldn't have used it anyway. Roads were his life and they'd always known better than him where he should be going. What Nicky did have was an old-fashioned ball compass on the dashboard and in the black hours of the early morning, he hit a motorway sign-posted for a town called Auch, heading directly west. He drove in silence through the shadowed landscape that drew in close and sped past, then gracefully breathed away into the slow distance, and his thoughts became indiscernible from the night.

Just before five he noticed the horizon turn dirty grey in the rear view mirror. He was exhausted and his eyes were closing on him. The petrol light had just come on and the rhythmic sound of Anna's breathing beside him for the last two hundred miles had finally broken him down and he knew he had to sleep. He saw signs for a motel and rolled down the off-ramp then veered up the small side road, signposted for Le Castagne Camping Ground. The prospect of waking Anna up, or getting into a miming and guessing game with an overzealous concierge, didn't appeal to him.

The track was lit by dim standard lamps and save for the light in a single caravan and another over a toilet block, he could see nothing but hedges, mowed grass and trees. He pulled straight into a secluded pitch and switched off the engine. He took a cushion and blanket from the back seat and slipped the pillow under Anna's head. She snuggled into it, then he spread the blanket over her. He let the window down a little and was overwhelmed by the noise that came pouring in from outside. The night air was thick with the whistles, hoots and croaks of small creatures. It was noisier than a city street in rush hour as a thousand unseen characters competed for their moment in the chaotic symphony. He slid down into the seat and was asleep within a minute.

It was warm and stuffy when he woke and flinched upright. Anna was gone from the seat beside him. It was ten-thirty on the dashboard clock.

'Shit!' He opened the door and stumbled out. Through the trees there were green fields and gentle rolling hills with thickets and copses on their crowns, much like home but bathed warmer in the golden sunshine. The night symphony had been replaced by a chorus of bird song that rang out from the trees.

'Good morning.'

He spun around and Anna was sitting on a wooden fence behind him in her underwear and a red cut off T-shirt she had obviously found in Nicky's gear and doctored for purpose. Her khaki shorts were hung on the fence beside her, steam rising from them in the heat of the morning. Her hair was fluffed up and almost dry from a shower she had taken, and she was smiling as brightly as ever.

'Wow!' He rubbed his face and shook his head. 'What a sight for sore eyes. You look much better.'

A flock of tiny birds took off from the bush behind her, flew a tight, low circle above the car then landed in the exact same spot to continue their singing.

'This place is like a Disney movie,' she laughed. 'I'm Snow White and you are Grumpy.'

She gestured around to the preened hedges that bordered lawns as smooth as putting greens. The orange gravel tracks were lined with lamps and wooden benches secreted in shaded recesses. Blossom trees, pink and white, gently shed their petals on the warm, fragrant breeze.

'The wicked witch is dead, Tomas.'

She stepped down from the fence and turned her leg for him to see. She had replaced the bandage with three large waterproof plasters.

'You did good, the wounds are spotless.'

She went to the back seat and retrieved a can of Sprite and an individually wrapped pan chocolat and handed it to him.

'Got it in a vending machine at the office, I paid her for the night. Told her we were too tired to pitch the tent. Said we drove from Cherbourg all day and night.'

'Nice,' he said through a mouthful of pastry.

She got him another from a little pack as he demolished the can of lemonade.

'Healthy and nutritious,' she quipped.

'Uhum,' he nodded, stuffing the next one in.

'There is blood and dirt on those jeans,' she said. 'Steep them in a basin while you take a shower, they'll be dry on the fence in an hour or two. I already washed your pretty shirt.' She pointed to where it was spread on a hedge close by.

'The water is beautiful and warm.' She gestured to the shower block close by.

'Sounds good,' he said, blowing pastry flakes everywhere. She laughed and when she stopped and smiled at him, she seemed happy enough for both of them.

'Do you think they're hunting us?'

'The law?' She shook her head and smirked from under her fringe. 'Maybe looking for a black car with a couple of gypsies, three hundred kilometres away, but not us—not here.'

He went into the shower with Nicky's towel and shower gel and over the rush of steaming water he heard a knock. Anna asked him for his jeans with her arm extended in the door. He leaned against the shower wall with rivers of warm water pouring from his head and shoulders and he recalled the mayhem of the preceding night.

'I'm free,' he sighed into the water. 'I won—you fuckers.' All they had to do now was disappear until the cops lost interest and chalked it all up to a night of gypsy madness.

Anna was behind him and she slid her hand up his stomach to his chest and pressed her body against his back. Her other hand came around his waist and slid down between his legs and took hold of him. Her fingers were dripping with thick soap and she squeezed and worked her fist up and down, it quickly swelled and stood up. She slid her hand all the way down till her firm grip rested at the base and she used it to pull him around to face her. Her arms went around his thick neck and she pulled herself from the ground wrapping her legs around his waist. He took hold of her bare ass and lifted her up higher until her breasts pressed his face. She tucked her hips in tight to his chest and her thick pubes rubbed against him, then she lowered herself until her lips came to rest on the tip. She closed her eyes as she commenced her slow descent, her hot belly taking him in, inch by inch.

'You're not big enough for me.'

She sighed. 'I'm sure that's the first time a man ever said that to a woman.' She slid further down and moaned.

He turned off the water and leaned back against the cold tiles. 'You're so small, I don't want to hurt you.'

She grunted and took another inch and nestled her face tight against his cheek. 'Shut up and give me the rest of it.'

He pushed his hips forward to present his full length and she loosed her grip and lay back. In small circular thrusts she slid down until her ass came to rest against his thighs. Her head lolled back and her mouth opened a little, as though she had passed out, but the vice-like grip of her legs around his waist tightened and loosened rhythmically, sliding her lips up and down. The heat deep inside her grew and the embrace of her walls tightened and sweat beaded beneath her eyes. The aroma made his head spin faster as she drew herself tight against him. Her mouth and tongue crushed into his and she licked her spit around his lips.

It went briefly through his head to ask her about contraception before his mind turned a bright white and he finished himself into her, as deeply inside as he could reach and she sucked hungrily for more.

THE LONG ARM

A phone rang behind a plain wooden door on a long deserted corridor.

'Yeh.'

'Detective, I've a caller ringing from a public payphone in France, he won't give a name. Says he wants to talk to whoever it was that handled the Flora Mac Carthy case. Says he's got information you need to hear.'

Jackie lay in his hospital bed, his jowls growing fatter and greyer by the day. He should have been released twice already but complications arising from a fluid buildup on his spine had set him back each time. Stuck in a bed, not knowing what had happened after Nicky left town, the silence had eaten away at him. He only knew that the takings stashed in the bus hadn't gone into the safe. Now there were two cars and a bus off the road and Fat Dave was turning a blind eye to his crew driving around town with their meters switched off. Jackie was bleeding money from the jugular and the shock of it all had reverted him into a near primeval state. He was just as likely to attack someone approaching his bed as he was to ignore them and stare blankly at the wall.

Detective Gerry Brehony pulled a stool up and a female police officer stood inside the door of the semi-private ward.

'Jackie,' the detective began, 'are you feeling any better than you look?'

'You better be here to tell me that ye found that hoor

and me money.'

'Not exactly.' Gerry Brehony, a veteran of the town's force, had had a busy morning. 'We got an anonymous phone call, from a town in France, of all places. Auch—y'ever hear of it?'

Jackie's nose screwed up and his bottom lip stuck out. A badly shaved gorilla would have had a friendlier profile. He didn't like cryptic sentences. In fact, Jackie didn't like anything at all.

'Nah, me neither,' Brehony continued. 'Had to Google it, and I hate Googlin—middle of nowhere. Well, you wouldn't believe the wild allegations the caller made against you.'

Jackie's beady eyes flicked back and forward. 'Was it that Nicky cunt? He stole three grand off me, ye know? I wouldn't pay much heed to a thievin bastard like that.'

'We don't know who it was, Jackie, that's why we call them anonymous phone calls. But he seemed to know you alright. Told us a story about a girl that got picked off the street and locked up in a shed with a chain around her neck for a week. Fed dog food, raped, drugged and dumped in a ditch on the sand flats, nothing but the rats for company.'

Jackie's eyes were fixed on the far wall now.

'Sick world, Jackie.' Brehony rubbed his furrowed brow and his tired eyes were red around the lids from having seen more than he wanted to see that morning. 'We got an emergency warrant and we turned your house over for the last four hours. I can confirm—present injuries aside—that you're not a well man.'

Jackie's scum-caked mouth cracked open.

'Shush now,' the detective said, 'ye have the right to remain silent. The videodisk we were told to look for was located and the girl on it has been positively identified as Flora Mac Carthy. The location of the video looks a lot like the sheds on your property and the animals used in the film are also yours. I'm gonna go out on a limb and suggest that at least one of the voices in the background is you.'

A long, slow gurgle escaped Jackie's throat as his mouth slowly closed again.

'We also found a Claddagh ring in the dirt in your shed. Showed it to her half-sister in London. Skype—did ye ever hear of that? Didn't know she had a sister, did ye?'

Jackie's bottom lip was trembling.

'She said the ring belongs to the wee girl, alright. Says she gave it to her years ago—in better times. Remember those, Jackie? Better times? Something sad about that phrase when you use it in a context like this. Well, that's what the sister said and she's some kind of a teacher, so who am I to argue?'

Brehony stood up and straightened himself. 'Better times Jackie—I think you've already had yours.'

He fingered through the assorted clutter on the bedside locker and there were some rosary beads wrapped around a bottle of lemonade. He retrieved them and tossed them onto Jackie's chest. 'Ye better start praying—cos there's no god where you're goin.'

END OF THE ROAD

Toady and Anna had reached the main visitors car park at three. Tucked in behind the dune, it sprawled away beneath the shade of the trees. They sat in the car in a secluded corner and Anna talked quietly as she amused herself.

If it were the high season the car park would have been full. A line of cars and coaches would have been backed up a mile out along the approach road with police controls everywhere. But this early in the season, they had simply driven straight in and parked.

They had come directly to the dune from Auch, having first stopped off in the town so Toady could make a cash withdrawal and fill up with petrol. Toady had gifted Anna some essentials as they walked around the small supermarket, hand in hand. She squeezed his fingers to bring his attention to a display. He pointed at the shelf and she nodded her head when he had the right item in his sights. She kissed his bruised knuckles and sighed each time he pulled an item from its place and dropped it in the little basket—a hairbrush, pretty ankle socks and a warm top with pink fleece lining. Then some make-up and sunglasses and a leather purse to put them in. A hypnotic flow in the sequence made him want to forget whatever he was thinking and just spend the afternoon making her happy with small ritual strokes of materialism. Whenever he turned to her she was looking back in seductive anticipation, willing him to imagine what she wanted next. He was afraid to do that in case he got swept away.

She applied black lipstick to her mouth in the wing mirror and used a pencil to colour her three moles blacker as she hummed tunes to herself and passed occasional comments to her dead dog. Then he made a lengthy call on a payphone as Anna watched from the car with little round shades balanced on her forehead.

The drive from Auch to Pilat was spent playing Anna's game of sharing intimate secrets and for the first and only time in his life Toady shared the story of his sexual inculcation while she stroked his thigh.

'Raped,' she sighed on the faintest of smiles. 'But would you change a single thing about it, Tomas?'

'No,' he said after a while. 'In fact—I think I loved her. Still do.'

As the moment of their separation drew nearer he felt butterflies in his stomach and found it hard to breathe as she insisted that there remained only one more thing that she wanted from their relationship.

'I want you to remember me in this way. I want to paint a picture of us together, for our future.'

'We have a future?'

She tapped him on the side of the head. 'When you are forty, fifty and sixty we will have a future. Whenever your wife can't make you come, when you are alone in bed. Every time you go hard, remember me, remember this.' She worked her hand up and down.

'You don't need to do it, I can remember enough to last me a lifetime.'

"I want to do it.' Her head went down.

'Wait,' he grabbed her, 'I'm not comfortable with this.'

'You have the girliest sex talk I ever heard.'

'Anna!' He pulled her face up beside his and darted glances out the window at the empty car park then back into her black eyes. 'I don't need anything else to remember you by. Jesus—you make my head spin just looking at you.'

'Stop panicking, I don't want to keep you,' she

whispered into his mouth. 'I just want one more bite before I give you back.'

'Wait—I mean it!' He took her hand and held it away and she slowly sat back in her seat. He fixed himself as she watched him like a scheming cat.

'Never got turned down before.'

'I'm surrendering—please—have mercy.'

'You're afraid she'll see us together, aren't you?'

'A bit.'

'You really think she's here?'

'Maybe.' He pointed at her face. 'I caught you out again.'

'How?'

'That expression, you haven't practiced it properly, it's funny—I like it.'

She frowned. 'Are you being mean to me now?'

'I could never be mean to you. I'm telling you that you're perfect and I won't forget you, ever.'

Her eyes sparkled from under her fringe and she bit her lip. 'Do you love me?'

'Yeh,' he laughed, 'like a kid loves explosions.'

'Seriously—tell me.' She grabbed him by the shirt. 'Could you love a crazy woman like me?'

He reached over and cupped her cheek in his hand and kissed the other one. 'I already do.'

She held him there for a moment in silence then let him go and turned her face to the world outside.

'So, what are you going to do?'

She gazed into the endless trees. 'Firstly—have a memory blackout. Then—report my missing husband to the police and inevitably endure a certain amount of sadness while I make some insurance claims. And after that—' she raised her finger, 'I will buy a little white dog and call her Sukie.'

She pulled the door lever.

'Wait, don't go yet. We can go up there together.'

'Now now, Tomas, be careful. If she's not there I might

have to eat you alive.' She made her hands into claws and snarled a grin.

'No,' he objected. 'I mean we can all be friends, spend more time together. Shelley would like that. We can take you somewhere. I'll drive you to Germany if you like.'

'How beautiful.' She stroked his chin. 'But I think I'll walk for a while. Maybe hitch when my leg hurts.'

She reached into the little pocket on her hip and produced two small pills. She popped one in her mouth and dropped the other in his hand.

'What is it?'

She tapped her head. 'It's the end of the road, Tomas.'

'What does it do?'

'Depends on what you find there.'

He made her take all the cash he had then she stood on her toes and squeezed him around the neck. 'Stop crying—you're worse than a woman.'

'Anna,' he called after her as she walked backwards away from him. 'Don't you want to see the dune?'

'Saw it before, it was nice.' She spun in a semi circle and kept walking.

'Anna.' She turned around again and he could see her beautiful smile even from that distance. 'Maybe I'll see ye around?'

'Definitely.' Her voice was faint. 'Don't worry, Tomas, she'll be there—I would be.' He could barely hear her words now. 'Stay away from the ghosts and don't do anything stupid.'

'There's nothing stupid left to do,' he called through his hands.

She dissolved into the golden light that danced through the canopy and he never saw her again.

For hours he sat on top of the yellow crest as time eroded hope and eventually Anna's pill found its way into his mouth. When the sun started dipping toward the horizon, loneliness and despair drove him down the hill and into the trees. Stumbling and tripping in the heavy sand, he found a place to hide until the shadows grew long across the beach and he watched as whispering ghouls emerged to patrol the space between him and the giant crashing waves. Mossy was standing in the shadows nearby, watching him trying to bury his head under his arms.

From the dark spaces, deep in the trees, he could hear a young girl whimper and beg for mercy. As the night bled out from under the canopy, the dogs started closing in, snarling and yelping, unseen in the bushes as they prepared to attack. He rocked back and forward tightly gripping his skull while it threatened to crack with the pressure. The bloodcurdling howl of a man being disemboweled came from up the hill, then his lonesome voice, crying for his wife on his dying breath. Her name haunted the stillness.

Toady curled up in a ball, defeated by terror, while rapists, murderers and torturers convened all around him. He called for his mother, but the gates of hell were no place for a saint. So he ran, pulling his clothes off, then tripping and tumbling as he tried to look back over his shoulder. Plunging into the sea, he disappeared into the thundering waves—and that was the last anyone ever saw of the grey man.

POSSESSED

The sound of waves crashing stirred her from her troubled dreams. Her sticky eyes opened to a bright blur and a familiar pain in the roof of her skull. She lay still as her eyes became accustomed to the brightness of the endless, blue sky. Large birds circled high overhead. A cool breeze licked the curls across her mouth and she smelt the ozone of the sea. The lonely call of the gulls came on the sound of crashing surf. She eased herself up and a quilt fell from her chest to her lap. A quick check told her she was unmolested, her clothes intact and her shoulder bag beside her. There were some people not far away by the water's edge, laughing and playing in the wash. A figure approached her out of the blur then knelt by her side. It was a young girl, fifteen at the oldest, with deeply tanned skin, sky blue eyes and bleached blonde hair. A necklace of beads and shells hanging on her bare chest, she spoke with a harsh Australian twang.

'Good day, I was told to git ye a drink o watuh when ye woke.' She slipped her a plastic bottle. Shelley emptied half of it into her without a word.

'Thusty wuhk, ay?'

'Where am I?' Shelley gasped.

'Pilat,' the girl said and Shelley shook her head. She pointed past Shelley's ear causing her to twist around and take note of the sand bank behind her, then she raised her head to see a mountain of gold and white sloping endlessly into the sky.

'Giant sand dune?'

'Reckon so—don't you?'

'How did I get here? Who brought me?'

'We did—me and my folks.'

'Where are they?'

The young girl pointed straight up in the sky.

'Dead?' Shelley whispered, shaking her head.

The girl took a fit of giggling, then reached out and put her fingertips under Shelley's chin and tilted it up till she was looking straight at the sky. Her vision had cleared and the birds she saw hovering earlier came into sharper focus. Blue, red, orange, stripy green and indigo parachutes wafted high above and the figures of people dangling beneath, swinging on twists and turns as they drifted higher on the thermals rising off the back of the giant sand dune in the early morning sun.

'That's them.'

Shelley dropped her head between her knees. 'God help me, I can't remember a thing.'

'Yih, Jeez, you wuh loike an escaped lunatic.'

The girl rooted in her pocket and produced a phone. 'My mum told me to show it to ye whin ye woke up.' She handed her the phone with a video playing. 'She said, it might help ya understand how demented yah.'

Shelley took the phone and brought it under her bowed face in the shadow of her hanging hair. There she was, at a bar, roaring. It was hard to make out the exact words over the laughter and the retorts coming from those out of sight. But the general theme of her rant revolved around the premise that Australian men were faggots, prisoners and wife bashers and that there were no real men left in the world.

'That was only six in the avvo, then ye got us all thrown out of that bah. One of the young guys said something to ye and ye went flippin bonkahs.'

The girl tinkered with the phone. 'Then ye stahted croyin.' Sure enough, there she was, balling in tears and bubbles of snot on some woman's shoulder. 'That's me mum. She said she could feel the huht pourin outa ye, said that yid been through a terrible wrongin.'

Then she was fast-forwarding the playback. 'Then ye asked us to take you with us to the dune.' She held up the phone again. 'Hih yah in the van—when ye went apeshit.'

Wild screaming as the picture hopped around and then she came into focus, her teeth clenched, the sinews on her neck stretched to breaking point as she writhed in torment. Two men strained to keep her under control, one each side. 'You're not gonna rape me,' she roared at the screen, '—I've got AIDS—I've got Ebola, you fuckers.'

'We nearly crashed at one stage. Vinny had to put a Judo hold on ye till ye passed out.' A short scene of her in a headlock turning purple, still trying to scream, but only managing to croak. 'Then ye calmed down.'

A sequence of her kneeling in the shallow sea, fully dressed. Big waves breaking and rolling in up to her waist. Two women kneeling beside her, one hugging her around her shoulders, the other holding her face.

'Lit it out, Dahlin.'

'Scream ye haht out, princess.'

And she was letting it out. Wailing like a woman giving birth, with the water bubbling around her, throwing her hands to the air then beating the water with her fists.

'Then ye went unconscious.'

A scene of her lying in a heap in the flickering campfire light, snoring with her mouth open and people singing songs in the background.

'Dear God almighty, forgive me, but I don't remember any of that.'

'Mum did a Biyani, said ye had a Malingee followin ya.'

Shelley shook her head frowning. 'I had no idea, I'm mortified.'

'She thinks it's gone now.'

'Thank God, tell her I said thanks, and your dad, oh—those judo men too.' She started to gather her stuff. 'What time is it?'

'Nine-thuddy.'

Shelley groaned and stood up.

'Wait.' The girl ran to the pile of effects arranged in the sand, surrounded by windbreakers and shrouded beneath a cluster of parasols. She dived her head into a freezer box and came back with a drink bottle and handed it to her. 'Mum said to give ye one of these if you were goin—it'll see ye roight.'

'What's in it?'

'Ginger, mango, carrots, ginseng—stuff—ye can live on it. Mum's a Karadji, she knows about things loike that.' The girl dug into her pocket. 'She told me to give ye this too.'

The large, flat, brown pebble was smooth underneath with lumps on its back and felt cool to the touch. 'We call it an animal totem, a spirit guide. She's been saving it for the right puhsun.' Shelley slid it into her pocket.

'Thanks.' She backed off and waved.

'Thanks for the laugh,' the girl called, doing a little curtsy, 'yuh fanny.'

Shelley waved up at the distant shapes overhead that had climbed ever higher into the endless blue, where they now wheeled and soared in big circles like majestic eagles. She tipped forward with her hands on her knees and roared as she threw up on the sand. 'Oh—fuck me,' she gasped in between retches, pointing upwards. 'That's not natural.'

'I'll lettem know ye said so.' The girl smiled and waved and Shelley mouthed the word 'thanks', then slung her bag and walked away down the beach.

POINT BREAK

Out beyond where the waves break there is a sacred place that is quieter than the inside of a confession box. Silent reverence hangs over the water as it rises on the backs of giant monsters passing in the darkness beneath. They head for shore one after the other, determined to take another bite from the world in a timeless war. The only way back to land from here is to ride in their open jaws.

He had spent most of his energy getting out this far, thrashing in the foaming break at first, before remembering to dive under as the waves battered past on the surface. Then further out, giant black walls surged towards him and he pulled his way up their faces, punching through the curling lip at the crest before plunging into the trough on the far side, only to see the next one loom towards him. The low rumbling of the break faded behind him as he made it further out to sea until the quietness of the deep ocean reigned.

Now his arms were heavy and he was cold. His teeth were locked and his temples ached as another big set came and lifted him high on the swell so that he could just about see the beach through the veil of spray, fading into the last scraps of daylight. He dipped his head underwater and rubbed his face. His arms were beginning to fail him; if he didn't go soon, he'd sink like a stone.

'If I did wrong then judge me,' he called to the sea and the sky and anything else that might hear him. 'I'm not sorry.' He gasped and sank below the water, where for an instant he saw Shelley's face smirking at him, daring him to live or die in that moment, then blowing him a cheeky kiss goodbye. He came back up coughing for air with a belly full of salt water. He strained his eyes ashore again but this time could see nothing but darkness and spray.

'I don't want to die,' he spluttered, his lips just above the water. 'But I don't want to live in shame either—so you decide.' It felt like the sea had attached its weight to him and was pulling downwards on his dead legs.

He struggled to the edge of the surf and the first wave carried him aloft, holding him between the sky and the deep, then dropped him skidding down its face. It turned him over and the sea bit down hard, folding herself over him with the wings of a cold dragon. He rolled along with the tangling weed, twirling in bubbles, swiping his way through the darkness.

No light painted the sky, nor could he feel gravity telling him which way to kick to get back to the world. Not a scrap of mercy to protect the intruder from the brutality of the place. He writhed and clawed then clutched at cold air as he broke the surface and gasped a precious breath. But the sea crashed down on his head again and drove him deep, to the sand, but before he could get his feet under him the long tentacles of the undercurrent took him by his ankles over gravel and stones, back out to the silent depths and held him there. He kicked and flayed at the dark veil until it released him and he climbed with a desperate cry back into the dusk. A straight cliff of water stood poised above him as he tried to fill his lungs then toppling over and taking him straight to the sea floor with a million tons of water trying to bury him there for good.

In the passing of an instant everything stopped.

There he stood at the bottom of the ocean in perfect stillness. He gazed into a strange and eerie light that seemed to draw closer as the fear in his heart faded. An amazing tunnel was extending towards him, smooth shiny walls in the night. Reaching his hand out to touch it, he wondered if he were to die in that moment, where the force of life inside him would go. His heart bursting with unspent love and the unexpected happiness in his soul just disappearing in the deep. Two more handfuls of salt dissolving into the ocean on a world unable to justify its own existence.

He heard a rushing sound as the sea inhaled again. Then a wall of sand and stones blew him off his feet and sent him back out, his last conscious thought escaping him in a long trail of bubbles.

'You can stop fighting now, Thomas, my love—it's over.'

He was swept away in strong arms that rocked him sweetly and held him to the sky under cold seething air. They rolled him through the grey and green hollows all the way down to the dark floor where he was gathered again from the seabed with armfuls of glittering shells and smooth pebbles. Then squeezing him till his chest burst with fire and the promise of cold heavy lungs already seemed like a sweet memory. He was dragged away through the swirling sand clouds.

He found himself back on a cold Halloween night, shivering in his short pants, while he had watched a crime unfold. The McNally brothers had just thrown Danny Redmond in the river. Tied in a sack like a mongrel, it was supposedly a joke, but the eldest brother had other plans. They left him there for the best part of five minutes, till the squirming stopped. They were arguing on the slipway about leaving him for the crabs as Toady watched them from the shadows at the end of New Street.

In an uncharacteristic fit of common sense, the youngest brother jumped in, grabbed hold of the rope and dragged it up the slope. He untied the cord and they all stood back and watched. After a minute the sack began to stir and out crawled Danny Redmond, silent as death and white as a ghost. Streaks of blood ran down his face from where he'd pulled lumps of hair out of his head to stop himself from breathing in the saltwater. He walked past the McNally Brothers without so much as a word, then past where Toady had slunk back into the dark laneway. Silent as a ghost, he crossed the street to his home and never spoke a right word again. After that, he turned up in school less and less and nobody ever knew why.

Toady and his mother were cornered on the steps of their home not long after by Danny Redmond's mum. She was trying to make sense of how her son went out the door a happy boy and came back some kind of half dead zombie with holes in his head. Like a vomit reflex Toady started talking, but before he had made a sentence, his own mother pulled him back up the steps and through the front door.

'Thomas, my love, come with me.' She stood him by the door under the staircase and knelt before him. 'Whatever it is you think you can do to change the way something is—ask yourself this first: Are things going to be better afterwards—or am I just looking for attention from the world?'

She took hold of him by the clothes on his chest and twisted till they were tight around his neck and shoulders.

'Do you want to be the next Danny Redmond?' She searched deeply in each of his eyes then pulled his face to her cheek and whispered in his ear. 'Nobody wants to know what happened to Danny—especially not his mother.'

She let him go, then pointed at his chest.

'Swallow it—and keep swallowing it—for the rest of your life.' She pushed him away with her fingertip until he was in the shadows under the stairs. 'This is not punishment, my love, this is how the world works. Make silence your friend, Thomas. Make the shadows your home, and be safe within them.'

She closed the door on him and left him in the dark for the afternoon until he was no more than a shadow himself.

When he came out, he was cured of the need to talk about what he'd seen done to little Danny Redmond. He was cured of the need to talk about many other things that he hadn't even seen yet.

The lonely sound of a gull came crying in the darkness. The rushing water lifted him a little and nudged him further onto the sand. Bubbles of wash spun tiny grains of shingle around his feet. He coughed salt water onto his face then rolled to his side and vomited the rest into the sand and lay back. The intense pain in his head bled out of his nose as warm water.

I'm alive, he thought and felt a smile tugging at his lips, his breath shallow on the warm air.

"Christ boy, but you're easily pleased." He heard her voice on the waves.

He tried to laugh and found he couldn't, but the smile on his face was the sweetest one he'd ever felt. For the first time since he was a kid, he only had the one thought in his head and it was still the same one now as he'd had back then. "Find Michelle Kelly, and make her kiss me." The wonderful simplicity of it felt like coming home after being away for a long time and walking through your own front door to find everything just the way you left it, and somehow better.

He raised his head from the sand to look up and down the empty beach then rolled onto his knees. The world spun, then steadied, as he staggered to his feet. He didn't know how long he'd been in the water but his muscles were exhausted and his legs shook beneath him.

To his right he could see land rise away into dense trees. In front and behind him the beach arced out of sight around a slow bend. Loud barrels of ocean crashed hollow onto smooth sandbanks.

'End of the road,' he whispered.

He tried to walk but his knees folded and he went down on his face with a soft thud and a grunt.

'There's nothing stupid left to do.'

He sniggered into the sand and watched his hand as it was swallowed into the soft shore. He didn't move for a long time and when he did the stars were starting to show. He rolled onto his back and lay quiet as a child, as time was obliterated into the night and a million galaxies spun upwards into the sky. The trees on the hill behind him began to ring with insects, and night birds clung to the shadows. The rumbling breath of the waves washed air in and out of his lungs through the death of the night. By the grey light of dawn he found himself empty—a hearth cleaned of ashes, awaiting the flame.

RENDEZVOUS

Shelley ambled along the beach and as time passed, her head cleared. The tonic the young girl had given her was doing its job. At first the heat of the ginger burned her throat but then it warmed her chest and cleared her breathing. The sweet mangos perked her mood and she felt a growing sense of relief come over her as yesterday's destructive pessimism failed to rear its head. She was free, she had escaped and only now was it becoming clear how much of her subconscious had been devoted to panic management for the last two weeks.

She rested frequently and bid hello to the passing couples that started to appear as the morning wore on. She hiked out onto the deserted flank to avoid company and sat and watched the sea shimmer around silvery sandbanks drying in the sun far below. A mile away to her left, where she had come from that morning, the numbers of parachutes circling the shoulders of the golden beast had doubled. Half a mile away and high up to her right, she could see streams of people issuing over its rump. She sat alone and tiny among the undulating ribs of sand and took another large mouthful of the secret elixir and smacked her lips.

'There's only one way to make that better.' She reached into her bag and pulled out the remains of her vodka and emptied it in, then swirled it around and took another draft. She fetched a joint from her magic menstrual box and the moment was as good as it could get.

Toady sat on top of a picnic table and stared at the space that had swallowed Anna the previous afternoon. He sat for hours with his heart becoming lighter than he could ever remember, too light to make a difference to anything. His form became fluid in the endless day as it poured in on molten light through the leaves. To stop himself from dissolving into nothing he repeated her name from time to time.

Shelley.

In the distance, through the trees, a river of people came and went in an endless flow on the track that leads to the ridge of the Dune du Pilat, Europe's highest Sand dune at 110 metres above sea level.

Creeping incessantly inland at a rate of three metres a year, it swallows trees, roads and even houses. People's lives are disappearing under the belly of the rolling monster and at that rate of advance it might take a hundred thousand years to reach Germany. But in reality it will probably crash like a collapsing wave across the Southwest of France long after we've made ourselves extinct. Well...so said the crusty hippie with the skinny whippet, as Shelley shared a joint with them at the top of the dune. Then man and hound wandered off in a philosophical blur across the long ridge into the azure sky with a parting salute.

Shelley.

She gazed out to sea, the evening sun starting to turn the sand banks autumn gold, a cool breath of air bringing goose bumps to her bare arms while she hugged them around her knees and rocked back and forth.

'You should have made it here by now,' she whispered onto her arm. She had a premonition of herself scaling back down the mountain, going in search of the Australians in the dark. Then another vision of her sitting right there, with the sun descending into the sea, a giant ball of flames setting fire to a blistering red sky on a purple horizon. Her lonely silhouette set timelessly against a full moon as she kept her brave vigil on top of a shimmering moonlit mountain of silver.

'Fuck that,' she muttered, 'I'm gaggin for a drink.'

She pushed her shades up onto the top of her head then dipped into her handbag and checked her phone. It was after half six and the crowds on the hill had thinned considerably. The para-gliders were gone from the other end and she was still alone in the middle.

'Where am I going to go?' It occurred to her that she hadn't got a clue what to do if Toady didn't turn up. How had she let him convince her that this was even a plan?

'Thank you so much, Thomas Fucking Brody. How do I know I'm not sat up here like a twat and you're not off havin a party in Spain?' She gazed over the vast expanse of the Atlantic Ocean then shook her head and laughed aloud. 'Nah, you didn't run away to Spain, you're in love with me, boy, and I can wait. Just hurry up.'

'Shelley—you're talking to yourself again.'

Standing over her with his blue shirt licking at the breeze and his arms hung by his side was her man. Just as she'd seen him in her head a thousand times since she was a child, but now he had a face.

'Thomas?'

She stood up and stepped into him checking the contours of his face. He put his hands on her waist and she slid hers around his neck and he buried himself in her curls. Pulling her in he breathed her into his lungs with every inch of his chest.

'What kept you?' she sighed.

'I've been standing here for the last fifteen minutes,' he protested. 'I was starting to think I was dead.'

He squeezed her tighter and her fragrance swarmed his vision with vivid colours. He kissed her warm neck and she moaned and squeezed his head.

'I love you, Thomas.'

MAGICAL BLUE

They drove straight up the coast for two hours, barely talking, until the pine forests all around them fell into shadows and the clear blue sky to the west turned red over the treetops. They came to a village called Carcans, sitting on a quiet crossroads signposted for Carcans-Plage.

'It's a beach.' Shelley pointed down the road. 'Good enough for me, so long as I can get a drink and something to eat.'

When they arrived at the coast it was dark. There were campsites and cabins and a village of restaurants and cafés alive with people. Young people, tanned and happy, walked in the plaza flooded with light and music, and surrounded by sand dunes.

'This is what I'm talking about.' She found a stool at a bar and ordered two beers and a vodka and coke. Toady sat beside her and put his arm around her waist and pulled her close.

'There's something peculiar about this.' He pulled a confused expression.

She pushed his beer in front of him. 'What's that?'

'It's normal.' He gestured around. 'Me and you, at a bar. Jesus, I feel like a real person.'

She lifted her bottle. 'Here's to normal.'

The two of them emptied their beers in one go as they eyed each other on with encouragement. When she smiled her face lit up and he noticed she wasn't wearing a tap of makeup.

'You're so young, Shell.'

'Oh my God.' She put her hands to her face. 'I must look awful.'

'You're more beautiful than I ever remember you.'

'Shut up!' And it actually seemed as though she may have blushed.

They sat at a table and one by one ordered all items from the starters menu. Garlic bread, mussels, mushrooms, goujons, chicken wings, cheeses and salad. They worked their way down the list until they came to Frog's legs and Toady forbade them.

'Relax,' she laughed, 'they're frogs not toads.'

'Same thing,' he replied.

'Well, I'm not going to call you that anymore, it doesn't suit you now. I like Thomas.' She lit a smoke and leaned her elbows on the table. 'Answer me one question, Thomas, are they all gone? Is it over now?'

'Yeh, but ye don't wanna know.'

'Nope.' She picked up her beer and they clinked bottles. 'I don't care.'

They got drunker and the night was warm and Shelley wanted to go to the beach, so he pulled the blanket from the car and found a brand new sleeping bag in the boot. They were overcharged for a bottle of wine at a bar before finding a long boardwalk that took them through the dunes until they overlooked the long straight beach. A few people sat by the water's edge or paddled in the wash. The moonless sky cast no light and it took a few minutes for their eyes to become accustomed to the cool white radiance of the sand.

'Where does this beach go?'

'Spain.'

'We could walk all the way to Spain from here—on a beach?'

'Come on,' he said. They walked towards Spain for a half-mile until they could hear nothing but the sound of the sea and the occasional call of a seagull, invisible in the dark sky. They spread the blanket in the sand at the edge of the dunes and she retrieved the last of her joints while he struggled with a cheap corkscrew. He swigged it by the neck and handed it to her and she swapped it for the joint.

'I wonder is the sea warm like the sand.'

'Off ye go,' he dared her.

She pulled off her top and stood bravely in her bra facing out to sea before kicking off her sandals and letting her loose bottoms fall to her ankles.

'Jesus you're not goin in, look at the size of the waves.'

She went over to him on her knees and took hold of his belt and tugged it open.

'I'm wet enough already.' She took his hand and slid his fingers over the moist fabric between her thighs.

'Thomas,' she whispered in his ear. 'How much do you love me?'

'I don't know.' His voice barely came out.

She pulled his shoes off then tugged his jeans down by the legs and pushed him back on the blanket till he rested on his elbows.

'Why don't you know?'

Straddling his shins she pulled his shorts down to his knees. Then working him with slow strokes she moved herself into position before sliding onto him. Once she had it all inside, her head hung limply and she sat calmly with her eyes closed, marihuana smoke trailing from her nostrils and a bottle of wine in her hand. She didn't move for a long time and he just stroked her hips and pressed her soft thighs with the air from the sea cooling the sweat on his chest and brow. He pushed up her bra to release her breasts and squeezed them until her hips began to move in time with him.

'Why don't you know, Thomas?'

She put her hand on his chest and forced him down then leant back and ground herself harder onto him.

'It's too much,' he said. 'I can't see the end of it.'

When he started to grunt, she lay forward with her hair covering his face and settled into a sliding motion, her cheek resting on his. Her breath was soft on his lips. 'What does it feel like?'

'Everything,' he whispered. 'It feels like my whole life.'

Wrapping one arm around her, he forced her down to met his thrusts. With a fistful of her hair he pulled her head back until he had her frozen in his embrace. They came together and he didn't move until she stopped shuddering. The passion seeping from his rigid body back into his heart, his muscles eventually letting go of her, she lay back down lifeless on top of him.

He felt her cheek, warm and wet against his, her breath quivering. He couldn't tell if she was laughing or crying. They kissed and stayed like that until he went soft inside her.

'Shell,' he said and couldn't stop himself laughing a little.

'Brody,' she sighed in his ear. 'Did nobody ever tell you to quit while you're ahead?'

'—but.'

'Now's your big chance.' She kissed him on the lips.

His mouth was open as he searched her face with words lodged in his throat. With her finger and thumb she pinched his lips together then kissed them. She got up and walked away to the water's edge while he watched, then he followed her.

A ghostly light hung over the world, save for the glow of a couple of small fires back up the beach towards the village. The only sound was the crash of the waves and the breath of its retreat over sand and pebbles.

'Oh my god, look at this.'

She stamped her foot on the damp sand and it lit up in a thousand blue sparkles. He thought he was seeing things. She did it again and on impact the sparkles scattered out from her foot like a universe expanding into the dark. She walked along the water's edge and each time her foot came down a new universe of tiny stars was born, shimmering then fading to black again. Reaching into the wet sand she pulled out a handful and held it up to his face and worked it through her fingers. She was a goddess and a galaxy was pouring from her fingertips. When it hit the sand below it flickered and died.

'It's magic,' she said and took another handful.

'It's that luminous algae stuff.'

'Does that mean it's not magic?'

'No.'

They went back to the dunes and she got dressed and threw the blanket over her shoulders and he sat down behind her and put his arms around her.

'I decided while I was waiting for you on top of that sand dune—I'm going back.'

'When?' His stomach went into a knot.

'Straight away. Tomorrow maybe.'

'Why for God's sake? What about this? Aren't you happy here?'

'Yes, but I can't get all the rubbish out of my head. I need to go back and deal with it. Get it over with. Close up the house, see Maeve, tell her what's going on. Then we can come back here and get a place, down the south.'

'We?' He hugged her close.

'Yeh, you and me, boy. We'll do something. Something brave.'

After a while the foam on the sea started to glow.

'Did you see that?' he whispered in her ear.

The tail ends of the surf glowed bright blue then washed out neon into the break. Then a whole barrel lit up, two hundred metres long, as though a switch had been flipped in the basement of the deep.

'It's getting stronger,' she sighed.

They sat for an hour, drinking wine in near silence until every wave rolled in neon blue and electrified the beach in front of them.

'This is the happiest I've ever been in my life.'

THE HONEYMOON

Pale, early morning light showed miles of endless beach evaporating into a sea haze in the distance. Here and there the tiny figures of people moved like lost ants on the grey sand. The sound of a dog barking came on the breeze and Shelley stirred and lifted her head.

'Hello,' he said from close by.

'Slept on the beach—I'm a free spirit,' she said shaking sand from her hair. 'Must tick that one from my bucket list.' They stood up and brushed themselves down.

'Where did you sleep last night?' He tapped sand from her ass.

'Ehh—on the beach,' she remembered. 'Okay so, I'm a tramp.'

'How do you feel?'

'I'm cold and I'd murder a cup of coffee, and a bed.' And with that she grabbed him by his shirt. 'Ooh Jesus, I'd love to get into a bed. Let's do that tonight. Before we leave France, get a hotel with a big four-poster bed and a Jacuzzi. Order room service. What d'ye say?'

'You had me at bed.'

'I'm bursting for a piss, wait up.'

She went into the dunes, pulled down her things and squatted. While a stream gushed out of her, an ice-cold shiver ran up her spine right to the tip of her head, like a ghoul had run a cold dead finger up her back. She spun left and right. 'Who's there?' she called over her shoulder. She was still pulling her jeans up as she stumbled out to where he was waiting.

'What's up? You're white as a ghost.'

She grabbed his hand and pulled him away down the beach. They got takeaway coffee and croissants from a stall and strolled back to the car while he considered a pocket map he'd just bought.

'I see a journey on a boat in your future.'

'No shit. I'm not even thinking about it. I'll only get depressed.'

'Not that, there's a big river in our way.' He showed her the map. It's either that, or all the way around through Bordeaux.'

'Not a chance. I have a feeling I'm not welcome in a few places back there and I don't want to find out which ones.'

They drove with the windows down and French music playing through endless scrappy pine forests in shimmering white sand and small towns sat on quiet crossroads with few people to see them pass. By noon they had reached the ferry at Point Grave. They waited in lines and Shelley sat on the boot and soaked up the warmth radiating from the hazy sky and they watched cars, bikers, cyclists and foot passengers of all ages and descriptions gather for embarkation.

'C'mere, tough guy.' She wrapped her two legs around his waist and pulled him close and kissed and hugged him until all he could do was smile.

They enjoyed a tranquil twenty minutes sitting on the deck, watching the turbulent brown waters of the Garonde swirl by underneath. Bright orange cargo ships slipped past into the vast estuary, headed inland to Bordeaux. He remembered the night he'd spent in captivity on the banks of the steamy river and it gave him a twist in his gut. Mossy was now dead and Arno motionless in a hospital bed and the river rolled on regardless.

'C'est la Guerre,' he whispered.

'What?' Shelley piped up, but he just shook his head.

Back on dry land they stopped in Rayon and had lunch.

'Let's just get up to within easy shooting distance of the ship and we'll get a hotel—then we'll party.' She winked.

'Sounds good to me.' He finished his coffee. 'Never been to a grown-ups party before, not unless you count funerals.'

Ile du Noirmoutier, a small island joined to the mainland by a bridge and a causeway, was the last stop on the coast before they would have to head inland to cross the Brittany peninsula on the passage north. Shelley liked the sound of it and didn't particularly care, so long as they had room service. They arrived over the crest of a long, high bridge that overlooked the island. A bank of mist could be seen rolling in from the sea and swallowing the western shoreline as they descended the long slow arc to land. The island was small and flat. Salt marshes and mud flats breathed steam into the afternoon air, and wisps of cold fog crept over the land.

'What's that?' She pointed to a large billboard at the side of a road with the picture of a car submerged in water and big red letters in German, French and English warning of imminent catastrophe.

'Is this island safe, does it sink or something?'

He laughed and pointed out the side road that became a causeway running over a wide sand flat, back to the mainland. 'I can only presume that the sea must cover it.'

'They don't seem too worried.' She pointed at the hundreds of people wandering the misty wilderness with buckets in hand.

'Mussels and periwinkles, we used to gather them from the river when the tide went out across the road from my house. Wanna try it?'

'Collecting sea slugs?' She pointed out the front window. 'Jog on, boy.'

They carried on to the end of the island and the town, with a large white castle at its centre.

'Wanna see a castle?'

'You're like a kid on holidays,' she laughed. 'I see it,

thanks. Onwards! I want a bath and a vodka and if you clean yourself up you never know what might happen for the rest of the evening.'

'Say no more.'

They followed signs for a hotel, down a long leafy road, past tree-shrouded gardens with chalets and villas. They arrived at a grand old building nestled in trees overlooking a crescent beach. A dilapidated pier projected into the mist surrounded by still water. On a cool, grey Monday afternoon there was nobody to be seen. A light drizzle hung on the air as he pulled their few things from the back seat then stood a moment, facing out to the sea.

Shelley wasted no time in heading in the front door. 'Bags, garcon!' she shouted over her shoulder. 'Oops! Not you, sweetheart,' she cooed to the man behind the desk.

They took the bridal suite as it was the only one that met the specification, with a four-poster bed, a Jacuzzi and a bar. As soon as she saw it she shrieked and slammed the door in the porter's face behind her.

'Thomas Brody,' she squealed, 'I love you!' She crossed the room oblivious to his humble apologies at the doorway. Then she was behind the bar while he carried the bags to the bed.

'Black Russians all round?'

He fell prostrate on the bed with his arms outstretched and released a long muffled expletive into the covers.

'Get me room service,' she shouted, a cocktail shaker in her hand and fag dangling from the corner of her mouth. 'Pronto—I want a tray full of chicken wings and chips up here before my ass hits that bed.'

An unintelligible string of noise came from where he lay, face still buried in the covers.

'Fuck that,' she shouted. 'What am I like? I want caviar and truffles—whatever that is.' She clicked her fingers in the air. 'Do it, bitch!' She swaggered her way to the bed, laughing at the sight of Brody still waffling into the sumptuous duvets.

The two of them reclined on the pillows for a long time and drank their cocktails and anything they said was harmless banter, making fun of each other or everyone else. They kissed and he fondled her before she squirmed away from him. He went to grab her but she dodged him and he fell back on the pillows.

'Next time I get hold of ye, you're never getting away from me again.'

'Better have that bath while I can so—ye can get in after a while.'

She went to the bathroom and started her bath while he opened the balcony window to watch the small bay succumb to the bank of fog. Running water echoed spaciously on marble tiles and steam swirled at the French windows where the lace curtains sighed on cold sea air.

When the bath was filled she came out pulling her top off and could see no sign of him anywhere. 'What the fuck boy? You're letting the cold in.' She walked to the edge of the balcony and peered out over the multi-coloured roofs of the beach huts. There he was, standing solitary at the end of the promenade, dissolving in the mist.

'Thomas,' she called to no response. 'Brody,' she cried.

He was motionless and grey like the fading posts of the pier itself.

'Toady!' she roared, two hands to her mouth and he looked back and waved.

'What are ye at, ya clown?' Her voice seemed dead in the thick air and his came back so distant.

'It's my mum—she's here. I just saw her.'

'Ah here—did he just say that?' She shook her head and mumbled, 'Don't get weird on me now, boy, not with the night I have planned.' She turned to the warmth of the room when a shiver ran up her back and made the skin at the crown of her head tingle so fiercely that it hurt. 'Jesus!' she gasped and spun around. 'What is that?' Down in the trees at the start of the pier, someone moved in the shadows.

Toady was heading back for the room. He'd definitely seen his mother from the balcony, but now there was just the cold dampness of the mist and the feeling that he had become detached from the world. The hotel seemed far away, painted on veils of grey, decaying in the lifeless air. In front of him emerged the lean figure of a man from the gnarled trees. He was wearing a long Mac, much too short in the sleeves, with streaks of dried black blood scrawled down the front to the belt. He advanced, the features of his face impossible to discern. One hand in his pocket, the other tucked inside the coat, he wheezed through his nose and the air seemed to stick in his throat. His face could be seen now as a mess of swirling blotches, red and purple skin, cracked and bruised. His whole right cheek was swollen into a brown and black mound. A sickly, sweet smell preceded him on the salty air.

'What's the problem?' came a voice, hissing from the side of his mouth. 'Don't recognise your old partner?'

Toady backed away, shaking his head. 'How?'

'This is what a man looks like after he's been shot in the face and set on fire.'

'No!' He pointed at the ghoul. 'You're dead.'

'Crawled out in a screamin ball of flames, had to roll in the snow and gravel. Have you any fucking idea of the pain?'

'This isn't right—you're not real.'

A dull thud sounded and Toady felt a punch in the gut that winded him.

'Is that convincing enough for ye?'

Toady was watching his shirt turning red, his mouth opening and closing on empty air.

'You have sixty seconds, Brody, but nothing you say is gonna save your life.'

A cushion dropped from under his coat and he produced the pistol from his pocket and held it by his side.

'Looks like you're gonna see your precious Flora before me. Tell her I said sorry. She wasn't supposed to die—not like that anyway.'

Just then Shelley came out of the trees running and the vibrations in the wood alerted Nicky to her approach just a second too late. He spun around, but she was on him with all her momentum and pushed him full force, tipping him over the handrail. Feet in the air, he somersaulted backwards and down into the water. Toady stood still, blood leaking through his fingers as she grabbed hold of him, shouting through a veil of silence He watched her face contorting and wondered what she was saying?

'Mother, why did you betray me?'

'Now, Thomas—don't be afraid.'

Shelley had his arm around her shoulder and was pulling him along the pier as she fumbled in his pocket for the key.

'But you let him kill me. You led me straight to him.'

'Hush now, Thomas, I did it for you. He was going to come in the night and kill you both. I saved her—because I knew you would want that. Now you live on, inside her, and she can love you forever. It's the best I could do.'

He stumbled with her to the car and she shoved him in the passenger seat.

'What are we doing, Shell?' he grunted. He could taste the blood in his mouth.

'I don't know—running?' She grabbed his face and kissed it, then ran around to the driver's side and started the engine in time to see Nicky coming as fast as he could up the beach. She spun the wheels in reverse and skidded around in an arc, then out of the car park. They made it back to the town, but he was gasping, one hand on his stomach and the other on the dash.

'Christ, help me, I don't wanna die.'

She put her hand on his leg and turned to him, her mascara running black down her cheeks and her mouth moving, spitting tears into his face on silent words.

'I can't hear you, Shelley.'

'She says she's taking you to a hospital as soon as she

gets you off this island. She says you're not going to die.' He could hear his heart beating and the rush of the blood in his veins.

'Make me live, I beg you, Mother, give me life.'

'I already gave you life, Thomas, isn't it sweet?'

Shelley's lips were moving and her head swung from side to side as she pulled on the wheel and the town flashed by outside the window.

'What about mercy?'

'There is no mercy, son—you know that by now.'

They made it through the narrow streets and out the far side of the town, tearing away into the grey light of the salt marshes.

'Stay with me, boy,' her voice came in echoes. She grabbed his collar and shook it with her free hand. 'I saved you before, I can do it again.'

The giant billboard approached and she brought the car to a screeching stop opposite the causeway. A dead light hung over the sand flats, almost deserted of people now. The tide lapped over the middle section but the far end could just be seen emerging from the water, half a mile away.

'How deep can it be?' She was shaking her head, then her eyes were back in the mirror on the solitary set of headlights closing in fast out of the fog. Her voice rang clear. 'We're takin a shortcut, baby, hold on.'

She slammed her foot on the accelerator and the car catapulted out onto the causeway. A man at the side of the road waved his hands in warning then had to jump out of the way as they sped past.

'Hang in there, Toady, it's gonna be fine.' Her voice was retreating again and her face blurring through the tears in his eyes. She shouted at the windscreen and banged on the steering wheel, then water sprayed up like a fountain behind her. Through the window a huge white arc blasted out into space.

When he turned to her for the last time, she was just

smiling back. The freckles sprayed across her nose, her thick, red lips and her gold-speckled cheeks. Her beautiful red hair was full of wild flowers and glistening in sunlight. Though her lips weren't moving anymore, he heard her voice ringing through his head.

'What are you looking at?' Her green eyes pierced his soul in sudden agony.

'I'm looking at you, Shelley.'

He reached his hand out to touch her but it was falling down. Everything was falling away from him, melting into streaks, flowing through his outstretched hand until the car was racing through the water below. Two huge arcs of water sprayed out either side, like wings about to take off and carry them both away to the mountains—to Switzerland maybe. He could hear her reckless laughter now, rising up to him from below like seagulls circling upwards into the sky. There was a familiar feeling as someone took his hand and he wasn't afraid of anything anymore.

'Come now, Thomas, I told you I'd make it easy in the end.'

THE DIVORCE

Shelley sat in the parking area at the eastern end of the Passage du Gois for two hours. She held Toady's hand as it grew colder and the dead minutes inched by. Out on the causeway the sea had advanced and most of the road was now out of sight beneath the choppy, grey water. Banks of mist rolled past between the mainland and the island and all the while the two yellow headlights of Nicky's stolen car were disappearing beneath the rising tide.

'What do ye reckon, Brody? Will it wash him away?'

Nicky had tried walking, after the car had stalled, but the water had grown treacherous around him and twice he'd stumbled off the causeway into the deeper water before he gave up. He swayed through the grey tide to one of the safety towers that lined the route and climbed the steel rungs to the platform. And there he sat, like Frankenstein's monster cast adrift, his dark form hunched over against the biting cold of the sea mist.

A knock on the window startled her. Outside a handsome young man stared out at the scene on the causeway. Fifty metres away, at the water's edge, a handful of locals had also gathered to watch the spectacle unfold. He tapped on the window again. Shelley pushed the button and it whined its way down. He bent his head and looked in at the pathetic sight. With black streaks from her eyes to her chin, Shelley sniffed and sobbed on her breath. Toady sat motionless staring at the dashboard, his stomach and the lap of his jeans soaked red.

'Is your friend dead, Mademoiselle?'

She made no response or movement other than to shudder on her breath. He reached in past her and put his hand to Toady's neck to feel for a pulse.

'He is gone, Michelle, I am sorry.'

Lieutenant Richard Laurent of the Saintes Gendarmerie was on a day off when he got a call from a strange number he didn't recognise. It was the young Irish woman he had met in his father's bar nearly two weeks previously with a rush of words in his ear. 'Do you remember me? Red curly hair? You said you would take me to dinner? I need your help, me and my friend. I can help you. I know who attacked your father. I know where he is right now.'

He pointed out across the water as the last beam of the car's headlight was swallowed by the sea. 'There is only one? Where is the other one?'

'Dead,' she whispered.

'You are sure of this?'

She nodded.

'Good.' He squeezed her arm.

'My colleagues are here now, we will take care of it. I am not so sure this one will make it to the station either, it is a long way back to Saintes.'

'I don't know how he found us,' she said, staring out the window, 'it's impossible.'

'Non, Michelle, I am sorry, it is not. This is his car, you said?'

He reached in the window and pulled on the lever for the bonnet, then went to the front and lifted it. After a moment he came back and showed her a package the size of a brick containing wires and a screen and a mobile phone.

'Home made tracking device, GPS. All the young guys put them on their cars now. He could have found you in Siberia with one text message.'

'Shit, Thomas, why didn't you think of that?' She glanced across at him.

'Madame please, we need to get your friend away from here.'

'How is your dad? I liked him. He was the first French person ever to be nice to me.'

'He is paralysed, for the rest of his life. A life which will be decidedly shorter than it should have been before he met this animal that you have captured for me.'

An engine revved and a large vehicle pulled up behind him, the giant tyres taller than the roof of Nicky's car.

'Okay, we better go and pick up this piece of shit. You need to go home. Take my car and leave it at the port. I will take care of your friend here. We will send his body back after the investigation.'

'Investigation?'

'Yes, very straight forward. This man was abducted and shot by that bastard who caused trouble when we tried to apprehend him. I don't want to know what happened here, but you needn't worry about him talking to anyone. Your friend's body will be home within a week.'

'I can't leave him.' She shook her head. 'Someone has to be here to hold his hand, he can't be on his own.'

The cop scratched his head then turned and jumped onto the step of the amphibious rig. Over the noise of the engine she could hear a shouted exchange and a woman's voice growing agitated.

'Merduh, Lieutenant!' She jumped down from the cab and landed at the door beside Shelley. She was dressed in a navy jumpsuit with boots laced up to her shins. On a thick leather belt, she wore an assortment of weaponry. Her long black ponytail swung wildly behind her as she gesticulated and shouted over the din into his face. He put his hands on her shoulders.

'Daysolay shoo, but this lady needs your help,' he said and gestured in the window.

'Merduh, Richard,' she punched him in the chest, 'juh mon foo.'

He smiled in the window. 'This is Officer Suzanne

Devin from the local police, she will sit with your friend.' The young woman tipped her head and forced a smile.

'I am terribly sorry for your loss, but you definitely must go now. We must move him away from here, it won't suit to have witnesses. Please, thank you for your help and rest assured you will never be bothered by this bastard again.'

The woman cop smiled sympathetically as she tried to help Shelley out of the car but she didn't want to go. The Lieutenant grew impatient and they pulled her out and stood her against the car.

'Do not make a scene, Miss Kelly, just go quietly. Suzanne will take him to the bridge and we will meet her there. He will not be on his own, I promise. In three or four days when it is all processed, I will call you.'

He walked her away to his car and she struggled, but she knew he was gone and her limbs felt like lead as the Lieutenant pinned her to the door of his car and the female cop rolled by in Nicky's BMW.

'Allay drwot oh pohn,' he shouted, then opened the door of his silver Toyota and sat her in. 'Go and forget about this and live your life, I'm sure this is as your friend would want.'

'Are you going to kill him?'

He looked out across the causeway without emotion then tapped the roof. 'Adieu Michelle.'

He ran back to the rescue vehicle and climbed up to the door and with a puff of smoke it set off into the water towards the distant steel tower.

That night Shelley went to the ferry port and discovered that the boat didn't leave until the next day. In a morose haze, she booked her ticket. She felt physically ill with the loneliness.

She had spoken briefly to Maeve on the phone, without telling her too much, and was going back to stay with her for a few days until she figured out what to do next.

Nothing worked inside her anymore.

Whilst driving the last hundred miles to the port from the island, her logic had become defunct and her emotions had thickened in her veins till her blood stopped. The crying also stopped and silence had taken over inside her head. Numbness had moved into her heart and the creeping mist of the island had somehow seeped into her pores, leaving her cold to the bone.

Outside the ferry port, at the door of the car, she fumbled with the key.

'Three days,' said a husky voice with a rough French accent. Shelley spun around and was met with jet black eyes that fixed her with a primordial hatred so intense she could feel it trying to smother the last flicker of light in her heart.

'Since the night you tried to murder my son, I have dreamt of it. And since the night you murdered my husband I have seen it, with every waking moment. I knew you would run like a rat for the boat, sooner or later. Three days I have sat in that cold building, dreaming of this moment. And now it is here, at last. Now it is my turn to be heard. Now you will understand how I feel.'

'Ellen?'

She lunged her fist into Shelley's stomach with a grimace. Then again as she stared in her eyes, and yet again as the corners of her mouth turned downwards and she bared her teeth like a rabid dog. Shelley slid down the car onto the damp tarmac holding her side. She looked up at Ellen towering over her, then held out her hand, covered in blood. 'But I didn't kill anyone.'

'Too late, cunt.'

The words fell on her head as her face tipped sideways onto the ground. The last thing she remembered were the sandals being pulled from her feet and the sight of her pretty painted toenails lying in an oily puddle.

'Don't look at me, Thomas. Don't see me like this. Why weren't you here to protect me?'

She woke in the night to see Toady and his mother sitting by her bed. His mother was giving out about something and Toady patiently asked her to be calm. 'Don't wake her mum, she's dreaming about me, we're together.'

When she woke again it was morning and a young doctor sat on the edge of her bed.

'Where am I?'

'Cherbourg Hospital.'

'Am I okay?'

'You are exceedingly lucky,' he smiled. 'You were attacked by the craziest mugger ever. He stole your shoes but left all this money.' He held up a large Ziploc plastic bag and in it, was none other than Gucci.

'It is true to say that money has saved your life,' he said pointing at the purse. 'At least two of the knife blows struck the purse. The third one glanced and cut you quite seriously, it took five stitches. But all in all, it is a miracle. You will be out in two or three days.'

'But I died—I saw Toady.'

'Non, Madame, you fainted from shock.'

He pointed at the bags on the chair opposite. 'They arrived from Noirmoutier this morning, delivered by a Lieutenant of police, no less. You must be important.'

He took her wrist and felt her pulse. 'Okay, I am finished my shift now, so regrettably, I will not see you again, Madame Kelly. Au Revoir et Bon Voyage.'

AU BAR L'IRLANDAISE.

Seven months later, in a bar called L'Irlandaise, in the picturesque Mediterranean town of Collioure, a woman sits at the bar with a notebook open. She is putting the finishing touches to the research for her book.

Kiera Mc Carthy came home from London when they found her sister's killers, then came out here to meet the people who won justice for her and to hear their story.

'I will immortalise the dead in words, Thomas and Flora, it's the least I can do.'

She is studying the framed drawing of Michelle Kelly behind the bar as she sips from her coffee.

'That is the one you did in the campsite, I presume?' she asks the girl behind the bar, who takes a little bow.

'You are talented,' she notes, not lying one bit to the pretty woman who has now fixed her with a perfect smile. A single flick of her rich dark hair curling in to touch her shiny, black lips.

'I have just one question left that I want to ask her, can I go out to her.'

The woman behind the bar checks her watch and the suave looking man sitting close by stands up and says it is time for his dinner.

'Ah,' she says and smiles to Flora's sister. 'This is our local law enforcement representative, Inspector Pascal. I don't know what we did to deserve so much of his time. He watches so closely over us, we couldn't possibly be any safer.' His jaunty smile seems a little forced as he salutes and leaves.

'Okay, wait here. I think it is time for her to come in anyway, the afternoons are quite cool but she still loves to just sit there. Please wait, I will get her.'

She goes out the door and crosses the plaza and steps over the wall to the sand and approaches a deckchair where she bends down and speaks to a person out of sight. Then her hand reaches down to help the woman from her chair. Tossed red curls and big sunglasses provide warm colour on the grey canvas of a January afternoon. She makes her way back to the bar, the two friends holding hands all the way, talking and smiling until Shelley is standing in front of Flora's sister. Her face is sprayed with freckles. Her green eyes glinting gold flecks in the subdued light of the bar.

'Sorry for disturbing you this last time, but I just had one more thing that I thought readers of my book might like to know.'

Shelley smiles and sits back on the stool, her two hands gripping her swollen belly.

'Thomas Brody; can you remember the first time you saw him?'

'Of course.' She frowns, as though it was a silly question to ask. 'First day in primary school, I was holding a ball in the playground. Some of the bigger boys came over to me and slapped it from my hand. They were laughing, calling me names: Carrot-head, Duracell—the usual. One of them pulled my hair then another one pushed me to the ground. And that's the first time I saw him.'

'Where?'

'Standing over me, in a striped T-shirt and short pants, hands by his side. They were twice his size,' she said, smiling, 'but he just waded in with those fists—knocking heads.'

'What happened?'

'I got away and he took a beating for me. But later, when no one was watching, I gave him a kiss and he went red as a berry and asked me to marry him.'

They all laugh, Flora's sister is scribbling it down.

On the glass shelf behind the bar there's a carved wooden box and in it, the returning folds of Shelley's red scarf around the folded photo of a dead girl with red, curly hair and no name. Shelley doesn't wear the scarf anymore, she has no need to.

Sitting on top of the scarf is a flat, brown pebble, smooth underneath with small lumps on its back. Cool, almost wet to the touch. It's what they call a totem. Ancient people used them to invoke their spirit animal, to act as a guide between the living world and those who have gone ahead. It enables us to watch over those we love.

I watch her when she brushes her hair and she talks to me about my son and she wonders aloud what she's going to tell him about me.

I suppose there's not much to tell. I wasn't particularly clever or brave, and in the end I did some things you're not supposed to do. But I always stood up and took what was coming to me—and that's got to be worth something.

FIN

A Fistful of Salt

EPILOGUE

HENRI'S CONVICTION

THE SHORT STORY COMPETITION 2015.

*** SHORTLISTED***

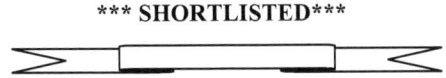

Older, and speaking a different language, his sweetheart Magdalena had come back from the dead in a campervan. Three days and nights without sleep and this conclusion had become his raison d'etre.

He could see the dark rings of his eye sockets at the periphery of his vision and he flinched when his clothes chafed against the large patches of raw skin on his ribs. His skull was being crushed in a formidable vice which tightened as his logic advanced, making it hard to concentrate, but the only alternative was sleep. When he slept, he saw a girl in a coffin, lips pursed for the wakening kiss, trapped in the frigid bosom of the earth awaiting her heroic rescue. But even in his dreams Henri had neither the academic nor the alchemical credentials to effect a resurrection. Frankenstein was a psychedelic butcher's story compared to this.

Upon their arrival at the campsite to commence work that Monday morning, they discovered the woman already ensconced at the end of a hillside track with the coy elegance of a mountain cat on a shaded lookout. A caravan, a table and three chairs with an empty wine bottle under one made for a modest lair with small garments adding pink and fuchsia pageantry to a pale fence rail. The fact that she seemed unaware of her previous life was to be expected, Henri reasoned, though it felt like broken glass in his heart when she did not recognize him staring intensely into her deep, green eyes early that first morning. In fact she had told him and the other boy where to stick their leaf-blowers.

It's not an easy thing to explain such a space-time anomaly but Henri would have to wrestle the evidence into logic then extrapolate his own weight in the equation. He needed to make this woman remember their past life if he was to have any chance of snatching his sweetheart back from the continuum.

He considered the direct approach: ask her had she dreamt recently of being pulverised by a cement truck and subsequently passing through a time tunnel; Henri's English was excellent, he anticipated no communication problems. But there was a practical weakness to the plan: the men would never allow it. They would throw him in the van, take him back to his room and Magdalena's dissolution in the ether would be a fait accompli shortly thereafter. He knew that their paths in time would not stay crossed for long and Magdalena's presence would be fleeting as is always the case with the purest miracles. But surely if nature had bent the rules of death this far it would also have an endgame, or her return made no sense; ergo, it was obvious that there had to be numerous undisclosed elements in the denouement. So he waited, and watched her closely; some might call it—stalking.

The day after Magdalena's roadside hanging, the event had been scrupulously described to Henri by the prison doctor who displayed an unreasonable zeal for the relaying of tragic reports. So now her final moments were as vivid in Henri's head as the sensual acts of an erotic dream and, perhaps, it was the same for the woman: the final trauma of her previous life etched somewhere in her unconscious as a reminder of who she really was and—critically—traces of him lingering there also.

Throughout the first night of her death (as his time on earth would thenceforth be recorded) he lay on his bed, her photo pressed to his face, the excruciating vice closing on his head and his nerves burrowing from beneath his skin into the captive light. In the immeasurable darkness of the corridors some of the boys would inevitably cry and the sound of it was like the futile whimper of a gateless hinge. But he was unwilling to share any of his agony. He had listened for the sound of his eyes blinking, or his tears sundering as they soaked into the pillow, until he eventually ran dry sometime just before dawn. He had given them nothing by the time the dead light of dawn came creeping across his ceiling once again, not so much as a quiver of his breath.

Within the granite walls of the Roussillon Juvenile Correctional Facility there is a metal bell that rings once every morning on the precise stroke of six awakening the beast with a faint groan followed by a chain of dull explosions drawing closer as doors slam, confining the inmates to their designated rat runs. A list of numbers repeated over a staccato loudspeaker preempts a buzz in the roof and the cell door skids on greasy wheels in a neon lightning storm revealing the belly of the whale that has swallowed them all whole. This beast was set on course over a hundred years ago, eating men's freedom and digesting the meat of their lives while it slides through an ocean of guilt, defecating chastened despots and silenced hooligans back into the streets from time to time.

On the first morning of her death he had an epiphany of guilt when he caught a glimpse of the rapist for the first time in the cracked mirror by his bed: a translucent face defined by hollows rather than substance and exuding a contagious moral decay that made him worry for his soul. The vice grip on his temples tightened another quarter turn before the guard's whistle frightened it away, but only to the margins of his thoughts, where he could sense it brood and mature. Though he had been in prison for two months of his two year sentence he had never been aware of its existence, but now, in hope's vacuum, the fiend abided.

Each morning he had no choice but to breathe the air that circled the prison balconies, pushed around by a ghost hag, it leaked into the cell when she passed: antiseptic robes, scrambled eggs with a twist of human excrement, oily margarine on burnt toast. He retched each time she breezed past his door but there was nothing left to come out of him since he was squeezed tight and dry at both ends in an uncontrollable bout of shitting and vomiting brought on by the doctor's account of Magdalena's decapitation. He had eaten nothing since.

Along with the bell, The Roussillon Juvenile Correction Facility, situated just outside Perpignan, has an unmarked van for taking the boys to work. On these excursions the guards don't wear uniforms, the boys are not chained because it's not supposed to be punishment and you don't have to do it if you don't want to; you can sit in your cell and invent new ways to masturbate for fifteen hours a day. But Henri would never masturbate again and on the fifth day of Magdalena's death he should have been in the infirmary—not in the van—but he kept his head down and nobody noticed his advanced mental decomposition, though his vacant expression and recent ramblings on resurrection had not gone entirely unnoticed by the guards.

Two lines of bowed heads nodded in unison as they were ferried to the campsite. Some words passed back and forth in the darkness. Bernard, the works supervisor, watched from the door with a smile on his face. His eyes and teeth were visible beneath the dim light coming through the mesh. He had a half-hearted liking for the boys that manifested similarly to how a man treats a dog that has turned on him once or twice, accepting a share of the guilt for the defect, he will grudgingly give it some scraps of affection. These muggers and thieves and man-slaughtering misfits had bitten the master's hand. Heads down they traded insults with each other through cornered mouths and stifled grins; their spirits always dared to lift a little when they were packed closer together: commandoes, raiding at the fringes of the free world.

Bernard knew each boy by his crime and Henri was by far the most pathetic of his charges to date. Having bitten nobody he was simply an unwanted mongrel that had strayed on the wrong street. Upon conviction for the statutory rape of his girlfriend, Magdalena's father, a cruel and influential bastard, had wanted Henri removed from plain sight until his daughter acquired the acumen to see him for the hopeless wretch he was. Throughout his hour-long trial Magdalena had remained silent, her bowed face hidden in shadows, until an angry old man in a wig walloped a mallet on a wooden place mat then sent him away for two years for taking advantage of the girl. Exposing her adolescent fragilities to his own was a crime, and apparently—though it was also his first time to be naked with another person—Henri should have known better. Magdalena did not raise her head once as they took him down, not even when he called her name.

The prison van jerked to a halt and a guard outside hummed the national anthem in mock baritone while he unlocked and opened the door letting warm sunlight flood in.

'Voila,' he announced, 'another day breathing the sea air and serving your country. Such a lucky band of deviant bastards you are.'

The vehicle bounced as each one dismounted and they lined up their smirks and frowns for a quick inspection; one frown was missing.

'Henri!' Bernard called, and the shadows stirred in the corner of the van. 'Merde du monde, you look like you have brought the bubonic plague with you.'

Henri squinted into the light and Bernard beckoned him with a wave of his big hand. He sat him on the floor of the van in the open door and while the other boys retrieved tools from the back of the trailer, Bernard fetched his flask from the front seat and poured Henri a cup of coffee.

'Did you eat?'

Henri shook his head, so Bernard went to the front again and came back with a bread roll wrapped in paper and tore half off. 'Eat it, or I'm taking you back. I'm not having another one of you sons of bitches drop dead on my shift.' It went in his mouth and he sucked a few flakes from the crust with his dry lips then coughed them out.

'My wife made that. If I catch you dropping another crumb—' he said it with an excruciating twist of his head, '—I will extinguish you for good.' Henri sat with two full hands by his side and an open mouth while Bernard's final ultimatum dissipated in his face: 'No mental shit today, boy—stay well away from that red head.'

The municipal camping grounds at the seaside resort had opened for the summer season to find that an innocuous toilet block on the third terrace had become overgrown with ivy and wild roses and the steep banks around it crowded with brushwood. Day three of a five day operation and presently the painters disembarked from another unmarked van to booming laughter, resounding backslaps and vacuous roars. Henri's mouth tugged weakly on a tuft of roll while he regarded their phony camaraderie with a mild disgust from under his knitted eyebrows.

When Bernard returned he found Henri touching the girl's face in the photograph on his knee. The coffee cup was drained and sparrows chirped unseen in the bushes as they gorged on ham roll. Bernard reached down and took the photo from him without a word. Henri shifted his head sideways a little into the shade of Bernard's towering silhouette.

'You think your little Cherie would want you starving yourself to death—or going insane?'

Bernard looked up the slope to the next level, but the lone caravan was out of sight from where they now sat. Then he eyed the photo again. 'Okay, Henri, to be fair to you, the likeness is uncanny—supernatural even.' He waved his hands in the air and Henri saw his big white eyes roll. 'But she is *not* a ghost, and she has *not* come back from the dead, or the future—or whatever the fuck you say. Hear?' The boy blinked the torrent of words into his shrinking skull. 'This woman is a stranger,' Bernard ranted, 'and you will end up in the lunatic asylum if you persist with these delusions. In fact, I will drop you there myself at lunchtime.'

'But I need to explain—'

Bernard's finger snapped in Henri's face. 'Shut up.'

Henri complied.

'Do not dare to approach those people with your zombie, time-travel bullshit.'

'Not a zombie,' Henri grumbled.

'*Good*!' Bernard rejoiced. 'I'm delighted to hear it. Now pick up those branches and get them in the truck.'

Seventy-two uninterrupted hours of extrapolation had not left Henri without an explanation of the phenomenon at hand. Very little space remained in his brain for further conclusions—but—to put it in layman's terms :

When Magdalena killed herself, the violent intensity of the event had rent the natural fabric of things and projected her being into an alternate past, far, far away from the trauma.

'Henri?'

Now, as is well known, energy cannot be created or destroyed—so—in that instant (but approximately thirty years previously) a baby girl was born. The new child then advanced on an independent but inexorably converging route towards this inevitable intersection point in the present time and location.

'Henri?'

'Huh?'

'Branches.'

Perhaps the migration began at the very moment Magdalena had jumped from the bridge. Maybe that heinous covenant alone had frightened her soul away. But more likely, it was in the moment that the razor wire snapped taut and her head came off that her spirit took flight, just in that instant when head and heart were divorced and immediately before her body was vapourised in a pink cloud in the speeding traffic below.

'For the love of God, boy—'

'Huh?'

"Will you pick up the damn branches?'

Scientists would think him a fool, physicists would laugh, but Henri's theory was above all derision because he had the proof that the soul *could* transmigrate space and time, and it was quaffing drinks in a deckchair not thirty meters away.

And with that summation his brain was full to the brim and the vice grips on his skull tightened another quarter turn as the heat of the sun gathered to a pinpoint over his head and his presence crystallised in a pitiless desert.

'Huh?'

'For fuck's sake, Henri. Pick up the branches!'

Elevenses, and the three guards would now be sitting at the plastic table vying for her attention. Her bright-red bikini and her colourful sarong hugging soft curves, sunglasses sitting on top of her head and her flaming curls cascading to her freckled shoulders. Henri smiled for the first time in a week. Magdalena had certainly come out of herself in her new life. Each day she had all three guards in the palm of her hand as she laughed, winked, and blew smoke rings over their heads.

Worth noting at this point is the fact that she had not come back alone; there was a man with her: short, stocky and muscular in the functional sense as opposed to the aesthetic. Henri had listened as the guards spoke of him over coffee and cigarettes.

'He's her cousin and he's a halfwit, so she's still fair game in my book. I'm going to invite her to The Rendezvous for a romantic dinner.'

'You don't know which half of his wits he has about him, so don't push your luck too far.'

'He didn't get those raw fists playing piano. Whatever else he may be, he is definitely a fighter and they've come straight from trouble.'

'He's definitely a simpleton, isn't that what she told you, Bernard?'

'Yes—if you are to believe anything she says.'

'So why else with the public sponge bath?'

'Well, if she offered to wash me all over, I would happily be her idiot.'

They had all cheered wildly at that prospect, but Henri knew different. He had sat and watched this man execute his martial arts manoeuvres in silence at the end of the track and had instantly understood from his vacant expression that nothing would be spilled from a half-empty glass and only in the emptiness can the wine breathe and exude its essence.

On the very first day they had all sat on the fence and watched her shave his head and dress the injury on his crown. They sniggered as she washed his body, while he seemed oblivious to them eating lunch close by. The man had been through a war and she tended his wounds jealously. There was melodrama about the pair, in how they interacted within their modest ballet of whispers, the unbearable tenderness as she pushed the sponge into the welts on his ribs and the bruises on his back. He remained unaffected when he eventually turned, naked, and saw them all sitting on the fence.

The next day he walked around in his shorts, conducted slow motion attacks on invisible demons in the shade, then stood silently watching as the boys hacked and sawed in the trees in front of him and finally, like a despondent child, he had sunk into the dust and let the sparrows hop around him. A sacred silence had descended by the third day, each pursuing their own end: the inmates, the guards, the fighter and Magdalena. Henri presumed that an outsider wandering into it might have considered the gathering a coincidence, but he could feel the interwoven strands of their destinies tangled in the static air. At one stage Henri stopped involuntarily in his tracks, just to scrutinize him. The man stood up so that they were eye to eye, madman to madman, as is more often than not the case.

'What's your problem?' His tone was tranquil.

'I want to be you.' Henri could only think the words as the man looked him up and down then sat back in the dust with the sparrows.

Life without sleep soon becomes the onset of death and the place in between is a cornfield slowly obliterating to an untended wasteland. By afternoon, Henri was getting lost in the weeds with dead grass and vines catching his feet and threatening to tip him over at every moment. Eyes glued to the ground, he wandered from trance to oblivion in search of a path to the alternate reality he knew eluded him just beyond the thickening haze. He waded in liquid gold, up crumbling marble steps to where the haze retreated and found that he was standing near the table with a branch in one hand and a white dove in the other—or was it a sparrow? No, it was toilet paper.

'Rise, Magdalena, and take my hand as the day congeals like an oil painting in the sun and we will take flight as swans lifting from the frozen surface of a lake.'

He took a step towards the group but the fighter appeared on the opposite side of the scene in the same moment, shirt open, his chest tattooed with lacerations. The guards greeted him noisily to the table, offering him brioche and coffee. Henri watched the sultry curl of the woman's lips as he took his place beside her.

'Who's the simpleton now?' he whispered.

The red haired woman had been reading the future from the palms of their hands, promising them fame and fortune and long mystical voyages. She played with them and they fawned for her touch, eager to laugh out loud and feel the slow stroke of her charming indifference. They jostled for a moment of her attention, as she regarded them sweetly from under the smooth arc of her eyebrow. As Henri drew closer inwards he could see the redness of her lips and when she lifted her head and laughed, Henri instantly recognized the sweet sound and the golden flecks in the green of her eyes. The invisible vice on his head tightened another quarter turn and his tightly packed extrapolations began to bleed into his throat.

'Magdalena,' he said, 'the time has come.'

A Fistful of Salt

Then the fighter's chest cracked open and glowed, but instead of going into the light Henri was sucked instantly back into the shade above the steps where the day poured into his senses once again.

'Henri!' Bernard's voice was replete with the authority of the state as he stood up straight, a giant bear towering over a picnic scene. Sparrows chirped, boys laughed and people talked gaily at the plastic table where Magdalena was still a thirty-year-old woman completely oblivious to his presence.

'Shit,' he mumbled, 'I really thought that was it.' But then a low rumble of thunder signaled the true onset of the transitional phase from prisoner to fighter, or perhaps, boy to man.

Down below, the work crew bustled away in the thickening air. The sky was turning to black as a storm rolled in from the sea, pushing mist through the canopy that cloaked the foothills of the Pyrenees. Perhaps it was the gathering storm that was causing the unbearable pressure and giving rise to hallucinations but more likely it was static from the temporal gate that was preparing to open close by.

The heavens erupted in a single breath with the carpet of red roofs disappearing in a veil of rain that set the treetops rattling and a billion leaves dancing. The guards shouted as they hurtled past him down the steps, bundling into the dark interior of the toilet block.

Criminals, guards and painters communed noisily as thunder rolled down from the mountains and out onto the sea. Before long, rivers of white and brown storm water were cascading down the faces of the terraced tracks. Mud and leaves spluttered from dry pipe ends along the slopes and extended outward into arcs of water. Singing brewed up from inside the half-painted building as the besieged men struck up a chorus and white streaks trailed down the walls forming milky puddles around abandoned buckets and trays. In all the casual mayhem Henri's absence went unnoticed.

At the back of the toilet block, a stump of the wild rose bush that had smothered the building still offered a few remaining blossoms against the glistening stone. Their scarlet petals shivered in the rain as he picked the sweetest one using the penknife he had taken from the painter's van.

'Magdalena!' he cried out against a crash of thunder and his tortured eyes rolled skyward.

At the top of the steps stood the fighter, staring into the distance, naked to the waist. Water rushed over his skin and sprang from his fingertips. He was talking to the storm and Henri heard it answer in the soothing voice of an old woman.

'This is chaos.'

He watched a smile break out over the man's face who now held his upturned arms out to his gods. A gust of wind rushed up the hill and struck him like a tsunami making landfall. It set the trees writhing at their trunks and the fighter rocking on his feet. He spoke to the sky even as the words were snatched away from him. Then he was looking at Henri and his voice came down the slope.

'Do it now.'

Henri's dementia lifted and without a second thought he took off from his hiding place for the far end of the bank then clambered up through the undergrowth to where the caravan swayed on its wheels. At first he could see nothing but the dark shapes of the trees and a ghoul reflected in the glass. His hollow face and translucent skin were dissolving as he divested from the world in streaks that melted into the mud puddles. Magdalena appeared to him gradually in the insipid light of the dying storm, edging forward until she was framed in the window, as though in a portrait. She smiled, and by her side her scarlet fingernails fluttered in a childish wave. The bashful angle of her head made her long copper curls lie on her pale cheek. He silently mouthed her name and she nodded to confirm that she could at last see him.

He raised his borrowed blossom to the glass and the girl's face was illuminated with joy. Yes, she was older now, just as his youth was also leaving him, with all the years that had been stolen from them crumbling and the beautiful light leeching into the darkness, his pain recalibrating to levels that could be withstood from this point forward. She reached out to take the flower and now he only had to pass through the mirror and they would be reunited.

'What do you want?'

He felt a hand on his shoulder and opened his eyes to find the man standing beside him and Henri could see him perfectly now. Not just the texture of his skin and the line of his stubble, slashed through with a half-healed wound, but the brooding anger in a face defined by adversity and frustration. That familiar desperation, in the eyes of a man who also knew he was living the defining moments of his life, struggling to exist on his own narrow terms in a world that was suddenly intent on extinguishing him at every turn. He could taste the brutality of survival in the salted raindrops.

'What do you want?'

'I want to be you, and this is my moment.'

The man looked straight at him, then past him to the woman in the window frame.

'You want to have all my problems too?'

'You have no problems. You are a free man.'

'And you will be too,' the man replied.

Henri reached into his pocket where he found the wooden handle of the knife and understood that only one of them could survive from this point forward if Magdalena was to remain. The man shifted his weight to his back foot to reveal the killer in his stance and Henri knew it would be his coup de grace the instant he pulled the blade.

'I can never be free; my condition is permanent,' Henri whispered.

'Not even death is permanent,' the man assured him, 'but it can be painful.'

'More painful than life?'

Henri's conviction was finally crumbling at the point where his logic ran thin. In that moment he had no hatred for this usurper and could feel no love for himself and his destiny felt more like a narrowing passage than an opening gate. His fingers slipped from the knife to the furled corners of the Magdalena's picture as the guards' voices reached him from the thinning rain. His hand extended and the man gripped it, freezing them together like statues—the door swung open between them flooding the trees with light as the young girl's portrait passed out of Henri's reach.

The fighter stumbled back and lifted his hand to reveal his lover's face at the age of seventeen, exactly as she had looked on that day, fifteen years ago, when he had proposed to marry her and she had laughed in his face. Her expression was intact: a superfluous mixture of mirth and sympathy, now handed to him a generation later by a crazy kid in a place he'd never been before and would never be again. The passing of time felt like a curse and his belligerence in the world a sin against the only thing he ever truly desired. He looked from the photo to his sweetheart's face and, as always, found a patient promise.

'She was dead,' the boy said, his eyes spilling tears. 'I brought her back.'

The door was closing as the guards took the boy by the shoulders.

'Is there something you want me to do, Henri?'

The boy produced the rose and the man plucked it from his open palm.

'You must keep her for me.' The kid's eyes froze, then emptied, with the guards catching him before he fell into the mud. The fighter watched them carry the insane kid away and pledged to devote whatever little time he had left to embracing the tyranny of his freedom, for his sweetheart, and perhaps, even for the kid.

In the dim light of the unmarked van used by the guards of The Roussillon Juvenile Correctional Facility for the occasional transportation of stray dogs, the boy stirred, but Bernard didn't like the look in his eyes. Okay, he was smiling for the first time since he'd known him but he had the look of a simpleton about him and when he clicked his fingers in front of his face, his expression faded to bitterness and his features hollowed out.

That night, deep in the belly of the beast, the painter's knife was used in a murder. The convicted rapist would be found in the locked cell with his head almost cut off.

'An inhuman feat of strength and determination to do that to oneself,' the doctor's report would proclaim with far too much gusto for an audience of nil.

Before the beast awakened that morning, the prison hag came by to check on Henri, but he had not returned from the work excursion the previous day, deciding instead to watch the sunrise from the shade of a secluded lookout with his lifelong sweetheart.

****

ABOUT THE AUTHOR

Kevin Keely is a native of Dublin City, Ireland, now living in the Rural North West in a modest cottage surrounded by soggy hills and occasional, glorious sunshine.
With Short Stories published in the *2017 Book a Break Anthology* and longlisted in Fish Publishing in 2017, 2016 and short listed in the international Short Story Competition in 2015, this is Kevin's first novel.

His next Novel and a collection of Short Stories and Flash Fiction are currently under construction.

***

Thank you, good friend, for having read the book and I hope you enjoyed it..

Please leave a review on Amazon if you can find the time, as it does make a difference.

Made in the USA
Columbia, SC
07 June 2022